ANNALS OF THE OMEGA PROJECT

Ω

A TRILOGY

BY THOMAS A. CAHILL

Published by EditPros LLC
423 F Street, suite 206
Davis, CA 95616
www.editpros.com

ISBN-10: 193731703X
ISBN-13: 978-1-937317-03-4

Library of Congress Control Number: 2012939470

Printed in the United States of America

CATALOGING INFORMATION:

Cahill, Thomas A.

Annals of the Omega Project – A Trilogy

Filing categories:
    Fiction Thriller
    Occult
    Paranormal
    Psychic
    Science Fiction
    Supernatural

CONTENTS

3

For my darling wife, Ginny.

The view from the penthouse was magnificent. Fog rolled in across the Golden Gate, diffused with a golden glow from the sodium vapor lights in the bridge. The penthouse deck, festooned with expensive pieces of garden art and beautifully sculpted topiary trees, was connected through a wall of glass into a large room full of opulent furnishings, walls of book cases, rich tapestries covering additional windows, and 22 comfortable leather chairs. Most of the chairs were formed into a large circle with a gap centered on the fireplace, in which aged blue oak burned quietly. Directly in front of them and facing the fire was a single chair, very plush and expensive. The two chairs on each side of the fireplace were somewhat larger than the others. One was occupied, one empty, except for a pair of wire-rimmed glasses.

All the rest of the chairs were occupied, all by men, none too young and none older than perhaps their mid 60s. These men exuded power and wealth with sharply tailored Italian suits and Rolex watches. In the central chair a somewhat younger man sat, dressed in an expensive suit a tad more modish than the rest, still without being flamboyant. All were silent until the grandfather clock finished striking 9.

The man next to the fireplace spoke. He was known only as 1A, the most powerful telepath in the group. As senior member, he spoke first as was his prerogative.

"Tonight we attend to the most important activity we ever do, namely the joining of a new member to our Coven. Steven, we will soon welcome you into our midst in a way that will give you power and influence over other lesser folk for the rest of your life, guaranteeing you a life of success and luxury, and enormous influence over the affairs of the city, state, even country. You have shown nascent powers as a telepath, and we can help you grow and develop these powers. In a few minutes, we will all be one entity."

Steven could sense the eagerness of the Coven. He was honored by their obvious excitement at the ceremony about to happen. He had always known that he could somehow sense the feelings of others, sense their moods and emotions, and use it for his many romantic conquests. But these men were special, and soon he would be one of them. His mind was at a high pitch of excitement. He took another sip of what was without doubt the most delicious (and expensive) champagne he had ever tasted.

He had been honored that a senior member of his law firm, with its 260 lawyers spread over five cities, would take the time to notice a new summer legal intern. But when he was asked to join a very select and secretive upper tier of the power elite of San Francisco, he was stunned. He was assured that this was being done because of his outstanding promise for a legal or political career, and because only by recruiting the best and brightest early in their careers could they really learn and mature into a partner in the powers behind the scenes that really ran San Francisco and much of the Bay Area. It did require that he suddenly take three weeks from his internship for an unpaid compassion leave and craft a story about a dying relative in Florida, but they assured him that this was an essential step in his training. And this evening, during a splendid meal, he started to learn how powerful and influential these people really were. Decision after decision, advantage after advantage, flowed to this nameless group of powerbrokers – never in the limelight, always pulling the strings. This was heady stuff for a 23-year-old intern.

1A smiled at him, and just for an instant, he felt something cold, dangerous, in that smile. A tiny thread of fear sifted into his excitement. But no. 1A was actually laughing, smiling at the other members behind Steven, clearly relaxed and enjoying the moment. Then he turned to Steven again, and this time the dread was more palpable. Without consciously meaning to, Steven tried to raise his right hand, almost as if to shield his face from that ominous smile, but suddenly clamps sprang out of the arms and legs of the chair, and he was held fast.

Now 1A's smile was a yawning pit into which Steven's mind was being sucked. "No," he screamed, in dread and fear, "No!" He slashed back at that smile with all the hate and anger he could muster in his fear, and felt 1A recoil ever so slightly. But then other minds were there, like leaches, draining his thoughts, feeding off his fear. Steven's screams rose to a crescendo that could have been heard blocks away, were it not for the very expensive sound-deadening of the walls, the tapestries, bookcases, and the triple-paned xenon-filed windows.

In a few minutes, it was all over. For a few minutes, 20 members of the Coven had been as one, "feeding" and growing in power and strength.

Now they slumped back in their chairs in a post-prandial stupor. In a few minutes, their youngest member would clean up the mess that had been Steven, using equipment of such quiet efficiency that all parts of the late Steven would soon be flushed as a thin, uniform soup into the San Francisco sewers.

A few weeks later, when the police were finally notified by the worried law firm and became interested in Steven as a missing person, a variety of evidence was uncovered in his apartment and phone records that indicated he was lost in Mexico on a drug deal gone bad. The San Francisco Police Department soon lost interest, and somehow the case never made the newspapers.

BOOK 1
THE AWAKENING

CHAPTER ONE

United 217 climbed smoothly through 15,000 feet on its way to Denver. The captain had turned off the seat belt sign, and flight attendants began dispensing drinks forward in the coach cabin. Ken had the aisle seat in row 17 and recalled the afternoon with unrestrained delight.

It had been an important colloquium at the Department of Physics at the University of California, Berkeley, and Ken was absolutely on top of his game. He had blown them away with a whole new way of looking at thin-film superconductivity, with important implications for layered room-temperature superconductors. His analysis flew in the face of current theory, but he had his key and very original experiments to make the case convincingly. If this worked, and it did lead to a cheap, high-current room-temperature superconductor, it was the stuff of which Nobel Prizes were made.

Old Kauffman, long protagonist of conventional wisdom, had asked at the end exactly the question Ken had anticipated, and Ken neatly put him away with not only a proven error in an earlier Kauffman paper but a re-evaluation of the same data Kauffman had used, explaining a problem Kauffman had alluded to but left unexplained. He could sense a certain pleasure among the younger faculty at seeing the old curmudgeon simply leveled by this much younger professor from that nascent cow college, the new University of California, Merced campus. Ken felt the audience was with him, some through nods and smiles, others just by rapt attention as he showed them a whole new way of using data and theory, opening up new opportunities for many in the audience.

The only minor annoyance in this picture was that he would be unable to share and exult with his beloved Jill, wife of 13 years. He had to rush to catch the plane, and Jill had that seminar. In fact, he was probably not that far from Merced and Jill right now. A yearning far beyond the physical flowed through him, and he could picture a wonderful evening and delicious night as they reveled in Ken's success and each other's presence. Alas, a long-promised colloquium at the University of Colorado was too important to avoid or delay. So Ken quietly sat, but his mind was both furiously active and emotionally bereft by Jill's absence.

A flight attendant was coming down the aisle, tall like Jill and good looking, with a wisp of hair that kept falling in front of her face. Her nameplate said M. Kolberg, but that could simply be a noncommittal way of avoiding stating her marital status. Sort of like "Ms." Ken had not the slightest romantic interest in her, but appreciated her style. She was passing out drinks with an unusual flair. She addressed each person as though he or she were the only person on the plane, smiling, joking, exuding confidence and competence. Ken liked that whenever he saw it in his students, fostered it, encouraged it and in the processes won the coveted Academic Senate Teaching Award with its $25,000 prize.

Michelle Kolberg was indeed alive with good humor and anticipation of her upcoming vacation. She was on the last shift before a two-week vacation with Karen hiking in the Maroon Bells wilderness in Colorado. Michelle really liked being a flight attendant, liked the people, liked the travel, and liked the other girls. She had been at this for two-and-a-half years, and the kick she got out of the whole scene had never faded. Her ratings were sky high, and she was destined for a better route in three months.

She smiled and chatted, and many of the passengers responded with smiles. She really liked people, which made it all the more troubling that her love life was zero. Worse than zero. Zilch! She had had numerous boyfriends and had been willing, even eager, to have sex with some of them, but somehow it all went wrong at the last minute. This resulted in three or four occasions that could have been legally called attempted rape, but Michelle was athletic and quick and determined, and thus one more relationship would end badly. This actually had some advantages in the career of the flight attendant as this reduced the number of attempts from unsuitable (one-night-stand specialist) co-workers as the word got out that she was an iceberg. Still, sometimes she wondered whether she was the only 24-year-old virgin among the United flight attendants.

She had just finished serving a grandmotherly type in 16D, who was clearly nervous at flying, and giving her hand a squeeze and a wink, reclined the back of her seat, to be rewarded with a lovely smile and visible relaxation. Michelle could sense her success, and turned to serve the passenger in the next row, 17D. She was still bent over from helping the

11

lady, and thus her head was very close to his. He was in fact a great-looking older guy with a glorious smile alive with feelings as she looked into his eyes. Why can't I find a guy like this, she thought, and in her loneliness reached out her feelings.

Suddenly she was seeing herself, standing there, transfixed, like in a mirror, but it was not a mirror. She was seeing herself in the eyes of this guy. In Ken's eyes.

Ken was stunned. Suddenly he was not seeing this flight attendant, but himself, in her eyes. In Michelle's eyes.

For long seconds neither could, or wanted, to move, to breathe. Emotions surged uncontrollably through each, neither wanting this moment to pass. But it had to.

Ken said, or thought he said, "We must meet again as soon as you get a chance." But, in fact, his lips hadn't moved. "Yes, yes yes," thought Michelle. But why hadn't his lips moved? Stunned, she went into autopilot, serving the people in 17E and 17F, and moving on, averting her eyes, but feeling him still in her mind and he in hers. How had this happened?

By row 20, she had lost all contact with Ken. Her mind worked furiously. Somehow they had transcended some incredible barrier and could read, share each other's thoughts. She yearned to repeat the moment again, and again, and forever. This was way beyond love, beyond yearning.

Ken, ever analytical, was way ahead of her. There had been some transcending of a barrier between their minds. He had to get close and do it again, as soon as possible, but while Michelle worked her way down the plane, he had time to think. The best analogy he could think of was that at that moment when their eyes met he had sort of blown a kiss at her mentally, in appreciation of her enthusiasm, appreciation of her smile, her attention to the passengers, her athletic good looks.

He was aware of the recent work on brain functions, since some of it used the hypersensitive thin-film electric devices he both designed and used. The technical term for what just occurred was telepathy, and unlike most of the paranormal trash that so many of his students accepted as real, telepathy violated none of the laws of physics. He had long had a subscription to the The *Skeptical Inquirer*, just to anticipate such questions from lower-division students, but he was careful to base his arguments on sound science. Telepathy in fact had some scientific support for its potential existence. Contrary to prior thought, it was now proven that thoughts did not originate at a point in the brain but seemed to occur simultaneously at many spots that were too far apart to be in chemical communication via synapses. Thus, there had to be some sort of electrical signal passing through the brain, and these could be picked up outside the skull. The same studies showed that women's minds were more dispersed in memory than men's, with far more left-hemisphere, right-hemisphere interconnectivity than men's. It was just that previous attempts to probe these signals had been rather crude – EEGs, for example. Could it be that some combination of great intelligence (he was realistic about his capabilities) and a yearning to reach out could link the signals across the barrier of skull and skin. He was also aware that the range of contact was short, and by the time Michelle was 10 feet down the aisle, all contact was lost.

This was a stunning development, and he could scarcely contain himself until Michelle had finished her drink service. The lavatories were at the back of the plane, and at the first opportunity, he headed down the aisle. He was wracked with all the doubts and fears of a high school junior on a prom date, eager and emotionally driven by self-doubts and self-worth.

Michelle was sideways to him, doing something totally inconsequential, not looking at Ken, fearing that the moment would never occur again.

But as he approached, she could feel his mind, which was in a state of wild longing and near panic of doubt. Their eyes never met.

"Where and when," asked Ken audibly.

"At the Starbuck stand, south side of the main concourse, 30 minutes after we touch down," Michelle responded.

For the rest of the flight, Ken was in some state of torture. Clearly, either something extraordinary had just occurred or he was loosing his mind. But every time Michelle passed by on the aisle, he could sense her mind and sense her panic, facing the unknown with both profound longing and fear of what might come of it. Every time Michelle passed by, it seemed easier to regain contact, a skill once mastered never forgotten, sort of like riding a bike.

The first point was that no one must know what had happened

13

between them. If they were wrong, misled, daydreaming, they would be laughingstocks, ruining his career and probably hers, too. Thus, there must be total secrecy until they could work out what had happened.

Then there was Jill. Ken was totally and completely bonded to Jill in every way a man could, through friendship, admiration, love, marriage, body, and soul. Yet he could sense Michelle's longing, and he would not, could not hurt Jill who had shared his very thoughts and feelings, and who knew that he could not help but love her in return. Thus, immediately, there had to be a resolution involving Jill. And there could be no physical relationship with Michelle.

However, he couldn't easily drop his colloquium tomorrow, and so he had to tough out one night in Boulder, attending the scheduled dinner in his honor this evening, teaching a graduate class at 11:00 a.m., and then the colloquium at 3:30 p.m. It would be a challenge to his intellect to focus on the talks that had meant so much to him just an hour ago, and now were inconsequential to his recent experience. Then he and Michelle would take the 7:55 to Sacramento, and then the long drive to Merced for a midnight arrival. He would call Jill first and tell her everything. It would be a weird phone call, but a lifetime of total truthfulness would be a foundation for understanding. Far better than showing up at midnight with an attractive young woman in tow.

Ken got to Starbucks in about 15 minutes, about as fast as the Denver train shuttle would allow. Of course, he was using a roller board and laptop carrier and had no checked luggage. The next minutes were pure torture. What if Michelle didn't show up? What if she, too, was married, and simply ran away from a potentially disastrous situation?

But 10 minutes later, there she was, still in uniform with her carry-on over her shoulder. She wordlessly motioned for Ken to follow, and passing behind the ticket counters used her pass to enter a door marked "Authorized Personnel Only." It was a set of small rooms, designed for aircrews between flights, which were generally used mostly late at night (except for brief liaisons of a romantic nature). Michelle chose one, motioned Ken inside, and closed the door. There was one chair and the bed, and Michelle chose the chair. Ken sat on the bed, about as far from Michelle as the room would allow and out of mental contact.

"What happened to us? What do we do now?" said Michelle in an anguished voice clearly looking at the wedding ring on Ken's hand.

"We have had some sort of telepathic breakthrough," said Ken. "Contrary to popular belief, this does not violate any of the laws of physics and indeed recent research has hinted at some sort of inner-brain electrical communication. No one has made any sense of the signals that have been seen for decades, and no one has even hinted at person-to-person telepathic contact. My analysis is that it was only a very unusual coincidence of circumstances that occurred between two highly intelligent people that allowed this to occur. First, you are clearly very smart and empathetic, interacting with and responding to your passengers in an especially effective manner. Second, I was in a high state of excitement, longing for a chance to communicate with Jill, my darling wife, and also appreciating your sympathy for the old woman. Third, by accident, our heads were very close when our eyes met.

"I have to accept what happened as fact, and act thusly. I could not help loving you, and you me, as we knew each other more intimately than any married couple, any lovers ever could. I have an enormous desire to know more of you, to protect you, and to see us grow in grace and wisdom with this enormous gift we have been given. But I propose we move very slowly, in total secrecy, and with no physical intimacy, until we understand what has happened and plot the best course for our joint future."

Michelle's heart plummeted with the words "Jill, my darling wife," as Ken feared it would. But she stuck with it, and at the end merely nodded concurrence.

Ken laid out his plans, and Michelle dreaded having to cancel the long-planned trip with Karen, her best friend. Some excuse had to be found, and soon. The death of a relative, her old aunt with whom Karen had had no contact, was decided upon. Conveniently, she lived just north of Sacramento.

This done, Ken said, asked, prayed, "Do we dare to get close together here?" Michelle nodded yes, so they decided that Ken would sit on the floor and Michelle would bring her head near his. For about 15 minutes, they communed, each gripping the chair so hard their hands became numb, as they talked and saw and felt as one. Ken remembered Jill, and instantly

Michelle was in love with her, too. She vowed never, never, to interfere with this love of 13 years, no matter what hurt it cost her.

It became clear that they could read only current thoughts, and had no access to past memories. It was also clear that they shared all the physical sensations each was experiencing: sight, hearing, smell, taste, and touch. Emotions were deeply shared.

After about 15 minutes, some sort of mental exhaustion set in, and regretfully all contact ceased. They sat, still apart physically but deeply and permanently bonded. They were drenched in sweat, as though they had been in heavy exercise. They both had headaches, and their foreheads were hot and blushed.

Fearful of physical contact, they each went their way, with a scheduled meeting just before the flight back. They agreed to sit apart and refrain from communicating.

CHAPTER TWO

By Ken's insistence, Jill was firmly planted on his lap. Michelle was across the room, looking very young and very scared. The events were described, and Jill was stashed somewhere in the ozone, trusting Ken totally but wracked by a future suddenly uncharted. She was intensely jealous that this woman had, seemingly without effort, achieved in moments a level of intimacy with her husband that she could never achieve in a lifetime of loving. Trust was one thing, but Ken insisted on demonstrations. Michelle, with fear and trembling, moved close to Ken. Jill asked Ken questions, that Michelle, without any hesitation, answered. They could recite long passages that Ken remembered with each of them reciting the words alternately, just as fast as Ken could talk (which was fast, indeed).

Ken was simply radiating his love for Jill, and Michelle picked it up, reinforcing her commitment never to come between this couple.

So well into the night, they discussed what came next. Ken described a theory of the Jesuit anthropologist Pierre Teilhard de Chardin, who hypothesized that mankind was destined to gradually become a single thinking entity as communication between people improved and became global in scope, eventually joining with God in the end at the omega (Ω) point, last letter in the Greek alphabet.

Was this the beginning of this transition? Ken could scarcely believe that he and Michelle were unique. Would it be possible to search for others? Could their communications be enhanced by training and perhaps even technology? These were questions that required an urgent answer, and they coined the effort "The Omega Project."

But the first problem was how to derive a plausible story that explained the sudden presence of Michelle in their household, a story that would not lead to raised eyebrows. By dawn, they had a plan. Michelle would become the daughter of an old school classmate and dear friend from Brown University, "married" to a fictitious U.S. State Department staffer on a long assignment of some sensitivity (hint: CIA operative) in Pakistan. Michelle has come to take classes at the University of California, Merced, and help with housework for Jill, whose teaching and administrative duties were steadily expanding. Michelle immediately and without regrets resigned from her job.

For the next weeks, all three went about their duties with as much attention to detail as they could, and each night spent several hours of research and training. It was clear that recognition of actual words was one of the most difficult tasks, and required concentration and close proximity to work. Thus, they designed tests to see how far apart they could be while still able to read a list. Jill became a mentor in this work, and designed the rating system. It was clear that Michelle had the greatest ability, greater than Ken's, to read the words. Defining Michelle as a "10," Ken was an 8.8, based on the distance at which he could read the words. Sight was perhaps not surprisingly the next most difficult task, while other feelings and emotions were the easiest to sense, and at several times the range of reading words. The presence of a mind, but no details, could be sensed at greater distances, yet several times that of emotions. It was also clear that the effort was exhausting, and could rarely be continued for more than 30 minutes.

It also became clear that when Ken and Michelle were far apart, their ability to sense other minds improved. When close, they only sensed themselves, even when Jill was close. Separated by 10 to 15 feet, Jill was clearly perceived as a mind present, although without any detail. It also became clear that if they wanted to, they could hurt each other by sharply focused and broadcast negative thoughts, sort of like a mental slap. Finally, the act of consciously trying to project thoughts enabled detection from much greater distances.

Ken began very quietly a series of studies on the phenomenon. It was immediately evident that a layer of aluminum foil completely blocked the thoughts, and in fact made even Jill's mind invisible even under close probing. Thus, the phenomenon, as expected, was electromagnetic. However, every attempt to enhance the signal with AM or FM narrow- or wide-band amplifiers failed. This was going to be tricky!

Finally, it was clear that they had succeeded in making a connection, based upon a desire to communicate an affection and love that they both possessed in abundance. They decided to try to see if there were other "sensitives" among students who had exhibited similar feelings and altruistic love in their daily lives.

Ken and Jill were committed Catholics, products of Jesuit colleges and thus sort of free thinkers in the Catholic community. Jill, in particular, had a thing on the need for female priests. They were co-founders of the UC Merced Newman Center, which attracted about the nicest and most altruist bunch of students imaginable. Thus, after about six weeks, Michelle joined them at Mass, which bothered her not one bit as the Mass was so similar to the Lutheran Christianity with which she had grown up. Jill sat with Ken (as they always had) and Michelle came in later and sat about 15 feet away.

The effect was stunning. This group, about 75 students in all, were alive with positive feelings and love for one another. Several stood out as potential contacts, and their names were noted. It was also clear in Ken's heightening sensitivity that this community was in some sort of low-level contact already, amplifying the feelings of others and reinforcing love and communication and commitment. They called it "grace" but it was real, and it was there. Could it be that several minds could work together, with powers beyond that of a pair? Back at the house, shared perceptions were turned into a list of seven students (five women, two men) for contact next week.

Next week rolled around, the last weekend before the Thanksgiving break. All seven potential "sensitives" were present at the 9:00 a.m. Mass, and Ken deliberately volunteered as a Eucharistic minister so that he could address the students one at a time. One shy young woman in particular, Diane, had responded with a resonant smile to his mental blessing, and she was immediately added to the list. As they left the chapel, each was contacted and asked to come for a few moments to the Newman house next door for an important meeting.

"We need your help," began Ken. "Each of you has extraordinary gifts of grace, and we want to pray as you have never prayed before. Let us kneel in a circle, and lean forward until your heads are almost touching. Hold hands, and blank from your minds all thoughts, and then I want all of your to focus with all the intensity you can muster love for the people on each side of you. I want us all to be one in grace and prayer and love."

Ken was not at all sure this would work. Michelle was at the far side of the circle. They leaned forward, and Ken intoned, "Peace I leave you, my peace I give to you," and reached out across the circle to Michelle with all the love in his heart and mind. In an instant, he felt Michelle's beautiful mind merge into his, and their joy was without limit. He could sense

19

all the other minds in the circle, and one in particular had this enormous yearning to be loved, yearning for acceptance, yearning. It was Diane. He and Michelle focused on her, and suddenly they sensed in her a joy beyond yearning, a leaping of love and acceptance, of communion. Michelle and Ken gathered her love into their fold, and focused on others in the ring with renewed power and intensity. One by one they joined, and with each, the barriers between their minds fell away. Within minutes tears of joy were pouring off everybody's cheeks, minutes that lasted and then gradually faded one by one as exhaustion set in.

"Welcome to the Omega Project," intoned Ken, exulting in their success. "What you have just experienced is telepathic communication driven by the highest levels of human achievement, the altruistic love offered and demanded by Jesus when he said, "Love one another as you love yourself." For 2,000 years, this has been simply thought an unachievable goal, hyperbole that was impossible to live. Today, for a few moments, you lived it. This is for you all, as for us, a life-changing event. But you must not change what you are doing. What we have done must be a profound secret, for we are weak and young and have no idea what lies ahead. But before we talk about the future, sit back and look around at each other, for you now see you as you are. There is no "they" in this group."

They tried to sit back, but it was easier said than done. Their legs didn't seem to work, several had to almost crawl to the bathroom, others staggered to the nearest couch. They looked stunned, wrung out, exhausted. But in every eye shown a transparent exultation, a hymn of joy, knowing that they would never, ever, be alone again. They joined then in a short prayer of thanksgiving for the incredible gift they had been given.

"You are going to have to be great actors, all," said Ken. "There is probably no way to hide the change that has come over you. I would, when pressed, mention a secret love that cannot yet be revealed. We will meet here two evenings a week and still attend the 9:00 a.m. Mass. You will not sit close to each other. No matter how profound your love, you must not get physical with others in this team, for we fear it will stunt your development. You must get your joy by reaching out with your minds." Ken, ever the teacher, then assigned reading material, including Teilhard de Chardin's *The Phenomenon of Man* and Arthur C. Clarke's, brilliant science fiction novel,

Childhood's End. In 30 minutes it was over, and they returned to their houses and dorms, looking at the world with new and awakened eyes.

Weeks passed until the Christmas break. The Omega group was making rapid progress, and on the third week of December, each was ranked according to Jill's "reading words" scale as first calibrated. The relative results were interesting:

Michelle 10.0
Ken 8.8
Diane, the first recruit 8.2
Tiffany..................................... 6.7
Michael 6.2
Roger 5.6
Joanne..................................... 5.4
Phyllis 5.4
Mary 5.2
Nancy 5.0

However, it was also clear that each differed in important ways. Michael, for example, could "see" almost as well as Diane. The absolute scores were also interesting. Michelle could now pick up Ken's words at almost 30 feet away, and sense minds to 100 feet. Finally, it was clear that the group as a unit had capabilities far beyond the individuals that made it up.

At each Mass, they were able to start to sense in some detail members of the Newman Center. A number were slated for the next recruitment effort, set tentatively for February. They went sequentially to all Masses at Newman, and started working through the Lutheran and Episcopal groups, with some potential recruits in each. Other groups seemed to lack the inner yearning, some because they were so sure of their "salvation" that no yearning was needed, others because their religious practice was all external.

The dynamics of the group had also developed. The two men were sort of by consensus tentatively paired with two of the women, although of course everybody wanted and loved them profoundly. Diane with Michael, and Roger with Joanne, were slated to eventually marry but until then they needed to stay strictly platonic. There was some fear that their group capabilities might wane if they became too closely pair-bonded too soon.

Training proceeded, especially in those tactics that were important for safety. The technique "dark mind" was developed in which each could instantly shut off all telepathic broadcasting and simply accept signals as a sponge with none of the spontaneous response so normal even in non-sensitives. It turned out that most people were modestly sensitive, and only about 30 percent of the population in and around the Merced campus was totally non-sensitive. By suppressing all mental emissions, "dark mind" had the beneficial effect of increasing the range at which thoughts could be received.

Michelle, Ken, and Diane found they could cause non-sensitives to do innocuous actions, like raise their left hand and wipe their forehead, even at some distance. This led Ken to propose a new test, namely to determine what fraction of the population at large you could compel to brush their foreheads with their left hand. In this Ken was slightly better than Michelle, at about a 75 percent rate, although nobody below a 6.0 could do this at all. Some effort was made at defense via a mental slap, which worked only if the recipient was a sensitive.

But the greatest progress was made in increasing the range and diagnostic capabilities of members working as a team, which then allowed the group to search for sensitives in a large number of non-sensitives. The number was discouragingly small, but seven new sensitives were identified, often in groups that specialized in religious activities, charity work, medicine, or teaching, but they were not yet contacted since they appeared to be in stable situations.

Ken maintained his normal schedule in the Department of Physics, including regretfully the interminable faculty meetings as hiring decisions were hashed out, departmental directions chosen, and decisions made about the future of the small but growing department. His recent success pretty much guaranteed him additional hires of young faculty in his field of condensed matter, so he could sit back and observe. He could by now sense all their minds, and they were all very sharp, but he came nowhere close to reading any of them. Their external actions and internal emotions were often surprisingly de-coupled. Some of the most urgent faculty debaters were actually fairly calm inside, while there were a few who never opened their mouths but were in a state of internal turmoil for reasons he could not guess. There were no real sensitives in the entire faculty or staff. However, there was a senior faculty member in theory, vice chair of the department in charge of teaching, Jonathan Campbell, who had some stirrings of capability. His present research was solid but modest, but he served a key role in making the department educationally competent. He was very good with students, patient and helpful. He and his wife were wonderful people, practicing Episcopalians, with both acting as foster parents to numerous disadvantaged kids. He could become an ally in the future.

He tried the compulsion test, and could make only about half of the faculty wipe their foreheads, less than the population at large. Too bad. Perhaps the commitment to a highly rational science dimmed and extinguished any capabilities toward telepathic communication.

CHAPTER FOUR

Ken was pursuing his scientific breakthroughs vigorously, with a fine bunch of graduate students who were smart enough to realize that they were on the ground floor of a very big thing. Ken made every effort to make them feel appreciated, even in little things like the Monday group lunch. Today they were down at the Carl's Jr. near Highway 99, which had a good Santa Fe chicken sandwich. He was sitting back relaxed enjoying the camaraderie of the group when he suddenly realized that some new mind was probing his. In panic, he went into "dark mind" and waited as the signal grew, passed, and faded, clearly in a car on the highway moving south to Fresno. He could follow the mind down the highway for perhaps a minute, a long way, as it was making no attempt at concealment. He sat with beads or perspiration on his brow, sensing that the foreign mind was cold and hard, even cruel, and in its interrogation, sort of deliberately abusive.

Shaken, he toughed out the rest of the lunch, but at the first opportunity, called Omega together by e-mail and phone. By 4:15 p.m., they were all assembled in the Newman House.

The group could sense a serious problem. "I have just been probed by a foreign telepathic mind, dark, hard, and cruel. I will now remember as best I can the feeling." He ran through his memory very carefully, all the way through the departure of the foreign mind toward Fresno. "I had the sense that the mind was deliberately probing to get a response of some sort," said Ken. "I am not sure whether he sensed my mind, but I believe he did, although I went to "dark mind" as fast as I could. I sensed an uncertainty as he passed that he reached out for a mind he had momentarily sensed. He may well return."

"There was something else. He was contemplating some sinister plan for someone named Gabriella, a telephone operator in San Francisco, who appears to be some sort of sensitive. It is scheduled for this Friday, when he will pick her up after work. Someone named Greg was in his thoughts, and the thoughts were grim and brutal. I have no details beyond that. What are we to do?"

A long discussion followed, knowing that any attempt to intervene could result in exposure to, and perhaps destruction of, the Omega group. Yet the thought of standing by idle while a life was (most likely) destroyed was repugnant. The decision was made to keep all members of the group in groups of three for better defense, and keep away from Highway 99, while Jill, Ken, and Michelle went to San Francisco to learn what they could and intervene if they must. Ken carefully got out his 22 caliber semi-automatic pistol, unused in a decade and then only to put a trapped rattlesnake out of its misery.

He knew he had sufficient time to seek additional help. Ken called Jonathan for a meeting in his department office. Jonathan listened intently to this unbelievable tale.

"If this gets out, we are both academic road kill!" Jonathan said. "It will make "cold fusion" look like a picnic in the park in comparison. You are certain of this?" Jonathan pleaded, hoping it was some arcane joke.

"No question whatsoever. Given enough time, I could prove it to you with compete scientific certainty. Remember, I had to convince an equally skeptical Jill, with a comely young woman in tow to further muddy the waters. But we don't have any more time. I need you to mentor Omega if somehow we fail. We will die rather than reveal the presence of Omega, and if that happens I want you to step into the place of Jill, who is just barely sensitive but learning. Provide guidance, structure, and support, wisdom, and stability. I am sorry that I have not done this earlier, as I always planned to have you join the project, but events have moved awfully rapidly."

A faint flicker of what this all could mean crossed Jonathan's consciousness, along with the enormous gamble Ken was taking if it all should fall apart. Jonathan always felt Ken had Nobel Laureate potential, and it all could be lost in an instant if Omega was some fluke or error.

"I accept," Jonathan said, "although you are really pushing the envelope of my credibility. I want to see those tests when you return."

"If I return," Ken said. Ken gave him the group list, asked him to cover a class, and headed out to get ready. He had never been so frightened in his life. That mind he had felt was awful to contemplate, and he was about to challenge it.

They arrived in San Francisco on Wednesday, carefully using "dark mind" but sensing no threat. They stayed in an obscure but nice pensione off Van Ness, not far from downtown. Gabriella was actually rather easy to find, as she was a relatively new bi-lingual telephone operator at AT&T. All that was required was to wander into the AT&T building and "convince" a staffer 40 feet away to check up on the confidential list of operators by name. Her shift schedule was of course noted. That evening, at 5:30, they were all waiting as Gabriella appeared from the bowels of the AT&T building. While they had a rough picture from her employment form in their mind, there were an awful lot of women and they were afraid that they would miss her.

It was not a problem. Gabriella was broadcasting anguish so profoundly that they could have picked her up at 300 feet. She was clearly a sensitive and a powerful one at that. The interest of the hostile mind in Gabriella became more understandable and yet more sinister. Gabriella was anguishing over a romantic rendezvous of last weekend with this neat, rich, unmarried lawyer who claimed to be in love with her. They had gone to his apartment and made love, and then somehow Gabriella was doing things, awful things, with him. When they parted, he gave her $500 as a gift, sensing perhaps her disgust in how the evening had turned out. For the last four days, Gabriella had felt dirty, like a prostitute. She would tell him this Friday that there was no way that she was going on another date with him if this was what he wanted from her, and give him back the $500. What had she been thinking of when she accepted? She was not on her way to her apartment but to Saint Francis Assisi in North Beach, to go to a confession previously scheduled with the pastor.

They fell in behind her, and once they were free of the crowd, Michelle addressed her. "Peace be to you, Gabriella Martinez. We need to talk to you, now, for your own safety."

Gabriella paused, looked at them, and defenseless and open in her anguish, suddenly she was together with them, and it was beautiful. She almost fainted, but a bench was near and they helped her to it.

"Now you know," said Michelle. "We are a group of sensitive people with telepathic capabilities, steeped in Christian love. We have learned that dire plans are being laid for you this Friday, and you must flee evil people who have the power to control your mind. What you did last weekend was not your fault. You were forced to do them. You have great powers, and they plan to use them for some awful purpose whose details we do not know."

Gabriella was quick and smart. "I cannot leave you, now, or ever. I love you all. You know that. What must I do?"

"You must find an excuse to not show up Friday – one that gives no hint that you are doing anything to break off the engagement. Have a trusted friend meet your date and give him your profound regrets that an aunt in Orange County has just gone into the hospital and needs your help. Offer to re-schedule it for a week later, same time, same place. Then leave with us, taking only what you would take for a short visit to Orange County, get permission from AT&T as a medical emergency, pay all bills, and promise a quick return. Then later you will extend that date. You must never return here."

By 10:15 p.m., it was done, and they headed out of the city, Ken driving with Jill at his side. Gabriella lay back on the cushions of the back seat next to Michelle, deliberately not touching each other, immersed in a love that she had never believed possible. Suddenly Jill broke into tears. "What is wrong," Ken asked worriedly.

"Nothing, nothing at all," said Jill, and snuggled closer to Ken.

They got back to Merced by 1:00 a.m., and installed Gabriella in the second bedroom. He wryly contemplated the growing harem of gorgeous young women in his house, all profoundly in love with him. His explanation to his friends and department had better be convincing! He would leave this problem to Jill.

Once in bed, and despite the late hour, he and Jill made tender love that seemed especially sensitive and comfortable. As they lay together in each other's arms, Jill said, "In the car, coming back from San Francisco, I was so proud of you, I was loving you to bits! Then suddenly I felt something else, not Gabriella or Michelle, but their mutual love, sort of filling the car like perfume. And I felt you."

Tears of joy came to Ken's eyes, and they kissed. And so they fell asleep, and slept like that for hours.

CHAPTER FIVE

The view from the penthouse was magnificent. Fog rolled in across the Golden Gate, diffused with a golden glow from the sodium vapor lights in the bridge. The penthouse deck, festooned with expensive pieces of garden art and beautifully sculpted topiary trees, was connected through a wall of glass into a large room full of opulent furnishings, walls of book cases, and 21 comfortable leather chairs. The latter were formed into a large circle with a gap centered on the fireplace, in which aged blue oak burned quietly. The two chairs on each side of the fireplace were somewhat larger than the others. One was occupied, one empty except for a pair of wire-rimmed glasses.

All the rest of the 21 chairs were occupied, all by men, none too young and none older than perhaps their mid 60s. These men exuded power and wealth with sharply tailored Italian suits and Rolex watches. All were silent until the grandfather clock finished striking 9.

The man next to the fireplace spoke. He was known only as 1A, the most powerful telepath in the Coven. "We have been called to address a problem of Group 4." There was now only one "A" in the Coven, sitting next to the fireplace. Their founder and teacher, the late and great Matt Friedman, was an A+, but five years ago, he suddenly went insane and in response to fears that his babblings might reveal details of the Coven, he was quietly dispatched in a medical "accident." His glasses had been retrieved and became a permanent reminder.

Friedman had been a brilliant trial lawyer, extremely successful and very persuasive, but he had had a dark side of carefully planned killings. He had originally chosen gay men as his targets, because from their death throes he got some sort of powerful impulse. Gradually, he realized that he got the most effect when his victims had certain psychological strengths, and as he persisted, his own powers grew. The "summer of love" in 1967 presented easy victims for several years thereafter, men and women, usually young. He met and recruited a companion around 1975, and they jointly continued, always choosing victims who showed special sensitivity. Realizing that they were telepathic at some level, they started to "troll" for sensitives, and thus gathered more victims. The joint "feeding" at the death of a sensitive resulted in augmentation of their dark powers, and they grew.

In 1980, they were suddenly contacted by a powerful telepath from the eastern United States, who had been unaware of new telepaths in San Francisco. A prior Coven had died out in the 1930s. He brought them information and techniques, showing that they were only the latest in a long history of telepaths, never numerous at any one place or time, but usually dominant in their careers. Techniques of secrecy, self-preservation and contact, communication, and training were transmitted, along with a clear message that the eastern telepath, known only as A Prime, was the absolute leader. A quick demonstration of his capabilities left Friedman shaken and his companion retching out his guts.

With the new knowledge, the Coven grew faster and recruitment was stressed. All members were extremely successful in business: lawyers, investment bankers, a few CEOs, and a politician, as their powers of persuasion became ever more formidable. However they deliberately tried to avoid publicity, staying slightly in the background of their professions. At present, there were 20 members divided into four groups, and all 20 met together but rarely for questions of mutual concern. They never used each other's names, but group and rank only, with the group number 1 to 4, set by order of formation, and the rank, A through D, by mental capacity. 1A was actually grateful that he came to his full powers when Friedman was clearly in decline. There was a rumor that Friedman had once come upon another A-level telepath in the city, and arranged to have him eliminated.

Group 4 consisted of five members; two Bs, two Cs, and a D, the newest recruit, Greg, who was still thought of as Greg but was now officially just 4D.

4B1 began, "I sensed for just an instant a sensitive in Merced as I was trolling on my way to Fresno Monday, around noon. Then suddenly, in a fraction of a second, it was gone. Completely gone. And I never picked it up again. Admittedly the signal was weak, but I have never felt such a shutdown before. I see two possibilities: 1) error on my part that for some reason my ability to sense suddenly decreased, and I lost the signal. If so, there is no problem; 2) there was indeed a sensitive there, he sensed my probe, and rather than emit the instinctive echo of a probed sensitive mind, shut down. This shows both an ability to sense our thoughts and the discipline to block further reception. If this is true, there is something going on in Merced that needs to be studied, and soon, as it could pose a threat to our existence."

"There is something else," 4B1 continued, "I had a date last Saturday with a highly sensitive but naïve telephone operator named Gabriella. All was going well, and she was a major candidate for a Group 4 'feeding.' Regretfully, I pushed her too far sexually, and once my compulsion waned, she felt revulsion at what she had done. She is a fervent Catholic, and I should have known better. I gave her a gift of $500, but that may have simply compounded the error. The only reason I bring this up is that Thursday she suddenly left town to help a sick aunt in Orange County. No such relative is listed on her employment form, but with these big extended Mexican families, this is not necessarily a surprise. She rescheduled our date through a friend. Why I bring this up was that I was thinking about the 'feeding' on Gabriella as I drove through Merced. Could our plans have been picked up? If so, the situation is yet more serious."

There was a long pause. 1A responded, "I concur with 4B1 in this analysis, and I do not think that it was an error on his part. We must however proceed with great caution, for the sensitive in Merced could be either a new recruit or a useful victim, as well as a threat. I believe that the level of concern is adequate to propose a joint visit of Group 4 in its entirety as soon as it can be arranged. The first effort must be a passive survey of the entire region, especially including the university and its students, as I don't expect to find many sensitives among the farmers and migrant workers of that depressing region. Be patient. Whoever it is may have been scared away by your contact."

"If on the other hand, the sensitive somehow has interfered with the Gabriella 'feeding,' he shows a level of competence that is at a very worrisome level. Be careful, be very careful. We have never before had to contemplate such a threat to our group. If the sensitive learned about Gabriella, could he have learned about us all?"

"I don't think so," said 4B1. "I was only thinking of the 'feeding' and of Group 4."

1A responded. "Anyway, great caution. I want twice daily reports to 2B1, your designated backup."

31

CHAPTER SIX

Group 4 traveled in a rented white Chevy Suburban, big enough to easily hold them all, their luggage, and if necessary one or more of their quarry if that could be accomplished. Greg also drove a used convertible, useful for probing since the fabric top didn't block the signal the way steel did. They traveled to Merced two weeks after the group meeting, and rented two rooms in about the best motel that the city had to offer. They had already obtained excellent maps of the entire region, phone books electronically on their laptops and in hard copy, U.S. census demographic data, and a full list of all UC Merced faculty, students, and staff. They all had secure communication via cell phone to cell phone on encrypted lines. With some difficulty, they had all cleared their calendars for about 10 days.

On the second day, they went for a group breakfast to the Carl's Jr. near Highway 99, the closest place to the earlier contact. They were in a totally passive mode with no attempt to probe.

Nothing.

For the next four days, they covered essentially every street in Merced, out into the country for about 10 miles, and even wandered among the students in the temporary Student Union on the UC Merced campus.

Nothing.

Frustration, and perhaps a bit of relief, began to permeate Group 4, and Greg in particular was aching to start active probing. That noon, they decided to repeat their entire four-day survey with two actively probing (4B2, 4C1) and the rest listening only, which improved their ability to sense a response. In order to further enhance the possibilities of contact, they traveled in two cars, with the two probers in the van and the three receptors in a rented convertible closely trailing the van. All were armed.

Four more days passed.

Nothing.

Most of Omega was high in the foothills of the Sierra Nevada in a rented house, carefully chosen for a good view of the terrain below and at the end of a long, difficult road leading north out of Merced, just beyond Hornitos. Jonathan was taking care of local concerns, and only Michelle, Ken, and Jill moved around Merced in a complete "dark mind" mode. After about two weeks, they sensed some presence but it came and went, nothing of great strength, and no fix was obtained. However, it was unusual enough to alert them that the feared presence was looking for them. Jonathan made useful contacts with the Merced Police, purportedly about a threat by crazy enviros over some of the research in the Physics Department, and had a list of all motel customers and any other unusual doings. He had placed video cameras on the entrances to UC Merced, and every evening checked the tapes for suspicious cars. Each evening he called a number in Modesto and left a message on the machine. The evening Ken and Michelle first sensed the presence, a short message was on Jonathan's work number.

"They are here and appear to be moving about the city," was what he meant, but what the message said was that a student was asking to have a midterm rescheduled due to sickness, a flu that kept moving around her body.

Three days later, Jonathan noticed a white van had appeared in several pictures and at two separate entrances to the central campus. In one photo he was able to make out a license number, reported it to the campus and Merced Police, and promptly received confirmation that it had been rented in San Francisco by two men, driving a convertible despite the season. The driver's license was traced and found to be fraudulent, and the credit card was to an account with fictitious names. Merced Police offered to pick them up for questioning of this information alone, but Jonathan recommended waiting to see what developed. Still, Merced Police found where they were staying, and surreptitiously took good pictures of them.

Two days later, Merced Police reported that the van and convertible had been seen cruising the streets of Merced, one following the other by about 50 yards, a notable event since it was approaching winter and convertibles were rare in the Central Valley in any case.

That evening, Jonathan got a message. "They are actively searching Merced for us, with active mind probes from the van and receptors in the convertible since the fabric top would not interfere with weak electromagnetic signals. Please tell the police not to interfere, as we are gathering valuable information from them."

Any lingering doubts of Jonathan about the seriousness of the search for Omega were rapidly being dispelled by the unusual events predicted by

Ken and confirmed by the van and convertible.

After three days, Group 4 had gotten into a pattern of taking a break at the Carl's Jr. closest to where the original contact had been made. Whenever possible, Ken and Michelle tried to be near, and were picking up a lot of valuable information on the group, including past behavior and future plans as part of a Coven of telepaths in San Francisco. The appalling history of the group and their need to "feed" on the deaths of sensitives were passed to Omega and to Jonathan. It also became clear that while the individuals were powerful, they really could not work well in concert. It was also true that they tired easily from the strain of probing and control, and even while alternating responsibilities, they needed regular breaks.

It was during one afternoon break, with Ken and Michelle nowhere in the vicinity, that Greg, the youngest and hungriest of Group 4, probed the mind of a cute waitress. Her name was Bonny, a sophomore at UC Merced in social studies, and a marginal sensitive. He mentioned this to Group 4, and since they were almost at the end of their survey, with zero contacts, and already together as a group, they decided to act. Group 4 was both frustrated by over a week of hard work and secretly relieved that this unpromising berg was not harboring crypto-telepaths. They were expert at capture procedures as they had used them repeatedly in San Francisco.

Bonny was about finished with her shift, and Group 4 timed it perfectly. Bonny came to deliver the food bill, checked off her shift, and then suddenly had an irresistible urge to join her new friends in the white van for some fun. They left together, and drove east into the hills. All during this time, Group 4 alternated in convincing Bonny that she was having the time of her life with a bunch of witty companions. The van began to climb switchbacks into the foothills on the way to Yosemite on Highway 140, past Catheys Valley, and into steeper terrain skirting a deep canyon, until they turned off on a dirt road that led to a clearing in the blue oaks.

Bonny's scream was heard by Ken and Michelle from many miles away. Michelle was ashen faced, Ken furious.

"They have killed Bonny," whispered Michelle.

"I sensed that it was far away, east, and I sense a clearing and blue oaks. Bonny was one of our potential recruits," said Ken to Jill, "and modestly sensitive."

"They have ripped her mind apart," whispered Michelle.

"There is no way that Bonny alone could have projected that scream so far, no matter how awful her terror. It must have been amplified by the Coven, probably all of them for once working in concert," said Ken.

"They ate Bonny's mind," whispered Michelle.

So that was what we saved Gabriella from, thought Ken. They jumped into their car and headed east, toward the sound, although they knew that they were too late to help Bonny. They drove up Highway 140, one of the few roads in the direction from which the scream had come. Winding steeply up into the blue oak forest, they kept in a "dark mind" condition. The first twinge of dread alerted them and they slowed down, moving up the switchbacks until only perhaps a half mile away. Group 4 was just finished burying Bonny's body in a deep grave, covered with plastic, and arranging the ground surface and cover so that no animal or policemen would ever find it. The Coven was fastidious in cleaning up on the scenes of their "feeding" activities, but it did take a lot of time and effort. Their minds were in a state of exhausted euphoria.

Ken pulled the car off a short dirt spur on one of the switchbacks. Ken and Michelle recoiled in horror over the naked and uncontrolled emanations from this truly evil group. It was also clear that this group was searching for Omega and that if they discovered Omega, they would not quit until it was destroyed.

However, any attempt to eradicate the group would be a red flag back in San Francisco confirming Omega's existence and, until now, their search for Omega had come up negative. Further, the absence of Bonny and the discovery that she had left with five men who often ate at Carl's Jr. and drove a white van would result in instant police action, driving them away from Merced for months, if not longer. Ken guessed that this unscheduled "feeding" of a traceable person would not be viewed positively at the Coven, and that would further reduce efforts at discovery. Perhaps they would give up entirely, and assume that the original contact had been some sort of fluke.

Carefully, Ken and Michelle walked toward Group 4 as it completed the burial process. Jill stayed with the car. There was brush for excellent cover, and they could cut across the switchbacks that made the road so

35

tortuous. They climbed to within about 100 feet of the group in a "dark mind" mode, and began to pick up details of Group 4 thought patterns. Group 4 was anxious to finish the task because almost by accident they learned from Bonny on the drive up that there was a small group of cool people who were very close, meeting regularly and deep into some spiritual quest. Bonny provided several names, some of them her friends, and hoped to join this group soon. Group 4 had a strong suspicion that this might be the source of the telepathic response at Merced, since Bonny was clearly a sensitive at a low to moderate level. Not wanting to use their cell phones, which could be traced to the scene of the "feeding," they were anxious to get back to Merced and pass the information back to San Francisco.

Ken and Michelle were horrified. All would be lost if such contact were made. They raced back to the car and consulted with Jill on what to do.

Greg as junior in Group 4 was given the task of driving the van back to Merced. Group 4 members were in their post-prandial euphoria, spiced by the knowledge that they may have also solved the problem of the telepathic response from Merced. The road was steep and winding, and the heavy Chevy suburban steered like a boat. It also had a pattern of picking up speed on the steep downgrades and needed continuous braking to keep the speed reasonable. As he turned through yet one more of the interminable switchbacks, Greg saw that he had finally reached the flat straight section that led across the grassy plains to Merced. He stomped on the gas to pick up speed for the quick trip back to Merced.

The van left the highway at more than 65 miles per hour, launching itself through a thin screen of bushes and into the void with at least a 500-foot drop to the canyon below. Once the van was airborne, Ken and Michelle released their control over Greg. All other members of Group 4 were screaming at Greg, grabbing for the wheel, when they heard a clear, grim message, "This is for Bonny!" Suddenly they knew all, and knew that the knowledge would be too late. Hate and anger spewed from their enraged minds, awful, beastly thoughts. The van struck the canyon wall, bursting into flame as it tumbled on and on. Ken and Michelle could sense the minds winking out, one by one, as they scrambled back to their car, anxious to get off the mountain road before the police arrived. Despite what they had learned about this group, they shared a profound sadness at having to deliberately kill five human beings.

CHAPTER SEVEN

The view from the penthouse was magnificent, but none of the members of the Coven was particularly aware of it. Twenty-one chairs were formed into a large circle with a gap centered on the fireplace, in which aged blue oak burned quietly. The two chairs on each side of the fireplace were somewhat larger than the others.

Fifteen of the 21 chairs were occupied, all by men, none too young and none older than perhaps their mid 60s. These men exuded power and wealth with sharply tailored Italian suits and Rolex watches. One of the two chairs by the fireplace was occupied only by a pair of old-fashioned glasses. The other five empty chairs were scattered seeming randomly around the circle, but one was directly opposite from, and therefore farthest from the fire. All were silent until the grandfather clock finished striking 9.

1A spoke. "We appear to have a problem at Merced. I would like 2B1 to summarize the situation"

"The Group 4 survey, passive and active, had been totally without contacts. Group 4, probably pushed by that psychopath Greg, decided to have a 'feeding' on a woman well known in the town and from a place where Group 4 had repeatedly dined. While this is poor procedure even in San Francisco, it was an especially bad mistake in a town as small as Merced. Rough descriptions could probably be developed by about 50 people, perhaps with permanent but low-quality records on video surveillance cameras. Our security thus depends on reliance on faked identification, and I trust it holds, but some Group 4 faces are well known in San Francisco and the local law enforcement in Merced is not under our control. We will have to expend considerable time and resources to bolster our defenses in the area, which in itself and in the present highly charged atmosphere has its own risks. Our only hope is that this woman's case is handled as a missing-person case and not a murder, and the destruction of the van as a driving accident. We understand that the van was totally destroyed and the bodies burned beyond recognition. We also must trust that the 'feeding' site in the mountains is secure, since the van crashed coming down the mountain, not going up into the mountain, and only five bodies were on board.

"We also need a series of stories to explain the deaths of five prominent business men in San Francisco. I propose a plane crash in the mountains while surveying a potential land purchase can cover three of them. The bodies could easily be incinerated beyond easy physical identification, but on the corpses there will be items that will aid the identification process. We should do this quickly. Group 2 will find a plane and Victor, our secure pilot, then will get four victims from the homeless population, and make it so. Greg is a loner and has few ties to the city. Minimal effort is needed to have him take a trip. That leaves only one additional death, perhaps a flaming crash off Devil's Slide on Highway 1. Schedule it for two weeks later, and we will cover the absences by other excuses," 2B1 concluded.

"We must get non-telepathic personnel into Merced immediately to monitor events," demanded 1A. "Group 2 will be in charge. Once a foundation is laid, bring in no more than two Group 2 personnel in the lowest conceivable profile. We must get all police reports on the crash to see if there was any possibility of foul play. No active probing at any time except to interfere with a police investigation if it appears to be going inappropriately."

But at that very minute in Merced, the police investigation was going "inappropriately."

The totally unexpected and uncharacteristic diversion of Bonny into the white van was immediately reported. The police, already highly suspicious of the strange behavior of the van and convertible, had taken high-quality surveillance photographs of the men at the motel. Fingerprints (and potential DNA samples from hair and nail filings) were taken at the motel, but no matches found to the fingerprints. The disappearance was labeled a kidnapping, and the FBI was called in. The white van had been sighted by several people going along the road up to the mountains. From the times involved, and the van crash site, a series of potential areas for crime had been plotted, and one was the actual crime scene. Tire tracks were mapped at the scene, and one officer noted that a large flat rock seemed out of place. They were very familiar with the site, a favorite "Lovers Lane" for Merced teenagers. Bonny's body was found within hours of her death, but other than the terror in her face, a face that would haunt the investigating officers for years, no mark was seen on her body as a cause of death.

The identification of the essentially destroyed white van was tied to the rental agency, but there was no way to find out who the five passengers were. All identification proved to be forged, and the bodies largely incinerated and crushed. Some dental information could probably be derived in the autopsies. An "all-points" bulletin was issued, with pictures of the suspects taken earlier at the motel, and transmitted to San Francisco, city of the fictitious identification used to rent the van and pay for the motel.

Within minutes of the report reaching San Francisco, the report and pictures were in a lawyer's private office high on Nob Hill. And a few minutes later, slightly altered pictures were returned to the San Francisco police for transmission to all points.

The convertible proved more interesting. It was found parked at the motel, and was not from any local rental agency. It was carefully searched for evidence, and dusted for prints. There were many. Quite a bit of other evidence was found, and carefully catalogued. The search to trace the origins of the vehicle was initiated.

CHAPTER EIGHT

Omega met up in the mountain house, this time with Gabriella and Jonathan. The mood was somber. Ken, Michelle, and Jill related all that had happened, saddened and troubled by what they had done. But even now in hindsight they could see no other way to avoid exposure and destruction of Omega.

Jonathan gave a report on the police investigation, to which he had contributed his research. All leads had dried up except perhaps the convertible, and they were hoping that when the pictures were circulated in San Francisco, someone might recognize the men. Jonathan had sent a set of pictures directly to a journalist at the *Chronicle*, with a report on the strange doings at Merced, but used the name of an investigating officer at the university. Ken and Jonathan would watch over the investigation and if anything surfaced that even hinted that it was anything but careless driving on a mountain road, they would intervene with the greatest of caution.

Ken then gave a technical report on his efforts to electronically enhance the signals, either in sending or receiving, totally without success. Clearly, the information, although electromagnetic, was varying in amplitude, frequency, and phase in a way hard to capture. He did by accident come across one old spark generator used in the physics labs, and when the megahertz ranges had been isolated and put through a broadband amplifier, it made telepathic transmission impossible. In fact, one got a headache without even sensing what the problem was. This could prove useful.

In the future, they had to continue training while living as normal a life as possible. Clearly, Bonny (and perhaps others) had sensed something special about this group, so they had better back off having regular meetings in public places. Jonathan was asked to develop surveillance of motel visitors, cars and other reconnaissance, because his earlier efforts had been so successful.

Then with Jonathan and Jill in the circle, they leaned back and tried to project love, peace, and comfort at Ken, Michelle, and Jill. Their minds linked effortlessly, bathing Jill and Jonathan with torrents of love barely perceived by either, although the resonances in Jill's mind were definitely stronger every time. Then Ken started to speak, and each member of

Omega said the words in sequence, as fast as Ken would normally speak, summarizing for Jonathan's benefit the theories of Teilhard de Chardin and the findings of current brain research.

Jonathan was stunned, thrilled, confused, and profoundly committed to this brave new world.

Gabriella turned out to be both powerful and complex. Her telepathic assets had been based on a profound religious commitment to the Virgin of Guadalupe. Clearly, the Coven had not understood this, or they wouldn't have proceeded as they had. She also had a hard edge to her mind, based on bitter resentment for the domination she had suffered and the degrading acts that had followed, and was keenly aware that she had barely avoided the fate of Bonny.

Ken began to wonder if the level of communication possible for Coven members was less than theirs. The Coven clearly had great powers of domination and excellent powers of probing and receiving the mental presence of sensitives, but detailed verbal and non-verbal communication might be weak. In the few cases he had penetrated their minds, they were never acting in concert but individually and sequentially.

Omega then had an extensive discussion of what should happen next. Ken was of the opinion that further attempts to find Omega would occur, and that their presence in Merced was risky. Thus, if work in Merced was essential, they should always be in twos and threes, always with "dark mind" in place, and always armed. But before drawing away, there must quickly be a survey of sensitives in Merced, as they wanted no repeats of the Bonny tragedy. They divided the university and town into zones, and assigned pairs to search, first passively, then actively using the probe and automatic response technique they had learned from the Coven.

Further it was decided that Omega should be split in two, with each half roughly balanced and at a location secret from the other. Communication was only to be through secure channels that could not allow the source to be traced. They would periodically meet as a group but only when essential and then in secure locations.

Jill was the head of Omega-alpha, with Ken, Michelle, Roger and Joanne, who were clearly becoming a committed pair, and Mary and Nancy, whose relative rating was rising steadily. Jonathan was the head of Omega-beta, with Diane and Michael, a potent pair, Gabriella, Tiffany, and Phyllis. Several, including Ken, Jill, and Jonathan, could not neglect their university duties, while the students were committed to classes.

CHAPTER NINE

The view from the penthouse was magnificent, but none of the members of the Coven was particularly aware of it. Twenty-one chairs were formed into a large circle with a gap centered on the fireplace, in which aged blue oak burned quietly. The two chairs on each side of the fireplace were somewhat larger than the others.

Fifteen of the 21 chairs were occupied, all by men, none too young and none older than perhaps their mid 60s. One of the two chairs by the fireplace was occupied only by a pair of old fashioned glasses. The other five empty chairs were scattered seeming randomly around the circle, but one was directly opposite from, and therefore farthest from the fire. Three chairs had been added in the center of the ring, facing the fireplace, and these were occupied by two men and a woman. All were silent until the grandfather clock finished striking 9.

1A spoke. "We appear to be handling the problem at Merced at this time. Photographs of Group 4, of distressingly good quality, were intercepted and subtly morphed to prevent identification of Group 4 members. The Merced police were already aware of and suspicious of Group 4. This is the kind of problem that one can encounter in a small town. We must be much more circumspect. Secure non-sensitive personnel will be on site to assist in the investigation by tomorrow, and the police have met dead ends in trying to trace the false identification. Plans are in place for providing more suitable deaths for Group 4 members.

"But I am still concerned over the accident itself. The timing and place are both highly suspicious, and we have survived undetected for the past 50 years because we have taken extraordinary steps to prevent our discovery. In this crisis, I have taken the liberty of inviting three members of the Los Angeles Coven to attend this briefing, to see if they have encountered similar problems and to advise us of additional steps we can take in the present and future. They will be addressed as L1, L2, and L3, from left to right. I want to thank them for the assistance they have offered."

L1 spoke, "The Coven in Los Angeles has not been as successful as we had all hoped. There is an enormous population to draw from, but there appears to be a smaller proportion of 'sensitives.' We are not finding it easy to duplicate your frequent 'feedings' here in San Francisco, although the best area appears to be West Hollywood. However, it is a small area, and the unexplained loss of too many members of the gay community would be noticed. We have had only modest success building up a non-sensitive infrastructure in the police department and elsewhere, and we have a long way to go to duplicate your situation here in San Francisco.

"We are surveying San Diego in the hopes for a better sensitives ratio. However, we have also found two single telepaths in Los Angeles, one a well-known politician, who appear to operate in a rather passive mode, dominating those around them, forcing small modifications of behavior, just enough to ensure their own success. They do not have anything like the techniques and capabilities of the San Francisco Coven, and essentially pose no threat. On the other hand, they would provide a satisfying 'feeding' and so we let them be until the need arises. They appear to have no ability to sense our thought probes, and thus are not candidates for your Merced event.

"We of course would welcome any members of your Coven, and provide material support, cover, secure houses, and the like. We also offer our members as part of your investigatory team in Merced, and in return desire to be kept in touch with anything you learn as we share your concern about the threat to our organization and life style."

"Much appreciated," said 1A. "Could you assign one of your members to stay with us here as a temporary liaison? We would prefer L3 as we have no women in our Coven at this time."

"Done," said L1. "L3, although a relatively recent recruit, has capabilities that are both considerable and differ in significant ways from our male members. She had already volunteered for such a task as she could learn a lot from you. We also have a new recruit, LA 3C, named Edward, who could pass as a UC Merced student."

CHAPTER TEN

The 54-foot yacht rested quietly at anchor in Monterey Bay. However, the sky, though blue, had cirrus and horsetail clouds at high elevation, and the wind was blowing from the southeast, the direction that predicted the arrival of a storm in a few hours. The caterer's boat had left more than an hour ago, and the remains of a sumptuous lunch were scattered on the teak table in the dining room. Coven members 2B1, 2B2, 3C1, and 3C2 were present, with the latter three dressed and carefully made up to closely resemble 4B1, 4B2, and 4C2. In addition, Victor Tagliaferro, a short dark man with a weathered complexion that comes from many hours in the sun, lounged in a large leather chair chewing a toothpick.

Victor spoke first, "All is in readiness. The weather is turning bad, with a large storm approaching, and I propose we make the flight today at 3:00 p.m. I have rented the Beechcraft, capable of carrying four people with ease, and have already filed a flight plan down over Big Sur, and then into King City. I believe this is much safer than trying to stage a flaming crash in the Sierra Nevada, because the snow could preserve evidence for a police investigation, which none of us desire." No one mentioned, and no one cared, that this approach would spare the lives of four of San Francisco's homeless population. Non-sensitives simply did not count.

"Excellent," responded 2B1. "We have the duffels packed with the necessary gear. Pickup is waiting on the road you selected in the hills behind the Soledad Mission. I have passed around to a number of people who knew Group 4 members the reason for this surreptitious over-flight of a potential major land purchase inland of Big Sur, following days of negotiations at a secret location. As you have seen, there is $1 million in smallish bills already transferred to your bank vault in Albuquerque, and $2 million in your Aruba account. Your new identification papers are complete, and we have already obtained for you a house at Key West under your new identity. All is ready on our end."

Victor kind of grunted, for although he liked the money, he was not really keen on leaving the Bay Area. He checked for the third time the duffel, his hand-made ejectable autopilot system, a high-quality life jacket designed for ocean rescue, donated by these businessmen, complete with built-in GPS locator. This was the fourth time he had worked for this group that had no name but had tremendous clout in San Francisco. They had saved him from ruin and jail time several years ago, while paying him handsomely for his work.

At 2:15 p.m., Victor and his passengers left for shore with the launch, picked up the rented car (all with legitimate identification for Group 4 members) and proceeded to Monterey Regional Airport. The plane was ready, Victor checked his flight plan, and brushed aside warnings of the impending storm, saying they would land safely at the King City airport well before serious weather arrived. The flight down the coast was bumpy as the winds picked up, and as they had seen on the satellite, a low stratus already hid the land below about Point Lobos. They flew directly to the lonely road in a valley west of Soledad in the hills, landed, and quickly dropped off the passengers at a waiting delivery van which was, as their pattern, windowless in the back. Victor took off immediately, and then maintained for about an hour a pattern back and forth across the foothills that would mimic a land survey. Then he started to climb and move west, over the mountains that by now were cloud covered.

At the chosen time, and exact location over the Big Sur Mountains, he radioed King City. "King City, I request an emergency approach vector. One of my passengers is having trouble breathing, and I am trying to resuscitate. Please have an ambulance standing by."

"Roger. Your vector is 280 true. We will clear all local air for your approach." This would not be much of a problem at that tiny airport with its essentially volunteer tower personnel from the local flying club.

Victor then carefully put the plane on exactly the opposite direction from King City, shut off the radio, and flew straight out over the coastline. forty-five minutes later, safely out of radar range, he had installed his ejectable autopilot in the pilot's seat, with the window open so that in 30 minutes it would be flung out of the plane and fall safely into the ocean. The locator beacon showed that he was almost exactly over the yacht. He figured the wind drift, and put on the parachute and then the life vest. Forcing open the passenger side door, he jumped from the plane and went into free fall, soon entering the clouds. He watched his altimeter carefully and at 2,000 feet, he pulled the ripcord and opened his chute. There was a period of disorientation as he drifted down inside the clouds, and so it was a great relief to come out of the stratus at 500 feet and see the yacht perhaps a mile off but in easy range. He hit the water and went under, but soon came to the surface. The sea was rough, but with his super life jacket, he rode high in the water. The yacht turned and came toward him. He would be safe and dry in a matter of minutes. The plane would never be recovered because they were over water thousands of feet deep even here and the plane would be out another 60 miles before it crashed and sank.

A small wave slapped him in the face. The sea was getting rougher, and he was anxious to be back in the yacht. It didn't seem to be moving any closer, and he was definitely getting a lot more water in his face. He was riding lower in the water, and his jacket didn't seem to be holding him up very well. Perhaps it was the parachute that was weighing him down. Struggling and working, he sank lower and lower. He tried to get his boots off, but they were laced, a larger wave hit, and he barely re-surfaced. Why was the yacht so slow? It didn't seem any closer. A horrible though occurred. Was this a double cross? Was the life vest the group had provided from the yacht deliberately defective? Another wave hit, and this time he never surfaced.

2B1 watched as the last part of the parachute was pulled under water, then took the yacht controls and headed back to port at Palo Alto as the storm grew ever more intense. It would be a rough trip through the "potato patch" of rough water just outside the Golden Gate Bridge, but 2B1 was an expert yachtsman and the tide was favorable. He actually looked forward to the challenge.

CHAPTER ELEVEN

Jonathan made his daily visit to the Merced Police Department to check on progress of the investigation. He was introduced to a visiting policeman from San Francisco, Sergeant Robert Teller, who was helping track down the San Francisco connection through the much greater resources of the San Francisco Police Department (SFPD). There really seemed no reason to have Teller actually stay at Merced, since the computers and labs were in San Francisco, but he settled down for what by all appearances was going to be an extended stay.

There was nothing much new to report yet. The convertible was proving hard to tie to any person, because it was bought used in Seattle about a year ago for cash, and with faked identification. The conclusion was that the perpetrators had gone to extraordinary care to hide their tracks, and this raised the whole case profile higher. Now it was not just who they were, but what did they have to hide? Why had they spent nine days covering Merced like a blanket? It was certainly not just to kidnap and kill a waitress that they had probably seen a dozen times during the previous week. And how did Bonny die in such terror with no mark of violence on her body and no unusual chemicals in her blood? The FBI was solicitous but equally stumped as their standard tracing techniques came up blank. No fingerprint matches, no DNA, no dental records. It was as though these five men had never existed.

It was not a great surprise, then, when that evening Jonathan came across Teller's picture spending a great deal of time at the site. Jonathan had placed a hidden, solar-powered digital camera at the crash site and crime scene, and reviewed the pictures each evening in his faculty office. Teller especially seemed to be tracing out the route the van must have taken, searching for skid marks. He then went somewhere behind the camera site and was invisible for more than 30 minutes, only to reappear. More interestingly, he was not wearing his SFPD uniform and he never appeared in the camera shots at the actual crime scene of Bonny's death.

It took but a short time on the Internet to locate Robert's name on the SFPD roster. He was indeed a sergeant, but in an "at large" position moving from project to project. Jonathan would have to check this out with his buddy at the *San Francisco Chronicle*.

At that moment, his buddy at the *Chron* was not a happy camper. His article on the mysterious five men and the Bonny murder was uncharacteristically rejected for publication. So he went to a friend at the *North Beach Voice*, and peddled it to him for basically beer money. The editor thought it a neat piece, and next Monday, the story was all over the Bay Area in free newspaper stands, super markets, and other locations. The pictures from Jonathan came out pretty good (the paper was actually printed on the *Chronicle's* presses as a contract job) and immediately any number of cops noted that the pictures did not quite jibe with the shots in the official "all-points" bulletin. A call was made to Merced, and the originals were sent up to San Francisco by fax. The differences were indeed real, and what is more, two of the mysterious persons were quickly recognized as a mid-level local politician and a well-known trial lawyer.

Now the *Chronicle* went into high gear, and immediately ran the original story (reluctantly with credit to the *North Beach Voice*), along with in-depth analysis of the identified men. Within a day, all five men were identified. This was the very same day that three of these men were reported missing in a plane crash off Big Sur. The press had a field day, and the *Chronicle's* front page read like the *National Enquirer.* Conspiracy theories sprouted like mushrooms in the hills of Napa County.

Sergeant Robert Teller failed to report to work at Merced on the next day, and passed quickly into an alternate identity long prepared for him in Spokane, Washington.

CHAPTER TWELVE

The view from the penthouse was magnificent, but none of the members of the Coven was particularly aware of it. Twenty-one chairs were formed into a large circle with a gap centered on the fireplace, in which aged blue oak burned quietly. The two chairs on each side of the fireplace were somewhat larger than the others. Three chairs had been added in the center of the ring, facing the fireplace, and these were occupied by two men and a woman.

Seven of the 21 chairs were occupied, all by men, none too young and none older than perhaps their mid 60s. One of the two chairs by the fireplace was occupied only by a pair of old-fashioned glasses, the other by an older man. He looked tired. The empty chairs were scattered seeming randomly around the circle. All were silent until the grandfather clock finished striking 9.

1A spoke. "We are facing disaster. Only you remaining members appear to have impeccable credentials and no connection to the 4B Group. We have had to promulgate the ultimate story involving real estate speculation, theft of clients' funds, and the like, adequate to cause nine of our members to flee the city, and some to flee the country. I would like to express my deep appreciation for our Los Angeles colleagues for their support in these dire times.

"But that is not all. The report from our agent in Merced, now departed, was that there was no trace of skid marks at the crash site. It appears on the contrary that the van turned the corner and accelerated to the one point where there was no guardrail because of the bushes. We have to at least consider the possibility that some very powerful telepath took control of the driver's mind – the unstable Greg, our newest recruit – and caused the crash. If that is the case, we have serious trouble indeed. We have to cease all activities, cease active mind probing, cease all 'feeding' activities, and basically hunker down until a counter response can be mounted. This will take some time. I will be relocated to Los Angeles, and all meetings here will cease."

"That is all."

The men and one woman left the apartment in the usual staggered mode after re-arranging the chairs into a more natural looking clubby configuration. After 10 minutes with no activity in the room, the motion sensors shut off the lights and locked the doors.

CHAPTER THIRTEEN

Spring had come to the Central Valley. The winter's rains had been good, the grass was green, the oaks healthy, and the famous vernal pools that almost blocked the formation of UC Merced were full. There was still a lot of mud around the campus from the frenetic construction going on, but in between were carefully preserved areas of oaks and meadows, as beautiful with wildflowers for these few weeks as any place in the world.

Edward Jones, a recently enrolled student in the Graduate School of Administration, was thoroughly enjoying the scene. He had heard so many negative things about the Central Valley in general and UC Merced in particular at UCLA that he was frankly surprised how pleasant it was here. Students of all ages were reveling in the warm, soft air and the smell of grass and flowers, lounging on the grass singly and in groups, pretending to study.

He had been here now for two-and-a-half months on the order of the Los Angeles Coven, with never a trace of telepathic activity detected. He had, according to Coven instructions, strictly refrained from being anything but a student, passively alert to any trace of sensitives and refraining from any active probing. He was, however, becoming hungry, and while not about to violate the terms and conditions of his stay at Merced, and clearly aware that he was not the only Coven member here, he was becoming more alert to potential victims in the future once these restrictions were lifted. There was a nice looking student about 35 feet away, alone, leaning against the trunk of a valley oak. He had a rather refined face, his movements were easy and fluid, and clothes showed considerable flair. Really, it couldn't hurt to check his receptivity, perhaps even just for a standard date. Just then, the student looked roughly in his direction and gave a beautiful smile. Edward responded immediately with a mental probe probably somewhat stronger than needed, verging on a level that would generate compulsion in any sort of reasonable sensitive. He was sure that the guy was a sensitive and seemed to be smiling at him.

A blast of pure hatred from a woman not 10 feet behind him smashed into his brain, shortly followed by an almost equal blast from the guy. Every muscle was frozen, his mind was a wreck. Then slowly he felt his legs begin to move, standing him up, then walking arm in arm with the girl toward the parking lot, into a car, then they drove into the hills. Each person alternated in controlling him, about 15 minutes at a time, the guy driving, the woman next to him in the back seat. Edward saw that she was armed, and a semiautomatic pistol was pointed at his left ear. Somehow it didn't matter. He was in a sort of dream state but with an awful headache.

After about 30 minutes, his sight suddenly failed him and his mind was filled with of all things Walt Disney's *Fantasia*. That was always a favorite of his, shown repeatedly in his West Hollywood apartment for his guests, and he dreamed his way through three or four of the scenes.

Suddenly he woke up. He was in a small room with no windows, and four people were present, including the guy and girl who had captured him. The furniture was comfortable, and it had a lived-in look. All compulsion was gone but he had a splitting headache. This was noted, and after some discussion, he was given two pills to swallow. They all left the room.

What had happened? Clearly, he had been hit with massive compulsion stronger by far than anything he had experienced in the training session of the Los Angeles Coven. It had occurred just after he attempted to probe the guy's mind, and it came from of all persons – a woman. He had never known such pain! This was the group that he had been sent to find, and they found him first. In despair, he had no doubt what was coming next. He was a reasonably strong natural sensitive, and the "feeding" would enhance the powers of up to a dozen people. He remembered the terror on the faces of the victims as their minds were torn apart, and the explosive thrill he felt as his powers peaked with those of his colleagues. After the "feeding," they all went into a post-prandial stupor as their minds digested what had happened. When testing came, usually three days later, he had sometimes gained a full 8 percent in overall power of compulsion. Why had he violated his orders? Had he been lulled into complacency by two-and-a-half months of null results? Now he would pay the price! He began to cry out of terror and frustration, great tears of sorrow for his failure and fear of what would now happen. Where was 1A and his powerful presence when he needed him? Without his recognizing it, his headache had abated and, in his exhaustion, he fell asleep.

Omega-alpha lounged in chairs and on cushions in the large room next to the training room. Two members rotated to surveillance duty on the sleeping Edward.

Ken said, "Well, it worked. With Jonathan's help, we identified all new mature students enrolled in spring quarter, especially those with last-minute applications, and Edward stood out like a sore thumb. We have had passive surveillance on him for periods, and noticed his penchant for young men. Michael acted as bait, and Diane was close behind him when he finally attempted a probe. Since the results would most likely be positive from a strong probe at short range, no matter how quickly we attempted to go to 'dark mind,' we had no choice but to incapacitate and control. Diane may have overdone it in her hatred for this monster probing Michael's mind, but we could allow no chance for him to recover. Well done, Diane and Michael. You took a big chance, and performed splendidly. I only regret that Michelle and I got no response from him at all, and had to leave you two to do our dirty work," he said.

"Now we must face the options we have discussed:

Kill him; keep him captive; or let him loose, in the hope that he will somehow betray more members of the Coven.

"There is no way to hide the fact we exist and have controlled or killed a Coven-trained telepath. As we decided before, we will keep him captive under sensory deprivation conditions, manipulating time and experience, and testing his powers. While we cannot read all his thoughts, we can get some emotions, images, and information by mental probing that might prove useful.

"The price we pay, however, is that all our minds will be awash in the most horrific negative images, which will never leave our memories. This is a price that I am not willing for any of Omega to pay. Thus, we will use standard techniques, including repeated questioning by unseen questioners, to learn what we can, with food and books as the only rewards.

"The cell we have prepared is mentally shielded by three layers of aluminum foil, so he cannot sense us or project out of the room. Execute our plan. Meanwhile, I will alert Omega-beta about Jonathan and prepare for an expected response from the Coven."

CHAPTER FOURTEEN

The view from the patio deck was magnificent, with the San Fernando Valley awash in light and patterns. Sixteen chairs were formed into a circle around an elevated gas fire with artificial logs. Fourteen chairs were occupied – all by men.

All were silent until the electronic clock finished sounding 9 bell-like tones.

2B1 spoke first, "What is your evaluation of the threat, 1A?"

1A, although from San Francisco, spoke. "So it continues. We have had two-and-a-half months of null results from either of our two telepaths at UC Merced, and then Edward disappears suddenly with no trace.

"This leaves us with a series of problems – not the least of which is that Edward is alive in their control and may be encouraged by any number of telepathic and non-telepathic means to reveal our presence, rough numbers, location of meeting place, and other clandestine details, despite our efforts to keep inter-personnel information to a minimum. It is to our advantage that you are not nearly was well known in L.A. as we are in San Francisco.

"Our analysis of their capabilities is not comforting. One of them sensed a mind probe at a considerable distance and shut down all response in fractions of a second. All attempts to re-find that mind were futile. This shows great self-control and a trained mind. They were able to control the visual stimulus seen by 4D1, Greg, to the point that he drove the van off a cliff. They have captured or killed a mid-level telepath. Thus we have to assume, much as we dislike this conclusion, that they are probably powerful enough to fend off our attempts at telepathic control. Thus, we must find them by whatever means we have and eliminate them by physical methods, all without revealing our existence.

"Still, we have learned in this process. One fact is that they have a secure base and resources in that miserable excuse for a city, Merced, and its pathetic attempt at a university. It is proving very difficult for us to work in the area without being spotted, and clearly the loss of six Coven members was on their part a remarkable achievement. It is also interesting that they made no attempt to 'feed' on our Coven members, which would have

55

greatly increased their powers since all were mid- to high-level telepaths. Most likely is that they were not powerful enough to control the whole of Group 4, and thus chose to kill them through control of the weakest member. Is it that they do not need the assist? I can scarcely believe that. Perhaps they were not aware of the 'feeding' procedure at the beginning, but with Edward in their control – I do hope that he is dead – we have to assume they now know much more and perhaps have gained strength.

"Another likely supposition is that there is a potential non-sensitive associate of the telepaths, Jonathan Campbell of the Physics Department. He turned up daily at the Merced Police Department, purportedly to help the investigation of the death of the UC Merced student, and Teller found him awfully suspicious. We sent 3B1 from L.A. up there for one day and checked to find Jonathan totally insensitive to our mind probes. Campbell sent the true photos to a friend at the *Chronicle*, which despite our squelching the project, later became public at a most inopportune time, essentially gutting the San Francisco Coven.

"I want him tracked electronically, where he goes, what he does. I want tracers on his vehicles, tapped phone lines, intercepted cell phone messages, correspondence he receives, and all without revealing that it is happening. We will continue our existing telepath, but try to have her get into closer proximity with Campbell. Campbell provides a way of following the precepts of the great Chinese strategist Sun-Tzu, that if the enemy is in too strong a position, take something he wants badly and force him to come to you. Eventually, I want Campbell kidnapped, and then we will encounter them on our home ground in the full power of our united Covens, recently fed.

"Finally, I want to know more about Bonny. Why did the telepaths respond so definitively to her killing? Why did they care? Was she of some interest to them? How did they know where the 'feeding' took place? Their response to Bonny's death shows a vulnerability. We will exploit this weakness through Campbell.

"Take the greatest care. I believe that Edward got careless. Do so, and you may be their next victim. All that Edward knew, including this site, must be changed, now.

"I will arrange for the physical methods through some convenient and absolutely ruthless contacts in Los Angeles," finished 1A.

Edward actually didn't know very much, or he was a very good actor. In only five days of sleep deprivation in the small cell, random interrogation at all times, day and night, by unseen voices, bright lights, and other well-proven techniques, he was saying anything they wanted. His life was laid out in nauseating detail, but Omega-alpha was very circumspect about checking on his story except through public and printed records. They feared electronic surveillance of Edward's e-mail and websites. Still, his birth record was found, Social Security number, educational record, arrest record (minor) all checked with what Edward was so eagerly telling them. In reward, he got a book, eight hours of uninterrupted light at a moderate level, plus a vegetarian wrap sandwich to go along with his unvarying diet of vitamin-laced oatmeal.

The most fascinating part of Edward's story regarded his recruitment and training, first in San Francisco (details jibed with recent police reports) and then in Los Angeles, at a site in the Santa Monica Mountains above the San Fernando Valley. It appears that the Coven really did not work as an integrated unit, but in a detection-dominance-capture "feeding" cycle that was essentially individual. It was clear that they could not read minds, only feelings and emotions. They had nothing remotely approaching the rapport of Ken and Michelle, and now significantly Diane and Michael.

Since they were not sure that Edward was telling all, and had said little about his activities at UC Merced, they went back to the deprivation scheme. Edward immediately folded, and told them about a person known to him only as L3. She was a student here at Merced, and he knew no details about her other than that she and he would meet once a week at a very open site on a farm road south of Merced for sharing information. Each received instructions via the oldest spy communication device, a drop box, his in a beer can under a fence post near Highway 99, and L3's was somewhere else. There had been a drop box scheduled meeting only one day after his abduction, and thus L3 would know of his absence by now.

For the moment, they let Edward be, but increased surveillance to counter any attempt at a rescue, even by force such as an armed helicopter attempt although as far as they knew, their foothills center was still undetected. Ken had made major progress on his mental interference device, miniaturizing the package to about the size of a cigarette pack, and they were placed all around the perimeter should they be needed. Panic buttons were set up at multiple locations inside and outside the perimeter, but use of the devices would also illuminate the fact that they own telepathic capabilities, too.

Omega-alpha was now facing the fact that the training of the past four months had brought most of the members close to their telepathic potential, and that further progress would be slow. They also were interested in learning at what age they developed the potential. If training could be started earlier, perhaps greater growth would be possible. One reason this had come up was that a number of pairings had naturally developed.

Because the group sharings, which were done every other day since the effort, were so exhausting the longing of Diane and Michael for each other was evident to all, but their physical restraint was appreciated. Neither appeared to be gaining in strength by staying apart, so the question of their marriage arose rather naturally. Consensus was immediate, and a date was set in early June, while the hills were just turning brown (golden, as Californians called it). Joy permeated the group, tears of happiness washing away for a while the worry about their powerful but unseen antagonists.

Ken, Jill, and Michelle sat once again in the living room of Ken's house. It was quiet, and the classical music public radio station was playing something by Vivaldi.

Jill spoke up, "I have been thinking about Diane and Michael, and about how much you, Michelle, love Ken, yet have done absolutely nothing but support our marriage. I love you, too, Michelle, very deeply, and I cannot be truly happy as long as you bear this heroic burden. In what I am about to propose, I have not consulted with Ken. I think you deserve to bear Ken's child, and I would love you all the more for doing it."

Ken quietly left the room, stunned by Jill's generosity, and thinking back to the movie *The Big Chill* and a similar solution to an intractable relationship. Michelle and Jill were in each other's arms, crying torrents of happy tears.

One hour later, Ken was back in his garden when Jill and Michelle strolled up looking like a pair of schoolgirls, hand in hand, big grins on their faces, eyes still a bit red from all the weeping.

Jill took the lead, "Now we will ask you jointly, will you be father to Michelle's baby?"

Ken looked at Jill with eyes full of love, and said, "If my darling wife so wishes, I will consent," sort of assuming this would be an artificial insemination procedure.

Then Jill sat down and they filled in Ken on what had been a well-thought-out plan, down to where it would take place and what each would wear. This was to be no artificial insemination but a three-day weekend up in the foothills house, alone in the house but with security around the perimeter. They decided to wait until the next fertility cycle after Diane and Michael's wedding, roughly in the first week of July.

Diane and Michael's wedding was held in the Newman Chapel. It was a beautiful Mass with readings chosen by the couple, and a large crowd in attendance. Jonathan deliberately stayed away, because he was not part of the Newman scene and wanted to keep his association with Ken to be, from all appearances, strictly professional. Their honeymoon location was not announced, but it was clearly to be close to Merced, because they still had classes to handle.

They were both present for the Omega-alpha group meeting two weeks later. Ken was interested in how their potential would have changed by the marriage, and feared a loss of group consciousness because of the ever-closer pair binding, but little change was experienced. After the meeting had broken up, they took Ken and Michelle aside.

Diane spoke, "It was transcendental. I have never believed such integration of two minds and bodies was possible. It seems to have happened as we slept and dreamed together. Next morning, I could read Michael's thoughts at 100 feet and feelings for over 200 feet, about three times what I had done before." Then they drifted off, hand in hand, mind in mind, as much in love as any two human beings had ever been in love."

Ken murmured the Biblical admonition "Love each other as I have loved you." Those two were there. Now for the rest of us, thought Ken.

CHAPTER FIFTEEN

Whatever thoughts L3 had regarding the boredom of this miserable town and the interminable classes in English Literature 106B were dispelled by the sudden absence of Edward. He had missed their weekly meeting at the edge of town, at a place where the presence of anyone else would be easily detected. She put the note in her drop box, and three days later received a short note. "Do nothing. Your colleague is not responding. Be careful, especially around Jonathan Campbell." L3 suddenly knew fear. Clearly, she was in a dangerous situation, saved perhaps only by the fact that she was one of only two female Coven members and thus less likely to be discovered.

In the beginning, it seemed so special when she was noticed by the senior lawyer in her firm and singled out for special attention. She had made a name for herself as a regular Amazon in the courtroom, with a special talent for reading and resonating with a jury. She fully expected that at some time, she would have to be involved sexually with him, and she was willing if the price were right. But no such sexual request came. What did come was a sense of being observed even when no one was visible, and enhancement in her long appreciated ability to sense emotions even when a person was hiding them.

Then came the first night, when she was invited to a "political scoping party" for a potential Assembly candidate and found herself in the heart of the L.A. Coven. She was offered success without limit, the ability to dominate others, protection in the secure network, and powers beyond those of ordinary people. She was enthralled, honored, and appreciative, and accepted the requirement of total lifelong obedience or death. Then came the first "feeding." It was awful, but it was only a gay man with AIDS, and she could feel her sensitivity grow in the mental death throes of the victim. In the post-prandial stupor, she bonded with the Coven, and was accepted. Still, she had to carefully hide the inherent horror of what they did to increase their powers. Then they "fed" on their first woman. At that moment, she shared the crushing pain of the victim without hope as her mind was shattered, and L3 was never the same again. The effort at hiding her inherent horror required more and more of her energies, and her progress in the training slowed. Her nightmares required massive doses of sleeping pills to have any rest at all.

The Coven hoped that the trip to San Francisco and the powerful presence of 1A would buck her up into the dominant and ruthless warrior that attracted them to her in the first place.

Now L3 was all alone in the den of the enemy. She did not feel like a warrior but a little girl, little Barbie, lost and frightened. She didn't want to go back to the L.A. Coven, and she was deathly afraid of the unseen menace lurking in these barren hills. The comment about Jonathan Campbell was interesting. She had originally been told to observe him surreptitiously, and she had done so. He seemed to be an extraordinarily nice guy, loved by his students, with a wife who was a wonder with disturbed foster children. How could he be dangerous to anyone? In her mind, she began to contrast Jonathan with the members of the Coven, vicious sharks all. Had she made a wise choice? Was it irretrievable? Clearly, whatever was lurking in Merced was very powerful, for they had essentially destroyed the San Francisco Coven, oldest one on the West Coast, killing five members and killing or capturing a sixth. If she defected, could it protect her from the wrath of the Coven?

L3 was tormented, and took a day out of classes to drive into the mountains. It was early summer, but still not too hot. The view was beautiful beyond all measure. She pulled off onto an area that had a great view down on the Central Valley, bathed in rich greens of the oaks and golden grass, and with incredibly regular farmland beginning in the distance. Why did the farmers care that their fields were so regular, so trim? Was it a sort of homage to the soil? She could see Mount Diablo, dark in the distance. Mount Diablo, the Devil's Mountain, thrusting incongruously out of the Valley foothills. Somehow it was foreign, out of place. She, an urban woman, had never spent much time out of a city, except to rush to another city. She was foreign, out of place, like the mountain. Suddenly it was all too much and she bowed her head and began weeping copiously, wracked with guilt and remorse, lost and adrift, caught up and thrust into something awful. She needed help, and none was to be had. She cried and cried, until exhaustion took over and she fell asleep over the steering wheel of the car, this time without any pills.

It was the sun that woke her. It had moved into the west and now shone directly into the windshield, a blinding light that could not be denied. She got out of the car, walked over onto the grass, and sat down. She would defect. Whatever awaited her in Merced was less fearful than the deceit and disgust of her life in the Coven. She would go to Jonathan and confess, throw herself on their mercy (until now, she had done nothing to hurt them) and tell them all. All she could hope for and ask for was a clean death, not a "feeding." She had to trust that someone as good as Jonathan could promise her that.

She stood up and faced the sun. Somehow inside of her a shadow had lifted. She did not know what the future held, but she was on a new path, one of her choosing. She lifted her arms up and let the sun shine on her, figuratively and physically.

She then turned to go back to her car, and there was Jonathan, leaning on the driver' side door.

"You have chosen well," he said with a smile. "We can and will help you, and we can and will protect you."

"I am Barbara, and I am yours," she said, enormously thankful that she had made the decision she had. This group clearly had had her in their power, for how long she couldn't guess. When did they know? How did Jonathan get here? Can they read my thoughts?"

"Let's go back to where you were sitting. It is so beautiful up here," Jonathan said.

"You have many questions, and I will answer them truthfully. Where shall I start? We knew from Edward that there was another Coven member in Merced, a woman, but you learned of his disappearance before we could locate you. Still, we had only about 120 female candidates for the Coven member, based on time of enrollment, nature of your pre-enrollment records, and other factors. We were in the process of checking through all the records, one by one, and your record as you know was carefully faked. It would not, however, have survived close scrutiny. We would have had you in about a week."

"Is Edward alive?" asked Barbara.

"Very much so. By an accident, you drove past our members, while powerfully broadcasting anguish on about every wavelength (actually she had driven past the secure house of Omega-beta north of Catheys Valley but had been picked up on the main road over a quarter of a mile away). You clearly are a powerful telepath. We followed you, observed you stop, observed your anguish. I was called to come up here, but by the time I made it, you had cried yourself out and fallen asleep. I waited out of sight for over two hours until you awoke. You got out, and clearly made a life-changing decision. Then you stood up and greeted the sun with arms outstretched. It was time for me to come and help you through the next stage."

"Are you a telepath? I can't sense you," said Barbara.

"Regretfully, no," answered Jonathan. "I am but a midwife and foster parent to something wonderful that is aborning."

"Then how did you know what I was thinking? I might have decided to do something awful," said Barbara.

Gabriella strolled nonchalantly out from behind a tree. Immediately, Barbara sensed her presence, her power, her, her... love? "How could she love me after what I have done, what I was trying to do until just now? How?"

"Peace be to you," smiled Gabriella, and Barbara, at that echo of a lost childhood and a promise of a redemptive future, could take it no more. She threw herself into Gabriella's arms, crying – this time tears of relief, of joy.

"It was awful," she said. "I was awful, but what happened to the victims was bestial. Long before I came here, I was being destroyed by nightmares of what I had seen, what I had done. The only way out I could see was suicide."

"There is a better way," said Gabriella.

Jonathan made a slight motion to Gabriella, who nodded "yes." Barbara was theirs, now. They drove back to the safe house, and Gabriella walked into a room alive with good feelings, alive with love, and tinged with relief that the second telepath had not only been found, but had defected to them.

The difference between the Coven and this group, which was called Omega-beta, could not have been more profound. First, they were mostly women, young women, with only Jonathan, who was older, and a young guy firmly ensconced in the lap of an equally adoring young woman. They all looked relaxed, but she had never sensed such communication among a group. It was as though all their mental shields were down, each confident that they would receive nothing but love in return for their trust.

Barbara spoke, "After what I have done, I do not deserve your love. Please let me tell you all the awful things I have done before you accept me."

And so Barbara began, and made a public confession of all her errors, her destruction of innocent people, her manipulation of others, cheating in law school, sleeping with professors, lying, until she came in contact with Coven members. Then it got worse. She could tell of the first "feeding," a man, but broke down totally trying to relate the horror of the "feeding" on the woman. She cried and cried, and Phyllis and Tiffany held her, one on each side, and could only think of poor Bonny.

Later, after supper, she borrowed Jonathan's laptop and began to record everything she knew. And unlike the basically clueless Edward, she had observed and remembered a lot. License plates, addresses, phone numbers, every meeting, the San Francisco Coven members – five or six remained there, she noted. She remembered their boasting about successes they had achieved, even where Teller had suddenly gone, the death of the trusting pilot off Big Sur (how they chortled at that), but the secrecy of the Coven set strict limits beyond which she could not pass. She did note that they had widely dispersed around the L.A. basin and even San Diego, and would be hard to track down. But they also would be simply terrified by L3s disappearance so shortly after Edward's. They would come to the conclusion, a correct one at that, that Edward was alive long enough to betray L3. Hopefully they would never learn of L3's defection, until it was too late to matter.

Thus, whatever the Coven would do next, it would be different. Barbara predicted that they would sacrifice no additional Coven members to the mysterious and powerful Merced telepaths.

Two weeks later, Jill, Ken, and Michelle drove up on a lovely Friday afternoon to the Omega-alpha safe house, high in the foothills. All of nature appeared ready to complete its tasks as the hot, dry summer set in. The last of the vernal pools around Merced had dried up already, leaving concentric rings of brilliant spring flowers as the water receded to just a memory.

Edward, still locked up in the back room, was given a massive dose of sleeping powder in his food, and soon dropped off for what eventually turned out to be 15 hours of sleep. Dinner that evening was a bit strained, with all in total consensus as to what would happen next but unable to control racing emotions of all sorts. Jill dressed Michelle in a white terry cloth robe that, when Jill wore it, almost provoked spousal rape in the amorous Ken. Jill gave Michelle a big hug, then left to go out onto the deck as Michelle, with all the fear and uncertainty of a long delayed wedding night, went back to meet Ken, roughly equally nervous. Ken saw Michelle in the terry cloth robe, and sensing each other's quasi-panic, broke into gales of laughter.

Jill sat on the deck, watching the evening get darker and lights twinkle in the valley. It was beautiful, but somehow she felt very much alone. She loved them both so much, and now she had given them a gift of love beyond all measure. She yearned to be in Ken's arms, and big tears slowly trickled down her cheeks.

And then he was there, in her mind, loving her, calling to her. Never, never had she felt like this. She got up slowly, weaving slightly as though unable to control all her muscles, and headed back to the bedroom.

Jill didn't wake until almost 9:00 a.m., and she felt somehow exhausted. Ken and Michelle were gone, so she gathered her clothes, still in a hasty pile on the floor by the bed, and walked out to the breakfast room. Ken and Michelle smiled, wonderful radiant smiles, and Ken said, "Hi, beautiful." But his lips hadn't moved. Suddenly it was as though the sun was through her mind, she could see them, feel them, they in her, she in them. She threw herself into Ken's arms and broke down completely in tears of joy.

"Welcome to life," said Michelle. "We have been waiting for you to awake for months. Now it begins."

All that long weekend, the three loved and laughed and grew, and it was clear that the intercourse of Michelle and Ken was secondary to the awakening of Jill.

Monday morning, Michelle sat alone on the deck as Ken and Jill drove back to Merced, with barely enough time to make Ken's first class. But Michelle was not alone. Minute after minute, mile after mile, she could read Ken, then just Ken's emotions, then just Ken's presence, but by then he was probably two to three miles away. Something else. She could let her mind range over the hills below, and sense perhaps hundreds, maybe thousands of individuals going about their normal chores. Something had changed, and she felt nothing like this when she was close to Ken. Did somehow their separation force her mind to project, to range out?

Miles below, Ken was amazed that he still sensed Michelle's mind, Michelle's love, much farther than ever before. And as he went past houses, he could sense the people inside them. He stopped in a driveway, amazed. A nice-looking older woman came out on the porch, about 200 feet away, and they waved at each other. Then the woman wiped her brow with her left hand, despite the fact she was right handed. With a final cheery wave, Ken drove away.

"What was that all about," asked Jill? "Something has changed," Ken said. "I can still sense Michelle miles behind us, and I also sense people within about a few hundred feet of the road. This weekend has greatly increased my telepathic capabilities as well as yours. Wow!"

CHAPTER SIXTEEN

At the next meeting of the whole Omega Project, several major issues were raised. First, since the spring quarter had ended, the students (those with any sense at all) had scattered to the four winds to avoid the incendiary summer of Merced. Thus, some of the seven sensitive candidates were gone, some perhaps to never return. It was decided that, after analyzing them one by one, the five that remained should be contacted and asked to join. Teams of two were selected, and scheduled contacts would occur before more were lost.

Second, a report was given by Ken and Michelle, Diane and Michael, about their experiences. The sharp increase in paired capabilities and the first ability, especially in Michelle, to sense hundreds of ordinary minds and their emotions, was greeted with wonder and joy. Further progress was possible. Bilateral pairings were positive and a method of growth. Ken noted wryly the shared glances of Roger and Joanne, who now yearned to move their scheduled September wedding earlier (family constraints had pushed it to September, and it was probably immovable) and between Mary and Nancy, who had clearly bonded deeply. This decision would have to wait until after the group's mental communion later that day.

Third, what should be done about Edward? He was providing no new information, and was polluting the mental atmosphere around the Omega-alpha house with his negativism. It was decided to move him to yet another safe house, rented for the occasion, after having prepared a secure cell with more amenities to make his life at least passable until resolution could be achieved. If this were done well, security would be largely electronic and most of the time no one need be at the house.

Fourth, what to do about L3 – Betsy, as she asked to be called – since she had long hated the name Barbara and detested the associations inherent in the name Barbie, the doll whose unrealistic dimensions she could never aspire to. Omega-beta was unanimous in wishing to offer her full membership in the group, so long as she never, never recalled her past, and especially the "feedings." Betsy had a fine, trained mind, and hated those memories, so Omega agreed to offer her this opportunity.

Decision made, she was called in from next door and told that today would be her first group communion. She looked so young, now that she was dressing like a UC Merced student. She did not know what would be involved, and was scared to death that once this group was in her mind, they would recoil in horror and eject her. She wanted into this group so badly. She had never seen such unselfish love between people. She yearned to fill the vast void in her own life that had driven her to evil in hope of unconditional acceptance.

Jonathan and Ken summarized their technical progress, which was slow, and enhanced security measures for the anticipated Coven response. "Their best plan," said Ken, "is somehow to get us to come to them, where they have the resources and advantages. We must be careful. No one should contact Jonathan but me, since I have innocuous Physics Department contact opportunities available, and Jonathan should no longer go to the Omega-beta safe house. We have some safety equipment that we will have ready for all of you at our next group meeting."

At the end of what was called the "Business Meeting," all members, including Jonathan, Jill, and Betsy formed a large circle. Ken held Jill close, their heads almost touching. Without realizing what they were doing, no one sat too close to Betsy since they still feared what might happen.

They all said the traditional prayer, emptied their minds of daily concerns, and reached out to one another in love. Michelle was looking directly at Jill with this glorious smile on her face, somehow broadcasting anticipation. Jill smiled back, and then 30 minutes later, exhausted, they all lay back, each hating to lose contact but drained by what had been without a doubt the most intense communion they had ever had. All felt the warm glow of a success at all levels.

Jill had blossomed immediately into their midst and took wing, loving them all, clenching Ken in her arms, crying and laughing.

Betsy was so scared she was almost in a faint. All had reached out to her, but Betsy could not give up her individuality easily. She felt like a little girl going on her first rollercoaster ride, wanting some way to jump off before it got to the top but couldn't because she was strapped into her seat. Minute after minute, the battle went on, ego against super ego, until Betsy, exhausted by the battle with these incredible minds, gave up. Suddenly all was glorious and full of light, of love, and the group exulted at the birth of a new member of the common consciousness that was Omega.

Betsy lay totally passive in these loving, supported minds – like a baby. All pretensions of her powers were swept away as though they were nothing. For the first time in her life, she was alive.

A week later, a wedding was held for Mary and Nancy, deeply in love. Ken could not believe that such love and commitment was not a gift of God. Two weeks later, the chosen recruits were initiated, and four of the five made the transition, including another guy, to universal joy and much hugging. The failed initiate, Alice, was desolate, crying great buckets of tears. Jill especially was able to comfort her that progress could be made and her time would surely come.

It was also clear that Mary and Nancy had grown a lot since their wedding, and that somehow this growth was somewhat different from that between Ken and Michelle, for example. The whole group was growing not only stronger but more diverse in their growth, which seemed to be a sign of growing maturity. The aborning infant had become a small child, one that was capable of walking on its own.

CHAPTER SEVENTEEN

The house was a very ordinary ranch house, about three miles north of the Fresno city center just off First Street. A nice older couple had rented it for a year, and went about their lives chatting with neighbors, mowing the lawn, and fitting in seamlessly in the community. The house had a garage, but the 1998 vintage Taurus was always parked on the street, as they, like most of their neighbors, had a garage so full of stuff that they couldn't fit the car in.

But this garage was full of different sorts of stuff. The garage had no windows, the garage door was nailed shut, and the only entry was through the kitchen. Two large satellite dishes were in the garage, mounted just below the wood and asphalt shingled roof that would in no way block the signals. On the south wall were banks of electronic equipment, tape drives and computers, and a large table was in the middle of the room. Fluorescent lights were crudely hung from the ceiling.

The west bedroom had aluminum foil in the windows, a common ploy of Fresno residents to reject the blistering afternoon sun. In that bedroom were three beds – a bunk bed and a mattress on the floor – that served to sleep three men at the same time, if necessary, but one was always on rotating duty watch in the garage. Another bedroom had twin beds, and a third bedroom was occupied by the elderly couple. Five youngish men slipped into the house late one night, and were never seen outside the house. The couple prepared their meals and served them in the garage.

Once a week, in the evening, Alexander, who was clearly in charge, would be smuggled out of the house lying on the back floor of the Taurus under a blanket, to emerge about two to three miles away at one of a number of local malls, pick up a car parked there (a different car each week), and start the long drive to Los Angeles. That next evening, at 9:00 p.m., he would give the report. The first three reports were purely logistical, as they arranged for the house, set up the equipment, and moved selected members of the Russian Mafia, as they were called, to Fresno. This time he had news.

The house in Beverly Hills he reported to have once belonged to a famous and beloved television comedian, had become available because of his death, and a Saudi prince bought it and then promptly outraged his neighbors by setting up statuary all around the property, mostly naked women, each painted with red nipples and pubic hair. After that problem had been resolved, mostly by intense peer pressure from famous people, the house had bounced around on the market with a number of buyers, the last of which defaulted on the mortgage when the dot-com bubble burst in 2001. Now, devoid of all statuary, it sat back on its enormous and heavily vegetated lot, almost invisible from any road. Served by no less than three driveways, it had very good access from different roads, one of which was the very heavily traveled Sunset Boulevard.

At precisely 9:00 p.m., the doors opened and Alexander walked in. There were chairs behind him, out of the light, and a number of people in them, but the only person he could see was in front of him leaning back in a large, leather chair, and his face, too, was hard to see. Alexander was the only person in the room well lit. These men made him nervous, but they paid awfully well.

Report Week No. 4

"We have established taps on the phone lines of Jonathan Campbell, but have received no calls that were anything other than what appear to be legitimate departmental business. The majority of the calls are to the department chair, then to people associated with the teaching program, and then with diminishing frequency to other faculty in the department, his wife – twice a day – some students, and other routine business calls. No statistical pattern has shown up in these calls showing any particular location or any particular collaborator.

"Due to the large number of calls to his home, we tapped it just two days ago, but have no statistical record yet. We have attempted repeatedly to hack his computer, but he used exclusively an IBM laptop that is relatively rarely on line and has excellent protection codes in place. This software is a bit suspicious since it is much better than that available to most casual users. On the other hand, he is a stickler about privacy of students' grades, and there are a number of highly confidential tasks he has in the department that do require security.

"We have placed a transponder for his cell phone, but while it had been operational for five days, nothing unusual has occurred. Most of these calls are to his wife and the others local calls for dry cleaning, car repair, and so forth.

"Our greatest success is that we have placed a miniaturized GPS locator on his car, hidden in the rear bumper. Once a week we can now interrogate the system and get a complete map of his travel for the previous 10 days merely by driving past the parked car at a range of under 30 meters.

"It is hard to access his incoming mail, and he gets a lot of it, much of which when we can see it, we can't decipher. He is a theoretical physicist, after all. The campus has not had any opening in the department that we could exploit. Thus, we have one of our members on the UC Merced staff that might be able to move into that slot should an opening occur. UC hiring rules are a major barrier in this regard, and no promises can be made. Should we create such an opening?

"That is all."

1A smiled ever so slightly. "You have done well. No, don't artificially create openings in the department at this time. It is unlikely that there would be any useful information and the possibility of exposure if an employee were caught opening mail is too great. You may go."

Once Alexander had left, 1A continued, "It is now several weeks since we lost contact with L3. We have to assume the worst, that Edward exposed her. I am slightly nervous about L3, as she was clearly having trouble at the 'feeding' – so essential for us to maintain and grow in capabilities. She is also much smarter than Edward. They may have had ways to learn yet more about our operations. We must assume that our capabilities are now well known to them, and perhaps they are copying some of them for their own purposes. Thus, the uniqueness of the Covens is now lost, and our futures clouded. We must continue to develop non-telepathic responses necessary to eventually eradicate them all. This will not be easy, but we have made some progress."

CHAPTER EIGHTEEN

Once again, Alexander was waiting outside the main room of the house in Beverly Hills. He had become curious about all the concern for this very ordinary physicist at UC Merced, but had picked up hints that he and some of his students had stumbled on a discovery so stupendous that it would change the face of electronics for the next 30 years. However, the Merced group did not yet know the implications of what they had found, and his patrons were working furiously and in secret to duplicate their work and obtain key patents before they wised up. It was also clear that they were not picky about the means they employed, but then all his people would happily kill their sisters if the pay was good enough.

At 9:20 p.m., Alexander was called in.

Report Week No. 6

Nothing unusual was seen in the past week on any of the physical or electronic surveillance modes. However, when they downloaded the GPS system last Saturday, it had been clear that Campbell had been driving around the eastern suburbs of Merced. Further inquiries would be made.

Report Week No. 7

Nothing unusual was seen in the past week on any of the physical or electronic surveillance modes. However, several phone calls were made to real estate agents on his cell phone, and Campbell had ended up renting for one year (with option to buy) an old farmhouse on the end of a long dirt road near Planada. Before they had been able to ascertain these facts, Campbell and a group of students, names unknown because surveillance had not been established, had gone into the house last weekend and done some serious construction. At present, a graduate student couple was living in the house, but because they were both students, there was a lot of time each day when the house was unoccupied. Alexander proposed electronic surveillance of the house and video surveillance of the road leading up to it. 1A suggested adding infrared cameras, too, as approaches might be at night.

Report Week No. 8

Nothing unusual was seen in the past week on any of the physical or electronic surveillance modes. The house had been entered and surveillance established, as requested. There were audio pickups in every room, and video in the two main rooms. One interior room had been modified and made almost cell-like, but at present it was empty. Surveillance had been established on the roads leading to the house. The graduate student couple had been identified, and they were third-year students of Campbell's in the department who were from all evidence shacked up. He called her his fiancée, and in fact they might marry after graduating about two years in the future. However, neither seemed eager to leave the comforting confines of academia, and their joint salary was more than adequate to live well in the low-cost housing market of Merced. Discrete inquiries indicated that Campbell bought the property because of foreknowledge of UC Merced expansion plans, namely an agricultural department that would need lots of land south and east of the present campus.

Al was grimly satisfied in this report. So there had been unusual activity, additional people, and what appeared to be a cover story. Something was up. And they were, this time, ready.

CHAPTER NINETEEN

"We have company again," Jonathan reported to Ken while sitting on the lawn next to the English Department where Jill taught. "You know that beginning about five weeks ago, I detected repeated attempts to penetrate my laptop, with the source of the attack coming from, of all places, Moscow. I suspect my lines are tapped, and ran a pulse generator in the system and found out where it is. I have left it in place. It might prove useful. I, of course, assume that my cell phone is compromised. Someone is very interested in me, probably because of my role in the departmental investigation after Bonny's death.

"I did a sweep of the Planada safe house, and it is most assuredly not safe. There are bugs everywhere, inside and outside, added last week when Tim and Jennifer were in classes. I made no effort to cover my tracks in renting the house with option to buy, purportedly as an investment, and it appears we have a hit on our line. I am worried about Tim and Jennifer, who know nothing of our project. I trust them totally, and request that they be told of Omega if they are to be in danger because of it."

"I am worried about you as well as them, my friend," Ken responded. "What if they try to kidnap you? With enough muscle, it would be hard to prevent. I shudder to think of what they could, and would do to get you to spill the beans."

"Perhaps we should try a little counterpunching, then," said Jonathan. "We can get no more information from Edward, and he knows little of us other than how he was captured. We can fill him up with misleading information and give him back to them, fully compromised and thus useless to use against us. In doing so, they could reveal to us their location in Los Angeles and their resources."

"The information I would like to get back into the Coven's hands is that L3 died during the capture effort," said Ken. "It is also true that having to suddenly run down to L.A. chasing a kidnapping is inherently dangerous. I can see many good reasons to translocate a small, powerful group into Los Angeles before the crisis arises. Besides, it is hot here and L.A. weather is better. I used to live there, you know. We lived in Beverly Hills. It was the cheapest apartment Jill and I could find while we were at UCLA.

"So let's get set up in L.A. as soon as classes end. You stay here and stay careful. You have your surgically implanted location device, and the batteries are good for six months. We have the psi-blanking modules, now in some quantity, and small enough to fit easily in your pocket. The more powerful ones run off the cigarette lighter in a car. You don't do anything. I will handle it," said Ken. "We are all armed, but I expect their muscle is better armed than we are. Let's aim for moving Edward on September 25."

It was a happy day when Edward was dispatched to "La-La Land" with a suitable injection, and was moved from the Omega-alpha safe house to the Planada safe house. It was as though a cloud had been removed from the site of so many joyous events. Tim and Jennifer had told the department that they had left for a three-week vacation in Oregon, until just before classes were to start, and the house was empty. Jonathan had visited the house after their departure and in about three hours converted the inner room into a cell, complete with neck and leg steel shackles, sound-deadening panels, and audio and video surveillance equipment "carelessly" powered by the house electrical lines. Edward was comfortable with a recliner, bed, and toilet, a television set behind a heavy plastic panel in the wall, on all the time, but he had a channel control and a mute button that he could use. As far as Edward was concerned, it was a much better system, more room, and television. He had lost all sense of the passing of time at the Omega-alpha safe house. But the shackles were annoying and there was nothing in the room that could be remotely turned into a tool to cut through them.

After he had made a survey of the new abode, he was testing the strength of the ankle chain. A disembodied voice said "Any interference with the security system will result in your immediate removal to a subterranean cell with no amenities." That was adequate to quell Edward, who had no idea of how much surveillance was active. He settled in as best he could, and after a few days actually started to follow the daytime soap operas. Food was delivered each evening through a slot in the wall, actually quite good fast food, plus milk, cereal, a cold sandwich, and fruit for the next day's breakfast and lunch. Life could be worse. He was allowed to communicate only in writing, placed on the returned tray the following day.

Report Week No. 12

Once again, Alexander was waiting, but this time he was admitted immediately at 9:00 p.m. Funny how he never saw anybody else in the house, coming or going.

Alexander started immediately, "We have found Edward. He is held captive in a secure room in the house Campbell rented and modified. The graduate students are on vacation, and until they return next week, Campbell takes Edward his meals every evening at 7:00 p.m. He is cautious, but we have operational plans ready to both free Edward and kidnap Campbell. We await your instructions."

Although there were a variable number of people present, all were behind Alexander and he could never see their faces well as they were, he suspected, deliberately in shadows. He heard them stir in their chairs, however. 1A responded.

"Leave us and wait outside." Alexander was only too glad to leave this group, and did so promptly.

1A spoke. "Too easy. They know we are watching. Edward is the bait. This whole activity is designed to make us show our hand prematurely. But we are getting nowhere simply monitoring Campbell, who appears not to be in communication with the telepaths except, perhaps…"

He paused. "What if Campbell himself is a telepath, and very clever at hiding it, getting and perhaps giving instructions telepathically? In which case he would be enormously valuable to us."

A rare open discussion followed, options weighed, and a plan developed. The final decision may have been a consequence of their frustration and, yes, the apprehension they all felt at the slow pace of the investigation.

Quite a bit of time had passed, almost 45 minutes, when Alexander was called again into the room.

1A spoke, "Give us the detailed plan you have developed. We will proceed with it within the next two weeks. Continue to be ready to move at our word. That is all."

CHAPTER TWENTY

Ken and Jill knew Los Angeles pretty well. The city in which one meets, woos, and wins one's bride always is someplace special. They had a whole host of special places around UCLA, old-fashioned hamburger and pie places like The Apple Pan, the Westwood Village Delicatessen (called universally the "VD" in those simpler times), those long, lonely, lovely roads in the Angeles National Forest (yes, there really were trees there), neat winding roads that dated from the Civilian Conservation Corps in the 1930s, and so many more. But now L.A. seemed menacing, with unknown threats and unseen dangers never dreamt when they were students. Perhaps the menace had always been there, and they just were too much "head in the clouds" to notice. Certainly the Raymond Chandler mysteries showed a dark face to L.A., even in the 1930s.

Thus, Ken, Jill, Michelle, Gabriella, Diane, and Michael rolled into L.A. to set up a secure site close to what they assumed would soon be the scene of a lot of action. They deliberately did not try to sense minds in the teeming metropolis, because it would be most unlikely that they could pull one mind from a thousand mixed with hundreds of thousands of insensitives. Finding a lonely spot in the L.A. basin would not be easy, but they wanted to be near West Hollywood, mentioned by Edward as a large gay community and the site of many Coven "feedings." Surprisingly, such a place did exist, on a sliver of land between two freeways and jammed against a large normally dry drainage ditch just west of the Los Angeles River and near the edge of Griffith Park, itself a large uninhabited area. The road to the house was almost half a mile from the feeder street, and the freeways guarded both edges, since cars were not allowed to even stop along that section.

The house was rented for a full year, using impeccably forged documentation. The rent was reasonable because the freeway noise was constant, day and night, and even fairly careful soundproofing couldn't block much of the sound, especially the big diesels as they used their engine to brake. Audio and video surveillance was set up, telepathic blockers were set up and keyed to switches in all rooms, a satellite dish was placed in the upstairs bedroom, and weapons were emplaced should a brute force attack take place. The possibility of a missile ejected from a vehicle on the freeways was analyzed, and escape routes developed (a drainage tunnel led under the freeway to the river, and one of their vehicles was parked across the way in a local driveway, for a fee, available for immediate use.)

Then there began a series of forays into West Hollywood, using "dark mind" techniques for passive surveillance. It was found that if each was about a half block apart, with Michelle on the point and Ken at the rear, and Diane and Michael on the neighboring streets, they could survey a four-block wide strip and check essentially every person for telepathic sensitivity. And there was quite a bit of it, but all at low levels. No wonder the L.A. Coven hunted here.

They were almost at the western edge of West Hollywood, only a couple of blocks from Beverly Hills and about two blocks south of Sunset Boulevard, when Ken felt that dreaded icy mental probing that, once experienced, never leaves your memory. It was in a vehicle moving rapidly out of Beverly Hills into West Hollywood, and it was most certainly probing. At their next scheduled stopping point, Ken asked, "Did you feel that?"

None had, since Michelle was two bocks father away from Sunset Boulevard than Ken, and only Ken, knew exactly what he was feeling.

"I think we should take a look at Beverly Hills, but since nobody walks in that town, we had better get the car." This would seriously limit their search range laterally since the metal car blocked to some degree the mental signals. But there was another option. They could just go into Beverly Hills in a "dark mind" mode and wait as the car returned, assuming it would return. The first place they could stop and rest was the parking lot of the Beverly Wilshire hotel on Wilshire Boulevard, and they set up shop there.

Nothing!

For hours they patiently waited until early evening, then decided to move back to the safe house, presently staffed by Jill (they would never leave the house unoccupied and the surveillance unsupported). Either the telepathic person, who from the probing was almost certainly a Coven member, had not returned or their destination lay between the Beverly Wilshire and West Hollywood. Tomorrow they would find a spot between West Hollywood and the Beverly Wilshire Hotel and hope to catch a Coven member in transit.

Three days passed before the next contact, but this was a much weaker signal in a car going into Beverly Hills and clearly not probing. They moved the surveillance closer to Sunset Boulevard, which was not easy because that snooty community didn't appreciate unknown cars parked on their streets. They had already been interrogated twice, ever so nicely, by the Beverly Hills police until they hit on the scheme of simply riding the bus back and forth on Sunset Boulevard. Thus one was either waiting at a bus stop or moving up and down the street. Coverage was complete. Two people worked the bus, one in each direction and alternating, and two were on backup in cell phone contact in legitimate parking lots.

It was Monday evening, at around 8:30, when the boulevard lit up with contacts. Nine were counted, none probing but all were powerful, and they headed for a large mansion on the north side of Sunset.

"I can scarcely believe it, but I think the Coven is using the old Jack Benny mansion," said Ken.

Surveillance was established on Sunset on both sides of the mansion, and on the driveways used for deliveries on the north side of the house. A rather inconspicuous car entered the ground through the northeast driveway about 8:45 p.m., and then left again at 9:30 p.m. The license plate and description were noted, to be later called in to Jonathan in the form of a call from a student who was so sick he simply couldn't take the test scheduled for next week. In the discussion of re-scheduling, the license numbers and letters would be transmitted.

Jonathan would get Tim and Jennifer onto Highway 99 at places where the car would arrive in about two hours, and hope to pick it up as it passed. Jonathan himself would take a post about 30 minutes south of Merced, but north of Fresno. It was a pity that it would be dark, but the number of cars, especially older cars of that type, would be few after midnight. Jonathan himself had a night-vision detector attached to a reflecting telescope that he used in photography (he was expert). The cars, while lacking color, were as clear as day and the licenses easily read.

Regretfully, while a few cars of this type were seen, the license plates were not the one they wanted. Still, only five cars of this type passed Tim and Jennifer, and three passed Jonathan.

CHAPTER TWENTY-ONE

Report Week No. 13

At 9:00 p.m., Alexander could barely restrain himself. However, it was almost 30 minutes before he was called.

"We have found the group you want destroyed. Campbell was the key. They have a safe house where they have their research meetings in secret, in the hills east of Merced, at 7:00 p.m. on Tuesdays and Thursdays. Other than that, they strictly keep apart.

"Three days ago, we were alerted when Campbell began getting an unusual number of calls on his University of California, Davis, phone referring to a make-up final exam at 7:00 p.m. Jonathan would confirm the time, but never the room. One girl, however, responded "Tuesday?" and Campbell did not answer. The girl did not repeat the question and hung up quickly.

"We deviated from our usual hands-off approach, and we posted our people to trail Campbell. He went to the UC Merced garage and took out a university car, and headed east on a road into the foothills. Regretfully, our vehicles were too far away to get to him and tail, but we alerted the Fresno house and they found two satellites in position to photograph, IKONOS and the EOS Thematic Mapper, both of which will provide pictures for a price. The next day we pored over the pictures and picked out Campbell's car well along on a road that had few turn-offs because it was in the foothills already. The car had been returned to the garage by early the next morning, probably late in the evening, and we were able to get the total mileage traveled on the garage charge slip. At exactly that amount of mileage, only a few options existed: one, a house on the end of a long, dirt driveway well away from the main road. We went there the next night, very carefully, and found, to our surprise, Tim and Jennifer, supposedly on vacation in Oregon.

"We established surveillance, but they never left the house. Finally, late the following night, we were able to penetrate under the house and place plastic explosives with minimum post-burn residue keyed to a cell phone. We also deliberately cracked the line from the propane tank and sealed it with paraffin and paper, both easily and totally destroyed in a fire, so that it would look at first glance that the explosion and fire were caused by a gas leak. Finally, we put audio bugs under the floor at several places, and then escaped undetected.

"At your order, the house and all in it can be annihilated with all their research notes, and other material. With Jonathan missing, that should end the Merced project." Alexander by now had an idea that the story he had been given was a cover, and he was clueless as to why they wanted this group dead. But he would play along as long as the funding continued.

This time, 1A left Alexander in the room. "Any comments or suggestions?" Murmurs of assent came from behind Alexander, and 1A said, "Execute the plan. I want Campbell here by midnight next Tuesday. Also Edward," he said, as in a distinct afterthought.

"This will end our contract, then, and at that time I want final payment," Alexander said, wanting the whole thing to be over.

"It shall be waiting for you," said 1A. "We of course need Campbell alive."

The Coven had really little option but to do as promised, as Alexander had all sorts of "dead man's switches" set up that would blow their cover to the police if they tried to double-cross him.

Next Tuesday, Omega-beta quietly slipped out of Merced and made their way to the Omega-beta safe house. They were a little earlier than the 7:00 p.m. scheduled time, and at the house, each slipped into the main room and began chatting animatedly. They all had brought large bundles, wrapped in coarse brown paper, which they placed next to the spot where normally they would sit. A CD called *Chant*, a Gregorian chant from Spain, began to play in the corner.

Jonathan went to pick up a Greek pizza at 6:45 p.m., which used to be a tradition most Tuesday nights until the excitement of the past few months, when Tuesday nights had other tasks at 7:00 p.m. Now, and for the last four weeks, he had returned to the old pattern. This was not much of a sacrifice, as the Forum made the best pizza in town, with lots of feta cheese. He was going to deliver some of it to Edward at 7:00 p.m. and take the rest home.

He walked to his car, opened the door, got in, and in seconds felt enormously sleepy and fell unconscious across the steering wheel. He was quickly pushed to the passenger's seat by a young man wearing a nose clip, who was suddenly right there, and the car drove off with all the windows open. No one was around to see anything.

At 7:05 p.m., in the hills east of Merced, a sudden flare lit up the foothills, to be shortly followed by the wail of California Department of Forestry (CDF) fire crews racing to head off a major conflagration in the tinder-dry grass and brush.

Report Week No. 14

At precisely 9:00 p.m., the doors opened and Alexander walked in. There were chairs behind him, more than usual, out of the light, and a number of people in them, probably more than a dozen, but the only person he could see was in front of him leaning back in a large, leather chair, and his face, too, was hard to see. Alexander was the only person in the room well lit. These men made Alexander nervous, but they paid awfully well. Today he would see the rest of that pay and be done with this lucrative but disturbing task.

He had noticed on the way in a larger-than-usual number of security guards patrolling the grounds. These "businessmen" were taking no chances even if they believed the situation was resolving itself satisfactorily.

He didn't even wait for 1A to start the program. 1A was not pleased, but right now he needed this insolent thug. Perhaps later he would learn, the hard way, of the Coven's power.

"I have received reports from Merced. All has gone according to plan. The group, somewhat larger than we expected, about a dozen in all, came to the house and joined three, including Tim and Jennifer, who were already there. They chatted and got some food, sat down in the main room in a group, and began some sort of joint music. At 7:05 p.m., we detonated the explosives. We were observing from as close as we dared, about a half-mile away. The house, and many of the cars, were eradicated. No sign of motion from the wreckage, no hint of anyone escaping. The CDF fire crews responded, so we had to get down the hill before they came up the only road.

"The kidnapping of Campbell went flawlessly, and in addition we found his laptop computer in the back seat of his car. It is coming down with him, and should be intensely interesting for you. We had simultaneously released Edward. Both have been sedated and blindfolded, as you requested. We anticipate their arrival here around midnight. I will wait out back and bring them to you once my people arrive. We will then return to Fresno, remove the equipment late at night, destroy any evidence, leave a gas vent open, and leave. I presume you want the geezers to leave with us and never arrive anyplace else?

"Yes," 1A responded. "We will stay here until you bring them to us. Then we want you to remain outside but within range of this cell phone. He gave the phone to Alexander. You have four people coming, I believe."

"Yes," said Alexander, "but this wasn't in our contract."

1A responded, "It won't be long, a few hours, and then you can go with all of your payment. We are just cautious about a possible rescue attempt by Campbell's industrial partners, who are more aware of the importance of his findings than is he himself. We suspect an eventual double cross against Campbell, from which we have rescued him."

Once Alexander had left, 1A addressed the Coven. "Are you ready with any and all telepathic and non-telepathic "incentives" designed to encourage Campbell to talk? You will each have your opportunity." All of the remaining San Francisco Coven members in Los Angeles were present, and most of the L.A. Coven. One high-level L.A. member, 2B1, was in San Diego, and several of the missing members were new low-level recruits who could be disturbed by a "feeding" on a mid-level telepath. He remembered their concerns over L3.

"Save any information about the destruction of Campbell's group in the Merced safe house for the proper moment, when despair is most useful for us. We are all very hungry, and Campbell's witness of what we do 'feeding' on Edward, a mid-level telepath, may well break any residual resistance. We will offer him merely a clean death in return for the full story of their ultimately futile experiments in telepathy. After all, with their members all dead, he can no longer betray anyone.

"3B1, give a coded call to the San Francisco Coven, which is waiting for news at the usual location. 3B2, monitor the information from the Merced Police and fire department radio, and CDF radio, too."

By 9:45 p.m., CDF notified Merced fire that there were seven cars in front of the building, which by now had been reduced to a cooling pile of ash. Four of the cars were destroyed, but their plates could be read, and were transmitted over the air to Merced Police. They in turn were running checks on the license plates, but any names would be withheld until next of kin were notified. By 10:15 p.m., it was clear that several cars appeared to be registered to UC Merced students, so UC Merced Police were notified. No signs of survivors, but extensive skeletal remains were seen in the ashes. There could be at least seven fatalities, probably a lot more. The investigation was centering on the propane tanks.

In addition, there was an unrelated report on the police radio to look out for Professor Jonathan Campbell, who was reported hours overdue by his wife when he had just gone out for a pizza.

A sense or relief swept over the Coven, as things were going well. The Russian Mafia had indeed lived up to their reputation of ruthlessness and had proved equal to the task.

It was actually 12:20 a.m. before the cars arrived from Merced. The guards and passengers were ushered quickly into the main room with two men sort of walking the barely conscious Campbell, two assisting Edward, who kept trying to brush off their hands but without success. One Coven member came forward, gave an injection to Campbell, and freed Edward from his captors. Campbell was then placed in a plain wooden chair and handcuffed to the arms, facing the Coven as a whole with his back to 1A.

Alexander, with a bit of flourish, handed over Campbell's laptop to 1A.

"Our tasks are complete. We will wait at the end of the north driveway, under cover, to support your guards if any attempt is to be made. I would like our payment, now."

1A motioned, and a different Coven member rolled up a large box. Alexander opened it, pawed deeply among the stacks of bills, broke apart one bundle, selected an interior bill, and tested it with the disappearing ink pen used at most stores to detect counterfeits. 1A looked amused. "Not very trusting, as always. That was why we hired you. Suspicious people make fewer mistakes. Now leave us, and you will never see us again unless you start blabbing. We will know, and you will regret it as you have never regretted anything else in your life."

1A showed, just for an instant, his powers, and Alexander blanched in fear. Without saying a word, he rolled the box out of the room.

"Edward, we are so pleased to have you return to the fold. Please take your rightful place in chair five." Edward, staggering slightly as the drugs wore off, did so, collapsing with a thump into the rich leather upholstery.

"While our Professor Campbell is recovering, and our dear member Edward regains his strength for what is to come, let us take a look at the laptop." Edward did not like the sound of that at all, and as he tried to raise his arm to ask permission to inquire what was next, he found that he was suddenly held by clamps hidden in the arms and legs of the chair.

"No," he screamed, in pure terror.

1A smiled slightly. "Excellent. Now it begins, but let's wait to make sure that Professor Campbell is fully awake to see the entire process. In the meantime, let us see what the laptop holds. 3D1, do the honors. One of your companies builds these things, I am told."

3D1 flipped open the case.

Horrible screams ripped through the room as 15 members of the Coven grabbed their foreheads, and lurching off their chairs, writhed in anguish on the ground. Edward, unable to move, just writhed in place and gave piercing soprano screams. The room, was, of course, carefully shielded for sound and about everything else, so no one outside could hear anything.

Six shadowy figures, all with heads and faces covered by hoods, leaving only eye and mouth holes, were suddenly in the room. The hoods hid the fact that each head was almost entirely covered with aluminum foil, essential to block the intense telepathic interference field of the fake laptop. Actually, it was also a real laptop, but had a three-hour time delay built in before the trigger of the interference generator was enabled, set to go into action as soon as one attempted to start the computer. Ken had also put in a radio-controlled switch, but that was not needed as it turned out.

Diane freed Jonathan, and after throwing a black cloak over essentially his entire body, ushered him toward the door. Each Coven member was given some sort of injection by an air injection system, and they became still, unconscious but very much alive. Gabriella and Jill bound 1A. The laptop was secured, the lid closed, and the shadowy members removed their masks because, for the next stage, they would all be needing their mental powers to escape unseen. One hood was secured around the head of 1A, and he was hustled out of the room, too, also shrouded in a dark cloak.

A cardboard box full of what appeared to be paper half-gallon milk boxes, but all covered with frost crystals, was placed in the center of the room. Candles were burning at several places in the room, and all were extinguished except the one in the farthest corner, away from the box. Ken checked the containers, pulled off the liquid nitrogen-filled insulated shroud, and left the room.

In under three minutes, all the figures had left the room as silently as they came. Fifteen bodies lay sprawled on the floor. The only sound was the tall grandfather clock.

No one saw them leave – not even the guards posted on the driveway, who at important times, suddenly heard a sound that urgently needed to be investigated somewhere else. One simply kept wiping his forehead with his left hand, again and again, and was oblivious to all else. Alexander and his thugs were more of a problem. They were posted right at the end of the northeast driveway, in a windowless white van backed into a shaded area in the bushes. They would have to get past them somehow.

The liquid hydrogen in the milk containers, chosen so as to leave no residue in the fire, boiled off quickly. The room filled with gaseous hydrogen, and in a matter of minutes achieved a critical air-hydrogen explosive mixture. The last candle burning did the rest.

A tremendous explosion tore through the mansion, and in its wake, fire flared up. All inside were instantly killed, which was a blessing in disguise for Edward. The hired security guards ran toward the mansion, while Alexander almost peeled rubber leaving the driveway and out onto the street. With the way open, all seven Omega members, dragging and carrying the still unconscious 1A, sprinted out the gate, across the street, and against a shadowy wall that led to their car. Michelle and Ken, sensitive to every mind within two blocks, carefully checked the thoughts of anyone who might notice them, but so far they were unseen. Lights were coming on in houses, but most houses were set back well away from the road, and carefully shielded by walls and shrubbery from the prying eyes of tourists. All eyes were on the mansion, with a growing red glow as the fire took hold. In two blocks, they came to their rented SUV, and drove off, carefully obeying the speed limit and with their headlights on.

Because no other source was uncovered, and because the 15 bodies found were all alive when they died in the explosion, the blast was eventually ascribed to a gas leak in the old and corroded gas pipes, dating from the 1920s.

Back at the Griffith Park safe house, 1A was tied into a chair. He was gradually coming to. Jonathan stood directly behind him with a .22-caliber semiautomatic pistol pointed directly at the back of his skull. The Omega team stood in front of him, and Ken motioned to take off 1A's hood.

"I know that man," Ken exclaimed. "He used to be a powerful investment banker in San Francisco, a political mover and shaker, who got into some legal trouble five or six years ago. He was found dead after a car accident on Highway 1 near Devil's Slide. I think it was registered as a suicide at that time, but we can check the newspapers."

1A looked at this bunch of children, with one older guy in whom he sensed some power. But their minds were all closed to him. So this was how they avoided detection. They have trained themselves in some blanking technique. Rage and frustration swept through 1A, hating these children who had caused him so much trouble. He knew without question that, if not he, others in the Covens would destroy these insects. But what a "feeding" it would be, then, with minds so potent! He could only imagine.

His dark thoughts were shredded in an instant as a mentality stronger by far than anything he had even conceived of smashed though his mental defenses. His mind was enmeshed in the strangest web of thoughts, and he couldn't dominate them in any way. It was sort of like trying to run a race through deep mud. He was in slow motion, forced to feel emotions he detested, sadness for his numerous victims, tolerance of others less capable, a chance to change his ways, and, and…pity. They pitied him! As the mind control of Omega was slowly relaxed, 1A remained fixed on this – Pity! He, the most powerful man in San Francisco, the West Coast, who could move others to do his bidding whenever he wished, to kill without impunity, to "feed." Pity! His mind recoiled and lashed out at these cretins, these children. They had no idea of his power, strengthened by the memory of more than a thousand "feedings." Powerful images surged through his brain.

"Now" said Ken, and Jonathan shot 1A precisely at the point a .22-caliber bullet would kill instantly.

Michelle lurched toward the bathroom, and threw up in the toilet, again and again, until nothing was left but dry heaves. Diane and Gabriella were furious with rage, Michael was ashen faced, Jill stunned and horrified, although she could not read the words like the others. But what evil she had sensed, beyond anything she had ever conceived of.

Ken, barely controlling his own guts, tried to bring them back from the brink.

"He would not have survived that last effort, and certainly is not sane. We killed a dead man."

Continuing, he said, "Our job is easier because he is also already legally dead. We will wrap his body with tire chains, using gloves so as not to leave fingerprints. We should slit his gut so he wouldn't float in any case, and then dump him in the Don Pedro Reservoir where Highway 49 crosses it on the high bridge. The water is hundreds of feet deep there, and it was discovered by and became the favorite spot where the Russian Mafia used to dispose of their victims."

"This L.A. house is awfully convenient, and I think we should grow a serious presence in Los Angeles. We will bring the seven known 'victims' of the Omega-beta house bombing here, give them new identities, and they can go back to school if they so choose. All seven were chosen because family ties were weak, and we have passed the rumor that they were going off the deep end in some spiritual quest, wished to definitely break all ties with Merced, and join a Tibetan Buddhist monastery somewhere in Oregon.

"Jonathan, you have got to call Louise right away. What excuse do you have? The Merced Police were alerted and are searching for you. I will say I was called to a crisis in Fresno by Sam, one of our foster children with whom we keep in touch. This would not be the first time I have done this. I will say I attempted to leave a message using my cell phone, failed to do so once I got to Fresno, and apologize deeply. I will call Sam and ask him to confirm my story if, which is most unlikely, he is ever asked. But later, Louise will have to be brought into the loop. She already suspects more than she says. Besides, it is just possible that such a generous and loving person may be a sensitive. You will have to check her out."

"I should have thought of it months ago," said Ken, "Will do."

Early the next morning, the seven "victims" of the Merced safe house bombing arrived in Los Angeles. All had gone well. They had very quietly started a tape recorder just before 7:00 p.m., but continued their chatter as each carried a paper-wrapped bundle to the place where they would normally sit, put it down, and then had slipped out of the house through a little-used lower deck patio door that led directly into thick bushes. They then worked their way along a path in the hillside, out of the setting sun and well below and out of sight of the driveway where their cars were parked.

At seven o'clock, Tim quickly left the house as the tape started a program of "Gregorian Chant" and made his way stealthily to join the rest who by now were a quarter mile away. At 7:05, the entire hillside erupted in a shattering explosion, followed by a fire, which soon spread to the tinder-dry brush. Omega-beta and recruits arrived at the windowless van parked on an inconspicuous dirt spur, got in, and continued up the mountain, eventually to arrive unseen at the Omega-alpha safe house beyond Hornitos at around 9:00 p.m.

By the time the CDF crews arrived at the site, the entire house was leveled. They concentrated in trying to contain the spreading fire in the thick, dry brush under the blue oak trees.

"Right now, I think we all need to give thanks and ask for divine assistance." All six Omega sensitives and the Merced safe house "victims" knelt in a circle, hands joined, heads bowed. Ken said, "Let us pray." And then all was silent. Jonathan sat back, still exhausted by his ordeal, but loving Omega — his latest foster child. What they are and what they will become is still unclear. They were so young in their quest, so vulnerable, so loving, but they were the hope of mankind and, he believed sincerely, of God. Well, he could pray too, in his own way. He got up, knelt down next to the circle. For just a second, there came over him such a sense of love and peace that brought tears to his eyes, but it was instantly gone.

CHAPTER TWENTY-TWO

The view from the penthouse was magnificent. Fog rolled in across the Golden Gate, diffused with a golden glow from the sodium vapor lights in the bridge. The penthouse deck, festooned with expensive pieces of garden art and beautifully sculpted topiary trees, was connected through a wall of glass into a large room full of opulent furnishings, walls of bookcases, and 21 comfortable leather chairs. The latter were formed into a large circle with a gap centered on the fireplace, in which aged blue oak burned quietly. The two chairs on each side of the fireplace were somewhat larger than the others. Neither was occupied, one empty except for a pair of wire-rimmed glasses.

Only six of the 21 chairs were occupied, all by men, none too young and none older than perhaps their mid 60s. These men exuded power and wealth with sharply tailored Italian suits and Rolex watches. All were silent until the grandfather clock finished striking 9.

3C1, the senior surviving member of the Coven, spoke first, as was his right.

"Only 15 bodies were recovered from the Beverly Hills mansion, not the 16 Coven members we know were present. No bones were found near the fireplace chair. Thus, they have captured 1A. In addition, one set of bones was found secured within steel constraints in one of the chairs. The police are getting very curious. There is no way that we can cover for the deaths of so many prominent people in such a short time, in San Francisco and Los Angeles. We must withdraw from any contact with other Coven members. Finally, the bones discovered in the Merced safe house were not human, but came from pigs. No one died in that fire."

"Notify New York that 2C2 and I are coming to consult with A Prime," he said, with obviously reluctance and dread clearly evident in every word.

CHAPTER TWENTY-THREE

The Hamptons in eastern Long Island are beautiful in late October. The summer crowds are gone, fall color tinges many of the trees, but the days are still warm and the sea usually calm. Ducks and geese are migrating through the ponds and marshes, and their calls echo over the bays and inlets. The houses, very expensive and very discreet, sit back on their large lots. Some fortunate ones have lawns and gardens that reach all the way down to the bays and inlets. In the summer, the view is cluttered by interloping boats, but now in October, the bay is empty.

The house was well set back from the road and had a large frontage on the bay, facing northeast. It was about as large and splendid as one could get without drawing too much attention to itself. The patio was large and beautifully finished in native New England granite, with a wall around much of it adequate to block the view of sightseers on the bay in summer. A large stone fireplace and grill dominated the center of the patio, and built-in niches with padded cushions faced the fireplace. The patio could have absorbed easily 50 or 60 people, but on this afternoon, only six were present, which meant that all could be close to the oak fire.

A man perhaps in his mid 60s, thin and ascetic looking, certainly no younger and perhaps considerably older, sat next to the fireplace and periodically warmed his hands.

Three other men sat on the benches, representing the three eastern U.S. Coven "provinces," listening carefully to every word, but saying nothing.

3C1 and 2C2, more formally labeled SF3C1 and SF2C2 once out of their home Coven, sat facing the fireplace, but about as far as the benches would allow. They had finished a detailed accounting of the entire past year, with as much accuracy as they could. No attempt was made to hide blunders and missed opportunities. One did not dissimulate in the presence of A Prime, who could read minds better than any other member of the Covens and who had honed his methods of mental punishment to a very high order.

"Why wasn't I notified earlier, as soon as it became evident that you were facing something entirely new to you? I have records going back centuries that could have helped you avoid your disastrous actions. I have capabilities that could have saved the Covens. Now the West Coast is a disaster, and in that disaster is a danger to all the rest of us. Names will be discovered, crimes uncovered, and inevitably it will become clear that there was some sort of strange connection between the dead. It is possible that the numerous missing victims of your excessive 'feedings' could be traced to the dead Coven members. That is about the last thing we want."

A Prime looked up blandly at 3C1 and 2C2, and smiled slightly as they recoiled in pain, covering their faces from the vision of horror and destruction that they knew he could intensify at any moment. But he needed them to tell him more, things they hadn't guessed themselves but things he wanted explored.

He waited a minute or so until they gathered some composure, ashen faced but willing to bear the modest punishment A Prime had handed out so far.

A Prime worked them back through their testimony. The first contact – at what distance? How did they know about Gabriella? How powerful was this Bonny? Not very, it turns out. Why did this Merced group care enough to expose their presence over a low-order sensitive like Bonny? Why no attempt at "feeding" off of 4C or Edward?

He especially went over what they had learned about the house in the hills that they had destroyed. How many people? What ages and sexes? A Prime was especially interested that Edward had told them on the way down to L.A. that he had been captured by a man-woman pair, and the woman was the more powerful. In fact, he had only seen five people whom he felt were telepaths, but three of them were women.

A Prime was also very interested that the Beverly Hills house had clearly been penetrated, and 1A captured, despite what he assumed were the usual psychic disincentives for sensitives and the long-range detection of non-sensitives possible when the Coven was assembled en masse.

A Prime decided to be forthcoming. "Our way, though ancient, is not the only way to telepathic capabilities. We have examples in the past where other telepathic groups were encountered, inevitably exclusively composed of women. When such groups collided, it always resulted in the destruction of one or the other, usually the women. Our predecessors use claims of witchcraft and the like to destroy them whenever possible, with some success. Further, our techniques were much more suited to dominance

93

than theirs, and so our methods prevailed. But our ancestors were never numerous, and there are examples when a well-founded Coven suddenly disappeared without a trace.

"The destruction of the Beverly Hills house is troublesome because the assembled Covens would have been very powerful and were clearly alert for, and in fact anticipated, interference with their evening's activities. Yet they were eradicated. I suspect that there may have been some technology involved, radio-controlled explosives, for example, seeing the connection of Jonathan to the Physics Department at UC Merced. This could be a problem, since for some reason, our members tend to be non-scientific, and in fact very few sensitives are found among scientists.

"The capture of Edward is troublesome because for the first time in recorded history we have alternative telepaths who are clearly a mixed group of men and woman, who worked seamlessly in concert.

"Finally, we come back to Bonny. This is the most troublesome aspect of all, for the risks taken by the Merced telepaths to avenge Bonny were enormous for a person who was only modestly sensitive. We know this because the reports back to the San Francisco Coven identified only very low-level sensitives, and they must have seen Bonny repeatedly at the restaurant. So why did the Merced telepaths care? All indications were that they did not plan a 'feeding.' Therefore, other than some misguided compassion, we must assume that Bonny was either a potential recruit or had given information to Group 4 that would have identified the Merced telepaths.

"If the Merced telepaths can recruit and train such a low-level sensitive, then they open up a much larger population of telepaths than the mid- to high-level telepaths our Covens require. The lack of natural telepaths and high-level sensitives is the Achilles' heel of our Covens, since our numbers are of necessity always small. I trust this hypothesis is incorrect.

"Thus, we must assume that before Bonny died, she had given Group 4 information that would have jeopardized the Merced telepaths. Thus, Group 4 would have to be annihilated before the information could be sent back to San Francisco, and so the Merced telepaths acted, using the weakest and newest recruit, Greg, who would have been the easiest to deceive.

"Finally, by their carefully planned responses, I sense that the Merced

94

telepaths are very intelligent, unlike some of the members here present who seem to have made every possible blunder in this sorry affair, not the least of which was keeping the rest of us in the dark."

Once again, 3C1 and 2C2 felt a dead, icy chill permeate their minds, like a hand from the tomb.

Long minutes passed. No one dared break the silence. The sun was setting, and A Prime's face could no longer be clearly seen. This merely intensified the sense of menace all felt.

Finally A Prime spoke. "Information. We lack adequate and reliable information. SF3C1, you mentioned that the San Francisco Coven still had potential informational resources.

"We have a non-sensitive as a graduate student at UC Merced in the Department of Environmental Engineering. This is a new program run in conjunction with UC Davis. The student is Linda Malcolm from Palo Alto. We supported her father to do engineering studies for us on electronic enhancement of telepathic capabilities (all failures) and in general built up a cover as a secretive international technology conglomerate doing what amounts to industrial espionage in Silicon Valley. She did a number of perfectly legal but useful tasks for us when she was a student at Stanford University, for which we paid handsomely. She was working in a dot-com that was barely staying afloat when we asked her to return to graduate school at Merced, paying her more than the dot-com paid. We provided a cover that some new, bright faculty at UC Merced were doing neat things, and we wanted early information. At the moment, she is taking classes, attending seminars in many departments, including physics, and generally playing student. In fact, there is some new stuff at Merced, including a guy who is working toward thin-film room-temperature superconductors in the Physics Department, so the cover is plausible."

"Tell her to stay away from Jonathan Campbell specifically and the Physics Department in general until we are better prepared," said A Prime. "She could be useful.

"I want Coven members in a totally non-telepathic mode to form legitimate business addresses in Pasadena, Fresno, Sacramento, and Oakland. Once you have set up these addresses, set up computers with absolute security and total lack of traceability. Then use public and non-traceable information sources such as the web. I want to know everything about anybody and everybody at UC Merced and the city of Merced. Each group should have a different cover story as to why this interest in Merced. The one used by the L.A. Coven was not bad – some new super-sensitive invention. Do nothing to let the Merced telepaths know that surveillance is being re-established. No line taps or hacking attempts. Be patient, be very patient. Once we have achieved this, we will very carefully increase our efforts. P1, P2, and P3, survey your provinces for personnel and resources."

Silence returned. The interview was clearly over. A Prime turned and began warming his hands by the fire. His own thoughts returned to a familiar line of inquiry. Why had the only A+ on the West Coast, Friedman, gone mad? Was there something about the repeated "feedings" that were eventually self-destructive? Certainly the San Francisco Coven had used the technique extensively, probably excessively, greatly increasing their powers, but at what price? He himself had not "fed" in four months, and he could feel the hunger gnawing at him. He could not last much longer without sustenance.

3C1 and 2C2, along with P1, P2, and P3, slipped away, all thankful the ordeal was over.

CHAPTER TWENTY-FOUR

The problem was Jonathan. He was the only known contact between the Covens and the Merced telepaths, and he had to be made to disappear. First, Louise was brought into the circle and Ken, Jill, and Michelle convinced her almost immediately that Omega was truly a breakthrough and that Merced was no longer safe. She indeed was a low-level sensitive. Jonathan came up with a "health problem" that resulted in early retirement, and told all that he was going to Oregon. He set up house near Eugene, and lived a completely normal life there, even including some casual contact with the Physics Department at the University of Oregon. But he had extensive security surrounding him to detect any attempt to tap his phones, hack his computers, or bug his house. There was nothing to connect him with Merced in any way, and he professed to one and all that he was happy to be away from the place. However, he took up a modest interest in gambling, and he and Louise would travel to Reno on gamblers' busses about once a month. They always chose a seat on the right side, just behind the rear stairway, and in the packet of freebees provided each gambler were instructions on the contact in or near Reno. At these meetings, the training of Louise was continued. Indeed, she had potential, but they would take this slowly, carefully. Older minds had so much more to unlearn.

As for the future, it was found that the best results were with about four Merced telepaths and no more than four recruits in a single group. In fact, the group communion was best with no more than six to eight persons – beyond that no gain was achieved as the mental patterns became too confusing. Despite that fact, total group communions were held about quarterly, as it bound everybody more closely together in a sort of profound but inarticulate joy, even if it did not increase individual capabilities.

Thus, the ultimate plan was to have Omega Project cells of six to 10 people, all living within a few blocks of each other so that there was constant awareness of each other's presence and the ability to sense sensitive minds out for several hundred yards in all directions. Each cell was provided with telepathy blanking units and metallic hoods that protected the wearer. Every effort was made to make the group look typical and blend in with the town. Only rarely and with great care did the entire

97

project gather together for important decisions. These always occurred at the new Omega beta safe house near Midpines, northeast of Mariposa in the ponderosa forest, much higher and cooler than at Merced or even the Omega alpha house.

Spring arrived in Los Angeles, although in the region around Beverly Hills, the weather was almost always spring-like, so spring was no big deal. Several months had passed since the Beverly Hills coup, and while some recruitment had occurred in L.A., the results were disappointing. With perfect weather, people seemed to live for the day and really yearned for little of import. The small cadre left in the L.A. safe house had settled into a pattern. Tim and Jennifer, with slightly modified resumes, had both been accepted at UCLA for the fall quarter. Regretfully, they would have to re-take two difficult first-year graduate courses – courses they had already passed at UC Merced. Two others were enrolled at University of Southern California, where there also seemed to be potential recruits. Scans at CalTech were unremittingly negative, so no efforts were to be expended in that direction.

Spring arrived in Merced, deeply appreciated by all as by far the best time of the year. The vernal pools, filled with adequate winter rains, bloomed their garlands of flowers. The grass was an intense, almost Kelly green, and the oaks a darker hue. There were hillsides that alternated with lupine and California poppy, one of the most brilliant displays of flowers seen anywhere in the world, ever. Sierra Club photographers were prowling the hills to get the perfect shot for next year's calendars.

Spring heralded the arrival of the first children of Omega. Michelle and Diane gave birth within days of each other, and the babies were completely normal with no trace of telepathic capabilities. This was not totally unexpected, since babies' brains rapidly wire themselves together until about the age of 2. For mutual support, they shared the Omega beta safe house. What would happen later to the forming minds as they grew washed with telepathically enhanced love remained to be seen. There was some anxiety, because the effect might be disastrous, sort of an administered form of autism. Or it could be wonderful. They placed their trust in God that loving one another was the way to grace and to Teilhard's Omega Point.

The effect of the Omega Project on the communities around Merced was by now tangible. Members in twos and threes visited various religious, social, and charitable groups on a rotating basis, leaving behind warm feelings and generous impulses and taking back occasionally new recruits. Volunteering was on the increase, and previously moribund groups were showing greatly increased activity and enthusiasm. Potential recruits were also found in Mariposa, through which Omega members often passed getting to the Midpines safe house. In spring, many prospective students came through UC Merced from all over California for a campus visit, and many were impressed by the high level of social involvement and generally positive vibes on the campus. The critical rate of undergraduate applications to UC Merced started to rise, to the delight of administrators, and those choosing to come were often those most committed to social causes.

The recruitment protocols had been modified in important ways. The nature of the Omega group was held back from new recruits, who joined merely to fulfill a spiritual growth or quest, drawn by what were clearly extraordinary people with extraordinary charisma. There was at least a month of strictly non-telepathic evaluation, reading, and discussions, before the first joint telepathic communion, now named "The Awakening," was attempted. Through this procedure, the failed attempts to awaken had dropped to essentially zero.

Gabriella was highly effective among the migrant and second-generation Mexican agricultural workers, tapping a strong current of religious belief and historically strong social group interactions coming from the extended family structure. Jonathan had sold the Planada safe house to a third party, after his retirement, and it was easily re-purchased by Omega through a university-associated intermediary. It became the safe house of the third Merced group, Omega-delta, in which Spanish was the preferred language of the group communions. Ken really missed Michelle's presence, but he and Gabriella alternated with Diane and Michael for Merced security, checking the campus and Highway 99 for any sign of telepathic activity.

It was late spring when Ken, Jill, Gabriella, Mary, and Nancy drove up to Davis, and visited the Newman Center. It was housed in an old brick church, which had long since been too small for the normal Catholic parish in Davis. It was perfect, however, for the UC Davis Newman Center, close to campus, large enough, sort of homey, with the old parish residence next door. And it had a real bell in its tower. The Newman Sunday Mass was a joy, compared to their months of frustration in L.A. – the chapel was alive with joy and peace. A good fraction of the entire congregation was sensitive to some degree, and a few were really impressive. The plan was to form another strong base for Omega in a sympathetic university community. Ken thought that he might be recognized at Newman, since he had given a seminar there two years ago in the Physics Department, but no familiar faces were seen. The scene seemed so promising that he arranged to work that summer with a colleague at the Physics Department. They rented two houses about a block apart in old East Davis for summer, and planned a systematic recruitment effort.

It was early summer when Michelle brought her baby, Dawn, up to Davis. Jill went instantly major maternal, and Michelle was able to get some time away. After some serious discussion, they decided to do a "dark mind" passive survey in San Francisco, because they knew from Edward that there were several Coven members still in the Bay Area. Ken, Gabriella, Michelle, Mary, and Nancy drove down one Saturday in late July. It was a miserable day in what San Francisco laughingly calls "summer." Fog was pouring across the city, driven by about a 25 mph winds, and it was raw and cold. They first worked their way up Market Street and Mission Street, sauntering, stopping at shop windows, taking their time.

Nothing.

After passing the Civic Center with its permanent retinue of semi-affluent homeless panhandlers, they moved onto Castro Street, traditional heart of the San Francisco's gay community. Gaudy storefronts offered highly visual ways to "make your statement," although few on the street, even obviously gay couples, seemed to dress like that. There were a lot of low-level "sensitives," but nothing major.

Suddenly they felt the old, cold dread again. A Coven member was trolling, and making no effort to hide his probes. This was the first time that Mary and Nancy had felt the dreaded, polluted touch of a Coven-trained mind, and it was with some effort that they kept "dark mind" intact against the instinctive urge to mentally recoil and thus give away their capabilities and potential victimhood. Then they saw him, dressed in what could well have been gay-inspired attire, walking slowly in a straight line on the west sidewalk so he would be in shadows of the stores.

Ken had prepared for the moment, and took excellent pictures with his mirror-lensed SLR camera, equipped with a 90-degree mirror that permitted photos to be taken without looking directly at the target.

The Coven member was not that old in his gait and demeanor, but his face was deeply lined and his eyes sunken. He somehow looked dissolute, wasted, older than his years. He passed within 20 feet of Ken, who picked up easily his thoughts as he surveyed for victims of the Coven's next "feeding." He was hungry, as they had lain very low for months after the Beverly Hills disaster, and had only recently begun more active trolling, partly out of desperation. They had been so used to frequent "feedings" that they could not bear the withdrawal symptoms of a long fast. They had fed twice in the past two months, which had helped, but they still had a lot to catch up on.

Ken learned essentially nothing beyond this. The Coven member was totally focused on his task, and never strayed from the effort to find a victim. Ken casually started to follow, staying about a block back, but suddenly realized that there was a second Coven member behind him, trying to pick up responses from the first member's probes. The "prober" tended to be less sensitive to responses because of the effort to send out a powerful signal, and the trailing member "sensor" gained sensitivity by keeping a blank mind. Blank, but by no means "dark mind." The second Coven member was younger, inconspicuously dressed in jeans, but equally focused on picking up that instinctive recoil from the prober's signal. Ken stared at a local window until the second Coven member passed, then started to follow. He could easily sense the first member even at 100 feet. A name, "2C2" suddenly came through. As 2C2 stopped, he looked directly back at 3C1, and motioned to go to a café on the south side of the street. He had clearly seen Ken, but there was no mental response to anything but a faceless man with no sensitivity in a crowd of sheep. 2C2 was exhausted, and had to rest.

Since they were both well settled getting lattes, Ken wandered back and rounded up the others. He related what he had seen, and proposed that they bracket the café and see what they could learn. Regretfully, women were fairly rare on Castro, so Mary and Nancy, holding hands and looking very lesbian, went into a tea shop down the road, ordered a chai, and waited.

Ken, Michelle, and Gabriella found that they could be more than 50 feet away and still get a good reading of the Coven's minds. 2C2 was so exhausted that he was essentially non-telepathic and hard to read. 3C1, on the other hand, was gratuitously broadcasting all sorts of information. Ken learned the names of both people, one phone number, a work address, and that six Coven members were marginally active in the city. There would be no trouble finding them in the future. 2C2 was doing most of the talking, but what he was saying seemed very ordinary and made no particular sense to other people at the café.

"The plan is well in motion," said 2C2, "and we have business establishments set up everywhere but Sacramento. The provinces are being generous with personnel and resources, since ours are somewhat battered. We are to have one member in Oakland, and that is all. We are told to go nowhere near Merced, since we may be known to "them."" The last word was clearly a code word, and then the conversation went on to trivialities about the latest hot restaurant.

With the word "Merced," the hairs stood up on Ken's arms.

Circling around the block, he picked up Michelle and Gabriella, who had a hard look on her face. She had picked up enough words also to know that something was up, and she hated Coven people with a vengeance. Comparing notes, Michelle had additional facts Ken hadn't received, including what appeared to be a clear mental picture of the Coven's headquarters on Nob Hill in enough detail to probably find it. This information had to be passed to all members, and quickly. Because they believed that they would learn little more from these two low-level Coven members, they headed back to Davis.

CHAPTER TWENTY-FIVE

Jonathan and Louise had slipped away from their gamblers' special bus and driven down Highway 395 from Reno to Mono Lake, across Tioga Pass into Yosemite, and hence to the Midpines Omega-beta safe house. It was a lovely drive, with Mono Lake now fuller due to the court victories against the Los Angeles Department of Water and Power that saved Mono Lake from becoming a sterile saline sump. But the beauty of the drive was dimmed by the sense of foreboding in the otherwise innocuous message on the phone to go to Reno, and in the freebee pack with the keys to a rented car and directions.

Almost all the original Omega Project members were present, while still leaving at least one principal and three recruits to cover each safe house. This was the first time Ken had seen Victor, one of Gabriella's Hispanic recruits to Omega-delta. Ken could sense another pairing happening, which could be very good for Gabriella, whose progress had been slowed by the hate she felt for the Coven members. If only he could express the damage hate could do to Gabriella as well as Yoda did to Luke in *Star Wars*. Well, he would leave that task to Victor. Just then, Gabriella turned to Ken and gave this beatific smile. Laughing, Ken got up and called the meeting to order. How ordinary this seems, Ken thought, in such an extraordinary situation, sort of like Rotary without the bell ringing and contribution jars.

"Omega, we have a problem," Ken began. He related what they had learned on their survey of San Francisco, including all the names and addresses, all of which had been checked through open web-based sources via untraceable computer inquiries.

Michelle continued, "We were able to use the San Francisco Chamber of Commerce website to do a virtual flyover of San Francisco from all angles. We identified the apartment I sensed, and even the apartment of 2C2 from which he had viewed their headquarters house. After some checking, it turned out to have belonged to 1A, and now is owned by a strange group of front companies with indecipherable economic connections, one to another. I was able, by the way, to get enough information that we could if necessary probably hack into the computers that control these funds, which appear to be considerable, based on the number of properties owned."

This was no mean accomplishment, for Omega was usually almost broke. They had more and more properties to maintain, and their total incomes, including Ken's and contributions from Jonathan, were modest. Stealing from the Coven would merely compensate Omega for the destruction of the Omega-beta house and loss of Bonny, with massive "pain and suffering" and "punitive" bonuses added.

Ken continued, "We have to assume that some other Covens are setting up an operation against us, and the term "provinces" implies a major association of Covens, probably in the eastern United States but perhaps even including overseas. They are setting up several sites, including Sacramento and Oakland, to act as bases of operations. The two sites chosen are interesting. We have done nothing in Sacramento yet, although it was our next planned recruitment effort. Oakland, but not San Francisco. Interesting. It is almost as though they are drawing a noose around Merced. On this basis, I would expect a center in Fresno, too. After their losses, I believe they will be patient and cautious. We have to re-examine all the ways that they could pick up our trail using non-telepathic means. I suspect they are seriously disturbed that we captured the most powerful telepath on the West Coast and defeated easily the extensive security of the Beverly Hills mansion. Their uncertainty in what we can and can't to is a major asset. Let's keep it that way. On the other hand, we know little about the group that provided their muscle in Merced, except that it was expert and ruthless. What little we saw of them indicates that it may be the Russian Mafia of Los Angeles.

"There are only two verified Coven contacts with Omega: Jonathan and the seven Omega-beta victims. Taking the victims first, they have maintained the fiction of fleeing to a commune in Oregon, and after their narrow escape from some murderous group, they insist on keeping their whereabouts secret. They say they will become public once the perpetrators are found, but until then shun any contact even with Merced Police, who dearly want to interview them. Still, the only crime now is arson, not murder. The victims have rare personal contacts by phone – prepaid phone cards at public phone booths in Oregon – to loved ones if absolutely necessary. But their names are all known, now that they are listed as missing persons. I expect that and the Covens will find the names and try to contact next of kin, and learn that they are alive but hiding.

"I propose we should alert the kin to the threat to their loved ones, put on electronic and video surveillance, and see what we can learn when the attempt at contact is made.

"In terms of police, we have found where Sergeant Robert Teller is living in Idaho, and I propose we put surveillance on him, too. But we must be careful. It is a lonely area, and strangers will be spotted. Miniature battery-powered devices that can be flash interrogated from far away would be best.

"And then there is Sergeant Roberto Morales of Merced. He knows an awful lot, much of which is not in the official record. According to Jonathan, he continues to try to work out what has happened without any real police departmental support. He was the only one to grasp the possible connection with two major house explosions with massive fatalities only six hours apart, about the time one could drive from Merced to Beverly Hills. First, with what he knows and suspects, he is in great danger. Teller knows he was in charge of the Bonny car crash events, and I expect an early move against Morales. Kidnapping, then some awful form of interrogation. Jonathan, the Covens are clearly not yet ready to move. I want you and Gabriella to drive down to Merced, get Morales alone, and tell him enough to make him realize the danger he is in and his importance to something new and wonderful. I want Gabriella near but invisible, since we can't risk Morales knowing any more Omega members than is absolutely necessary."

The meeting with Morales did not start well. They were outside the police station on a park bench, in shade to avoid the blazing sun and scorching heat of a Merced summer, but still both were sweating profusely. Roberto knew and liked Jonathan, but he was nobody's fool. He was more than a little suspicious about Jonathan's sudden "health" problem, retirement, and departure from Merced, especially since he and Louise were developing such strong ties to the area.

"Roberto, I left because I was in grave danger. My sudden departure to Fresno was a kidnapping. I was taken to Beverly Hills by what I suspect was the Russian Mafia. I barely escaped before the house blew, and rushed back to Fresno as fast as I could in the car of friends who had rescued me. I am sure they will try to get me again, and the same people will try to get you because of what you know or suspect."

"And just what do I suspect?" answered Roberto, pleased that Jonathan had confirmed connections he had seen that others had missed.

"I don't know," answered Jonathan, "You tell me."

Roberto laughed, "This whole affair seems awfully deep and awfully important to lots of powerful people for reasons that escape me completely. The body count is pretty substantial by now – 21 deaths and seven faked deaths, two buildings incinerated. And no motives that tie it all together."

Jonathan sat back, and thought a bit. Nothing he could say could convince Roberto adequately.

"Let's take a short walk," Jonathan said. Around the corner of the City Hall garage, Gabriella lounged against the wall in whatever shade the place offered. She was waiting as they came up, for she had known what was up.

"I am Gabriella, and I among others, am the motive that ties the deaths together," said Gabriella, "and the body count will grow again, inevitably. I don't want you to be part of that count, but I can also assure you that death is enormously preferable to what will happen to you if you are captured."

Roberto thought Gabriella was the most beautiful woman in the world. Too bad he was not 20 years younger and unmarried to boot, but then he and Rosa had a wonderful marriage and great kids. But she had just quoted back to him his own words, and while in principle this could have been accomplished with a hidden transmitter-receiver, somehow he knew that this was not the case. Could Gabriella read his mind?

"Yes," she answered promptly. "That is why we are being hounded by truly evil people with some of our capabilities. We are part of a loving group of telepaths that has sprung up by accident in Merced. We share and grow and love, with our powers always used for the purposes a loving Lord would have chosen. However, we are viewed by the San Francisco Coven as either a threat or food, taken in horrific 'feedings' that tear the mind apart. A significant number of unsolved murders and missing person cases in San Francisco in the past four decades are the work of this group."

Roberto, stunned, but believing, could only think to ask "The word 'Coven,' what does it mean?" She replied, "A grouping of witches, male or female, is the standard meaning. It was the name they chose for themselves. It seems to fit."

"What can I do? What should I do?" stammered Roberto. He would have probably jumped from El Capitan in Yosemite if she but asked him to do it.

Jonathan answered, "Protect yourself and be alert. The file you have developed, it must be given to us and replaced by misleading data that we will provide you. You must, for your own safety, lose interest in this case. After all, it is only arson now that the victims have come forward through their relatives. I want surveillance on you at all times, house and work, and we will provide you with a method to protect yourself from mental attack. I expect that any kidnap attempt would occur as you do chores around Merced, as I was kidnapped picking up a pizza. They used an anesthetic gas in my car. However, I expect that they will first attempt to try to get to your files, because if you were kidnapped, access to your papers would be much harder to get. When the opportunity arises, we will have you meet other members, but realize that the very survival of something new and precious is at stake and we must keep information about our members secret. But by helping us, you become part of something wonderful that is coming into existence. "

"I will do exactly as you say," answered Roberto, almost echoing the words of the Virgin Mary, deeply learned in his Catholic youth. Gabriella, seeing his resolve, rewarded him with "Peace be with you," and a brilliant smile that somehow went all the way to his heart. Roberto and Jonathan talked details for a while and arranged for secure communications. Jonathan gave Roberto telepathic blanking units to be used only in an emergency. Each item was about the size of a flat brick, and would fit easily into a pocket.

Roberto walked back to the station forever a changed man.

CHAPTER TWENTY-SIX

A Prime always liked to be near the ocean, and had the wealth to pick whatever ocean he desired. Even so, the view from the deck of his rented house was splendid by any measure. Morro Rock spectacularly defined the entrance to Morro Bay, and a long sand spit trended south. To the east, he could see the first two of a series of extinct volcanic plugs that ran all the way to San Luis Obispo. To the north, the sweep of the bay ended in dramatic forested headlands, while behind him fields of golden grass swept up to groves of dark green live oaks. The scent of sea salt and eucalyptus filled the air, and the weather had been simply splendid in the week he had been here.

It was also clear that this area was much more private than the ever more crowded Hamptons. He could follow his own driveway down the hill for almost half a mile, and open fields and cattle were his only neighbors. The steel free-standing fireplace on the deck was a late addition, and not nearly up to the standard of the one at his Hampton home, but he appreciated the warmth it gave in the brisk September winds.

He saw their car and felt their presence even before they turned off Highway 1. This would be the first meeting of the Covens' West Coast Strike Team (the term seemed a bit dramatic, but the provinces were worried). He himself was enjoying life more than he had in years. He sensed that they were stalking worthy quarry, and the thrill of the hunt was in his blood.

Two common vehicles of the region, a full-sized Ford Taurus and a Jeep Grand Cherokee, worked their way up the driveway, far enough apart so they didn't look like the convoy they actually were. He wanted reports every two weeks from all participant teams, and this was the first. He wanted nothing to be initiated without his personal approval.

Eight men walked up the steps to the deck, and sort of clustered at the top of the stairs until A Prime motioned them to the deck chairs surrounding the fireplace, facing the ocean. A Prime sat with his back to the ocean so the afternoon sun would shine in their eyes. The men included the leaders of each of the new support sites, Pasadena, Fresno, Oakland, and Sacramento, representatives of the decimated Los Angeles and San Francisco Covens (the latter 2C2), and the same three personal representatives from the three provinces present at the original meeting at the Hampton house. They all waited patiently and a bit fearfully until the clock struck 3.

A Prime spoke. "The reports will be numbered from this day on every other week, starting with Report 1 today. These reports will rotate through the sites in order of siting, and the members of the West Coast Covens. The letters P, O, F, and S will represent your sites, while SF and LA will label the Coven representatives. P1, P2, and P3 will identify Province representatives. I will start each reporting session with analysis of what we have learned, and then the chosen representative will present the overall report for the entire project. Others will then have an opportunity to add additional information.

"Since our meeting last fall, many months have passed with no further contact with members of the San Francisco or Los Angeles Covens. SF2C2, that is still correct, I presume?" He nodded affirmative. Or Los Angeles? Again an affirmative. "SF2C2, how many 'feedings' have you had?" "Five," he answered, "mostly low-level sensitives whose absence would not be noticed, and all from the Castro District. All had AIDS."

"How often have you met as a group, and where is your new meeting site?" A Prime immediately knew he had hit a nerve, as SF2C2, seeing his error too late, mumbled, "Seven times, at 1A's old apartment that was sold and re-purchased by the Coven through secure financial arrangements."

"You blundering idiot!" shouted A Prime, with a hard mental slap at SF2C2. "That is exactly the sort of action that will let you all be identified. Immediately cease all activities at that site, as it could have been compromised by either 1A, which I doubt, or Edward, which is barely possible since he had not been there often and only under security. Sell it immediately and get it out of any Coven ownership, no matter how carefully hidden." Sarcasm dripped from every word. SF2C2 was almost in tears from fear and shame. What a way to start.

It had never occurred to A Prime that other Coven members in the Beverly Hills house might have compromised the site, as he had assumed that all had been killed by some carefully hidden explosive, remotely triggered. The thought that the entire Coven, including 1A, had been instantly mentally incapacitated was simply unthinkable.

A Prime continued, "On a more positive note, we have not been inactive these past months. We have identified statistical associations between students, faculty, and staff at UC Merced, based on classes and housing, focusing on the so-called 'victims' of the house explosion. Little is similar among the seven, but one association that did jump out was that four of them regularly attended the UC Merced Newman Center, a Catholic indoctrination center on many college campuses. Two were, of course, Jonathan Campbell's graduate students, two were roommates in the special Honors Dormitory, several had one class together. We suspect the seven are in Oregon somewhere, which in fact was exactly the story they leaked to their friends. We have also found where Jonathan Campbell went after he left Merced – Eugene, Oregon – that state keeps popping up in our analysis. We have the names and numbers of next of kin, and propose to institute surveillance and eventually openly approach the kin. Then there is the strange case of the pig bones. This was a crude attempt to confuse authorities that would soon be discovered. Thus, it must have been designed to merely act as cover until their plans could be achieved that evening – namely the attack on the Beverly Hills mansion timed for the one period when maximum Coven members were present. This shows detailed knowledge of the Coven's plans, very suspicious indeed since other than the Coven members, only the Mafia knew the details. The need to rescue Jonathan doubtless made these plans more difficult. Perhaps not coincidentally, we have not been able to find the Russian Mafia people that were the muscle in the earlier operation. They appear to have vanished from the face of the Earth. They could be scared and in hiding, possibly because they were part of a double-cross. This seems a likely explanation. In this case, we have to assume that the Merced group has serious financial resources to turn the Mafia from a well-paid program. Alternately, the Mafia may have learned too much about the reasons for the operation and fled from fear of the Coven's revenge at their failure.

"Getting back to Jonathan Campbell, we could find nothing in his medical records that could have led to his sudden heath emergency, retirement, and precipitous departure from Merced. When someone acts like this, it is either out of an urgent need to be at the new place or a desperate need to leave the old place. I suspect the former, with the Merced telepaths desperate to leave Merced for fear of the Coven and their mentor soon to follow. We must have secure sites in Oregon. P2, you have offered more resources than we have needed to date; could you see to it? If this is their new headquarters, be very cautious. Still, we cannot exclude the possibility that there are still members of the Merced telepaths at UC Merced. Continue developing your plans."

The remainder of the time concerned logistical and communication matters, and in this period A Prime sat back and observed. The other members largely ignored his presence as best they could, partially because the sun was getting low in the sky and shone directly in their eyes when they tried to look at A Prime, partially out of dread.

CHAPTER TWENTY-SEVEN

It was Sergeant Morales who spotted the sign – ever so discrete – offering a prime San Francisco apartment for sale. He was in the city for unrelated police business when he checked the address given him by Jonathan. He immediately phoned a number, which in turn called another number he did not know but knew it existed in Merced itself, not Oregon. A male voice answered, "Speak." Roberto said the emergency code word, identifying himself in the process, and told what he had seen. "Received," was the answer, followed by an immediate hang up.

Ken, Diane, Michael, and Jill went to San Francisco the next day, and inquired about the property. They seemed to have impeccable credentials at one of the banks that was in fact holding the property, so they got a grand tour. When they reached the main room and patio, they all stood silent, fearful that the walls would speak the unspeakable things that had happened here. Two of the chairs on either side of the fireplace were larger than the rest scattered about the room, and while they now each faced the fire, the marks on the rug showed that typically they had faced into the room. Ken sort of poked around and under the chair, and found a set of old wire-rimmed glasses between the cushions. He casually pocketed them.

Ken asked a series of well-planned questions, indicating serious interest but somewhat put off by the stiff price. Still, the patio was splendid, and the view of the Golden Gate Bridge worthy of a wall poster. A sort of casual offer was made, realistic but well below the asking price, and then they left. Only 35 minutes later, a call was made to 2C2's apartment, long since remotely tapped, from the real estate agent. Ken's laptop beeped at him, and as they got on the Bay Bridge on-ramp, a number was written on his screen. Ken smiled. And then another, and another, until six numbers scrawled across the screen. He could no longer restrain himself. "Bingo," he said. And one was in Oakland.

One week later, surveillance of the Oakland Coven house had established a fixed pattern, with three unknown Coven members of serious telepathic capabilities (probably Bs, they decided), and 2C2 himself was in daily attendance. Unlike 2C2's own car, which merely went around the Bay Area, the Oakland house had several cars, including a Jeep Grand Cherokee that, while brand new, had lots of miles on it already. It was pathetically easy one early evening for Ken, Michelle, and Gabriella to emplace under the bumper one of the very same high-tech tracking units discovered on Jonathan's car in Merced. All were in "dark mind" mode, but no one came even close enough to notice the playful but tipsy threesome as they fumbled for keys, dropped some, retrieved, then forgot where the car was parked. Since things were going so smoothly, Ken also emplaced a digital surveillance camera and microphone with a good view of the garage exit. The latest units looked like a standard double wall socket in one of several designs, and it could be simply glued onto any wall at the proper height. It even would take a plug, without of course giving any voltage.

Two weeks later, Roberto noticed that his files on the Merced house bombing, the car wreck, and Bonny's murder had been taken out and then carefully replaced. Clearly, what Jonathan and Gabriella had told him was going to happen was panning out almost on schedule. He made a short phone message, this time to Oregon, on the pay phone in the police headquarters and using a prepaid phone card.

Students were back, and the town, without ever admitting it publicly, was glad to see them. The start of the fall quarter also was the start of cooler weather, affluence for pizza joints and copying services, and generally an uptempo feeling throughout the town. The town was full of new people, and then came the call from Diane and Michael to Ken. "Company's here."

The gathering that evening was at the Planada safe house of Omega-delta, since it was closest to town and still remote. Careful surveillance was made of all vehicles on Highway 140, but no tails were detected. All cars were checked for electronic bugs. None was found. Almost 20 people were present.

Ken began with a short prayer, "The hour of trial has come. Let us all pray for divine guidance, as we struggle with both the need to preserve our lives and our mandate to love our enemies even as they try to destroy us."

Ken summarized what was known to date. There were cells of eastern Coven members set up in Oakland, Sacramento, Fresno, and Pasadena. We only know the address and have faces for the Oakland cell. In addition, some Coven members survive from San Francisco, six, whose names and addresses are known to us, and five in Los Angeles, unknown to us although we have pictures of two of them. The latter two Covens have been very passive recently. The action is being driven by eastern U.S. Covens in three provinces. They fear us, are uncertain of our powers, and are trying all the non-telepathic methods they have to learn about us. They are starting to contact the relatives of the Merced seven, and as they do, we will learn more names. Yesterday, the files on Bonny, the van wreck, and the Merced house explosion were lifted from police files, doubtless copied, and carefully replaced. These files are filled with misleading information, hinting that there were only seven Merced telepaths and they have fled to Oregon after wreaking vengeance on the Beverly Hills mansion.

"Now Diane and Michael have spotted a Coven member trolling for victims openly in Merced. This is either stupidity beyond understanding or a trap. I suspect the latter. They are deliberately stirring the Merced pot to see what comes to the surface. I expect that they will do this for a couple of weeks and see if anyone flees the town or does something unusual. But after that, they will escalate the plan and raise the stakes. So what do we do if they zero in on some low-level sensitive and kidnap him or her for a 'feeding?' We have to respond, to protect an innocent life. By doing so, we will reveal our presence and we will all be at much greater danger. Another point worth noting. We are no longer just in Fresno, but have Omega groups also in Davis, Midpines, and Los Angeles. This offers us some advantages, and we plan to use them to the fullest."

CHAPTER TWENTY-EIGHT

A Prime always liked to be near the ocean, and had the wealth to pick whatever ocean he desired. Even so, the view from the deck of his rented house was splendid by any measure, and the scent of sea salt and eucalyptus filled the air. The weather had been simply splendid in the three weeks he had been here. This area was starting to attract him for a future residence. He might consider it once California (and perhaps Oregon) had been cleansed. The steel free-standing fireplace was not nearly up to the standard of the one at his Hampton home, but he appreciated the warmth it gave in the brisk October afternoon.

Two cars, the same two cars he noted with distaste, wound up the driveway. He wondered how well the new recruits were being trained in stealthcraft. They were taking their present security under A Prime's wings a little to casually.

They waited until the clock struck 3.

Then A Prime began, "Never again come to this house with those two cars. Rotate them, and arrive farther apart in time Even a 5-minute separation makes people forget the prior vehicle. Never forget that these are dangerous times. Never before have more than one or two Coven members died in a given year. Last year we had 21, all from hostile action, all in California. At that rate, we would be eradicated in just a few years, and long before that we would be dispersed, vulnerable, weak!"

All were chastened by A Prime's comments.

"F1 – your report."

F1 gathered his somewhat scattered thoughts, his carefully rehearsed presentation is disarray. A Prime did that to people.

Report Week No. 3

"All base sites are established, and electronic surveillance established at the Merced Police Department. The files on the past year's events was taken, copied, and carefully replaced. The data in the files is more extensive than we had realized. But the last entry was four months ago, and according to the duty roster, no one is presently assigned to the case. The police have been contacted by all but one of the relatives of the Merced house 'victims' and the police have closed those missing-person files. They are still very interested as to what tied these people together, and they present some evidence that they were in some sort of secret non-university sponsored research for an industrial client that went sour big time. The files contain some data provided by Jonathan Campbell, mainly on the students' majors and official research projects. We have checked these data with UC Merced records, and they are accurate. The record sheds little light on Campbell's role in the matter. They have his current address, which also checks with our records. In summary, it appears that the police were initially very curious, and then backed off as the 'victims' surfaced. There is no hint of a Beverly Hills-Merced connection.

"We examined closely the Newman Center because of the statistical association, and found it full of starry eyed do-gooders. No hint of telepathic activity. A week of passive Coven presence in Merced was easy because of all the new students and staff at the rapidly growing university, all without any contacts, and the first active probe was initiated. A Coven 'prober' drove through Merced, with three other Coven members inconspicuously wandering the streets on foot in the same area in a pure 'sensor' mode. We received no response other than a fairly high frequency of low and low-to-moderate sensitives. For some reason, the area is surprisingly rich in sensitives. Once the present problems are resolved, it could be a good 'feeding' area."

"We will feed exactly when and where it is most likely to flush any hidden telepaths out of the woodwork," interjected A Prime. "Remember this pathetic Bonny creature, and the violent response of the telepaths. Continue what you are doing on and off for two more weeks, going into outlying areas as they may have moved their base out of Merced proper for fear of us."

Contingency plans were discussed, the establishment of the Oregon cell confirmed. Standing orders were that at all times there would be three Coven members together and one well away to act as backup support (they were all well armed) or at least report any setbacks to higher authority.

Plans for the first "feeding" in Merced were then discussed, with a site picked out with excellent defensive characteristics, close to the city but remote enough to spot and deter interlopers.

It was on a dirt road just before a sorry excuse of a burg called Planada.

A Prime broke in, "How did the Merced telepaths detect Bonny's death?

116

Her powers were far too weak to have broadcast very far, and Group 4 had taken her well into sparsely populated hills. Were they followed? We find no evidence of that, but it cannot be totally ruled out. In the one satellite photo that shows the Group 4 van on the way into the mountains, no other cars are within a mile of it going up the hill. This bothers me. Be careful. There are things we are missing in our analysis."

A Prime turned away and warmed his hands at the fire. It was the signal that the meeting was over, and the rest filed out, grateful to leave his presence.

Omega was on a war footing. The decision was made that the first attempt at a "feeding" in Merced would draw many of the Coven members to the site. The trigger was to be the location of the newly discovered telepath in Morro Bay, recently arrived from the east with unlimited money. The car tracker worked perfectly, and a satellite photograph showed the Grand Cherokee tailed by a second vehicle the entire way. Two cars, perhaps 10 people? All were clearly in consultation with the new telepath, for after only three hours, they turned around. Regretfully, this information was not known until two days after it occurred, since the GPS tracker had to be triggered to release its records.

Since nothing had happened in the past three days after the visit, perhaps there would be either additional consultations at Morro Bay or perhaps the telepath would come to Merced. They would certainly want their best capabilities present for the inevitable attempt to flush out Omega, probability by a "feeding" on an innocent, perhaps by capturing Jonathan in Oregon. The latter possibility was reduced when Jonathan and Louise went into hiding at the Davis safe house, after leaving a detailed message at the University of Oregon and with neighbors about a trip back East to see an ailing sister (which was true in a way, but the sister had been stable for about a decade).

The site of the new center of the San Francisco Coven was easily found, thanks to the ever-incautious 2C2. Even before the first group meeting, Ken and Michael had broken in pretending to be part of the security installation teams (three separate companies were being used in any case) and slipped non-metallic "bugs" into the feet of three of the chairs taken from the previous Coven headquarters on Nob Hill. Cameras were placed outside, audio pickups in the garage.

Very carefully, Tim and Jennifer came up from the Los Angeles safe house to San Luis Obispo, and then after two days of long-range surveillance, were able to place "bugs" at the entry to the driveway and back in the oaks. The latter were recording and transmitting continuously on a tight CO_2 laser beam to a relay transmitter more than two miles away, and then to a cell phone and land lines to Merced.

Personnel were brought into secret locations all over Merced, always in pairs or threes. Even Michelle and Diane left their babies at the Midpines safe house, because they might be needed in the crunch. At night, when activity was low, the entire town of Merced was covered by a telepathic web. All people could be at least sensed as to presence, some far more, and about half of the ones close to the safe houses telepathically read. Gabriella's Omega-delta teams proved a major asset, fitting naturally into the large Hispanic population and ready, even eager, for the battle they defined in black-and-white terms.

Because it was the protocol of the Covens to always leave someone at their safe houses, plans were made to take them out, too, and non-telepathic resources were assigned to this task.

The hope was that the disappearance of large numbers of Coven members, powerful Coven members, well-prepared Coven members, by the Merced telepaths in hopefully as mysterious a manner as possible would force the eastern Covens to relinquish the West Coast and lick their wounds in secret back at their home bases. The one advantage they had was that they were sure that the Covens feared public exposure as much or more as they did, and so every effort would be made to keep this secret war from the general public.

Then came the waiting.

It was the ever-observant Sergeant Morales who noticed it first. He had arranged for all motel operators in the city to report anything unusual, especially young to middle-aged men without obvious tasks staying more than one day. On November 5, two motels alerted Morales, and the day after that, three more. Using just one trusted friend on the force, pictures were surreptitiously taken, fingerprints recorded, even nail clippings and such for DNA analysis were gathered when the men left to go into the town.

Finally, tracers were put on every vehicle, one of which was lost when a previously suspicious man upped and left with a woman clearly not his wife.

Tiffany came to Ken and said, "Rather than just any old innocent sensitive, I would rather offer myself as the bait. I have some defensive skills (indeed, thought Ken, both mentally and black belt judo) and I would be a preferred target. Let me pose in some job where they will come in contact with me." Ken was troubled but saw the logic. "You are taking a terrible chance," Ken said. "For Bonny," was Tiffany's terse reply. Tiffany was given the temporary job of mail clerk assistant in the downtown post office handling stamp sales, a job that had her at her desk for eight hours a day. Sergeant Morales arranged for police surveillance, Ken for Omega surveillance.

CHAPTER TWENTY-NINE

A Prime always liked to be near the ocean, but now the view interested him not at all. More important things were brewing, and the Covens were united in the largest and most carefully planned operation they had ever encountered. He could follow his own driveway down the hill for almost half a mile, and open fields and cattle were his only neighbors. He appreciated the warmth the steel fireplace gave in the brisk November winds. A little before the appointed time, and this time separately, two cars worked their way up Highway 1 from San Luis Obispo, and one came down from the north via Atascadero. All were slightly older models of very common brands, all in non-descript colors.

"Good," thought A Prime. "They are learning."

At 3:00 p.m., Prime spoke. "Your report, O2."

Week 5, Report No. 3

"We have had no active contacts at all in Merced, but there is a moderate level of sensitivity among what seems to be a rather socially conscious student body. More important, we have found one sensitive who shows quite a bit more potential, even enough perhaps as a recruit but certainly a splendid candidate for a major Class A 'feeding.'" The assembled members stirred slightly, for such events are rare and powerful. Once experienced, they are addictive.

"She had a somewhat anomalous response to our probe, slightly delayed and confused, but after all she is a woman," said P2 redundantly. "It is just possible that she is sensitive enough to sense my probe as I was close and excited. But she did not hesitate in the task she was working on, and never looked up."

"Lucky for you," said A Prime, with sarcasm in his voice but a sudden hunger in his mind. This decided it. He, too, would go to Merced.

"We had our non-telepathic operative, Linda, check up on her, confirm her schedule, and generally scout for any signs that she might be other than what she seems – a UC Merced student looking for part-time work. She checks out clean."

A Prime continued, "What do you have for 'muscle' should our activities become known?"

"We recruited an entire chapter of Hells Angels, 26 members, based in Modesto but claiming Merced as their turf. We offered them tons of money merely to guard our flanks as we interrogated this scientist. We spun the usual yarn of industrial espionage, but it seems they hardly cared. What they wanted was an excuse to fight."

And the Merced Police? "We have arranged for a disastrous hostage standoff up on Highway 140 toward Gilroy, the opposite side of the town from our operations. The Hells Angels were only too happy to oblige, and they will of course flee as soon as the police get near. Finally, there will be a timed fuel explosion in the police headquarters' garage."

"And the Merced telepaths?" asked A Prime, somewhat impressed despite himself.

"Our members are in pairs on every road leading to the 'feeding' site. I promised them some pre-'feeding' interaction, one at a time, of course," said P2. "All are well armed and paired with two Hells Angels members, who are veritable walking arsenals."

"What day do you propose, and why?" asked A Prime, no longer able to hide his eagerness.

"Friday, November 10. It is a three-day weekend because of Veterans Day and students will leave town in droves. Two police officers are taking vacation, and they will be gone Thursday late. The victim has the shift that day until 4:00 p.m., and then is off until Tuesday. I propose we abduct her as she walks to her car after checking out of work. She has no roommate to alert police. The scheduled feeding time is 5:00 p.m., to allow for the 25-minute drive and uncertainties in timing. Sometimes she lingers in the post office for a few minutes talking with friends before leaving."

"Remember," said A Prime, "Our purpose is to flush out the Merced telepaths. The 'feeding' is secondary. I will come. Pick me up with LA2B1 at the Carl's Jr. on I-5 at Kettleman City at around 2:00 p.m. We will then proceed in my car with two Hells Angeles, dressed well but heavily armed. No other Hells Angel is to get within half a mile of the feeding site. These two will, of course, have to die. Expect me at 4:45, Friday, at the 'feeding' site."

Joy surged at this news. With the formidable A Prime present, they feared no telepathic threat.

A Prime turned to the fire, warming his hands. The rest slipped away. Finally this nightmare would end, with the Covens triumphant, of course.

CHAPTER THIRTY

Two days later, on Tuesday, November 12, Sergeant Morales had the entire Hells Angels plan in his hand. He had, of course, long since penetrated their operations with no less than three operatives, so he actually had two written plans and one set of transcribed notes to compare. Regretfully, none of them gave any hint at where in or near Merced this kidnapping and interrogation would take place, merely points all around the city where two Hells Angels would meet two businessmen and proceed in their cars to their appointed sites. There was some resistance at having to drop off their Harleys and proceed in cars, but the pay was very good. In addition, two were told to meet a car coming up from the south at the Kettleman City Carl's Jr. at I-5 at 2:00 p.m. to act as drivers and security for two obviously important businessmen.

The problem was that the Hells Angeles actually would outnumber the entire Merced Police force, and simply guarding businessmen gave the police no reason to pick them up. He could, however, alert the force to the fake hostage crises and protect the police garage from explosives. This was going to be tricky.

The post office was very quiet on Friday, and Tiffany had sold hardly any stamps. Thus, she backed up the staff any way she could, sorting and hauling packages, which dominated the mail that afternoon. She was intensely nervous, determined yet trying not to be scared. "Fear is the Mind Destroyer," came suddenly to her mind. That didn't sound like Yoda from *Star Wars*, more like the Bene Gesserit witches in *Dune*. Have I become a witch, she thought? Right now, she just wanted this whole thing to be over. She was kicking herself for blowing the first contact last week. Her response had not been correct, she knew. Maybe they would not come back. Anyway, she was maintaining pure "dark mind" protocol, and then at around 3:45 p.m., she felt them coming from over two blocks away. She rapidly punched in a cell phone number. Her moment of trial was about to arrive, with the real possibility of a horrendous death as they tore her mind apart. "For Bonny," she whispered, and then, "Mary, at the hour of my death, pray for me."

At 3:45 p.m., LA2B1 and P21B1 checked their pagers. All was well and they soon received the "Go" signal, which was delayed a bit. Linda confirmed that the victim, named Tiffany they had learned, was still in the post office at 4:10 p.m. They were getting nervous, as the timing was critical. Then she came out, dressed in warmer clothing and wearing a baseball cap, and went around the back where workers parked. Because the normal federal employees got off work at 4:30 p.m., and because it was a three-day weekend, state and federal, the parking lot was empty. They pulled into a parking place three slots away from Tiffany, who was searching for keys.

P21B1 struck, and Tiffany turned, smiled, and came readily into their car. P21B1 got into the back seat with her, and LA2B1 who had both a real and a fake California driver's license, pulled out of the parking lot and headed east.

It seemed so natural, Tiffany laughing and chatting, the two men smiling and joking, taking turns every 10 minutes to keep control. Indeed, Tiffany had serious potential. This would be a "feeding" to remember.

Gabriella was posted in the eastern quadrant, with Michelle, Ken, and Diane in the others. Michael was at the Merced airport. Mary and Nancy waited expectantly on a side road not far from the post office. As the car with Tiffany passed, it was clear that the Coven members were making no effort to hide their emanations, since keeping control of Tiffany used about all the effort they had. Both were clearly powerful. Controlling them would not be as easy as the pathetic but vicious Greg, who was only a D-class telepath. But because they were so powerful, they were easy to track, and as they turned onto Highway 140, Gabriella suddenly sensed the mental map and the "feeding" site.

She pulled out her cell phone and spoke into it. The key piece of information was now known, but the site was much farther out in the country than they had planned for and the roads to the site were long and open. She received confirmation from Ken that all the Coven-Hells Angels pairs were also heading east and south, toward an old abandoned farm airstrip that was probably still usable because the fall rains had been light. Something was up. Ken called Mary and Nancy, gave them instructions and warned them that tailing would not be easy but Tiffany must not be alone. They swung their old pickup, with gun racks but no guns that anyone could see, onto the highway a good half-mile behind Tiffany's car.

Almost at Planada, Tiffany's car turned off onto a paved but bumpy road, heading south. They were actually only about a half mile from the Planada safe house, with Gabriella's recruits anxious to play whatever role they could. Still, they persisted in "dark mind" as they sensed the car passing. They called Ken, and gave him a progress report. Mary and Nancy swung onto the road about a minute later, and this was also relayed.

Victor was in charge of Planada at that time, and could see that things were not going exactly to plan. They were way outside of the planned radius of operations. But he knew of a parallel road that went south then turned west past a farm, and then to a farm airstrip. Four grabbed weapons, and headed out, after telling Ken where they were going.

"Be careful!" he said. "These people are powerful. Stay back, use your mind shields, be well armed, but never let Tiffany alone with these monsters if you can possibly help it." One recruit was left manning the phone, and he had soon had an interesting report. Groups of four, including tough-looking types, were taking up positions in and around Planada, but most were not going down the road.

The ride seemed to go on forever. Tiffany was working as hard as the Coven members, hiding her ability to read their minds, playing dumb and happy. It was probably about 4:30 p.m. when they pulled up to an area with a few eucalyptus trees, a makeshift picnic table, and four men in a car waiting for them. She sensed relief in her captors, but not finality. Whatever was about to happen still was in the future. She got out, moved under their control to the table, and there waiting for her was a fish sandwich from McDonald's, fries, and a coke. She actually liked these things, and occasionally bought them for herself when her friends weren't looking. What a nice touch. She said "Thank you," and meant it, and sat down to eat. As she had hoped, her actions led to a lower effort at mind control, and for about 30 seconds, no one was controlling her. She just ate and chatted, and waited.

About 10 minutes later, she heard two cars come down the road behind her. She sensed a number of minds, some but not all potent, but the captors reinstituted control at a high level. She could not turn to look. About 5 minutes later, yet another car came down the road, with four people, two totally insensitive (muscle, she thought), one a quite powerful Coven member, and one, "He is the Beast" came to her mind. An awful, powerful, evil thing was approaching, his power somewhat muted by being inside the metal car, and suddenly everybody at the site was raised to extreme level of excitement and expectation.

The car stopped, and he started to get out. All eyes were on A Prime, all expectations, all eager, now it would begin. A Prime was here, and A Prime was always in charge!

Tiffany easily broke through the control, grabbed the visor of her baseball cap, and pulled it down hard. A silvery mesh was revealed under the cap and now over her face, but thin enough so that she could see through it, dimly. This engaged one of the three redundant triggers of the interference packs built into the soles of her tennis shoes, and a mental din filled the site. The power was limited, so instead of disability, there was confusion, chaos – mental and physical. Tiffany used the opportunity and sprinted away from the table, away from that awful unseen presence behind her.

A Prime was caught by surprise by the sudden mental change in the totally passive Tiffany. Before he could institute control, she had done something to her head and triggered a mental static device, powerful enough to confuse but not disabling.

Suddenly he realized, "they have telepathic technological resources. That was how they defeated the Covens."

This fact was so astounding, so unexpected, and so revolutionary, that nothing else mattered. "With merely the knowledge that such technology could be developed, we could duplicate it," he thought. "This information must get back, back to all the Covens, otherwise we face disaster." All thought of eradicating the Merced Coven ceased, and now all he wanted was to leave immediately with his knowledge. Even a cell phone would do it. "I must get the call to Oakland," he thought.

But first, he leveled all his powers to Tiffany, to punish, to destroy her mind totally. But she was shielded, and she was fighting back. Her mind was sort of ensnaring his in webs – it was hard to gather his full strength. He could feel her pain, but he did not feel fear. How did she control it? Fear was the key element in feedings, but he would win. He cut the legs out from under her, and Tiffany dropped to the ground, physically incapacitated but mentally fighting for her life. "For Bonny," she murmured.

Other minds hammered at A Prime, from a different direction. Over in the field, more than 100 yards away, two minds joined flooding his with unwanted but powerful images. Mary and Nancy, lovers, mentally united. This enemy he knew, the joining of women who throughout history had been almost the only barrier to the rule of the Covens – witches! I will destroy you too, once Tiffany is crushed. But there were other minds coming across the field. He and the Coven could handle them later. He turned again to Tiffany, and exulted in her exhaustion. She had been fighting, controlling, for so long, now there was nothing left to fight with. She was almost defenseless, but that damn shield on her head protected her somewhat, he could not totally eradicate the images forced on him by the witches in the field, and that infernal mental noise-maker made concentration difficult. One at a time.

"Take off her hat, now," yelled A Prime.

Three Coven members, pulled out of their confusion, jumped to do this and received a firm kick in the groin from Tiffany for their efforts. Two more came to their aid, and the five circled around her, ready to jump.

Unnoticed by all, a small plane swooped low over the site, and a package with a small parachute was dropped through an open window. It looked like a laptop computer.

Every telepath screamed and grabbed their foreheads, even A Prime. All but A Prime writhed in the dust, screaming. He, ever quick, jumped back into the car, the steel roof sharply cutting down the signal.

"Drive out of here fast," yelled A prime.

The Hells Angels, incongruously dressed in ill-fitting suits, floored the car and spun down the road with a plume of dust. About a quarter mile down the road, as they came up out of a dip, they suddenly saw that the road was blocked by two cars hastily driven across the lip of the rise, and five people, four women and one man, arrayed themselves in a line just in front of the cars. The Hells Angeles braked to a stop, grabbed their AK-47s, and went to make quick work of the problem.

Two shots rang out in quick succession, and dropped both thugs into the dust. Sergeant Morales stepped out behind his patrol car, happy that his militarily honed rifle skills and sharpshooter's badges were still viable 20 years later.

A Prime got out, his mind now clear of the interference behind him. Quickly he cut the legs out from under Morales, and left him thrashing helplessly in the dust. The two women on the right seemed to have the most power, and one also held an Uzi. She was next, and Jill dropped into the dust like a rock with a cry. Her mind was still sharp, though. So that was how they did it, she thought, control of motor actions.

A Prime turned to the others, a sneer on his lips. Too easy. The woman next to Jill was somehow familiar, somehow.

It was L3, alive, traitor to the L.A. Coven, turned against us. Raging at L3, he turned to destroy this thing before him.

At that very moment, when his guard was down from the effort to dispatch L3, Betsy, four minds as one crashed into his own, tearing into his thoughts, sewing confusion and uncertainty. A Prime was furious, and the battle raged for seconds that seemed like an eternity. Then the older man stepped forward and held out a pair of wire-rimmed glasses.

"Here, these may help you to concentrate," he said ever so casually.

Friedman's glasses! How did he get them? Were the Merced telepaths behind Friedman's madness and death? Fury fueled by the power of hundreds of deaths surged through his mind, driving out all other thoughts rising to a crescendo he had never known, with but one thought – Kill!

And so his mind died. Ken sensed it first, a sort of mental short circuit, and then there was nothing but a pathetic old man groveling in the dust and saying over and over again, "My name is Milton, my name is Milton."

CHAPTER THIRTY-ONE

They stood in silent horror. Morales was slowly regaining the use of his limbs, but Ken, Michelle, Gabriella, and Betsy just stood, stunned. It was as though they had looked into the Chernobyl reactor core at the very instant it had gone critical, generating as much energy as all the rest of the USSR for a few seconds before it blew. And the images! Luckily, it was so fast and so incoherent, details did not linger. But the horror of it they would never forget. It was like the essence of death distilled from the despair of hundreds of victims.

Ken spoke first, "There is nothing left. His mind is totally gone."

Gabriella ran over to Jill, helped her to her feet, and picked up the Uzi. She was strongly tempted to empty an entire clip into what use to be A Prime, but somehow the victory had erased an old hurt and old fear in her. "Now I can love again," she thought. A Prime, regardless of his present condition, was given an anesthetic injection and hooded with a metallic hood, just in case he should revive and his powers return.

Back at the "feeding" site 13 Coven members now lay quietly, dispatched with anesthetic injections, tied, hooded, ready for transport. The Planada recruits had arrived across the field just in time to help control the Coven members.

Mary and Nancy gently picked up Tiffany, placed her on the bench, and held her close. Tiffany asked weakly, "Is it over?" Nancy said, "Yes, I felt an awful burst of horror, and now it is gone. Our people are coming, and that creature is no more."

They had almost finished loading the cars while keeping a sharp watch on the road for signs of a rescue. Morales' police radio chimed in.

"We have captured six suspicious individuals and a bunch of belligerent Hells Angels, who did not however put up much of a fight. The fake hostage crisis you anticipated did occur, as did the attempt to plant a bomb. The two perpetrators, Hells Angeles members from Modesto, are also in custody. What is going on around here? Has Merced become the crime capital of California?"

"Hold them carefully, and I'll be back soon to question them," responded Morales. "We are just booking them now, but on what charge? All we have on them is that their identification is faked," said the office. "That's enough," said Morales. "Until they can identify themselves, we must assume that they are wanted somewhere for something."

"I'll tell the booking sergeant – 10-4"

Gabriella gave him a big hug, and was then praising Victor and her recruits for their courage when a small plane made an approach to the farm strip. Ken cheerily waved. It flew over them repeatedly, clearly waiting for a signal that did not come, then flew off. Well before that time, however, all the captured Coven members had been safely hidden in the Omega vehicles.

"Non-telepathic," said Michelle, and Ken, Gabriella, and Diane nodded.

"Diane," Ken said, "tell Michael that he saved the day. This site was so remote that only a small plane could cover the territory, and with Michael being a pilot, it was the right choice. Tiffany, you were at your limit, but what a fight you put up! You wore him out so it was easier for us."

"He was known as A Prime," said Tiffany, "They were in awe of him and held him to be the most powerful telepath in the United States."

"We could read him clearly as he came up the road toward us," Ken mused. "He was amazed by the fact that we had technology, and he was racing to get the information out to the Covens. Nothing else mattered to him. We hastily set up the roadblock with Roberto hidden behind the car, armed and ready. We were counting on Roberto to be our ace in the hole should we encounter trouble, but the two Hells Angels' 'muscle' forced Roberto to take them out, and A Prime surprised us with his powers. Both Roberto and Jill can still barely walk."

The police radio crackled into life, "The six male suspects have disappeared. The booking sergeant thought they had all been booked, when none were. He said he turned them over to an officer to incarcerate, but we had no officer ready to do that yet. There are no photographs, no fingerprints, no suspects. They just walked out, and no one can say how."

Sergeant Morales would have some explaining to do. But he would do it well. He now understood what was happening, and burned with anger at how easily that guy dispatched him. He was on board all the way with this group, for he had seen the face of the Devil.

As Ken walked back to the car and Omega began to disperse to its safe house, Ken mused to Jill, "In the old days, they used to sing a 'Te Deum' as thanks to God for a victory. I'll try to find it in an old hymnal when we get home." Jill's legs were fine by now, but she pretended to be shaky so as to cling closer to Ken. "Our childhood has ended," thought Jill. "Now we have to grow up."

CHAPTER THIRTY-TWO

She was the archetypical domestic, probably Guatemalan, with a prominent nose and the air of someone whose immigration status is suspect. She was somewhat taller than average, was carrying a large carpet bag slung over one shoulder, and had a hearing aid in one ear. In San Francisco, their number is legion. She was walking along a sidewalk in a pricey district not far from Coit Tower, when she suddenly stopped, waited with her hand cupped over the ear with the "hearing aid." Then she pulled out a cell phone, and dialed a number. Checking her watch, she started to walk with some determination. Two blocks later, she walked into the lobby of an upscale apartment, checked the time on her watch, keyed a code into the elevator, and rode to the penthouse. There she put on ladylike white gloves (they were all she could find on short notice), pulled out a key, put a small cuplike device over her nose, opened the door and entered. Five men, all unconscious, were seated in large leather-covered chairs, circled around a short-wave radio and a speaker phone. She opened the sliding glass doors to air out the room. This would not be the place to fall unconscious under my own anesthetic and awake in the power of these monsters, she thought.

She quickly gave each one an injection of some fluid, quite a lot because she had to reload after each injection. Then she placed two large wrapped packages and one opened package onto the table, forced the hand of one of the men onto the packages to leave fingerprints. Next, she picked up the Coven's short-wave radio, which Omega had replaced with a duplicate model but complete with its cell phone-activated anesthetic release system, and put it into the bag. She carefully arranged drug paraphernalia on the table, including a small alcohol lamp, which she ignited. It looked like the men were sleeping, but they were in the process of dying of heroin overdoses from extraordinarily pure uncut China White.

She left in just under three minutes. Once around the building corner in a secluded alley, she took off the fake nose and wig and put them in her bag. She noticed that off across the bay, there seemed to be a large building fire in Oakland. Very good. Suddenly, she seemed much taller as she punched in a cell phone call to a pager with a three-number code. "What I won't do for my children," Louise thought. "What they are, I do not know, but I will do my best to be midwife and foster mother to something wonderful that is

132

coming into this world." She headed off to get her car, and thence off into an uncertain future but one filled with new hope.

Saturday morning saw all 14 Coven members, including the babbling wreck that was A Prime, jammed into the secure room of the old Planada house designed to hold Edward. Gabriella and Victor, looking ever more affectionate together, arranged for security. All Coven members had been photographed while they were under the anesthetic, any and all identification removed and checked, fingerprints and samples for DNA analysis taken. The facilities in the small Planada secure room, including the sink and toilet that Jonathan and Tim had hastily installed, were barely adequate, and several plastic chairs and sleeping bags were added. The food requirement would now be a bigger burden, but the same procedure was used as before – hot food at 7:00 p.m. with enough cold food and fruit to last though the next day. The television was on all the time but the mute button on the remote was operational. The picture was somewhat fuzzy and tuned only to NBC affiliate KSEE, Fresno, channel 24.

Omega was planning a serious debriefing schedule, one Coven member at a time, starting on Monday evening, after Roberto had a chance to run the identification through the police computers. Omega had to know who these strangers were and where they came from, or similar and perhaps more successful attacks would be launched in the future.

The Sunday evening meal was bought at a Subway store in Merced, and at 7:00 p.m., two of Gabriella's recruits, Steven and Manuel, entered the Planada house. A quick check on the computer logs and TVs showed nothing of great interest, but there had been a lot of conversation among Coven members, all recorded. A written summary of daily activities for the prisoners had been given to the Coven members at the Saturday night meal, and they were sitting around as best they could in the cramped and windowless room, waiting for dinner. The way the TV camera was placed, Steven couldn't see the entire room, and thus he was not nervous when only 10 or 11 people were visible on camera.

Steven went to the slot in the door, and flipped it open to slide in the plastic trays. Because of the amount of food needed, Manuel held the flap open while Steven inserted the food. Suddenly both froze. Two of the most powerful Coven members were just below the open slot, the only unshielded point in the room, and had taken control. Manuel remained frozen, holding the slot fully open, while Steve slowly turned to the door, slid back the dead bolt lock, and turned the handle to open the door. It didn't open. Steven tried ever more strongly, fighting the lock, pulling straining, thrashing about, kicking the door with his feet, as the Coven used all their powers to free themselves.

In fact, the door could never open. It was epoxied shut in such a way that the glue was invisible to people on either side of the door. The entire frame, subtly strengthened, would have to be destroyed before that door would open. The real door was on the other side of the room, visibly (but ineffectively) nailed shut but actually able to be opened after two people far apart had simultaneously punched in a code on electronic pads known only to a very few people.

With the release of the fake deadbolt and the turning of the knob, the external room ventilation fan turned off and anesthetic gas was released into the vent. In about a minute, the Coven members realized what was happening and in their anger slashed mentally at Steven and Manuel, dropping them both to the ground, unconscious.

After about 10 minutes, the gas input automatically ceased. By then, all Coven members were unconscious. The relay flipped on the room ventilation fan, but with all the electronic gear, the antique 10-ampere circuit was overloaded and the fuse burned out.

Silence ruled the Planada house as one by one, the combination of too little air and too much anesthetic killed the Coven members. About 7:45 p.m., alarmed by the non-return of Steven and Manuel, Omega delta members entered and found the scene. Steven and Manuel were recovering from awful headaches, and it became instantly clear what had happened. Quick consultations, a coded call, and by 3:00 a.m. Monday, 14 more bodies were immersed in the aquatic burial ground off the Highway 49 bridge in the Don Pedro Reservoir.

"This is UC Berkeley' drinking water," mused Ken. "I hope they are treating it adequately. The body count is growing, and for a peaceful and loving group that Omega is, we seem to have a lethal streak in us. We had better be careful. There is a 'dark side' to our 'force', too."

CHAPTER THIRTY-THREE

The view from the balcony was magnificent – the Eiffel Tower from a penthouse apartment in the 16th Arrondissement. The penthouse deck was in the miniature image of a formal French garden with every bush trimmed to geometric perfection. It was connected to the interior by French doors, with expensive draped curtains. The room was formal, Louis XIV, with chairs that looked like they couldn't take too much abuse. They were formed into a large circle with a gap centered on the fireplace, in which aged Limousin oak burned quietly. The two chairs on each side of the fireplace were somewhat larger than the others. Both were occupied.

All the rest of the chairs were occupied, too, all by men, none too young and none older than perhaps their mid 60s. These men exuded power and wealth with sharply tailored suits but were also discrete and unostentatious. The chair directly opposite the fireplace held a man who did not look French, and whose clothes somehow had no flair about them. His shoes had tassels, several noted with disdain. But what else would you expect from an American?

All were silent until the grandfather clock finished striking 9.

The man next to the fireplace spoke: "We have had an opportunity to go over your report thoroughly, and used the past three days to check some aspects of your story against public sources in California. Were you aware that the entire San Francisco Coven was also neatly dispatched, through heroin overdoses, says the police report, when we know that they were cleverly murdered? No Coven member has ever used drugs. Even wine, he sighed. Ah, the sacrifices we must make for power and wealth."

"What?" asked 2C2? "I did not know. How could it have been done?"

"Cleverly," was the answer.

2C2 continued his report, based upon the most recent information.

"The six provincial members who escaped from Merced have been thoroughly debriefed. They were well away from the 'feeding' site, acting as a trap for the rescue attempt if any Merced telepaths were still in Merced. Most of them felt that the Merced telepaths had scattered for fear of retribution after Beverly Hills, but they were prepared for anything, with their Hells Angel muscle in place if needed. They had been promised some pre-'feeding' interactions with the victim, but what actually happened was that police cars drove up to each site, almost simultaneously, and arrested them. Once they were all together at the police station, they had enough mental capability that they were able to convince the Merced Police to let them go.

"We still have a non-telepathic contact in Merced who seems to have avoided detection. Her name is Linda, and she has moved freely throughout the campus for the entire time and in fact assisted us in the capture of the sensitive. I am becoming more and more certain that she knows too much about us, or at least suspects something. Her father helped us in trying to use technology to amplify our powers. When he failed, he had an unfortunate 'accident,' and it is just possible as she gathers some hint of our powers, she may suspect we had something to do with his demise. However, she does not know the extent of the success or failure of the operation, and is following her usual patterns in Merced. We have continued her payments, and gave her a bonus for her recent work.

"Our analysis shows that the entire project had been completely compromised, most likely by the Hells Angels. The plane designed to fly out A Prime saw strangers and vehicles at the 'feeding' site, but no Coven members or bodies were visible. We have no idea where A Prime and 13 other Coven members are, but either captured or killed, it is a disaster. As for the plane, no landing signal was given, so it flew away. We killed the pilot after he landed at our request on a remote road.

"What is left of the Los Angeles Coven, now barely viable, has fled to San Diego. The eastern provinces are in a state of panic at the loss of A Prime, and are going into an underground mode, cutting all ties one with the other; suspicion is rife, trust, zero. We are destroyed! What can we do?"

"You will do nothing," was the answer. "We will have Linda captured or killed, immediately.

"Further response will take time and resources, but we too are greatly disturbed. A Prime was both one of the smartest as well as one of the most powerful telepaths in any Coven in the world. We trained him here, and have a great respect for his abilities. Stay with us. You probably know more than you realize, and we need time, much time, and information. Make no further contact with the United States."

He then turned toward the other large chair at the other side of the fireplace, and asked, "Do you think that this is a task for the entire Council?"

The other figure, looking immensely old, merely nodded.

"Then I will call London."

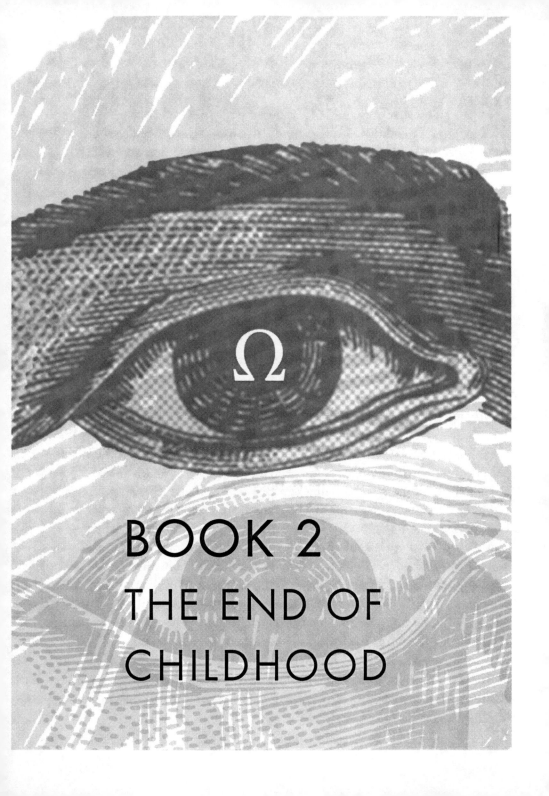

BOOK 2
THE END OF
CHILDHOOD

CHAPTER ONE

Ken should have been proud, for this was an honor rarely accorded a working physicist. A three-day session of the spring American Physical Society meeting in San Diego was entirely dedicated to an analysis of his recent work on thin-film semiconductors. He of course was keynote speaker, and speaker after speaker praised his breakthrough. However, they were also doing a lot of good and original work on their own – work that Ken could have done easily (and probably better) if he had not been so tied up in the Omega Project. His talk had gone well, however, and he revealed his most recent work, still one step ahead of everybody else. The last talk had been given this afternoon, and now he could relax. He was looking forward to dinner with Jonathan, who was down from Oregon and reporting on some of the work he had completed now that he was no longer tied up with the never-ending duties of vice chairman of the department. They had chosen a discrete location where he could bring Jonathan up to speed on their progress. Tim and Jennifer would be there, too, down from UCLA, where each was making splendid progress.

And the progress had been substantial. Louise was now a full participant, although her location in Oregon made communications more difficult. A new Omega cell was set up at the University of Oregon in Eugene, but they had not yet found a high-level sensitive to lead it. Periodically, Michael and Nancy went up there to move the project along. The University of California, Davis, now had three separate cells, making it larger than Merced, but then it was also a much larger campus. Saint Mary's College in Moraga had one cell, despite its small size. There were times when the Midpines safe house could barely hold all of Omega, now more than 50 strong. With such a large number, they had begun blanketing an entire town, sensing every sentient being in the vicinity and evaluating each for potential. Regretfully, in most towns, the result was nil. Clearly, the concentration of highly intelligent young altruistic people at universities and colleges was an important self-selector of psychic potential.

Ken arrived at the hotel attached to the conference center a little before the final rush, so no one else was at the elevator, and punched in his floor, number 15. The elevator stopped to get more people on the second floor, then again at the third. This was a bit unusual, and the people seemed a little better dressed than for a physics meeting with its seriously relaxed dress code. Perhaps they were sharing the hotel with something like a Chamber of Commerce meeting. It stopped again, on the fourth floor, and an additional press of people crammed the elevator. Ken was pushed hard against the back wall, arms pinned to his side, and suddenly he was concerned. He could still push the panic button secreted on his belt buckle, and use his toe to activate the mental interference system in one of his shoes. No effect, so at least these men were not Coven members. But then a cloth was suddenly pressed over his face, and he felt a stabbing pain on his arm. All he could think of was "Dumb, dumb, dumb! Why was I not more alert?" Then he lost consciousness.

In the elevator, one member pushed a key into the override switch normally used for firemen, and the elevator reversed to the sub-basement level. Quickly they carried Ken into a waiting Chevy Suburban, and with a second car they left the scene. They drove slowly and carefully, obeying all the traffic laws, down city streets until they picked up Interstate 8, east into the mountains. Forty-five minutes later, they turned off onto a road leading north, now in oaks and pines. In 30 minutes, they were in a pricey subdivision of houses on 10-acre lots, each well set back from the road.

Both vehicles pulled up, and Ken was carried into the family room at the back of the house, adjoining a kitchen with granite countertops and a large central island. Most of the men then left in one of the cars, but four men remained, all well armed, all positioned well outside the house to prevent interference. Five men were seated in chairs around a massive oak chair into which Ken was dumped, then bound to. He was frisked, (rather inexpertly, as these men were not pros at this sort of thing) and his jacket and tie were removed.

The Council had decided that the coincidence that a famous physicist in the department and friend of Jonathan's was deeply involved in the Newman Center to which several known telepaths belonged was too striking to ignore. They were not at all sure that Ken was a telepath himself, but they wanted to question him at length before they staged an unfortunate traffic "accident" for him in a rented car together with a comely young lady – not his wife.

Regretfully for them, Ken did not regain consciousness right away. They tried cold water, shaking, and slaps but they had probably overdone the injection. Two hours passed, and the Coven members were getting antsy. The accident could wait, and in fact night was useful in this regard, but Ken was well known and would be missed. Finally, Ken started to come to, and instinctively and immediately went into "dark mind" mode, as they had all trained for repeatedly as a major defense mode. He then feigned greater incapacity than he actually felt, delaying as much as possible until his Omega team could respond to his beacon. When he finally could delay no longer, he still pretended incapacity, blurring his speech, rambling, occasionally outraged, then fearful – all over the emotional map.

He was facing five men, all sharply dressed in somehow European style. Only one was questioning him, sort of a chief inquisitor, thought Ken, and he had a distinct upper-class British accent. A tape recorder sat on the table in front of Ken, recording all. An amateur's mistake, thought Ken – the recorder should have been invisible. These people were not professionals. The questioner refused to answer any of Ken's outraged declarations, but stated that unless he were totally honest and complete, his wife, Jill, presently in Merced, would die within the hour. The questioner stated that they were not really interested in Ken himself, but someone else far more important, and needed to know what he had observed in Merced. He would then be let go and as long as he kept his mouth closed, he would be allowed to live.

He started questioning Ken's association with Jonathan, then the Newman Center, and then individual members. Ken answered with feigned honesty, but rambling and with masses of useless detail, while soaking up as much information as he could.

It became clear to Ken that all five were European Coven members – two French, two British, and one Swiss – and that if Ken showed any sign of mental capacity, they planned a "feeding." It was also clear that they still didn't know very much about the Merced telepaths, but had in place a major plan to decimate the organization, even at the expense of a lot on innocent lives – "worthless sheep" was the term they used. Ken wondered if the suicide of a UC Merced student named Linda a few month's back was traceable to these people. Linda had, upon discrete inquiries, a very suspicious background, with fake credentials. She may have been part of the original plan last fall that now needed to be cleaned up.

The other members were getting restless. Several had flights leaving Los Angeles later that evening, and Ken was able to memorize an Air France flight number and even in one case the seat selection (in First Class, of course).

The British interrogator, getting nowhere with these questions, glanced at his colleagues, and then suddenly Ken was struck with a massive mental assault. As was usual, they were not well coordinated, but in their totality, adequate to cause a violent reaction even in a non-sensitive. He thrashed about and screamed, trying to meet their expectations, but it was hard to do. One in particular sensed something wrong in Ken's responses, and probed harder. A few muttered words in French, then there was a coordinated attack backed by horrific images designed to create fear. Ken was furious but not fearful, and fought off the first feeding attempt.

Now they all knew that they had in their hands a telepath, and a powerful and well-trained one at that. They all leaned forward straining, getting closer, completely focused, working jointly for the first time. Ken slashed back, stunning one of them who crumpled to the floor, but their counterblow got deeper into Ken's mind. And the images were frightful. Ken would not fear, but could not maintain their level of response much longer. He knew that at any point they could pull out a gun and shoot him dead, but they probably would not as long as there was some chance at a high-level "feeding."

He felt that he could destroy one or even two of them, but that would leave him open to the rest. He had to stay defensive, but for how long?

Suddenly it was over. The Coven members went to help their disabled colleague, who was vomiting all over the expensive carpet, and then moved away to the next room. Ken could read their dismay at the failed feeding, and the resolve that they would not take Ken lightly the second time. They were prepared, and once they were all at full potential, they would return and finish the job.

About 10 minutes passed, and then the Coven returned, with grim determination on their faces. They moved in very close to Ken, with two behind him, one on either side, and one, the most powerful British chief inquisitor, directly in front. Ken waited until the attack came, and once again he could handle it. The key seemed to be that the feeding needed fear, and Ken reused to be mastered. He was also tiring badly, so when they were fully extended, he triggered the interference device in his other shoe. The stunned response of the Coven members was just what he had waited for, and he struck through the interference to the inquisitor directly in front of him, struck hard, struck deep. The inquisitor screamed – the essence of pure pain, and now there was fear in the air.

Suddenly shots rang out from the front driveway, a long rattle of automatic rifle fire that ran on and on. The Coven members were simply overloaded by the rapidly escalating events, and this totally unprecedented failure to "feed," while mental static was hammering their brains. One of the members picked up the unconscious chief inquisitor, and yelled "To the car!" Another had enough foresight to grab the tape recorder. They were almost to the back door, when one of the French members stopped, pulled a small handgun, and turned to shoot. Ken, reading his intention, flung the heavy chair over so that it lay on top of him. Three shots rang out, and Ken felt one hard blow to his thigh, followed by a burning pain. Then it was over. They were gone, now in almost complete panic. Outside, the remaining four non-telepathic "muscle" leapt into the Suburban, and raced down the highway.

Ken was exhausted by the ordeal, but despite the bleeding thigh gradually worked his way out of the ropes that held him. From somewhere outside, a red glow could be seen reflecting on the ceiling. He was almost free when Jonathan was at his side, helping Ken out of the chair despite a clearly wounded leg.

"Thanks, it was a close thing, but what happened?" asked Ken.

"I got your homing signal and the psychic static trigger after you had left the elevator, so I picked up Tim and Jennifer, and followed you here. They are somewhere out in back, trying to get around and rescue you. But there were a bunch of goons out there with heavy weapons. I was waiting down the driveway. When I got the signal from your second static device, I gunned the car up the driveway. Just as I got close, they started shooting at the car, and I bailed out the driver's door with the car in cruise control and headed directly at them. I got winged, but they spayed the car with everything they had. Sort of a Bonnie and Clyde fusillade. It caught fire and is run up against a rock wall. Hertz will be really pissed, and I didn't get the insurance.

"Well, that fusillade scared the shit out of our boys." Tim and Jennifer scrambled in the back door, looking pretty panicked themselves. "Is everybody all right?" Actually, nobody looked all right, since Jonathan and Ken were both bloody, but things seemed to be under control.

"How are we going to handle this?" asked Jonathan.

"I think as a straight kidnapping effort, with industrial espionage overtones," said Ken. "This would let us put pressure on whomever they are, and make them more reluctant to try this again. Call 911 and get the San Diego Police Department up here, pronto. All our actions are legal. Just ignore the tracking information."

The questions of the SDPD were extensive, but there was plenty of physical evidence to back up the story. The bullet-riddled car, ropes, wounds, and the fictitious credentials of the European group that had rented the house, all confirmed the events. Jonathan had the license number, and the Chevy Suburban was found six hours later in a parking lot at Los Angeles International Airport. It too had been rented with forged identification. The newspapers, radio, and television had a field day. Conspiracy theories multiplied. The car alone made a great video background. Jonathan was made out to be the hero, and Ken was hailed as some sort of budding genius, since his work apparently was worthy of such dire attention from foreign mobsters.

Two days later, three new Omega recruits died in a car accident near Hornitos, and the safe house of Omega-alpha burned to the ground. Two Omega members got out of the house safely before it exploded into flames, but only by a lucky fluke – their cat had just run out of the door and they had followed it. Arson was suspected, but no cause was ever found.

On the following week, a meeting was held at the Omega Project Midpines safe house to evaluate events. Both Ken and Jonathan were still bandaged up, but were feeling well otherwise. The mood at the safe house was serious but not panicky. Ken took full responsibility for putting himself at undue risk, and appreciated how his required presence at the San Diego American Physical Society meeting was a perfect opportunity to abduct

145

him. Next time, he might not be so lucky.

The destruction of the Omega-alpha safe house, and loss of three recruits, caused great sadness. Everybody blamed themselves for any part they had in lapses of security. The sudden unexplained loss of the mysterious student named Linda was by now well accepted as the possible source of the information. The perpetrators were identified, unknown male Caucasians who had driven in, sabotaged the brakes on the van, wired the safe house with explosives, and left immediately for somewhere east of California.

Sergeant Roberto Morales gave a report on the European Coven members. From the seat assignment on Air France remembered by Ken, and after some FBI pressure, the names (or probably aliases) of two Coven members from France were known before they had landed in Paris. A private agency was hired to take surreptitious high-quality pictures of all passengers as they landed. Identifying the two Coven members was not that difficult. First Class passengers always exited the plane first, the two Coven members were identified by rough descriptions provided by Ken, and they were traveling together. They were tracked to a pricey apartment in the 16th Arrondissement. The agency was able to penetrate the garage, got registrations and license numbers of all cars, and found that the penthouse had telephone lines that were well protected and totally separate from the lines for all other apartments. The car licenses were checked, names and addresses identified, and transmitted to the Merced Police Department. None of the names matched the names provided by Air France.

CHAPTER TWO

As English country mansions went, this one was more comfortable than most. It was set well back from the nearest neighbor, with more than 1,200 acres of old-growth forest, plus some rolling farmland. The large living room had two fireplaces, one at each end, and the entire building had central heating (welcome in the damp Sussex spring) and even air conditioning for summer hot spells. The leather chairs and side tables were arranged in comfortable, clubby arrangements, roughly a circle with no obvious focal point. The art was extensive but uninspired – country scenes from lesser artists of the nineteenth century.

The living room was almost crowded with 23 men, most middle aged or older. They were a diverse group, with a variety of dressing styles, and conversations were usually going on in multiple languages. Two of the men sat together, Americans from their dress and dialect, 2C2 and P2. The former had been saved from the Merced massacre by being in transit from San Francisco, the latter by being in charge of the intercepting groups well outside the feeding site. They had finished more than a month of debriefing, and then helped plan the attempt to capture Professor O'Neal, who had surfaced as suspicious through a statistical analysis of associations with the known Merced telepathic students, the Physics Department, and the Newman Center. The assumption was that he was not a telepath himself, as scientists were never sensitives in their experience. But he could well be a supporter like Professor Campbell. The debriefing of Linda before her unfortunate "accident" provided the location of the Omega-alpha safe house, when by accident she had noticed an awful lot of student traffic on a little-traveled road to Hornitos.

The Council of Covens had been together now for five days, all staying in the sprawling mansion but carefully out of view when, each morning, the house was cleaned and serviced by servants from the nearby village. Breakfast, lunch, and dinner were catered from the village. The only other person present was a young Irish servant, Meagan, who served non-alcoholic drinks and snacks each hour on the hour for about 10 minutes, but was otherwise told to stay in the kitchen unless called. In fact, she was naive but moderately sensitive, and the scheduled victim for a group

147

"feeding" on the final evening, as was traditional at these rare gatherings of the full Council.

Gerard (the French and British used code names, not numbers) was summarizing results of the previous four days of effort. The Council was not displeased with the failed attempt in San Diego, because they had learned a great deal. First, no Coven members or Council Legionnaires – mostly Ulster Irish paramilitaries – were lost in the attempt. Security was holding, and no serious inquiries that could trace the perpetrators to Europe had been detected. Second, Professor O'Neal was surprisingly himself a telepath, and a powerful one, able to fend off five Coven attackers at once, at least for a while until the inevitable exhaustion would set in. His ability to avoid any trace of fear was remarkable, and showed a confidence in his powers and resources that was most disturbing. His use of a mind-blanking technique was unexpected, and caused serious discussion since it defeated the probe-response technique of the Covens that had been their mainstay for generations in sensing psychic potential. It also helped explain the original lost contact of Group 4 in Merced. Third, he had some sort of interference device that made a kind of mental static – not strong enough to be a serious problem, but a confounding and confusing effect that weakened their powers to concentrate. A full day was dedicated to evaluating this one factor, and several groups would re-institute the, until now, universally negative search for technological psychic enhancement. Professor O'Neal's expertise in micro-electronics was critical here, and the Council decided that as soon as possible he must be captured and killed, hopefully with the interference device hidden somewhere on him. Professor O'Neal clearly had supporters that had arrived on the scene, from press reports only the well-known Professor Campbell, but others were suspected to be involved. Finally, several Merced telepaths were killed and a safe house eliminated, hopefully causing fear and suspicion in the rest.

In this, their final day, Friday, they had become more relaxed, because they now had some hard information with which to work. There was a sense of danger and the thrill of the chase, with a worthy adversary that must be annihilated. Still, they were very careful to talk lightly of trivialities when Meagan was in the room serving drinks, regretfully all non-alcoholic, although according to plan she would never leave this house again. Many were looking forward to the evening's "feeding" in concert with this almost unprecedented full gathering of the Council of Covens.

Back in the kitchen after the 2:00 p.m. drink service, Meagan was worried sick. This job was paying enough money to support her for six months at Queen's University in Galway, where she was in the third year of the chemistry program. But back in the village, all the servants were scared to death of the reclusive owners of the mansion. And there were strange little things, such as that all the beverages were non-alcoholic. She did not like the predatory manner in which some of the members were looking at her. She had been always sensitive to the feelings of others, and now at times the hair stood up on her arms when she was near them. And the conversations she heard during service were clearly trivialities designed for her. But every so often, during the past four days, she would pick up a phrase that led her to believe there was something dire happening in California. The only specific words she heard involved the Newman Catholic student center at UC Merced, about as harmless an organization as she could conceive of. Yet these wealthy and powerful men from many different countries were focused on it.

Money or no money, she slipped off the maid's costume, gathered several hundred pounds from the catering fund stored in the kitchen (she had not yet received any of the promised pay), and slipped out the back. Running for her life, she cut through the woods to avoid the nearby village and arrived at the Stepford Village bus stop in time for the 3:10 p.m. bus to London. It was late by about seven minutes, which seemed an eternity to Meagan. By now, they would have discovered her absence, and she expected their response to be terrible. She rode through four bus stops, and then transferred to another bus that would connect up with a rural route of the London Underground.

Never had a bus moved more slowly. Never had every car seemed so ominous. Stumbling off the bus with her shoulder bag her only possession, she ran down the steps. Out here, however, the trains came only at long intervals. She perched behind a column far down the platform, and carefully examined every person who entered the station. Suddenly, just before the train was due to arrive, one of the "businessmen" from France appeared on the stairs to the platform. Reaching the turnstile, he fished frantically in his pocket for a token or change, but had neither. The station attendant was eyeing him suspiciously. Meagan buried her face against the cold, dirty concrete column and instinctively focused her mind on her beloved blanket she used for comfort as a child in Ireland. "Pierre," seeing no one on the platform, sent out a desultory psychic probe – expecting no response and getting nothing really definitive. He turned, and raced out of the station to intercept the next bus due to arrive any minute.

Finally the train came, but then it stayed at the platform for an interminable eight minutes more. Just as the doors were about to close, Meagan sprinted into the first car, and collapsed into the seat. What to do? The people who had hired her knew all about her normal haunts in Galway, knew her family, knew everything about her from the rather detailed questionnaire she had filled out. The sudden appearance of a "businessman" confirmed her suspicion that her absence would be the cause of a blistering response. She didn't understand why, but deep down she was petrified by fear of these people. Her assets were few – but she had her passport, typical identification, and about 22 pounds in her purse. She thumbed through the money she had hastily grabbed from the food fund in lieu of her salary, and found it more than she had expected – almost 1,200 pounds.

This opened a number of options. She could leave the country, go to some South American city and start working as an English nanny until the storm blew over. But in her heart, she knew that with this group, the storm would never abate, and she would be a fugitive for life. Even now, she was sure that all airports were being checked. But she had a friend at Gatwick, and had been told that on occasion last-minute standbys were accepted on some charters, with cheap fares. Thus, her name would never appear on a computer at the main airport at Heathrow. She changed Undergrounds again, and used a local bus from the end station to Gatwick. But where to go? She checked the flights – Frankfort, Rome, New York, Rio de Janeiro, and saw one to Oakland, California, that was just then loading. Suddenly she thought – I can warn these people at the Newman Center of what these monsters are planning. She had no idea where Merced was in relationship to Oakland, but they were both in California, so they couldn't be that far apart. She ran to the gate, and found lots of space available. She paid cash for the ticket, and was almost the last passenger to board. She slumped back in her seat, riven by uncertainty and a troublesome future hidden from her. But every mile she flew away from those people was a blessing.

The mood back at the mansion was fury. The Council of Covens had no idea how much she had learned. Every resource they had was directed to finding that girl, on the pretext that she had stolen 1,200 pounds and key scientific documents that had potential British national security implications. Computer searches were made of all flights, especially to Ireland, but the handwritten notation on the boarding list at Gatwick would not be computer posted for perhaps a day.

The U.S. Immigration Service was a brutal experience. Meagan had hit almost all the "hot buttons" for a terrorist:

- bought a one-way ticket to the United States with cash,
- without any sort of visa,
- traveled without luggage, and
- was from a known area of terrorist activity, Ireland.

Fortunately, calmer heads prevailed in the end, since the record showed that few young Irish Catholic girls seemed wedded to extremist Islamic causes. The question then arose as to why she was here? Meagan responded by saying that she wanted to be a volunteer intern at the Newman Center at UC Merced, but had no proof of the offer or contact person. Finally, a call was placed to the Newman Center, which bounced quickly to Ken's desk.

"An intern named Meagan O'Malley from Galway? Great. I'm glad she could finally make it," Ken lied through his teeth, but intrigued at this totally unexpected turn of events. He agreed to vouch for her in the visa process as part of a three-month internship. "Have her take the Altamont Commuter Express train to its valley terminus, and we will meet her there."

Thus, about an hour later, Ken, Jill, Michelle, and Jonathan were at the station. Michelle sensed her even before the train pulled into the station. "Mid- to high-level sensitive," she murmured, "and scared shitless of something." Meagan stepped off the train, saw the delegation, and ran straight into Michelle's arms, sobbing in relief. Ken sighed, and prepared to adopt yet one more comely young woman into his ever-growing harem. Jill was running out of long-lost college friends, but she would come up with something.

Back at Merced, Meagan sat in the living room with her hands wrapped around a cup of hot tea. Somehow she had absolutely no doubt that these were wonderful people who would protect her. After a light dinner, she started to tell her story. "Back to the beginning," said Jonathan, "Explain how the food server ad was placed and what the interview was like."

"It was in the student newspaper at Galway, and had a very high salary for helping host a two-week meeting of European businessmen negotiating confidential trade deals with the Common Market. Knowledge of languages was desirable, as was scientific and technical knowledge and about running computers, FAX machines, and other office equipment. It came during the Easter break at Queen's College, Galway, and I responded along with scores of other students, since the pay was high and the requirements so broad. There was a written application form, quite detailed, and for about 20 of us, a three-person panel for an interview. I was chosen, given an air ticket to London, and was told I would be picked up by a car at the airport. Actually, it was a limousine which also picked up two other people from a European flight. They said essentially nothing about who they were or where they were from."

Meagan then described in some detail the location, strange work schedules, and rumors of the townsfolk, and what little she had learned during the brief times she was in the room. There were perhaps a dozen men whose faces she never saw – they were always off in a corner somewhere in deep discussions when she was in the room. After a while, it became suspicious. Finally, there were the increasingly predatory glances and the strange feeling of dread she got when she was near some of them. This was especially true on the last day, when everybody seemed less worried about what she would hear.

A long silence ensued. Finally, Ken said. "You have no idea how valuable this information is to us for the survival of something new, beautiful, and holy, or the horrendous death you have so narrowly avoided. We will in all cases protect you from your enemies, and later when you are settled give you the choice of joining us in a way that transcends human experience up to this time."

Ken's face, and all the faces, just beamed a loving welcome, and Meagan reached out without reservation, without restraint, to them. She was suddenly with them all, in their minds and bodies, one in a communion she had so yearned for in her dreams and her prayers. Complete "awakening," and then a complete mental collapse into their arms. She was home.

"Wow! So much for our training program, Meagan. Welcome to the Omega Project. The people you fell in with wanted you for your psychic powers, and because of them, they would jointly that very evening 'feed' on your mind, tearing it apart and in doing so strengthen their unholy bonds and increase their powers to dominate, to terrorize, to kill. You were most likely in the den of our greatest enemy, probably reviewing all that they had learned during a recent attempt on our lives." Ken and Jonathan showed their bandages. "From what you describe, it appears to have been some pan-European gathering of Covens – yes, that is their name for themselves – dedicated to the eradication of the Omega Project. Your successful flight from them will put them into panic, but in their worst nightmares, they would never dream that you had fled directly to us.

"We must move swiftly, for they will try to erase all evidence of their existence. I expect by now not a single Coven member is left in England, and I will make a large wager that the house, held in trust by some secretive Swiss bank, is up for sale. Still, perhaps we can learn something even so. Fingerprints and the like are hard to totally eradicate from a week-long stay in a large mansion. But never, never, must they know that you are here. We will send you immediately to a safe house in the mountains, and then we will talk and your training will begin in earnest."

Meagan hardly heard a word. Home. She was home.

Discrete inquiries from a local real estate concern in Sussex found that the Bridgestone mansion was indeed available for the discriminating purchaser. Extensive but surreptitious searches of the house turned up a surprisingly large amount of useful information, including complete fingerprints from 27 persons, partials from probably a dozen more, several scraps of what appeared to be phone numbers found in the unburned residue from a fireplace, and quite a bit of hair and the like for future DNA matching. Equally discreet inquires in the local town from this potential purchaser elicited open statements of relief that these mysterious owners had left, and a lot of tales of uncertain accuracy about strange doings at the house.

CHAPTER FOUR

The view from the balcony was magnificent – the Eiffel Tower from a penthouse apartment in the 16th Arrondissement, but no one was in the mood for sightseeing. The room was formal, Louis XIV, with chairs that appeared unable to withstand much abuse, but additional chairs of all sorts of designs were added incongruously wherever they would fit. They were roughly incorporated into the large circle, with a gap centered on the fireplace, in which aged Limousin oak burned quietly. The two chairs on each side of the fireplace were somewhat larger than the others. Both were occupied.

Gerard, the senior French representative began, "The affair of Meagan O'Malley is not going well. Our analysis is that the designated victim was a more profound sensitive than we had appreciated. We believe she picked up the emanations of the combined Coven members, especially on Friday when our hunger and anticipation was most acute, to the point where she panicked and ran. We still have not picked up her trail, which considering our efforts, is in itself worrisome. One would expect a naive college girl to leave traces. We were careful to make sure she heard nothing of import, but the house was cleaned, all trash burned, and is on the real estate market. We expect to make a modest profit from the transaction.

"With regard to our plans for the Merced telepaths, we will follow our prior agreement to form the five multinational Coven teams who will operate essentially independently to eradicate the pests. Some will take a direct approach, others oblique, but we must be careful not to make the combined effort too obvious. The French team will take a direct approach as we have excellent industrial cover in our electronic operations. We will set up a business in Merced itself, without any telepaths involved. We will have the dual task of learning all we can about Professor O'Neal's electronics expertise to identify how he designed the mental static device, while researching him and his associates with the goal of his elimination in a credible "accident." We will maintain the three-person executive team here in Paris that will centralize information gained and must be notified prior to any, repeat any, field operation. We will follow our usual technique and insist on no electronic communication of information in any form."

It was a continuing regret of Coven members that in the sumptuous repast served that evening, no wine was involved. Still, some barely drinkable non-alcoholic wines were now available from U.S. sources (the Americans are so strange), and they were marginally better than water.

CHAPTER FIVE

The groundbreaking ceremony was a big deal for the city of Merced which, until UC Merced had arrived, was a permanent backwater in the Central Valley and in the shadow of Modesto (if such were possible). It was timed to occur during the Fourth of July weekend, and much was made of this new and promising U.S.-France collaboration in electronic research. The first fruits of UC Merced's successes in the field would now resonate in the community at large. The French company, L'Equipe de Nouveau Electroniques (ENE), had connections to many large French and Common Market industrial giants, and was clearly drawn by the work of the group headed by Professor O'Neal and his colleagues, themselves all good in their own right. The mayor and council, UC Merced chancellor, the chair and many of the physics faculty members (all eager for consultancies, new lab equipment, and other opportunities), Chamber of Commerce, Rotary – all the movers and shakers. The Chamber's president made a big deal of the role of the Chamber in attracting New Opportunities (the words were capitalized in his written speech the way he said it) to Merced, a new Silicon Valley in the Central Valley, and so on. In fact, the whole deal had come up suddenly only four weeks earlier, and the groundbreaking was largely ceremonial, because most of the buildings used by ENE in the beginning were unused agricultural buildings and the like on the west side of town. The groundbreaking really involved paving for a muddy dirt parking lot. But – what the hey – Merced needed an excuse to celebrate. Agriculture was in a semi-depression from international competition, and the California state budget was still in the tank.

Ken sat on the platform, thankfully shielded from the blazing sun and slightly cooled by the new evaporative misters, which were introduced in large scale during the 2000 Barcelona summer Olympics. Discreet inquiries from Jonathan confirmed Ken's suspicions that ENE was in fact controlled by the French Covens, at least insofar as its actual ownership was hopelessly hidden in a nested set of onshore and off-shore French consortia. Further, ENE didn't actually seem to make or do anything itself, shuttling stuff back and forth between larger companies – including what appeared to be, even in the pitifully incomplete public books necessary to meet the relaxed

157

standards of French commercial law, money laundering.

Now suddenly ENE made it out to be a research-based company, something totally new to it based upon past records. This and their obvious interest in Ken's work (and probably Ken himself) made the whole effort suspicious. Furthermore, despite all the public statements, ENE had actually committed very little money to this venture. While a 10-year contract and grandiose plans were in place, escape clauses were buried deep in the document that actually held them to only a one-year lease of the present buildings. The groundbreaking was really a sham.

The next Sunday, each mass of the Newman Center had a young French employee of ENE in attendance, sitting in the back, never identifying himself, as is usual for new visitors to Newman, and not taking communion. The local parish was also covered.

That weekend, a major meeting was held at the Midpines safe house. Almost half of all the members were present, plus Sergeant Roberto Morales and the Campbells, who were down from Oregon. These group meetings were a delight, as everybody was anxious to meet the new kids, Dawn, and the others, although most babies stayed with their parents in places like Davis. None of the children showed any signs of unusual behavior, but slightly more worrisome, they also seemed underdeveloped a bit in language abilities. Ken said not to worry – he didn't talk until 2½ years of age – to which Michelle tartly retorted, "Well, all boys are retarded until they are 10 – Dawn is a girl!" It was also the first chance for many to see Meagan, who had blossomed during the training and was already ranked among the top dozen in the entire Omega Project. Her whole demeanor had changed – she seemed much older, confident and with a profound calm about her that was way beyond her years. She and Jill had hit it off immediately, and while she really liked Michelle, she was also slightly in awe of her powers.

Ken reviewed all that they had learned from the San Diego kidnapping and Meagan's report of the Coven meeting in England, plus the recent French company setting up in Merced. His conclusion: "They know I am a telepath, they suspect I am behind the technology of the mind static device, although fortunately they have no clue as to our recent progress. The resources arrayed against me are too great. Last Sunday, ENE people started surveying the Newman Center and other sites in Merced. I can no longer attempt to operate openly as a professor and still be part of the Omega Project. Clearly, there is no real choice here. My life and career at Merced are over."

"And a potential Nobel Prize," said Jonathan, "but I fully agree with your priorities".

Ken continued, "The Omega Project is now my life, our lives, and we believe the life of the world. Thus, I will have to let them try to kill me and believe they have succeeded, or 'die' convincingly some other way. For the former, we will have to detect the attempt before it happens and then somehow make it non-fatal to me. There will have to be a body to take my place. I will have to have a new member of Omega capable of forging my death certificate. Roberto and Jonathan, any suggestions?"

Roberto chimed in, "There is a new doctor in town who has impressed me by the care she gives her largely Medicare practice. She has not much of a regular practice yet, and she is taking a lot of Police Department and San Joaquin County coroner business to make ends meet. Her name is Lucille Edwards. I propose that Jonathan and I arrange to meet her, and then have a few high-level telepaths present to both evaluate her state of mind and convince her of our capabilities."

He continued, "As to the attempt on your life, anyone with a high-powered rifle with a scope can kill anybody at any time. However, your murder would generate intense international investigations that would be dangerous to the Covens. One possible way is to give them an obvious opportunity so they don't get too creative and actually succeed in their attempt."

"I appreciate your concerns," said Ken.

Roberto continued, "I think they will try to kill you in an 'accident,' most likely a car problem. One possible response is that Ken could start some regular travel that involves steep and winding roads, perhaps to a fake safe house in the mountains. The car should be routinely parked far enough away from the house so that anyone could get to it sight unseen. We would institute surveillance of the car, and detect attempts to sabotage it, most likely by a timed or, better yet, radio-controlled failure of the brakes on a steep section of the road, plus compromised seat belts. The apparatus would have to be undetectable after the crash, so I would expect efforts to guarantee an intense fire after the crash. If we give them an obvious opportunity, then we may be able to direct their efforts into a form that will allow us to fake it. This will require a male cadaver and an electronics package so that the car can be driven by remote control. I would have to arrange to be the officer first on the scene, and the body would have to end up in Lucille's hands for the fake identification and Ken's death certificate. Thus, there are lots of steps, any one of which could involve failure."

Roberto continued, "A less risky option is a credible but fatal accident we create ourselves before the French team can get set up and operational. I am told Ken is a bit of daredevil with heights, and you do hike a lot in the Sierra. What about a 'fatal' hiking accident, a bad fall, with your body delivered directly to a doctor who will declare death to the coroner? With a bad enough fall, there would be no open casket."

Ken said, "It could be made credible, especially if ENE were told that the last few members were scattering to the far winds at my death. An announcement at the Newman funeral could achieve that purpose. It also helps that it is summer, Merced is hot as Hell, and that I have traditionally taken back-country hiking trips with Jill. Let's do it this way, and hope they bite. Even if they are suspicious, they would lose their only validated telepath, and picking up the trail would be difficult."

CHAPTER SIX

Modesto Bee, August 5
Physicist killed in Sierra fall
"Renowned physicist Kenneth O'Neal, a UC Merced faculty member, fell to his death down a 400-foot cliff yesterday afternoon at 6:45 a.m. while hiking near Carson Pass off Highway 88 with his wife, Jill, to whom he had been married for 15 years. A U.S. Forest Service crew based in the Eldorado National Forest believes O'Neal was caught in a small rockslide from an overhanging cliff and struck by a rock that either killed him on the spot or toppled him on the narrow ledge on which he was standing, causing his fall. Resuscitation efforts were not feasible, due to an apparent broken neck, and he was rushed to the small medical clinic at nearby Kirkwood Resort. Dr. Lucille Edwards of Merced, who was vacationing at the resort, was unable to revive O'Neal, and pronounced him dead. Funeral arrangements are pending.

Prof. O'Neal had recently gained international acclaim for his work....."

Modesto Bee, August 7
"A funeral will be held for Prof. Kenneth O'Neal at 9 a.m., Saturday, August 9, at the UC Merced Newman Center he helped found. In lieu of flowers, donations should be sent in his name to Catholic Relief Services."

The small chapel was packed to overflowing, and loudspeakers were set up so that the crowd outside could hear his words. Almost 1,000 people attended the campus memorial earlier in the day and many hundred attended the funeral service. The eulogies were effusive of both Ken and his bereaved widow Jill, and Jonathan came down from Oregon to add his comments on Ken's work in the Physics Department in teaching, research, and public service, and what a loss it was. He openly mentioned the potential for Ken to have won in the near future a Nobel Prize in Physics, now forever extinguished.

One student, a young woman, gave a moving eulogy about Ken's spiritual guidance to Newman students' promising beginnings tragically eradicated by a series of untimely deaths in the past years, and mentioning that she could no longer stay in Merced and bear the memory of what could have been. Ken's body had been cremated, half his ashes would be placed in a modest vault at the local Catholic cemetery, and the other half would be scattered in the Sierra Nevada he loved so much. The crowd dispersed in a somber mood over the tragic loss of a rising star in science and a wonderful teacher, friend, and colleague.

The mood that evening in the Midpines safe house was more of exhausted relief than any sadness. All had gone well. The key had been getting a suitable body, and when a dead indigent middle-aged Caucasian male was delivered to Dr. Edwards for an autopsy on August 1, the plan was executed. The standard autopsy was performed, and a pig's carcass was submitted for cremation in a closed wooden casket. The body, carefully packed on ice, was dressed in Ken's clothes and provided with all identification. The indigent's beard was shaved and some effort made to use hair styling and make up to get as much a resemblance to Ken as possible. Ken, Jill, Tim, and Jennifer, up from Los Angeles, drove the body to Carson Pass on Highway 88. Ken and Jill parked at the trail head and hiked up to the Little Round Top meadow, and camped for two nights, making sure Ken was seen and recognized by many campers. Early Monday morning, they packed up and returned to their car along the cliff trail, at which point the accident was staged by Tim and Jennifer who had carried the body up that trail very early Monday morning in the pitch dark – not an easy task without any light except a quarter moon. The face and head were deliberately smashed with a rock to make any identification difficult, the neck broken, and the body pitched over the edge. The distraught Jill raced down to the road, and used her cell phone to call 911, while a well-disguised Ken, white beard and all, hiked with Tim and Jennifer down to the State Park near Markleeville, where a non-descript Ford Taurus was parked. They then traveled through Yosemite National Park to the Midpines safe house.

Michelle reported on the funeral: "Jill and Louise were the only Omega members at the service, and they did a great job maintaining 'dark minds' for the ceremony. Both were probed on several occasions by a Coven telepath, British, who had driven down from Sacramento that day just for the service. None of the Merced ENE personnel are telepaths. Jacky did great with her eulogy, and had also been probed and had responded naturally, identifying her as a low-level sensitive well below the level of a trained telepath. I was able to get close to the telepath, unseen and unfelt, and took pictures of him. Roberto, thus alerted, broke into his car during the service, and copied anything he could find. It turns out he is British, and he has tickets for return to England (first class, no less) on a flight scheduled for tomorrow. The British telepath then drove around Merced in a probe-response mode, and returned to Sacramento. Roberto is working now to arrange to have him further identified upon his return to England, but we will not risk anything that could even remotely alert him to our surveillance. We may well lose track of him, but that is a risk we will accept."

"What about the future?" Ken asked. "I think that Gabriella and Victor at Planada and their growing cells in the San Joaquin Valley will not be picked up in the random sweeps that we expect the Covens to do in Merced proper."

Gabriella and Victor indeed had had success in the Valley, but the sensitives they recruited helped by forming sweeps using teams of six members – far more diverse groups that were scattered widely down the valley. They were often found in county health service offices, legal aid branches, a few from colleges, a few from church groups, all strongly altruistic but all profoundly lonely. The Omega Project also included a growing cadre of highly supportive non-sensitives. These cells would indeed be hard to find by the Covens.

Ken announced, "We will maintain one small cell in Merced to alert us to future Coven efforts, but I hope that the uncertainty will suppress Coven efforts to 'feed' on sensitives. The Midpines house is secure, as is the small cell in Mariposa. I propose that I move to the town of Winters, a rural community west of Davis, and support the rapidly growing cells in Davis while staying out of sight of the UC Davis physics community where I might be recognized. Jill and I have agreed on ways to alter my appearance to make that even less likely.

"It is Jonathan and Louise I worry about. You are the last contact with the Merced telepaths, and the Covens may decide on general principles to wipe you out. I hope that instead they merely keep an eye on you so as to be alerted to any new telepathic activity in Oregon.

"This then brings up the last point. It is all well and good to grow and thrive in secret, but it does nothing to stop the bestial 'feedings.' Eventually, we will have to surface again and destroy these monsters, and it may be sooner than later. The advantage that we will have in the future is that there will be no identifiable center that they can eliminate, as in Merced, only a widespread and amorphous network of cooperating cells. I am sure that they will maintain a presence in this area, alert to any strange tales of psychic doings, but as long as they don't have a large enough group to 'feed,' probably at least four members, they are not as dangerous.

"Still, our retreat from Merced is temporary and tactical in nature until we can pursue our own investigations of the European Covens, which by the way are going well. We have one of their centers, in Paris, penetrated and soon bugged."

Ten days later in Paris, a city largely deserted by its residents in the sticky summer heat, the Council of Covens' executive committee met in the secure apartment. They had decided on simply going by the letter E for Executive and 1, 2, and 3 for ranking. They had just finished listening for a second time to the tape-recorded eulogies from Ken's funeral.

Now E1 spoke, "She was a low- to mid-level sensitive, without the mind-blanking techniques used by O'Neal, and not capable of any serious telepathic activity. She is the highest-level sensitive we found anywhere in Merced, although the town had a lot of low-level uncoordinated sensitives. In her eulogy, she referred to 'spiritual guidance,' but we believe it was the Merced telepaths she was referring to. The additional deaths she mentioned were the three we killed this spring, exacerbated by the dispersion of seven members last year after the safe house explosion, and probably the death of the scheduled 'feeding' victim, Tiffany, last fall. We have checked up on her, and indeed she was a long-term Newman member who knew Professor O'Neal well. In fact, she should have graduated last year but stayed on and remained very active in the Newman Center. She left town immediately after the service, and we have not yet picked up her trail. O'Neal's wife, Jill, has put their house on the market. Note that Professor Campbell mentioned the possibility of a Nobel Prize for O'Neal if the early work on thin-film superconductivity continued to pan out. Our French scientists say this would have been a distinct possibility.

"The whole affair seems awfully suspicious, but we can find no hint of foul play. Professor O'Neal had everything to live for, and his death put an end to that. But it also puts an end to our search for the Merced telepaths, as there is now no trace of anything unusual in Merced or the vicinity. We have lost our last link, and either we have succeeded splendidly or they have deceived us and fled somewhere else, potentially to rise again. I will report this to all Council members, and close up the efforts, most of which had not really gotten started yet. But we should leave in place a constant research effort to trace any of the known or suspected Merced telepaths.

"Our analysis indicates that there was only one high-level telepath in Merced, Professor O'Neal, who, as an intelligent male, fits the model we have used to recruit new members. From the reports of the late and un-lamented Linda, we learn that he was in the habit of taking his graduate students for lunch at the Highway 99 Carl's Jr., where he was almost surely the mind probed by the San Francisco Coven.

"From the low level of sensitivity we have seen in his largely female associates and students, we believe that his failure is probably linked to his attempts to recruit young women, which we ourselves have found to be very difficult. His strength was technology, and his use of dedicated scientifically astute non-telepathic assistants. We have seen every evidence that he used it well – eradicating the California Covens by timed explosions, as the Beverly Hills massacre, avoiding the attempt at the first Merced safe house explosion, eliminating the rest of the San Francisco Coven via fake drug overdoses, and the killing of A Prime and the entire American effort – most likely by poison gas during the 'feeding' when the Coven alertness and defenses are low.

"Some of the other events, such as the San Francisco telephone operator and Alexander's comments about a female telepath, are unverifiable and unreliable, the latter since Alexander had every reason to lie about his incompetence that led to his capture. Thus, it appears that we had eliminated the greatest threat and scattered any low-level recruits and non-telepathic associates, who will live in dread for the rest of their lives. Professor O'Neal went to great effort to keep his activities secret, and I expect any adherents will follow that pattern for fear of their lives.

"I propose that we re-establish the San Francisco Coven from American members, and institute a permanent effort to maintain surveillance of any reports in the future from Merced and elsewhere. I also suggest that another center be set up in Oregon, since several members appear to have fled in that direction. We will of course continue efforts to duplicate the mind static device Professor O'Neal had discovered.

"Still, this whole affair bothers me, as it is also consistent with the Merced telepaths going underground. We have underestimated them in the past, and that led to disasters of unprecedented magnitude. I hope we are not repeating the same mistake. However, I see little else that we can do that is not being done at present. For the near future, when we are well prepared and no evidence of the Merced telepaths can be found by non-psychic means, and we have re-established the San Francisco Coven, we will resume 'feeding' activities in their area. That has produced a violent reaction on their part in the past, and it will establish that either they are destroyed or are so scared that they will remain underground."

Modesto Bee, September 16
ENE closes up shop
L'Equipe de Electronique Nouveau (ENE) of Merced unexpectedly announced today that it is "changing market forces" and that the untimely death of Prof. Kenneth O'Neal has prompted the company to terminate its plans to establish a major research operation in Fresno. All contracts and leases will of course be honored. This loss compounds the tragedy of Prof. O'Neal and...

CHAPTER SEVEN

The town of Winters, although only at about 6,000 population, was rapidly growing as a bedroom community for UC Davis, since housing prices in Davis were so outrageous. Very few senior faculty and no Physics Department faculty lived in the Winters area, with the new residents being mostly low-level associate professors who having finally achieved tenure could put down permanent roots. There was a lot of space in the foothills of the coastal range west of Winters, where one could get a 20- or 40-acre "ranchette" in the blue oak savannah characteristic of the area. The rolling hills and trees made the area very private, and in many cases no neighboring house could be seen. This was the case for the Omega property, which had no really close neighbors but was only five minutes from the center of town. Jill passed the word around that the house had been chosen for her semi-invalid husband. He was wheelchair bound and loved the extensive deck and veranda combination that was both shaded by lovely oaks and had a good view west to the mountains. Michelle then fit the pattern by being his live-in nurse as well as a single mother. A number of trips were made into town with Ken in a wheelchair, including a birthday dinner at the Staghorn Roadhouse. Diane and Michael with their child also moved into Winters, but in town, where Diane took a job as a waitress at the Staghorn, probably the largest single employer in Winters.

One of the best students Ken had ever had, Frank Kerns, was a young faculty member in the Davis Physics Department. Frank had been alert enough to know that Ken was into something new, and very secret. But Ken had never taken him into his confidence about Omega. Frank had had almost weekly phone calls to Ken about physics, asking questions, getting advice, suggesting new directions, carrying on the work. Frank was crushed at Ken's accident, attended the funeral, and felt the loss of far more than a mentor, an almost father figure who had guided him in both science and life.

Late one evening Frank, ever the bachelor, was still at work when the phone rang in his office. "Hello," said Frank, surprised at this late-night call to his university office. "Frank, it's Ken O'Neal. I was scheduled to be murdered, and had to fake my demise to save my life. I am living near Davis

167

in seclusion, but would be pleased to meet you at some neutral place where I would not be recognized. How about the Woodland Sizzler Steak House on West Court Street in 30 minutes?"

Frank, usually irrepressible, was for once almost speechless. "I'll be there!"

Thus it was in a car in the Sizzler parking lot that Ken told Frank about Omega. Frank had no problems and accepted it immediately as reality, based not only on what he knew of Ken but the mysterious, violent, and even lethal events that had swirled around UC Merced in the past two years, with the San Diego kidnapping attempt being the last straw. Also, the very concept that Ken, a veteran hiker and rock climber, could succumb to a bouncing rock was wildly improbable to Frank.

"I want three things of you," said Ken, "besides your complete silence on the matter. First, I want you to carry on my work as your own, with me as the ever-silent collaborator. Second, I may need your help in certain tasks, some of which are scientific. Finally, I want you to seriously consider some of the young women in our group as a possible spouse. We have far more women than men in Omega, and I can assure you of an exceptionally happy marriage if you fall in love with one of them."

Frank Replied, "With an offer like that, who could refuse? When and where can I meet these paragons of intelligence and beauty?"

"Better ease up on sarcasm with this group," mused Ken. "Some are getting pretty good at reading minds, and all of them can sense false emotions at 100 yards in a dense fog. Honesty is essential. Also, be very cautious. The Covens may well keep tabs on all my graduate students wherever they may be, and forever. I will give you all our stealthcraft tricks."

The following Tuesday, Frank was present at the Winters safe house with Michelle and Dawn, Diane and Michael, and four Omega women, including two representatives of the Davis cells (all of whom had been chosen by Ken and Jill, not totally at random). Frank was amazed that a large section of old East Davis was under constant psychic surveillance from the two-dozen or so Omega Project members. Also, the women were all awfully good-looking, vivacious and confident, strong women with a power he could sense. His courage left him in an instant, and suddenly he was the shy geek of his high school days, scared to death of these "paragons of intelligence and beauty." He would have done almost anything they wanted him to do to win their approval.

They all insisted on a demonstration of their powers, and Frank was simply stunned by what he saw and heard. So that was what this was all about. Somehow his physics wasn't so important anymore. Omega was what mattered.

During the evening, each of the Omega members had a chance to talk to Frank, one on one. The last one, Kelly, seemed a bit shy and uncertain, and Frank, who was in a state verging on panic, felt an instant empathy. As they talked, Kelly gradually opened up and described her lonely years of searching for acceptance, a longing for belonging, spiritual and physical comfort, but somehow everybody she met seemed shallow and selfish. In an hour, it was all over but the engagement. The other women sighed at what a great guy he seemed to be. Their search would continue, but they could sense the resonance between Kelly and Frank and wished them well.

CHAPTER EIGHT

Fall in the western Sacramento Valley is a special time. The first rains have come (usually) laying the summer's dust and cleansing the air. Ever since the routine burning of rice fields had been banned in the 1990s, the fall sky was often a lovely blue over the hills, already starting to show green in new grass. The hills themselves were abrupt, rising rapidly to 3,000 feet in a few miles, much steeper than the gentle western slopes of the much higher Sierra Nevada, seen dimly to the east. Through a gap in these hills, Putah Creek flowed east from the coast range into the Sacramento Valley, one of the very few streams to do so, as it followed an old fault line. The pleasant weather triggered hordes of people to visit the hills and creek each weekend, about the closest real scenery to many valley locations. Thus it was that the Staghorn was usually packed on weekend nights, and was always in need of charismatic servers for the overflow crowds, and with tips it paid well. Great plates of freshly baked sourdough bread complemented the prime rib for which the roadhouse was famous, with the staff singing birthday and anniversary greetings to celebrating families. In all, it was quite a scene, but oblivious to the score of mounted animal heads that ringed the walls for which the roadhouse was named.

Diane had taken a part-time job in September, now that a minimal but adequate surveillance network had been established in that section of Winters. She had become quickly one of the most popular servers, witty, sensitive, efficient, and even working part time she greatly supplemented the barely adequate income doled out by UC Davis to research associates. On the way back to the kitchen on a typically frantic late October evening, she stopped for an instant as she routinely went to "dark mind" for a few seconds to check for psychic activity. Instantly she picked them up, still almost a mile away, just making the turn off Interstate 505, and even at that distance, she knew that their destination was the Staghorn. Not 30 seconds later, even before she had a chance to code in her discovery, her pager beeped, confirming her detection and that the network had been alerted.

Closer and closer they came, searching for a parking place, and then just after 8:00 p.m., she saw them. Three men, sort of business men types but wearing badly fitting blue jeans and flannel shirts, went to the reception desk and explained that they were a little late for their 8:00 p.m. reservation. No problem, they were within the 15 minute "window" allowed for laggards, and they were taken to the back room, thankfully out of sight but very much present in Diane's mind. The next chance she had, Diane stepped aside into a small alcove and gathered her wits. This was the first contact in months, and somehow she had hoped never to again have to sense a Coven-trained mind. She had maintained strict "dark mind," but had been focusing only on these three men. Slipping back into trained responses, she realized that the protocol required a wide search for trailing Coven members, and immediately there he was, outside, standing near their car, clearly the "receptor" of the probe-response pair, waiting for any sort of signal.

Diane wanted nothing more than to somehow evaporate into thin air, but she had all the work to do. Back to the dishes, back to the tables, joking, and smiling as though nothing had changed, outwardly effervescent, inwardly "dark mind." She was just passing through the swinging doors when it came. A sharp probe by all three men, trying to be coincident, but in fact three independent probes that had as a consequence a confusing mental pattern for a few seconds. Diane froze for a second, staring deep into the blue velvet that was her "dark mind" target, and responded little if any to the probe. In a minute or so, the "receptor" strolled into the restaurant, nonchalant as could be and broadcasting an "all is safe" message. With a start, Diane realized she knew him. It was 2C2, the sole survivor of the San Francisco Coven, now returned to Northern California with new compatriots

It seemed forever, but in reality less than 10 minutes had passed before the Staghorn was ringed with some of the most powerful members of Omega. Ken slipped into the kitchen, and Diane briefed him on which was the Coven car. Michael soon had a tracer on it, and a new radio-triggered static device with auto self-destruct trigger. Ken and Michael then slipped into a booth in the bar only about 15 feet away from the oblivious Coven members, separated from them only by a plywood wall. Two beers and an order of roadhouse onions, and with their faded jeans, they were indistinguishable from the large bar crowd, so different from the more family-oriented dining room next door.

171

For some reason, the Coven members never realized how close they were to UC Davis, barely 12 miles away. If they had been smarter, they might have worried about a campus so much like UC Merced but much older, much bigger, and with a thriving Newman Center. Totally clueless, they had been told about this rural restaurant deep in the boonies, and had let their guard down completely once the probe had come out clear.

Ken and Michael spent one of the most fascinating hours of their lives listening in to a complete summary of the past two years from Coven perspective. What was hard was somehow nursing a beer and looking normal in the semi-riot that was the Staghorn bar scene on weekend nights. There were distractions. A couple of comely young women eventually decided Ken and Michael were so unresponsive to their obvious charms that they probably were gay. A fight broke out two booths down, but both were so drunk as to be harmless to each other. Despite these, the story unfolded, told by 2C2 as a triumph of Coven tactics in the face of an implacable foe eventually harassed, killed, and scattered to the four winds. San Francisco and its rich feeding grounds were deeded to them, a new beginning for its famous Coven. Ken and Michael were amused that the Council's strict cautions about a high level of surveillance and early restraint in feeding were ignored as unrealistic. It showed that some on the Council were worried that the Merced telepaths might have gone underground, and that later it planned an intense round of feedings all over Northern California to try to get a response. Clearly, their rescue of Gabriella from a scheduled feeding, at considerable risk, was taken as a weakness of the Merced telepaths that could be exploited.

When they finally left, Diane and Michael had the responsibility of tracing the car, aided by about a dozen Omega members strung out all along Interstate 80, assuming a San Francisco destination. However, at the Vallejo turnoff, the Coven car went west on Highway 37 along the northern shore of San Pablo Bay, and Michael and Diane were on their own. On south through San Rafael, then out to Tiburon and a pricey estate on a point that jutted south into San Francisco Bay. Carefully edging closer, they could see a boat dock just below the house. "Very nice," murmured Michael. "They can slip into San Francisco or Oakland at will." An entrance-exit beacon was placed by the gate, and seeing no further sign of activity, they headed back to Winters.

CHAPTER NINE

It was the largest gathering of Omega in six months, jammed into the Winters safe house, sleeping any old place – patio, lawn. Cooking duties were in a strict rotation, which resulted in some strange eclectic meals, such as homemade tamales and Chinese chicken salad. All cells were represented, a tangible recognition of the growth of Omega.

Ken let Diane and Michael do the full briefing, including the Covens' activities of the past two years. Intriguingly, the Coven members thought that the successes of the Merced telepaths were due mostly to better use of modern technology, not any unusual telepathic capabilities. They clearly had a low opinion of female telepaths, and totally misread the nature of the Merced telepaths as one powerful male (now dead) and a bunch of weak female followers. It was also clear that the four had just arrived in town yesterday, and were deliberately staying out of San Francisco itself for a few weeks.

When they were through, Michelle summarized the problem, "We can't stand by idle as the Covens resume their feeding activities. Yet to intervene when they are alert and ready to detect any Omega attempt at a rescue would be difficult and dangerous."

"I see a problem and an opportunity," said Ken. "But the problem is in the future, as Michelle so ably summarized, and the opportunity is now."

Expectation filled the packed room. The silence was deafening.

"Our friends have just arrived. If they were to immediately disappear without a trace, it would put fear and uncertainty into the Council. We were lucky to identify them so quickly, but the Council could assume an impenetrable surveillance net all over the area. In such confusion, they would surely hesitate to act again, only to lose yet more members to our unseen menace. I propose we move as soon as we can be ready – probably tomorrow night, with all our resources, perhaps aerial. That means you again, Michael, but there may be other options, including terrestrial and aquatic. I would propose that our boat approach their pier around 3:00 a.m. while others on the ground cut off all their power and phone lines just as we pitch a massive mental static attack on their house. I'll arrange for electronic blanking of all cell phone frequencies. I'll need Jonathan and

Frank's help in this. Then we and they must disappear without a trace.

"Omega, your thoughts? There is real risk in this action, and our attempt to lie low and fade away will be sacrificed. But without action, innocent lives will be lost in a ghastly manner."

By midnight, it was done, and prayers were intoned as Omega readied itself for the long day and night to come. There was almost a new moon, so the night was very dark. The ever-discreet citizens of Tiburon were not keen on street lights, so the *Chronicle* newspaper delivery truck had to carefully wend its way through dark and curvy roads, often with little help from street signs or house addresses. Still, papers were being efficiently delivered to all the right houses, as they were every morning around 3:00 a.m. But at one house, out on the point, suddenly it looked as though two papers were thrown at the house, one of which actually went over the wall. The truck ambled on, the driver totally unaware of his passenger and their surreptitious mission. About a mile later, the driver was once again by himself. He still had more than 300 houses to cover, and he was a bit behind.

San Francisco Bay was also very dark, but a surprisingly large number of lights streamed across the water from Sausalito. Ken would have liked fog, but in fall, fog was rare, so a new moon would have to do. Two boats approached the pier, small, open, and being pushed to shore by silent electric motors.

As they approached, they all sensed a sort of mental static. So the Covens were trying to match our technology, thought Ken. But upon analysis, the static was totally useless in interfering with telepathic activities while providing a splendid beacon to the presence of the Coven members. Nice try, but unclear on the principle.

They waited until 3:10 a.m., when all except Frank and Jonathan pulled down mesh caps that now had transparent eye patches designed to allow sight but block mental static. This was one of the first fruits of the collaboration with Frank and Jonathan. At 3:15 a.m., muffled screams rang from the house as the powerful mental static unit wrapped in a newspaper bundle went off. The team that had landed earlier cut power and phone lines, and ran to the front gate of the complex, only to suddenly encounter two Rottweilers bent on mayhem. The battle was short but noisy, as the land team was armed with silenced semiautomatic pistols. Rushing the pier, the boats landed and quickly checked the pier for standard defensive measures. None. They went to the large bay windows, and carefully removed a large circle of glass big enough for passage. Bedrooms were quickly found (the building plans were, of course, on file with the county), and the screaming, writhing Coven members neatly dispatched with anesthetic injections.

The four inert bundles were carried to the bay window and passed though one at a time, and put in the boats. A quick search of the house yielded laptop computers and briefcases, but it was clear that the Coven members had not had time to really become established in the house. The land team came around the side of the house and jumped in, and the boats silently moved out into the bay. Five minutes had passed, but there were only two sets of lighted windows in neighboring houses. Fifteen minutes later, in the lee of Angel Island, the two small boats were hoisted onto the deck of the rented 42-foot yacht, which headed off to an Oakland pier. The next morning, the rented boat was in its proper slip as nothing had happened, and somehow all the paperwork was misplaced at the yacht broker's office. However, payment had been made in advance, so no damage done.

Back in Tiburon, a silent alarm had been automatically triggered when power was lost, but since these events happen fairly often, it was almost an hour before ADT Security called Tiburon police. The police, using a mirror to see over the fence, could see one of the dead Rottweilers in the driveway, and called in a crime scene report. Since all attempts to contact the new renters were futile, at 4:25 a.m., the house was entered. The bedcovers in all four bedrooms had been violently displaced, and a small amount of blood was seen on the sharp corner of a bedside table. The cut phone and power lines, and the missing bay window, seemed to give a credible picture of a well-planned kidnapping. By next morning, several residents reported screams around 3:15 a.m. and the barking of dogs that suddenly ceased a few minutes later. The FBI was notified, the police began to trace the missing people, and the newspapers were notified, because crime of any sort (except perhaps tax fraud) is rare in Tiburon.

It was soon evident that these renters were not at all what they professed to be. All documentation used to rent the house was fraudulent, the bank account used for payments was under a false name, and the gold-plated references for their character and financial worth were carefully forged. In fact, the Tiburon police had never encountered such a professional effort to hide origins.

The *San Francisco Chronicle* had a field day, and soon it was all over the world. Four mysterious men arrived and were immediately kidnapped from a pricey and exclusive Bay Area enclave. Speculation abounded in the complete absence of fact. Even the *National Enquirer* (whose sources are checked, checked again, and re-checked, according to Jay Leno) found it hard to exceed the hype of the mainline papers, but they weighed in with "Aliens in our Midst? True Story of the Tiburon Abductions!"

In this case, the reality was almost as strange.

CHAPTER TEN

The four inert bundles, complete with metallic mesh head coverings, were quickly transferred to four older vehicles, all with impeccably forged license plates, registrations, insurance proof, and fake drivers' licenses. The newlyweds Gabriella and Victor had volunteered for this task, and they found it both easy and relatively cheap to accomplish.

The plan was for separate interrogation teams for each Coven member, located at widely spaced urban sites throughout Northern California rented for this purpose. All Omega members would participate, as it was an excellent chance for training defenses against what were sure to be future assaults. However, there had not been enough time to secure enough locations, so four adjacent apartments were rented in an old converted motel that allowed cars to drive directly to each door. The motel was in the Florin Road district of Sacramento, a lower- to middle-income area with a very diverse ethnic population and a lot of turnover. Bedrooms were soon made secure, and the gags modified so that the captives could drink through straws. They were still covered with mesh hoods and blindfolded.

Within a few hours, the drugs wore off and they woke up. They were all in a state of perfect panic, some whimpering with fear. All orders were given by women in the tersest and most authoritarian possible manner. No explanations were offered in response to their pitiful requests for information. Silence was ordered under the threat of immediate punishment. Two Coven members seemed unimpressed, but a fully charged electric cattle prod was adequate to make the point stick.

After three days of sensory derivation, they were once again drugged and dispersed to hastily rented rural sites well away from any neighbors. This task was made enormously easier by the discovery of more than $120,000 in $20s and $10s in a briefcase next to the bed of 2C2 in the rented Tiburon house. Meanwhile, Frank and Tim had worked with Jonathan and easily defeated the security in the one laptop computer found in the same briefcase as the cash. Regretfully, little of use was found that they didn't already know, but details of how the false identities were generated were included in great detail. It would not be well for the Coven team to forget who they were supposed to be, after all. There were also, however, a series

177

of 10-digit numbers that appeared to be random, each keyed to a day of a month. Clearly, it was the key to a one-time code pad. Finally, the miniature phone tap yielded just one potentially interesting phone call. It rang exactly twice, then never again. But the country code was France, and the number tracked to the 16th Arrondissement apartment already identified by Roberto's people in Paris.

CHAPTER ELEVEN

Gerard began the meeting at exactly 9:00 p.m. The 16th Arrondissement penthouse was close to capacity.

"We know now that our previous fears and suspicions were correct. We did not kill, harass, and disperse the Merced telepaths. They went to great efforts to appear to disband and disperse, when in fact they went underground to avoid us. Yet they immediately revealed themselves and struck as soon as we re-entered San Francisco, which shows either astounding luck on their part or, what is more likely, a level of regional surveillance that we cannot match. Our attempt to use mental static technology to protect our members failed, as did rather extensive but standard physical protection measures. Local witnesses speak of dogs barking and men screaming, both of which lasted less than three minutes. The intruders were never seen coming or going, but from the hole in the bay window, entrance and exit was by water. Until further notice, no Coven members shall get any closer to Northern California than Denver.

"We must assume the worst, that four of our members are now in the hands of the Merced telepaths. No secret of ours is safe. I want a full report of what each of the four knew about our activities, and then we must immediately close down those sites. This safe house must be considered compromised and must not be used in the future. Each of you as you entered received a packet of instructions. Memorize them while you are here, and then turn them in as you leave.

"There will be a full meeting of the Council of Covens in four weeks in Lauterbrunnen, when our future activities will be discussed. That is all!"

Back in California, the final cells were ready – rooms within rooms, carefully soundproofed and in basements, all invisible to anyone outside the house. Blindfolds and gags were removed, revealing totally featureless rooms with a sink and toilet in one corner. A television screen was in a wall at the end of the cot – the only furniture. The screen was dark, but a recessed light fixture in the ceiling flooded the room with intense fluorescent light.

One week was allowed to pass with the simplest food – apples and whole wheat bread – pushed once a day through a slot in the only door.

No communications were attempted. However, during this time, a major effort was made to understand the nature of their psychic powers, including low-level assaults to see what response was generated. Generally, the results were minimal – the Coven members were in a state of psychic exhaustion from continuous fear and uncertainty. If they ever had any psychic powers, they were not evident.

On day eight, a note and a tape recorder was sent in with the food. "Tell the entire story of your life from the present day working backward to your childhood and parents. You have one week. Leave nothing out. Omissions and lies will be severely punished."

Omissions and lies? Rather, was there any truth at all? Twenty-four hours later to the minute (the rooms had no clocks, and the lights were always on, so the inmates could not accurately gauge the passage of time) – each cell went dark, and stayed that way for three days. Water was cut off, and within hours they were all getting desperately thirsty. Room temperatures were raised to almost 100°F. By day three, the Coven members were really suffering, and then as quickly as it started, the lights came on, water flowed in the tap, and the temperature returned to normal. One day was allowed to pass, and then exactly the same note was introduced with the food as before, "Tell the entire story of your life from the present day working backward to your childhood and parents. You have one week. Leave nothing out. Omissions and lies will be severely punished."

At this point, 2C2, whose name was actually Eli, and a Coven member from England, Spencer, folded completely. Their stories agreed even in tiny details, and those parts that overlapped Omega information checked out well. A major effort was made to name names, dates, and places, and awful actions were detailed in disgusting details. Even their non-Coven lives were a real mess. These people were despicable long before they became Coven members. The sad thing was that they were also clearly intelligent, and to themselves they believed they were superior to the herd and that normal rules didn't apply to them.

The next day, a Snickers bar and a glass of milk accompanied the apple and bread.

Revelations continued from Eli and Spencer, but the other two, Otto from Germany and Sam from Atlanta, were made of sterner stuff. They filled the tapes with inconsequential ramblings but little real information. Otto in particular seemed really dangerous, and he gave the impression that he was the enforcer charged to keep 2C2 and the rest in line. After two days of this, Omega knew it had a problem.

Jonathan led the discussion that began, "What can we do with these monsters? We can't ever let them loose, and we can't keep them here forever. They deserve to die, for if they were released, they would kill again. We could have a trial of sorts and execute them with a clear conscience, because we would be saving lives."

Ken mused, "Is there any way that we could release them back to the Covens mentally emasculated? They could then be both harmless to others and scary to the Coven, hopefully then preventing many deaths. Remember A Prime? But would it harm us to use our powers, born in love, to mentally castrate these pathetic monsters?"

Jonathan replied, "But we are not killing, just stripping them of an unholy power that can be maintained only by the parasitic 'feedings.' It is also clear that without these 'feedings' their powers diminish."

"Could we keep them long enough so that they would emasculate themselves by a sort of mental starvation?" asked Roberto.

"Not really," said Jonathan, "One feeding revives them, it appears. I think we should try to burn out their psychic powers, very much as we were doing with A Prime, but very carefully, ready to back out if we are damaging ourselves."

Two days later, the six most powerful Omega members, all volunteers, waited outside of Otto's cell. Michelle, who was awesome in her ability to probe minds, acted as a passive observer as Otto provided his usual ramblings. She waited until he told an especially outrageous lie to the tape, then hit him hard with pain over-layered with sort of an omniscient disapproval. Otto, startled by the first hint that he was being observed psychically, struck back with viscous force. Bad mistake! Otto, furious at the unexpected attack, was putting out serious effort against Michelle. She was handling him easily, and sneeringly transmitted to Otto along with the information that it was a despised woman who was kicking his butt! As Otto reached a white-hot level, Ken, Gabriella, Diane, Tiffany, and Betsy struck. Fear racked Otto, as he pathetically fought the effort. Deeper and deeper burrowed Omega, until they reached a sort of point of origin. Then they all burned into his subconsciousness mind-destroying fear and loathing, so that any attempt to try psychic powers would result in an almost fatal level of abject panic. They all stayed there as Otto struggled, failed, and dropped into an exhausted despair. In about a minute, it was all over. Otto was unconscious, and all Omega members were bathed with sweat. Everybody had bad headaches.

Jonathan carefully pocketed the pistol he had carried in case by some awful happenstance Otto would have won and taken over one or more Omega members. Ken's instructions were clear. "Kill us immediately, then kill Otto."

The next day, it became clear what they had accomplished. The Omega members were tired but as far as they could tell, perfectly normal. But Otto was wreck. Even at the gentlest psychic probing, Otto recoiled in whimpering panic.

Once again, the note arrived with the food. "Tell the entire story of your life from the present day working backward to your childhood and parents. You have one week. Leave nothing out. Omissions and lies will be severely punished." Otto immediately began his life history with impeccable accuracy and in such nauseating detail that they could barely mine the tapes for useful information without feeling soiled, dirty, corrupted. Frank, Jonathan, and Tim volunteered for the task, a descent into evil such as they had not believed possible, which however led to a level of detail about the European Covens that far surpassed anything they had known before.

One month later, Otto was delivered to a flight from San Francisco to Frankfurt with his fake ID and about $100.

After the Otto affair, Jill knew Ken needed all the healing he could get, and the next Sunday, they slipped into the UC Davis Newman Center for Mass. There were about a dozen Omega members present, and at the precise moment the priest says, "Peace be to you," called "the kiss of peace," they all broadcast love, peace, and total acceptance to the entire community. This was still the best technique to achieve "awakening" in a small group of candidates, generally with at least one Omega member for every two candidates. In the church, the impact was spread among perhaps 250 people, so no "awakening" happened. Yet, the entire congregation resonated to the message, sort of like a bell that has been rung. Thus, the Masses were permeated with charisma even for non-telepaths, and the crowds were growing each month, with some new attendees who weren't even Catholic.

The old brick church that served as the Newman Center was more than 100 years old, and the brickwork was a bit rustic. Thus, no one would ever notice that four of the bricks, one at each corner of the building at about 3 meters above the ground, though nicely matched in color and texture, were slightly thicker than their neighboring bricks. However, they were quite efficient receivers and recorders for the burst of modulated electromagnetic energy emanating from the chapel at that precise moment of the psychic impetus and resonance at the "kiss of peace." Still, the signal was so weak and the overall electronic pollution of Davis was so extensive that nothing could have been made of it even by the best computers. However, four similar "bricks" were also placed in a similar pattern in the old City Hall, about 100 meters west of the chapel. It was just barely possible that by comparing the data carefully recorded from all the receivers, a signal could be extracted by high-level computers.

About two weeks later, a delivery truck carrying Perrier mineral water and other products drove slowly by the Newman chapel and the City Hall.

Roughly one week later, late at night, the enormous computers of the Service de Météorologie de France in Saclay, south of Paris, were engaged in a totally unauthorized task.

CHAPTER TWELVE

Gerard began the meeting at exactly 9:00 p.m. The new 7th Arrondissement rental was close to capacity.

"Disaster. Otto reappeared two days ago wandering around Frankfurt in a daze. He had on him the fake identification we gave him that, when checked, alerted us to his presence. We 'convinced' the police that he was harmless and simpleminded and had him released to our protection for transport to a fictitious sanitarium. He is now in the new Bavarian safe house.

"He once was one of our most powerful members, sent to oversee the re-establishment of the San Francisco Coven in full awareness of the potential dangers involved. He never believed that the Merced telepaths had been vanquished, which is why we included him in the initial survey team.

"We have evaluated his condition, and find that all trace of psychic ability has been erased from his brain. Worse than that, any attempt to even try to remember what he had been reduces him to abject panic and fear. Yet he retains all his knowledge and memories, which are an enormous danger to us. We have to assume he has told the Merced telepaths everything he knows. He has to be dispatched immediately. The Lauterbrunnen meeting is canceled. Whatever we do now must not in any way touch the places and people we knew as of a week ago. All we can do is to go underground as deeply as we can while trying to gather information on the Merced telepaths by non-traceable and non-psychic means.

"There will be no further meeting of the full Council in Paris. It is too dangerous. You will be contacted individually in a few weeks or months. Be very, very careful or you will end up like Otto.

"But we have learned a great deal about the Merced telepaths, and this information must be summarized and transmitted to the Eastern European Council of Covens. We must no longer assume anything based upon our prior experience. What we have encountered is new and incredibly dangerous to us and our ancient way of dominance.

"I suppose we will have to alert the Romanji. They have practiced their psychic ways for millennia, and will have a wealth of experience we cannot match. They will not be pleased, and their displeasure can be lethal. But I think we need them, now. This meeting is ended."

A somber group of men drifted away, still rich and powerful, but shaken to their core. But in some, at least, was a burning hatred of the Merced Coven and a cold, hard, lifelong commitment to revenge. And then there were the Romanji. They would know what to do, and they will be awesome in their vengeance.

CHAPTER THIRTEEN

Ken, Jill, and Michelle sat in comfortable couches opposite a nice blue oak wood fire. They all seemed tired and distracted by the events of the past week. Three Coven members were still being held, and now that Sam, too, had folded, were being kept in somewhat better conditions, including better food and television. No further effort was being made to extract information from them, and now they were deliberately being fed misinformation useful to Omega against the day of their release. The plan was to send them to New Zealand with enough money to start a new, non-Coven existence, an option that all three would probably take. Each had been shown Otto, and the effect on them was stunning. The threat was to reduce them to Otto's state if they regressed or tried to contact Coven members.

The Omega cells had drifted back to their normal haunts. There was a sense of triumph in the achievements of the past month, tempered by compassion for the six members who had had to use their powers to burn out Otto's mind. Full healing would take time, but all of Omega was determined to help them any way they could. The recent group communion was a wonderful start on the road to health, as love washed deeply over the wounded members. In a while all would be well, but the memories would linger forever.

Dawn wandered into the room. Although she was well over 2 years old, she still had not spoken a word, and this worried Michelle a bit. Could it be that their children would be damaged by their psychic powers? Sort of an induced autism? Yet Dawn was a lovely child, bright, affectionate, just not vocal. Ken was insistent that he had not spoken until he was 2½, to which Michelle responded with her usual snide remarks about "all young boys are retarded," but with less and less conviction.

Dawn saw that her mother and her friends were sad, worried, and wounded. She walked up to Michelle, and said, "Mommy, I love you dearly. Please don't be sad."

But her lips hadn't moved, of course.

CHAPTER FOURTEEN

"So now it must end," intoned Karla. "What you have described would have been dangerous enough, but your imbecilic intervention has made the situation far worse. Whether you meant to or not is beside the point. You have force-fed and trained these 'Merced telepaths' to a high level of competence when, if left by themselves, they would probably have spontaneously imploded in jealousy and hatred, as has happened countless times in the past with these mixed-sex abominations."

Gerard was startled. "You mean such groups are not a new development?"

"Nothing is totally new," snarled Karla, "but you have made an excellent start in making something new to us and unusually dangerous. We take this whole affair with the greatest seriousness. Further, we have no idea whatever about their designs and motives. All we have is their devastatingly effective responses to your blunders.

"I simply can't conceive of the stupidities that led to the execution of Otto, our best evidence of the Merced telepaths' capabilities. I strongly suspect whatever happened to Otto was a direct consequence of your so-called 'feeding activities.'"

The Romanji did not approve of Coven "feeding" activities, which they had abandoned almost 500 years ago, and in any case had never used extensively.

"We will end it for you, but it will cost some of you dearly."

Gerard sat silent. He had a good idea that some of their Coven would have to die in the upcoming battle, but he consoled himself that because of his stature and lack of direct involvement in the botched plans to eradicate the Merced telepaths, he would probably not be one of them. It was also some small comfort that neither the Romanji nor the Merced telepaths practiced "feedings," so the deaths would be clean.

They were seated in a rather modest room in a small and largely destroyed castle in the Carpathian forest. It was heated by a pair of fireplaces at each side, the walls had tapestries and the windows heavy drapes, now closed. The view was quite dramatic from the paved terrace outside when the weather was good, but today it was not. Low clouds and occasional showers made the area damp and depressing. In summer, tourists were routinely

187

paraded through the grounds and some of the rooms, and they were told about the life and times of Vlad the Impaler, source of the original Dracula myths, even though it was the wrong castle in the wrong forest.

About 30 men crowded into the room – more than it could hold comfortably. They represented the Eastern European Council of Covens and three separate branches of the Romanji kingdoms. Seven representatives of the American and Western European Covens were present, led by Gerard, and for once a document had been prepared summarizing the events up to the present. Two copies had been given out a week ago – one to the Romanji and one to the representative of the Eastern European Covens.

The Romanji representatives were clearly distinguishable by their shorter stature and darker skins. They were heirs to ancient traditions, and probably originated as a race in southern India millennia ago. No great evidence of wealth and power were visible among the Romanji or in fact anyone present, since in the unsettled times in Eastern Europe, a low profile was essential. The Romanji did not at present practice "feedings," although they had in the distant past which was the source of some horrific fairy tales involving children that were told even in present-day Eastern Europe. The Romanji decided that "feedings" were essentially a parasitic drug, destructive in the long term but giving Coven members who used it temporary powers that the Romanji could not match. Current Romanji methods were more subtle.

After a long pause, Karla continued, "What concerns us the most is the clear evidence of their use of high technology, which you continually underestimated. The combination of a potential Nobel Laureate in Physics from the University of California with a mixed-sex telepathic Coven is ominous in the extreme. Yes, Professor O'Neal is most certainly still alive.

"We will find him and eradicate him. All your resources and personnel must be put unquestioningly at my discretion."

The fires burned brightly, but there was a chill in the room far more profound than merely the temperature.

CHAPTER FIFTEEN

The signs on Highway 99 were a bit unusual but not too much out of the ordinary. "The Merced Psychic" read the sign, with a picture of a dark-skinned turbaned woman with closed eyes gently fondling a crystal ball. A telephone number was given with a Merced area code, and an address in a residential neighborhood just west of Highway 99 near 16th Street. Similar signs are seen up and down Highway 99 and even on Interstate 80, where one advertises "The Davis Psychic," an improbable juxtaposition for a town dominated by a scientific research university. But then there are people for whom science itself is mystical, and anyway, science rarely helps in matters of love and money.

The house at the address was a small one, but hard to miss. A white picket fence enclosed a lovingly tended flower garden rich in heritage perennial flowers like hollyhocks and peonies. The path led to a house painted entirely in a soft blue, with the windows outlined in white. A tulip tree provided welcome shade. The whole effect was sort of antique but reassuring.

Rosa set up her office, put ads in the telephone book, placed signs on the highways, and hundreds of small cardboard index cards that could be taped to power poles, and crossing signal lights. The cards had a rather modest message, "Perhaps I can help. You have loving allies you don't even know about," followed by a phone number and "Se habla Español."

Almost two weeks went by, and Rosa wandered around Merced getting a feel of the town. She read all the newspapers carefully, noted names, places, dates, obituaries, screened TV news, listened to radio talk shows, and in general became as knowledgeable as possible about the people and doings of Merced. The exception was that she went nowhere near the university.

Late one afternoon, she had her first client, a young Latina woman in a difficult relationship with a married man. Rosa felt deep sympathy, as her own family had been a discriminated minority in her native Spain for centuries, and truly wished to help in any way she could. In this Rosa was aided by her library research, which included both a recent legal notice she saw regarding bankruptcy proceedings initiated by the man and an action on an unrelated financial matter by his present wife. Rosa's client went away with tears of gratitude, and Rosa agreed to pocket only half of the $20 offered. From that point on, Rosa's clientele grew steadily, mostly in the Latino community but gradually expanding into the Caucasian world. The word was out that Rosa was very, very good (and perhaps even psychic). Her client list started to expand up and down the valley, and some even had to arrange to stay overnight to get an appointment. No one ever waited at Rosa's house. Each was called by phone when Rosa was ready, in some cases after two or three days.

Professor Vladimir Ionescu was the heir of a proud name in Bucharest, but he had shunned the financial opportunities that his family connections offered to study physics at Sofia University. He assumed that eventually the pull of family connections would suck him into the financial world, but for the present he was fascinated by the opportunities of electronics. Thus, he was thrilled to be selected as a Fulbright Fellow at the University of California, Merced (aided by the fact that there were relatively few solid-state physicists in Romania to begin with, and even fewer who could go abroad for a year, but even so the selection seemed premature and unusually rapid.)

The gap left by the death of Professor O'Neal was enormous, but the work continued at a surprisingly fast pace, immeasurably aided by the close and active collaboration with Professor Frank Kerns of UC Davis, one of Ken's best students ever. Frank and his Merced colleagues were delighted to accept a Fulbright Fellow, even if the depth of his solid-state physics was suspect because of the scientific weakness of the University of Sofia. Still, a willing worker and a bright mind were always welcome as long as he didn't use up too much time getting up to speed. In fact, Vladimir became immediately useful because he knew and understood the older electronic instrumentation that was still essential to keep the experiments working, but which few if any of the new graduate students understood. Many a time Vladimir would be seen rebuilding a Tektronix oscilloscope with its obsolescent but still workable cathode ray tube.

Vlady, as he insisted upon being called, fit in with the team seamlessly, personally popular and the kind of glue that every successful research group needs to keep everybody working together with a minimum of friction. He was a bit of a clown, but also played a serious violin. The weakness in

the string section of the university orchestra was pretty much a permanent millstone around the neck of the Music Department, and Vlady was soon recruited. Late in spring, with Vlady's capabilities fully appreciated, they even dared to present Bruch's Violin Concerto
no. 1, Vlady's favorite and a real crowd pleaser.

At the group parties, Vlady would bring out his violin and play Gypsy tunes with such fire and passion that it brought tears to the eyes of the audience. When pushed, he would relate how hard it was growing up as a suspect minority in an authoritarian country, and how it seemed to take about twice as much effort to get even part of the rewards others got so easily.

Valley Drayage was an old and well-regarded trucking firm based in Modesto. The elderly owner, however, was more than happy to sell the firm to a group of investors with big ideas and a modern computerized method of maximizing on-road profits by minimizing empty trips. Soon Valley Drayage was expanding, offering rates significantly below others by pioneering the use of bar-coded mini-pallets that made turning around trucks highly efficient. Ads were placed up and down the valley for drivers, with promises of good pay and more time off, plus full medical benefits. Soon a contract was signed with UC Merced to provide air freight shuttle service to the campus at much less than Federal Express and UPS charged for the same service. A local office was set up in Merced to provide snappy service. The local representative was a well-known and popular ex-trucker, Manuel. His computer-savvy assistant, Hector, who looked Hispanic, spoke a rather academic English and the elegant Castilian of Spain itself, rather than the local Spanish. But then local Latinos with high-level computer knowledge were already in short supply and great demand, so Hector seemed to fit in well enough.

CHAPTER SIXTEEN

It was one of those days when people fled the valley to cooler climates. Midpines, on Highway 140 at about 3,000 feet elevation in the Sierra foothills and in an east-sloping valley that leads directly to Yosemite National Park, was such a haven. The cooler, wetter climate allowed heavy forest growth, and even in July, the local stream still flowed past the three widely spaced rustic motels that lined the highway. The country store was selling impressive amounts of both ice and soft drinks, and somewhat less beer than one might think.

The Midpines Sierra Retreat Center, specializing in therapy for substance abuse, was set well back from the highway on a long wooded road that leads to a 280-acre property. A discrete but effective fence surrounded the property was designed to keep backsliding "clients" from leaving unaccompanied, local residents were told. In fact, the fence, while looking ordinary, was a marvel of electronic sensors that alerted the Retreat Center residents to any incursion long before they even got close to the fence. The house was set with its back in the pines looking directly east across a lawn designed precisely to give views of the Sierra Nevada and Yosemite National Park. Today, cumulus clouds were rapidly building in the late afternoon, promising thunderstorms and downpours that were always welcome as long as they were not accompanied by the dry lightning that is known to start fires.

Lawn chairs were set around the lawn in the shade of a large maple tree. A large but very ordinary-looking bunch of people, most in Bermuda shorts, many but not all young, lounged in the chairs. A bunch of small children frolicked in a sandbox, closer to the house, with one young woman acting as both playmate and nanny. It all seemed so prosaic.

Gabriella spoke first saying, "I think we have company in Merced. A Spanish Gypsy named Rosa set up shop in Merced about six months ago. I'm sure you have seen her signs 'The Merced Psychic,' which we all find enormously droll. If only people knew! But Rosa is more interesting than I first realized. She soon started building up a large and enthusiastic clientele that swore by her powers. After about four months of this, I started to test her with some of our least-sensitive associates, all Latino, all with real problems, none with any real knowledge of the Omega Project. After a session, we would download what Rosa suggested, in some cases utilizing a miniature digital audio recorder. Rosa clearly was very good with all the normal tricks psychics use, very intelligent, and extremely well versed in Merced and its environs. But beyond that, she seemed to really care about her clients, and had rarely taken her full fee when doing so would distress a poor client. But she hammered rich and greedy clients for all they were worth, while still giving good advice, some of which was clearly unwelcome but always accurate.

"But beyond all this, and especially with our female Latinas, Rosa would occasionally give a fact that there was no way she could have learned this side of telepathy. I think she is real. I would like to perform tests with higher-level sensitives, but knowing that these have more knowledge of Omega, the danger may be too great. What are we to do?"

The group sat in silence for probably 15 minutes or so.

Then Ken spoke, "I would not have brought this up, but the coincidence is too great to ignore. About six months ago, UC Merced was offered and accepted a Fulbright Fellow from Romania, a bright solid-state physicist named Vladimir Ionescu. He joined my old group, and immediately became a hit with all. He also plays the violin extremely well, and was the soloist in the violin concerto you may have heard about two months ago. He is of Gypsy extraction, but his family has done everything possible to hide this fact, even to a name change. He works routinely with Frank."

"There seem to be a lot of Gypsies around all of a sudden," said Jonathan. "The new UC Merced contractor for shipping has a computer-savvy European Gypsy named Hector scheduling the services of Valley Drayage, which had been bought about six months ago – that number keeps coming up – by a group of investors. They have pumped serious money into the line, won major contracts, and are hiring all up and down the valley. I came across this Hector because he asked to be linked with the UC Merced main computers to speed scheduling, shipping, and getting payments. My colleagues were not enthusiastic because of security concerns, and I was copied in the e-mails. UC Merced has said no, but provided him modem access to billing."

Ken mused, "I wonder if our European friends, having been so badly burned, have resorted to old alliances. Could it be that there is something to the old tales of Gypsy psychics, and more? Could they have been brought in to spy on us, preparatory to destroying us? How close is their alliance with the European Covens? What are their capabilities, their methods? We know too little to be able to plan intelligently."

The sun was going down, and the lawn was now mostly in shadow. However, the sky was still bright with evenglow, and would be for at least two hours. Jonathan got up and started the fire in the circular pit.

The silence continued.

It was only 7:30 a.m., and the sun already was pounding the valley with waves of heat and light. It was mid-August, almost the hottest time of the year, and finely ground dust was everywhere. The trees themselves seemed shrouded in gray, waiting for the first rains of autumn to wash them clean of the summer's fine dry debris. In west Merced, there was a surprising amount of activity as everybody raced through their chores as early as possible before the dreaded triple digits held the town in its unrelenting grip. Deliveries were being made, shoppers were at stores which themselves had taken to opening an hour earlier than usual. Gardeners were busily cutting lawns and raising an unholy and dusty din with their misnamed leaf blowers. The trash and recycled materials for the day had already been picked up by workers at first light.

Even at the quaint house of the "Merced Psychic," activity stirred. The grounds of the house had been upgraded, and a series of old-fashioned bushes and annuals planted along the path to the door. The net effect was a certain homey but prosperous look that simultaneously shielded the house from the view of neighbors. Even at this early hour, two gardeners were busy developing a new planting bed just east of the driveway, and the run-down garage was being painted by yet a second team of workers when the first client approached the front door. Like many who came to see Rosa, she was cautious, and looked around to make sure no one she knew was in sight. She was a young Hispanic woman, as so many were, bearing troubles far beyond her years.

Carmen Maria Jimenez was met at the door by Rosa, who immediately gave her a hug and brought her indoors.

The gardeners and the painters continued their work but at a slower and more deliberate pace. A postman appeared at the next house, and seemed to be having trouble sorting the mail. He stood there, checking and re-checking his mail pouch.

Inside, Carmen opened up with an all-too-familiar tale of exploitation. Her employer was aware of her immigration status, and while he increased her salary to levels never before attained, it was clear that there were favors to be exchanged. Carmen had played the delaying game as long as she could, but now he was insistent that they meet this weekend while his wife and children were away at their Tahoe Keys house.

There was a key fact, however, that Carmen hid, and hid well. One that changed everything. Carmen already had had the assignation, and then some, and was pregnant. This thought Carmen kept in the front of her mind, but never even hinted at it in her rambling, tearful tale.

Rosa's behavior started to change perceptibly, and she initiated questions that seemed to push the envelope of Carmen's carefully rehearsed and totally fictitious story. But Carmen never wavered.

Finally, Rosa stated flatly, "There is something you are not telling me, something very important."

Carmen immediately thought of her fictitious pregnancy.

Rosa said in amazement, "You are pregnant? So this whole story you are telling me is a lie?"

Carmen smiled calmly at Rosa, who was suddenly frightened. Just then, the two gardeners, one a Hispanic woman, all three painters, and the postman walked in her door. They greeted her courteously, and made themselves comfortable as they could, since furniture was lacking for a group so large.

Gabriella began, "Rosa, we really like you. However, we think you were sent here to spy on the Merced telepaths, probably by a Romanji but at the request of the European Covens."

Rosa was very sharp and very quick, but she was stunned at the casual accuracy with which Gabriella laid out so exactly the facts as she had been briefed six months ago. These must be the people she was sent to Merced to look out for, the dreaded and deadly Merced telepaths.

She knew she was in serious danger, and her electronic emergency switch was under the table next to her knee, only about 6 inches away. A slight body movement, and help would be on the way. She rearranged herself slightly, but hesitated.

Gabriella watched her, smiling ever so slightly.

"Why am I hesitating?" thought Rosa. "What was it in these people, a strange mix of latent power and spiritual peace." She had never felt such a feeling of peace in her troubled life, always the outcast, always the Gypsy, never safe except with her own people. Yet these people seemed to like her, love her. "How could this be?"

A fly that came in with the Omega team buzzed around the room. It finally found the biscuits that Rosa always had for her clients, along with strong, sweet tea, and settled down to feast on the pomegranate jelly. An old-fashioned mantlepiece clock, somewhat out of place as there was no fireplace and mantle, solemnly ticked off the seconds.

Nobody moved. Nobody spoke. There seemed to be no rush, just a sense of waiting.

"For what?" thought Rosa. "What are they waiting for? Were these the monstrous and mysterious people that burned out Otto's mind? Were they about to burn out mine? Or perhaps have one of those bestial feedings that the American and European Covens used to increase their powers?"

Still Rosa hesitated. In her briefings, there had been hints that the Merced telepaths had struck so hard and effectively only because they were threatened, and some even killed, by the local Covens. Specifically, there had been an early "feeding" of a Merced female student, which triggered the eradication of a Coven surveillance team. The strong association with religiously active college students, many of whom were women, was so different from the middle-aged sharks of the typical European Coven. And this Hispanic woman. She seemed to be in charge even though one of the men was clearly older. That would have never happened in the Covens, where women are an extreme rarity and always subservient to the men.

Finally, Rosa could stand it no longer. She moved her knee away from the panic button under the table, and asked, "What do you want of me?"

"That you give us a chance to let you learn the truth about us," answered Gabriella. There seemed to be a slight sense of relaxation among all present, but especially by Carmen, who had played her part perfectly. The Omega members now had an excellent read on Rosa's capabilities.

Gabriella continued, "The panic button next to your knee has of course been disconnected, but we wanted you to make the choice you did."

Jonathan barged into the room, which was now far beyond its occupant capacity, and said, "Time to boogie, children. This place is alive with surveillance. We just blanked any Wi-Fi, and picked up some interesting hardware. Your picket fence was far more capable than you realized, Rosa.

Our European buddies play for keeps. Move, now!"

Gabriella said, "Better come, Rosa. We defused a large bomb directly under the floorboards where you are sitting, but there could well be more."

Rosa was stunned. Nobody told her anything about this. So she had been a tool, a pawn, and disposable. Once again the victim, once again the outcast, once again a Gypsy bitch. Somehow she never thought of challenging Jonathan's statement. In her heart, she knew it was all too true.

Rosa gathered her purse and all left. In all, only 4½ minutes had elapsed, though it had seemed like an eternity to Rosa. Two white featureless delivery trucks were parked outside. Two young women and a man, with what looked like shopping bags full of junk, were already in the vans. Everybody jumped in, now moving swiftly, and the vans drove off. At the first intersection a city of Merced police cruiser was parked. It did not follow them as they moved southwest out of town on a secondary road that soon turned to dirt and headed across the fields.

Simon, in his rented house 500 meters south of Rosa's but invisible because of the street layout and trees, vented his frustration.

"Merde!"

Simon was beside himself with anxiety as the phone on the other end rang at least six times. It was finally automatically forwarded to a second line and immediately picked up. The voice spoke in accented English.

"Summary!" Not much chit-chat on this line.

"I lost Wi-Fi surveillance on Rosa three minutes ago. I did the analysis, and it indicated sophisticated jamming, not a system failure. I immediately went to Protocol 2, the anesthetic gas, and when I received no confirmation in 30 seconds on the landline, I then went to Protocol 3. We are only about a half kilometer away, and I could have easily heard the explosion. None occurred. I have alerted the surface surveillance teams, but they are dispersed around the city, and I expect no on-site support in less than 10 minutes."

"What next? I have no authority above Protocol 3, and the second surveillance ring was not yet on line."

"On your computer terminal, type in PROTOCOL4, no spaces, all capitals, and at the prompt, the password $$31416otto##."

Simon did so, was rewarded in a few seconds with a massive explosion.

He moved to the front room of the nondescript rented house, and saw a plume of black smoke already hundreds of feet high in the sky as the Claymore mines built into the wall of Rosa's newly renovated attached garage spayed a hail of metal darts and phosphorus incendiaries through her living room.

"Massive explosion, smoke," Simon related.

"Now execute extraction. Call off the land surveillance teams. Gather any hardware. All leave for Rendezvous Point 7." The line went dead.

Sirens wailed, but before they even got close to the neighborhood, Simon was out the door with the parts for the second surveillance ring, his laptop, and anything else that could possible survive the next 10 minutes. He was only about 100 meters down the street when his own house erupted in flames. In only three minutes, he too was on secondary roads leading west out of town, but fortunately not the ones used by the Omega team.

Michael, high above in his new and electronic highly capable Cessna, was running cover for the Omega team when he noted the first explosion. He was on the radio when a second explosion occurred not far from the first. Intrigued, he saw a car speeding west from the site of the second explosion. A few terse coded words, and he began tracking the second car. The Merced police cruiser, almost at the scene of Rosa's house, suddenly diverted west.

In the van with the Omega team, Rosa sat stunned and furious next to Gabriella. She had heard the explosion of what she assumed was her house. Bait. She had been nothing but bait. And like bait, destined to be eaten alive.

In 90 minutes, the Omega team had reached the small town of Hollister, near the San Juan Bautista Mission, south of San Jose. The mission had been made famous in Alfred Hitchcock's *Vertigo*. Hollister was famous because it is smack dab on a portion of the San Andreas Fault that crept continuously, resulting in off-sets on city streets. For some reason, perhaps because of the fault, house prices were moderate, and Omega had purchased a small ranch and safe house on a rural road south of the city with, as usual, no neighbors and excellent visibility of any approaching vehicles or persons.

It was actually very comfortable, especially compared to the heat and dust of Central Valley towns in summer, and because of this (and standard Omega Project security protocols) it was continuously inhabited. From it, surveillance teams periodically combed to the South Bay Area, up to Palo Alto, while Winters and Davis teams did the same for the North Bay Area and San Francisco. The new small Omega cell at Santa Clara University used the Hollister house for retreats.

Ken and Jill had immediately started to come down from Winters upon the news of Rosa's predicament, but they would not arrive until well after Gabriella, Victor, and Jonathan's Merced teams. In the interim, everybody was trying to act as normal as possible. A barbeque was started, sangria punch prepared, and all chattered on with trivialities. Rosa was offered snacks, but refused.

Rosa sat stiff and upright in a comfortable chair near the window. She could see the lush valley, the hills, and the neat rows of grapevines. She could see them, but that was not where her mind was. She was outwardly calm and inwardly both scared and furious. Furious at being trapped by the Merced telepaths, scared of what they could (viz., Otto) and might do to her, but especially furious at the clearly long-planned attempt at her eradication should she expose any of the Merced telepaths. She had been set up as bait! But by whom? So there she sat, outwardly neat and collected, inwardly in turmoil in the midst of what appeared to be a burgeoning party.

Finally Ken and Jill arrived, with Frank, Kelly, and Meagan in tow. Frank tried to look totally inconspicuous, but all could see that he had some of the newest Omega diagnostic technology with him.

Finally Ken and Jill sat down in front of Rosa, with Gabriella and Michelle close to one side forming a loose circle. Care was taken not to make Rosa feel trapped. Ken thought that by being the oldest, he might better mimic the Gypsy respect for elder males and authority. Frank and Kelly were completely out of sight behind Rosa, discreetly setting up equipment.

"Rosa, we have come to like and admire you in the past few months for the obvious concern you have shown to the most vulnerable members of our society. But we are also concerned that you are here to spy on any remnant of the Merced telepaths —our name for ourselves is the Omega Project — that might remain after the battles with the American and European Covens." That was scarcely an accurate estimate of the rapidly growing Omega Project, but there was no reason to provide Rosa or anyone else with a reality check.

"We are also concerned since we have come to the conclusion that you have significant psychic powers in the area loosely called 'mind reading,' in all cases for current thoughts. Carmen was merely the latest in a series of tests we have sent you."

Rosa said nothing, but suddenly she could guess some of these test cases based on what she might call premonitions she had while counseling them.

Ken continued, "None of the people we sent was an 'awakened' Omega member, just candidates in training."

Rosa caught the emphasis on "awakened." It was clear that this "awakening" was a key to these people, but she had no idea of what "awakening" entailed. Still, she liked the concept. It seemed very positive.

"Here you are in the presence of Omega Project personnel. You probably have been told about our efforts to neutralize a particularly dangerous and recalcitrant Coven member, Otto. Several of us participated in that, one of our most distasteful efforts, the eradication of Otto's psychic potential. In all other cases, we were able to come to agreements that spared their lives as long as they broke all connection with their prior existence. We keep constant check on them, and several have become modest successes in their new lives."

This was all new to Rosa. She had been told that the missing Coven members in Otto's team had almost certainly been killed, and probably by ghastly means.

"Because we want to avoid a whole new war with Gypsies, we are taking a major chance in bringing you into our confidence. Our hand was forced when Jonathan and his team suddenly realized this morning that your entire compound was booby-trapped, and that you had no knowledge of the fact.

"So we are going to give you an unprecedented insight into our capabilities, capabilities born of an altruistic love regretfully all too rare in this world, capabilities that by an amazing accident resulted in a breakthrough, an 'awakening,' with two people, Michelle and me, that could then be taught to others. Note that in this group women outnumber men by roughly three to one, and most are young. Thus, we use a whole different approach than that used by the largely middle-aged to aged male Coven members."

Rosa had already noted the large number of young woman and the fact that they seemed to have an important role in this group. She still was not going to use their self designation, "the Omega Project," even in her own mind, until she knew more about what it entailed.

"The first point is that the level of communication among 'awakened' Omega members is extraordinary – almost total, all current thoughts and emotions, physical and mental. Working together, we then have some capability on non-psychic persons, reading thoughts, and some modest ability to compel movement. We have no capability to access memories. We have no psychic powers of any other kind – no fortune telling, no telekinesis.

"We are going to start with a simple example of the first kind. Here is a newspaper. Please turn to any page, and mark a point where you want me to begin to read."

Rosa did so, in the middle of a long paragraph on in inner page. She still spoke no word.

Ken started, "The…." at which point the other three members, not looking at the page, then added each word in the right order as rapidly as Ken could read. They then got up and started to walk around the room, still speaking as though they were one person. After a few minutes, they stopped.

Rosa was stunned. "Never had I even dreamed," and then she stopped.

Ken gave her the paper, "Rosa, you pick a spot on any page, and start reading it to yourself. Do not move your lips; do not indicate where on the page you start." Rosa picked a paragraph even farther back in the paper, and started to read it silently to herself. To her amazement, the same four people were parroting her every word, again in sequence. When she stopped, startled, they stopped. When she started on a different paragraph, they started again.

Rosa was in a strange quandary, for in her heart of hearts, she had always hoped that her Gypsy training would raise her to that level, a level rumored to have existed in a very few Gypsy women each century, and even then it was selective. Some people, most people, simply could not be read. But Rosa was very good, among the best in the Spanish Calé Gypsy Kingdom, which was why she had been chosen, requested, by the Romanian Rom leaders.

Rosa was speechless, torn between too many emotions: fear, anger, amazement, envy. She simply couldn't sort them out. So much had happened, and clearly there was so much she had not been told, and lies, now clearly in great numbers.

After a couple of minutes, Jill said simply, "I think we can help each other."

Then suddenly Rosa asked Ken, "I worry about my comrades. Could they be in danger, too?" Ken replied, "You mean Vlady and Hector? I hope not. My guess is that there were parallel efforts: the Gypsy diagnostic effort and a non-psychic eradication effort mounted in secret. I don't think that the Covens would dare challenge the Gypsies too openly unless there was an immediate great benefit, as might have happened if Gabriella and Jonathan's teams had been simultaneously destroyed."

Once again, Rosa was amazed at the casual way Omega had penetrated the Gypsy effort.

Ken continued, "But while we are on the topic, they know of you and you of them. What must they think when your house is blown to smithereens? No accidental gas explosion. Then the fire department will soon learn that there are no bodies. This is bound to cause all sorts of repercussions."

From behind Rosa, Frank caught Ken's eye and shook his head side to side, the signal for negative. He then turned off the generator since it seemed to have no effect on Rosa and was causing everyone else headaches.

Rosa finally said, "There is a message I must send. Do not fear for its contents. Will you trust me in this?"

Ken glanced quickly at Gabriella and then Michelle. Both gave slight nods yes.

Ken gave her a satellite cell phone, and said, "The best reception is out on the patio. No one will eavesdrop on you."

Meanwhile, high above the valley floor, Michael had been well briefed by Sergeant Morales on the events of the hour. He was easily able to keep track of the car from the second Merced house as it drove south and west on country roads with Roberto following. The fleeing car was now heading for heavily traveled Interstate 5, and Michael feared he could easily lose it before Roberto could catch up. Moreover, the dust plumes from the dirt roads defeated any attempt to get high-quality digital photos of the car's license plate, even with Michael's excellent optical capabilities, and then there were also power and phone lines to avoid.

Simon's car eventually reached a rural onramp to Interstate 5, and merged with the traffic, heading south. Fortunately, traffic was light, and much of it was heavy trucks, so Michael could keep track of the car. Even better, there were no power or phone lines in or near the freeway right-of-way in this stretch, so Michael dropped down in elevation to only about 150 feet above and perhaps 500 feet behind Simon's car, got a lock with the auto-tracking device, and took seven high-quality pictures before he was forced to pull up above an overpass that he was rapidly approaching. He dropped back, fairly certain he had not been seen by the car because he was too high to be in the car's rear-view mirror.

Back at a safe 2,000-foot elevation, and staying well behind the car while maintaining the auto-track lock, he projected the seven shots on his cockpit laptop. All were acceptable, so he took the best, pulled up his advanced pre-release Adobe Photoshop program, and isolated the license plate. Then he went through a series of digital filters, enhancing, expanding, until he had a slightly blurry but fully legible license number.

He then locked into Roberto's non-police Omega radio frequency, and in a tersely coded message described car, license, and location.

Roberto immediately placed an all-points bulletin with the California Highway Patrol (CHP), based on the simultaneous explosions with probable cause of attempted murder and arson. Possible terrorist connections were hinted to get CHP attention. The request was for a tail, not a pickup, unless the vehicle attempted to leave the country or the occupants stopped and attempted to disperse.

Finally, he alerted Tim and Jennifer in the Los Angeles safe house. Jennifer was still at UCLA, and could not return fast enough, but she went to a nearby Sunset Boulevard bus stop for a potential pickup, if the fleeing car perchance used the San Diego Freeway just west of campus. Within about 20 minutes, Tim had gathered two other full Omega members in their Volvo sedan, drove to a point where they could access all three major north-south freeways and waited for directions.

In about 15 minutes, Roberto got a call on the standard CHP frequencies that the fleeing car had been spotted, and an off-duty CHP officer in his family car had a tail on it. Additional unmarked cars would be assigned, with the next coming on at Buttonwillow, in Kern County, and by the Tejon Pass, on Interstate 5, they would have a rotating set of three unmarked vehicles as a tail, with one CHP cruiser as backup roughly one mile back.

Roberto gave effusive thanks for the effort, and continued on I-5 south but well behind the fleeing car. Within about 15 minutes, he too joined the growing parade, also about one mile behind the fleeing car that, fortunately but probably intelligently, was driving right at the speed limit and was thus about the slowest vehicle on I-5. At the base of the Grapevine grade on I-5, Simon stopped for gas. As soon as he left, Roberto also topped off. This could be a long chase.

Michael by now was running low on fuel, and peeled off to land and get gas. He would be little help as they entered the congested air space of the Los Angeles basin, but the surface pursuit was now well in place.

By late afternoon, Simon's car was entering the Los Angeles area, and switched onto the San Diego Freeway to avoid the congested downtown L.A. freeway "stack." Tim was immediately alerted by Roberto on Omega frequencies. Traffic built up, but because it was a weekday in summer, it was not as bad as L.A.'s legendary traffic snarls. All cars continued to move south. Tim picked up Jennifer, and fell in behind Roberto's easy-to-spot Merced police car. It was too risky to try to get close enough for any psychic potential readings from Simon's car, and in any case the car's metal shell would reduce sensitivity.

By now it was clear that the fleeing car was headed south of L.A. and worries arose about a potential border crossing attempt at Tijuana. However, just north of San Diego, the fleeing car pulled off and moved east in the rough direction of El Cajon. It turned up several side streets, and finally ended up in the driveway of a very ordinary house tucked in among its neighbors. Surveillance responsibility was transferred to the El Cajon Police Department, with profuse thanks to the CHP for a job well done. Plain-clothed officers were posted at both ends of the street, covering all exits from the road the house was on, until Merced personnel could arrive.

Tim, Jennifer, and their team drove casually past the house. There seemed to be some sort of psychic potential in the people inside, but it was weak and confused. However, there were clearly several interesting folk present.

They had barely left the neighborhood when an older Buick drove up with four men on board. It parked directly behind the other car, and they all got out and walked into the house.

Tim and their team grabbed two rooms in a nearby motel, and waited. They would like to put a tracer on the car, but had to leave all that to Roberto, who was now briefing the El Cajon Police on the situation.

The next morning, they met Roberto for an early breakfast. There had been no signs of any activity at the house, and both cars remained parked in the driveway. With the approval of the El Cajon Police, Roberto had been able to place a tracer on the Buick, but the original car was impossible to approach because of placement and lighting.

El Cajon Police had information on the house, a one-year rental to an older couple from Pennsylvania. They had just started quiet inquiries in the neighborhood about the renters when at 9:16 a.m., the entire house exploded in a massive fireball. The blast was so large that it pushed the closest car into the one behind it and set it on fire. Wreckage came down on nearby houses, starting numerous small fires. In minutes, the whole scene was a chaos of panic evacuations, screaming sirens, and TV helicopters overhead. The conflagration even made the national news that night (if it bleeds, it leads…) especially because parts of five bodies were found in the smoking crater of debris.

It was only two days later that the coroner was able to determine that all were missing their hands.

Later that afternoon, police were able to determine that around 5:15 that morning, a car, probably a white Honda Civic, had been seen pulling out of the garage of another rented but unoccupied house directly behind and downhill from the house under surveillance. Records also showed that around 6:15 that morning, shortly after the San Ysidro border crossing into Mexico had opened, a similar vehicle had crossed into Mexico with three German tourists on board. They all had proper passports and Mexican visas, and the car license confirmed that it was a recent Hertz rental that had bought the proper Mexican insurance.

Within two days, arson investigators had identified the cause of the explosion to be at least 1,200 lbs. of plastic explosive RDX of military origin stored in the garage. Quite a bit of electronic debris, some of French origin, was found scattered around the neighborhood. No useful fingerprints were recoverable from any of it.

All further trace was lost at that point until almost a week later when the Hertz rental was identified in the parking lot of the Mexico City International Airport. It, too, was devoid of fingerprints other than a few in the trunk and under the hood that were quickly traced to Hertz maintenance employees.

CHAPTER EIGHTEEN

Repercussions, indeed!

The meeting took place in a villa outside of Trieste. There were beautiful gardens wrapped around and through an extensive grove of old olive trees. In the distance, a swath of the Adriatic Sea was visible. No other houses were visible in any direction, and in fact none existed for over a kilometer. The room had a dramatic view of the gardens and sea in one direction, but in all other directions, windows were covered and doors barred. A long and very narrow table was in the middle of the room, so placed that people on each side could reach out across the table and shake hands if they wished.

Right now, that was the last thing on anyone's mind.

Rather incongruously, three long, low centerpieces of flowers were spaced evenly along the middle of the table, lending a cheery effect somehow out of place with the gravity of all participants.

With their backs to the closed wall and a view of the sea sat nine Gypsies – six men and three women, with the latter carefully placed along the length of the table. The women were there to check on truthfulness, and it was because of them that the table had to be so narrow. On the wall behind the Gypsies and thus quite far from the table and well out of Coven compulsion range were three Gypsy men, each holding at the ready an AK-47 fully automatic rifle.

On the other side of the table were seven members of the European Covens, all looking distinctly nervous. They had been asked to remove their coats before entering the room, and were expertly frisked for hidden weapons. It was they who had called for this meeting at a time and place chosen by the dominant Gypsy kingdoms of Europe, the Spanish Calé, the French Manouches, the German Sinte, and the Eastern European Rom – by far the largest kingdom.

Karla was clearly in a cold fury. "I pledged my honor to the Calé for the safety of Rosa. Rosa is dead and I have been dishonored. You may now present what you know of the recent and tragic events," he spat out.

Gerard began, "We had nothing to do with the attempt on Rosa's life. In fact, we didn't even know about Rosa and what you were planning in Merced. We left this all to you and have laid low, mostly in Switzerland, until you could tell us more."

The eldest Gypsy woman in the center of the table moved her hand slightly in a calculated pattern, a movement invisible to Coven members because of the flower centerpieces. It was noted by Karla.

"However," Gerard continued, "after our first failed attempt to capture Professor O'Neal, the European and American Covens initiated parallel programs to eradicate the Merced telepaths by actions initiated by non-Coven scientists, including one group from in the Coven-controlled French company, L'Equipe de Nouveau Electroniques – ENE. These attempts were terminated by my order and to the best of my knowledge after the fake death of Professor O'Neal. But since there were several non-psychic informational and eradication efforts in parallel, and we did not share information on these in any detail, I am not certain of the status of the others, although I have been told they were all terminated. I know a little about one effort initiated by the German Covens, with Otto doubtless involved in at least an oversight role."

Karla barked out, "I want in writing the nature of all these activities, the people involved, and your active cooperation. You clearly had a role in controlling ENE, did you not?"

There were beads of perspiration on Gerard's forehead, beyond what one might anticipate based on the warmth of the room. "Some, perhaps at one time considerable, but not total." The eldest Gypsy woman made a different pattern on the table. Her index and middle fingers were held tightly together. Karla stopped, looked at it intently, then said in some amazement, "One of the high-level administrators of ENE was your male lover?"

Gerard instinctively slashed angrily at the woman's mind, and she visibly cringed. Karla raised his left hand slightly, and all three AK-47s were pointed at Gerard. The Gypsy to Karla's left moved laterally to get out of the trajectory of any bullet aimed at Gerard.

Gerard, seconds from death, immediately realizing his error, "I sincerely apologize. My action was involuntary. It shall not happen again."

"If it does, I can indeed assure you that it will never happen again," said Karla. "But we are now getting closer to the truth. So it appears that there are non-Coven ENE scientists, and almost surely other teams that we trust were more discretely controlled than ENE, who know enough about the

Merced telepaths to plan eradication efforts with or without your direct involvement? Did the Covens ever consider the damage that would be done if these scientists went public with what they know?"

"They know nothing of our powers, I swear!" moaned Gerard, whose shirt was now visibly stained with sweat. "It was always cast as an effort at industrial espionage and eradiation of potential competition."

"And I suppose you never used your powers to encourage your lover to do specific acts to especially please you," snarled Karla, "actions that might have alerted him to your powers of persuasion far beyond the ordinary? Or perhaps there were psychic threats involved?"

Gerard was silent, not daring to open his mouth. The eldest Gypsy woman made another surreptitious pattern. Karla noted it with open disgust.

"I should kill you right now, but I need your help to clean up this mess. I want your lover delivered to us for interrogation. You might be allowed to live if you are extremely honest and helpful. He must die!"

"I will meet you in Paris next Monday at a time and place we choose. Your lover will be with you. That is all. Get out of my sight!"

All the Coven members left quickly, happy to be alive, but aghast at Gerard's duplicity.

After a few minutes, the Gypsies relaxed, moved the tables to a more logical pattern, pulled the chairs into a comfortable ring, and opened the rest of the windows. The cross breeze soon cooled the room. The armed Gypsies moved out to take up guard positions around the villa.

Karla began, "Rosa is not dead." Stunned silence. "Further, her life was saved at the very last minute by the Merced telepaths, most of whom are young women."

He could not have startled his audience more if he had said Rosa had been saved by little green men from space ships.

The amazement was compounded as Karla continued, "Rosa proposes we meet the Merced telepaths at some neutral location. They do not have any quarrel with us, and Rosa says their powers are both impressive and benign. But they cannot tolerate Coven domination and 'feeding' activities that they rank as the worst sort of torture and murder, a position by the way close to the Gypsy consensus."

"Finally, they are fully aware of our activities, including Hector and Vlady, but will do nothing about them."

The room fell silent. Each was thinking long thoughts about their way of life, their history as wanderers and outcasts, the gratuitous slander, and the persecutions, some of which, however, were based on unfortunate activities by a few eastern European Gypsies involving peasant children. These medieval activities were not that different from the Covens' "feedings" until Gypsies realized that such activities were mental poison leading to madness, as well as generating legitimate hate and fear among the non-Gypsy populations. Some of these fears were mirrored even today in the surprisingly bloody "fairy tales" dating from those times.

Finally Karla continued, "I think it may be time for us to reconsider our relationship with the Covens. It is clear that much of what they told us about the Merced telepaths was at the very least slanted. But first, we must learn more about these Merced telepaths. I will contact Rosa and ask her to make the arrangements in Merced. I want all of you present at this meeting if it can be so arranged. Meanwhile, I want maximum effort in France, which seems to be the locus of the problem."

"But we must remember that we have always fostered the view that as Gypsies we have some psychic powers of a relatively harmless sort, fortune telling and such, as opposed to the brutal Coven tactics. We have relatively little to fear from public knowledge, but if Coven tactics became known, the backlash against them would be awful. Even so, go with great care. There are unknown people out there who are clearly capable of murder, and they would not hesitate to do so if we threatened their still-obscure goals."

CHAPTER NINETEEN

Three-weeks later, Roberto was sprawled in an easy chair on the patio of the Midpines safe house, reveling in the mountain coolness and the beautiful view of thunderheads building over Yosemite National Park. About half of all Omega members were present, mainly those already seen by Rosa and the rest of Gabriella and Victor's valley members, plus the small Maricopa group. Very few members were present from the Winters and Davis teams. Jonathan was down from Oregon. Rosa was seated next to Roberto.

Roberto began, "Well, kiddies, the plot thickens! We got lucky in that the fire department was able to save most of the second house, and useful fingerprints were obtained. We have a match among the prints to those we surreptitiously took of all the ENE members in Merced last year. It turns out he was a Frenchman named Simon, who appeared to be involved in setting up electronic surveillance at ENE's purported Merced headquarters. In any case, he was electronically capable, and all information from Rosa's house went to him directly, some by wireless, some by hidden landlines.

"Second piece of luck. Simon had a dental problem while he was here, and while we do not have full records, the dentist did take X-rays of the left side molars. They are a match to one of the bodies found in the El Cajon blast. Simon is no more. Our boys play lethal, it seems, even with their own. We suspect but cannot prove that the other four bodies were from Mexican illegals seen in Merced in the past few weeks that did not seem to have any gainful employment.

"The recollection of a Hertz rental agent at LAX confirms a German rented the Hertz car later seen crossing the border. The German had a passport, the credit card was real, and had funds, but the backup information was all forged. Further, it appears that same German had rented Hertz cars on two-week rentals often before, roughly every two weeks, according to the Hertz records, always with Mexican insurance. They had all been returned with roughly 125 miles on the odometers, too few for a Mexican visit.

"At the border, the white Honda held three men, all of whom appeared potentially Germanic and carrying German passports.

"Thus the most plausible hypothesis in my mind is that this was a German-run operation that hired Simon as Merced point man because of his prior ENE-based knowledge of Merced. They could then stay far away from Merced and close to the border, with plans permanently in place for a surreptitious exit via a backyard fence to the second car.

"The question then arises as to why they were so interested in Rosa? I think what occurred is Simon and his German handlers were aware of the Gypsy involvement from the inside, and were using Rosa as bait for Merced psychics. Their hope was that any remaining Merced psychics would be intrigued by Rosa and eventually make themselves known. We picked up a lot of sophisticated electronics surveillance stuff mounted so that any visitors to Rosa would be photographed, and if they came to see Rosa in any numbers, they could all be blown to bits. The loss of Rosa was just collateral damage. Regretfully, there is at least a possibility that Simon was successful and downloaded pictures from Rosa's cameras before we discovered and disabled the surveillance. This information may well now be in the hands of the Germans. At that point, with the surveillance disabled, Simon went lethal. The delay of several minutes between the disabling of the surveillance and the explosion could well have been caused by Simon needing additional authority. Or it could have been that he had to go to backups when the bomb under Rosa did not explode, since we had disarmed it several weeks ago. It was hooked, Rosa, to that switch near your knee.

"If this is true, then the motive appears to be vengeance, a freelance operation probably to strike back at those who burned out Otto's mind. I am really sorry that we were not able to get good psychic readings from the El Cajon house before they fled, but Tim and Jennifer did have indications that something was unusual at that house."

Ken chimed in, "Could it be that they had made an effort to shield the house from electromagnetic radiation once they learned that we had some psychic electronic hardware? Recall I had to use the interference device in the kidnap attempt, and that information certainly got back to the Covens in the Sussex meeting. If so, this is not good news."

Ken continued, "Thanks, Roberto. You have done wonders. I do regret that Merced keeps showing up as the hotbed of Central Valley terrorism in the Department of Homeland Security computers. Rosa, you have better news, I hear."

Rosa had by now lost all her reticence, and spoke freely. "I have a formal proposal for as many of you as you want to meet with leaders of the four major Gypsy Kingdoms at a site in Mexico near the Baja California "Parque Nacional Constitución de 1857," called by everyone San Pedro Mártir for the region. It is high up in the mountains in a pine forest. They have rented a local ranch for two weeks, starting October 1, under the condition that the owners and all the staff make themselves scarce. There is a dirt airstrip close to the ranch. No other people are within miles, and several young Gypsy men will act as guards, but they will be well away from the ranch buildings on the access road.

"There will be nine of them, plus myself, Hector, and Vlady. I propose to have Hector and Vlady fly down by themselves in a charter aircraft. Based on past meetings, at least three will be high-level Gypsy female psychics, one of whom may be my old Calé trainer, Victoria. She is a better psychic than I am, by far, but she could not handle the Merced assignment because her English is weak. They include these women to check on the truthfulness of the speakers. Their ability to sense lies is limited to about two meters at most, so they will want these women to sit close to you.

"I sense that the leadership, which has never liked Coven tactics, may be ready to switch sides completely in this matter. Loss of Gypsy support would be a serious blow to the European Covens, especially the Eastern European Covens, because we know so much about their activities. But beyond that, they are very interested in your goals, which I myself, while I think they are benign by all your actions, don't really know. They are giving no hint of this meeting to their Coven contacts. In fact, there seems to be some sort of Gypsy-Coven collaboration in France to clean up some sort of distasteful Coven mess."

CHAPTER TWENTY

Things were rapidly spinning out of control.

All of Karla's carefully detailed plans for this meeting, the tables, location of chairs, sight lines, security, all were in tatters.

The Americans had arrived almost simultaneously in two planes, one of which was clearly a charter, since the pilot of that plane stayed on the air strip with both planes; a third was expected at any moment with Hector and Vlady.

The Americans, all tall and casually dressed, bounced into the main room and promptly spread themselves out from wall to wall. Rosa was chattering away with Victoria like a schoolgirl, and a young, tall Hispanic couple was joining with them, all conversing in Spanish. Two young Americans, clearly an affectionate if not married pair, found the big overstuffed chair, into which they delightedly plopped, with the girl on the man's lap. One young man, the pilot of one of the planes, was busy stoking the fire in the large, rock fireplace because it was a bit chilly in the room.

Finally, an older-looking man, most likely the famous Professor O'Neal, wandered over in his polo shirt and Bermuda shorts, with what appeared to be his wife in tow.

"Welcome. I'll bet you are Karla. I am Ken O'Neal, and this is my wife, Jill. Thank you for arranging this meeting."

"It was my pleasure," responded Karla formally in good but slightly accented English.

One of the Gypsy women, Marta, looked at Karla in amazement, and shrugged her shoulders. She had no idea now where to place herself, so she grabbed about the next most comfortable chair. Since she knew little English and no Spanish, the swirl of conversation was just babble to her. But she had never felt such power as in this group of ebullient Americans. There was something new here. She sat, observed, and waited. She was good at observing and waiting.

"You must be thirsty after your trip. Would you like something to drink?" asked Karla. As on a signal, one of the other Gypsy women opened a rather ordinary cooler and started to pull out bottles of soft drinks, lemonade (she had heard all Americans like lemonade), ice tea (in her native Moroccan tradition, heavy with mint), and French wines, both red and white, including a very good Pouilly-Fuissé.

"Wonderful" said Professor O'Neal, and immediately went for the Pouilly-Fuissé. Good taste in wines, thought Karla. So, these Americans, unlike Coven members, drink wine. One more bit of information to add into the mix. Without hesitation, Professor O'Neal asked for the Pouilly-Fuissé in French, which was the native language of the Gypsy woman.

"How did he know?" asked Karla to himself. "Did he read her mind? Was that just a good guess?"

The Romanian Gypsy, Marta, seated in the chair, motioned secretly to Karla. Karla wandered over, and squatting next to her chair, had a low-voice conversation that lasted a couple of minutes. Everybody ignored them and bounced around the room as they pleased.

Karla stood up, walked over to near the fireplace, and clapped his hands three times, loudly.

The room quieted.

"I offer you all my apologies. I had carefully planned this meeting based on our prior experience with Coven members, who can be brutal and effective in domination when operating together. We fear their powers, and we feared you. But you have, in minutes, changed everything. I have been told by our best psychic that what is present here in this room is simply unprecedented in our long, long experience with psychic phenomena.

"It appears that you are continually in communication with each other, even across the room, and we expect farther yet.

"It appears that you are continually in love with each other, although that word does not seem to adequately reflect what is clearly a higher reality.

"We think that we are in the presence of a single entity with many parts.

"There is also just a tiny hint that your powers are so great that at any second you could instantly control all of us, even probably kill us by your psychic power alone.

"But it is also clear to us that you have no intentions here except to leave this meeting with us as your friends and confidants, helping you to achieve some truly transcendental goal of which we know nothing except that which you have already achieved.

"I salute you. I envy you. Please help us to be like you. I offer you all the resources of all the Gypsy people. Perhaps together we Gypsies can escape our centuries of exile and join the human race as full participants."

The room was silent. Nobody moved for long moments. Suddenly the Romanian Gypsy started to cry, sobbing uncontrollably, yet her face was creased with a massive smile. Rosa, Victoria and the other Gypsy woman went quickly to her side, holding her in a close embrace.

Rosa turned and said, "Marta says thank you. At the end of Karla's speech, she felt such a wave of love and acceptance as she had never dreamed was possible. We all felt it, too, at different levels. It was beautiful. We simply cannot conceive of people who could be something so beautiful as that to be anything but holy. We are yours, body and soul."

Ken said. "Everybody sit down. This may take some time. But before you do, can I recommend to any wine lovers this Pouilly-Fuissé? It is magnificent." There were a few moments of chaos, people grabbing drinks, moving chairs, but at the end there was a rough circle with the fireplace at the center where Ken stood. Gypsies and Americans were completely mingled at random.

"What we all felt was a partial "awakening" of the most sensitive Gypsy psychics. Regretfully, the effect didn't linger long, and when the bond was broken, there was an immense sadness for something beautiful lost. Marta felt it most, and suffered most when it vanished. I do not know enough about the nature of your powers to know how we might make the "awakening" more permanent. This is something we will work on with you. We will also want to survey your young people, especially women, to see if we can raise them to this level early in life, around age 16 to 22 years seems best.

"But I also want to correct a suggestion of Karla's. No, we could not kill you. Dominate? Yes. Killing you would essentially kill us, too.

"As for reading your current thoughts, Rosa has or will tell you that is easy for us, but we have not done it consciously here with you. I did catch a thought from Karla when I, without thinking, asked for the wine in French. My mistake."

Ken paused. The sound of an approaching aircraft was heard, getting louder by the second.

"I took the liberty of asking Hector and Vlady to fly down with about the nicest cold lunch available in Sacramento."

Michelle chimed in, "A few seconds after we heard the plane's engine, you may have felt something." Marta and Victoria both nodded yes.

"What you felt was all Omega Project members teaming up to scan for intelligent life. We were able to scan out several kilometers in all directions, assuring ourselves that the occupants and contents of the plane were as expected. By the way, you might run some of this tea to your guards down the road. They are getting both anxious and thirsty."

Ken continued, "On a more serious note, we have a bad problem with the Covens. It appears that the attempt on Rosa's life was a byproduct of the attempt of German Coven members to destroy us in retribution for what we did to Otto. Simon, an ENE employee, was merely used as a tool because of his knowledge of Merced. He was murdered, as were his four support personnel, in the San Diego house explosion. The Germans escaped with additional knowledge and probably pictures of at least some of our members.

"They are aware that we have some technology, a mind-interfering static device, that I was forced to use in their presence to save myself from a Coven 'feeding' in San Diego. They are trying to duplicate it while becoming more adept at electromagnetic shielding. They are a serious threat."

"Germans?" Karla exclaimed, now thankful that they had let Gerard live after they had killed his ENE lover in Paris.

Karla continued, "We have decided that our tolerance of Coven feeding activities must cease, as will all Gypsy-Coven cooperation. They will then certainly add us to their enemies list, and as you know, Coven resources are considerable. They have effective domination over many companies, especially in Europe, and have thus enormous non-psychic resources – resources we cannot come close to matching. So we, too, are at risk. I expect that they realize that the prevalence of psychic sensitivity in the Gypsy kingdoms make us attractive targets for their bestial 'feeding' activities."

"However, like you, we are tough, but unlike you, we are numerous. So now we must begin to chart a new joint future, free to evolve in the direction you have pioneered, careful to protect ourselves from Coven attacks."

Ken responded, "This may be harder than you think. We have great problems trying to launch preemptive actions, but we work best defensively defusing threats, even though in this defense we may and have ended up killing numerous Coven members.

"One of our most effective defenses is that we can detect any Coven 'feedings' from many miles away. While we try any way we can to block 'feeding' attempts, which by the way weakens Coven capabilities sort of like drug withdrawal symptoms, we can easily detect the entry of a new Coven into a new area as soon as they have their first 'feeding.' I propose one of our first actions is to map current Coven activities in America and Europe, identify all members, and examine their non-psychic capabilities before any attempt at suppression is attempted."

Karla responded, "Agreed. We will call this the San Pedro Mártir accords. Further, I pledge on my honor on our sacred kris that what I have learned today about your capabilities I will forever preserve in secret, and I ask all my colleagues to do the same."

Each Gypsy in turn swore an oath in the Romany language, followed by a strange gesture of arms and hands to the forehead.

"Karla continued, "This will take some serious planning. We will start setting up safe houses and resources for your members when they come to Europe. You will be amazed at how easily we avoid European surveillance of any kind, and especially our ability to somehow vanish from the computer files. Our Gypsy hackers are fantastic and extremely discreet."

By now Hector and Vlady were staggering in the door with boxes under their arms and large, wheeled coolers in tow, straight from Biba's fantastic Italian kitchen in Sacramento.

Karla said to them brightly, "We are finished. Let's throw a feast in honor of the San Pedro Mártir accords. Someone please bring the guards back to join the party, as they are clearly no longer needed."

Ken said, "They are already on their way back." Karla beamed approvingly.

Hector and Vlady looked at each other in amazement at the completely mixed American and Gypsy gatherings all around the room, chattering in several languages, completely at ease with each other. Vlady saw the famous Marta, their best Romanian psychic, head to head with Michelle, although

neither knew the other's language. Meagan was chattering animatedly with
a young Austrian Gypsy, who was clearly appreciating the attention. A
couple, whom they guessed must be Tim and Jennifer, who they knew were
on the Merced team, were in an overstuffed chair, each drinking wine from
the other's glass, oblivious of the party swirling around them.

This was not at all as they expected. What had happened? Where were
the formal tables, rows of psychics checking truthfulness, armed security?
Where was the traditional Gypsy caution and restraint? This looked like a
happy riot. What had happened in less than 30 minutes before their arrival
that had changed everything?

An older man wandered over and gave a glass of the Pouilly-Fuissé to
Vlady. "I want to thank you for all the help you have given my research
team. Please have this wine. It is great."

"Who are you," Vlady stammered? "Ken O'Neal," Ken replied. "But you
are dead!" Ken couldn't resist the old joke, usually and incorrectly ascribed
to Mark Twain, "The rumors of my death have been greatly exaggerated."

Sensing their wonder, Ken continued, "The San Pedro Mártir accords have
resulted in the Merced psychics – our name is the Omega Project – and the
Gypsy Kingdoms joining with all their spiritual and physical resources into
a binding accord. We pledge close collaboration for the advancement of
both groups and in defense against our shared enemies, the Covens. From
now on, we work together. You should talk to Karla. There as a Romany
oath you must swear to with all your hearts to be part of the effort."

The sun was starting to set. The Omega teams began to gather themselves
with many hugs and some tears. Rosa would return with the Gypsies, who
tomorrow would use circuitous land routes that would eventually lead them
to Mexico City and Europe. Hector and Vlady would return to and stay
in Merced to help coordination with the joint efforts while keeping their
eyes out for future non-psychic Coven actions. Several Omega members,
including the by-now quite powerful Meagan, planned to transfer to Europe
next spring (one might guess Austria would be her first choice). Gabriella,
Victor, and some others of their team would go to Spain next Spring to
initiate Gypsy training programs there with Rosa and Victoria, while Ken,
Jill, Betsy (because of her knowledge of Coven practices) and Michelle
would do the same in Austria, meeting there with Meagan, Karla, and
Marta.

Later that summer, these and roughly seven additional high-level Omega members would attempt their first passive scans for detection of "feeding" activity, first in Vienna, then Paris. Since this required at least seven Omega members to stay for a few weeks in a major city, this could be viewed as a vacation. Ken was quick to alert Omega members who had never sensed a feeding, "This is no vacation. Once you sense a Coven 'feeding' you will never sleep completely soundly again for the rest of your lives because of your nightmares."

If all goes well, they might even attempt by fall a partial city scan for Coven activities.

Karla stood at the end of the runway as the last of the three planes winged north. He felt simultaneously elated and emotionally drained. Marta stood by his side, tears streaming down her face. "I have tasted heaven," she said. "Now I want to die."

Karla said, "We need you, Marta, since through your powers many more of our people will be able to share what you have felt. You will taste heaven again, many times, before you die."

CHAPTER TWENTY-ONE

It was a week later. Jill and Ken slipped into UC Davis Newman Center for Mass, since they had been assured by Frank that no one who would recognize Ken would be present, even if they could penetrate his disguise. But Ken and Jill loved the service, the students, and the young parents. Omega members were attending these Masses and permeating them with psychic charisma so that the crowds were growing each month, some of whom weren't even Catholic. The students were the most socially conscious group on campus, using their vacation for projects in Tijuana, El Salvador, and migrant labor facilities in the Central Valley. Even though Newman had gone to five Masses each Sunday, it was often hard to get a seat. Forewarned, Jill and Ken came early.

Her name was Kate. She and her husband were but one of a growing number of young UC Davis parents who were bringing their families to the Newman Center. The parents had formed a "Children's Church" that took all the young children out of the chapel until after the homily was finished. Out they bounced, dozens of children, smiles on their faces. Back they came 25 minutes later, carrying their little projects in their hands, full of life and promise. And the parents were such a nice-looking group, several interracial, all joyous.

Kate had been very pregnant last time they had come about a month ago. Today she showed up with her baby, cradled in a kind of sling over her shoulders – surprisingly chic as well as clearly effective. The rumble of tiny feet subsided as the children left for their service, and Kate turned to look at her newest child. A beautiful smile highlighted a tender mother-child bond, and suddenly there she was, broadcasting telepathic love without any reserve, filling the chapel with her love for her child, without any hint that fully 20 surprised Omega members were tuned in to this the most profound joy that any woman will ever have. Ken and Jill instinctively held hands, not wanting this hymn to Kate's child to fade, not wishing to intrude, but fascinated that Kate, who had never shown more than marginal telepathic sensitivity, could now broadcast powerfully to the entire chapel.

Gently, Ken and Jill joined their love with Kate's, opening to Kate the joy that the entire community felt at this blessed mother-child moment. Slowly

222

Kate raised her eyes from her child, looked out, and saw Ken and Jill, beaming their love to her. Stunned, she suddenly felt the warm embrace of 20 loving minds, and she was with them and they with her.

"So now it begins," Ken murmured to Jill, and held her tightly.

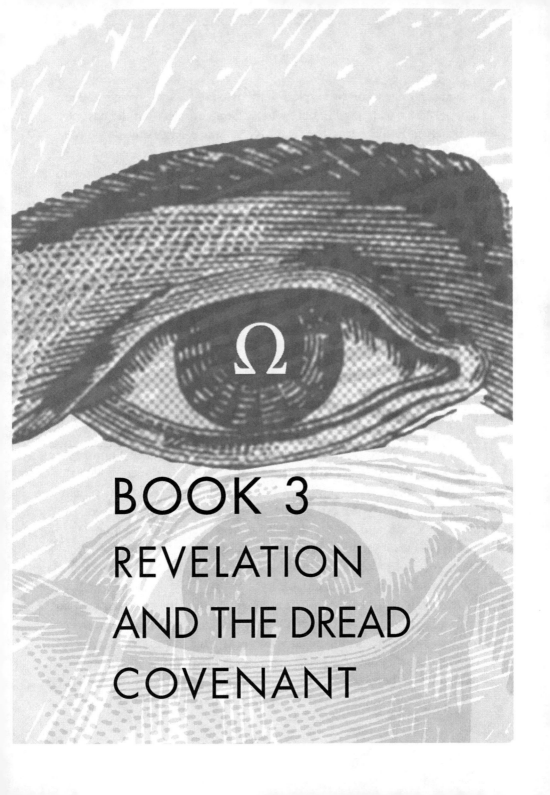

BOOK 3
REVELATION
AND THE DREAD
COVENANT

CHAPTER ONE

The gray and rainy day was typical of the late fall season. Visitors to the Hohenzollern Castle, traditional home of German royalty in the past but now safely in France, were few. The Alsatian grape harvest was long over, the tourists had all gone, and local inns and restaurants gave many of their people vacations since business was so slow. However, the Boar's Head Inn was fortunate to have a mixed French-German scientific planning group for a future international congress rent out the entire facility for a three-day mid-week retreat. Ten modestly affluent but geeky types filled all the inn's rooms, and they were taking all meals but one, the conference dinner downtown, in the inn's restaurant. While using the attached conference hall, they asked for, and got, confidentiality agreements from the staff.

Henri was over in the corner working with a young student named Philippe installing what looked like a complicated short-wave radio. Everyone else sat around with various forms of morning drinks, lattes and cappuccinos for the most part, while dipping into baskets of fresh croissants and other baked goods. The Germans in particular seemed to appreciate good French cooking. Finally, Henri turned to Jean, who nodded yes, and the unit was turned on. Nothing appeared to happen, and after a few looks at the dials, Henri and Philippe joined the others.

Jean began, "What we have installed is a unit developed by L'Equipe de Nouveau Electroniques (ENE) under suspicious circumstances earlier this year. We have no idea what it does, but it appears to be defensive in nature against some electromagnetic spying. One unit was shipped to Bayer, two more were made, and now all three have disappeared from ENE inventory. However, a prototype still existed that was scheduled to have been dismantled, but I intervened and saved it. It is operating now, but I have no idea if it is effective or what it does.

"Thank you all for coming in great secrecy to this, the first meeting of a group still without a name worried about strange happenings in French and German research companies. This meeting has arisen from a series of individual casual conversations among trusted friends about strange doings that involve at the very least gross misallocation of company funds and at the very most murder and psychic domination of an unknown sort. I

226

think we are all worried enough to take extreme care that our group remain secret. For I assure you, the discovery of this meeting could result promptly in the deaths of us all."

There were startled looks around the room. This was a new level of concern that had not been heard before.

Jean continued, "I propose that I begin the story, because I believe that the French teams got into the investigation earlier than the Germans and have learned the most. Six of us are associated with the firm ENE. But every one of you probably has vital information, as all of you have, on you own, noticed things and begun quiet inquiries. There are some others who seem also to be curious, but these we have not invited as we feel they were being incautious. We will watch with some interest whether these others have 'unfortunate accidents' in the near future.

"All of our comments are being recorded for wide distribution into secure 'dead drops' so that in case of our joint demise, what we have learned will become fully public."

There was a further nervous rearrangement of chairs. The baked goods and lattes were put down.

Jean continued, "This all began from the strange case of Pierre LaCoste, a casual friend of mine at ENE and a rising star among low-level administrators. About two years ago, we were having a drink when this gorgeous young woman walked by our table. Pierre nudged me and made some comment about not throwing her out of his bed. He then opened up to me his inner turmoil about his sexuality, that he was strongly attracted to all sorts of women, and had in fact a few year's back a young mistress from the secretarial pool, until he met one of ENE's high-level associate directors, Victor Catillon. Totally at variance with his entire prior sexual experience, he suddenly found himself in a homosexual relationship with Victor. After each session, he would go away with feelings of satisfaction and pleasure, which appeared totally at variance with all of his past feelings. He was of course excited to be a favorite of a powerful person who could advance his career, and always pretended to relish these assignations. His career indeed took off, and he became one of our youngest assistant directors in the Research Division within six months.

"Shortly after that, he started to get unusual requests from Victor for assistance in new and very hush-hush projects. Pierre was asked to initiate transfers of funds and duties, which Victor could then approve. The focus appeared to be on industrial espionage on the rapid technical advances of a professor at the University of California, Merced – yes, there are several campuses besides Berkeley. Kenneth O'Neal was doing new and important work on thin-film superconductors. This bothered Pierre not at all. Included was setting up a front company in a town called Merced. It took a long time to even find where this backwater town was – it was nowhere near Berkeley or UCLA. He couldn't figure out how Merced got a University of California campus in the Central Valley backwater with its awful weather and atrocious food. This task was accomplished quickly, and serious data mining was started in the UC Merced Physics Department. This included very carefully monitoring all radio emanations of the department, such as cell phones and wireless laptops, but little new was learned that was not already publicly available.

"What bothered him was that some of the tasks he did were weird. He was asked, for example, to secretly set up wide-band digital data ROMs at paired sites – four corners of buildings used as the Catholic student community center, and four equivalent units about a block away. These were set up in Merced, Davis, and Berkeley, and interrogated once every two weeks. The data was then shunted to the Service d'Météorologie de France at Gif-sur-Yvette, and unauthorized computer time was used to see if there were extraneous signals from the paired sites. Vast amounts of CPU time were used for the task, but after each session, the summaries went to Victor alone, and all record of the search were deleted and replaced by fake data tasks.

"In addition, he was asked to initiate a rush project on a wide-band noise generator, whose prototype we see here. He could not figure why this was being done, and in fact one had to be very careful not to violate broadcast regulations of ORTF. Periodically, Victor would come down to the project, whose funds were being provided via a circuitous route and a satellite company in Trieste, and make comments on whether it was going well or not. We had no way of telling how he knew it was going well, since we had no real output other than broad-band noise. Still, he kept pushing us into rapid phase, amplitude, and frequency modulations.

"All in all, something very strange was going on, and Pierre was getting very nervous, which is probably why he opened up to me.

"I didn't talk again to Pierre for several weeks, when he told me in passing that the ENE effort in Merced was being folded due to the death of Professor O'Neal in a climbing accident. Clearly, the way he said this indicated some suspicion that O'Neal's death was not an accident, and he suspected ENE involvement.

"All was quiet until about nine months later when suddenly Pierre appears to have committed suicide late one night in the Seine River. A week later, I received a packet from a local advocate addressed in Pierre's hand. The note said that in case of Pierre's death this was to be sent to me in complete confidentiality. It was about six months old, roughly the time of O'Neal's suspicious accident.

"In his note, he said that all this might be nothing, but he was still nervous, and I was the only one he had talked to about this matter. In it, he detailed five types of information.

"First, Victor had some sort of code name, Gerard.

"Second, he had been in charge of maintaining a very pricey penthouse apartment in the 16th Arrondissement, which was notable for the heavy use of ENE anti-spyware technology. Yet, that property was never involved in legitimate (the term as used by ENE was very broad) ENE business.

"Third, he had been asked to squelch an investigation of the death of a gay man in the Montparnasse area last fall. A locally known young gay man had been found dead in his apartment when his roommate returned unexpectedly. He had no apparent wounds but a ghastly look of terror frozen on his face. At about that time, a Mercedes-Benz had been seen leaving the street in some haste, almost hitting a pedestrian, who recorded its license number. It was Victor's private car, one of three he owned. Pierre was asked to drive Victor to the house of a well-known prostitute, who was soon willing to swear that Victor had been with her all that evening. Other proofs were forged, such as phone records, and presented to the police, who soon lost interest in Victor. In the process, however, I had learned from the officer that there had been a steady string of disappearances of young people, mostly male and gay, from Paris for years. He agreed to show me the file, but when he looked it up, it was devoid of any real information.

He was greatly disturbed by this fact, as he himself had taken part in some of these investigations and provided materials that should have been in the file.

"Fourth, Pierre was asked to transfer a really large amount of funds to a bank in Spain that was closely associated with the ultra-conservative Catholic 'Opus Dei' movement. Yes, the same one in *The DaVinci Code*. These funds were used to buy a modest but remote chateau near the town of Montrichard, near the famous Chateau of Chenonceau, and to provide for its maintenance and upkeep essentially in perpetuity. Pierre was responsible for hiring the house keeper-cook, and her gardener husband, who were fervent Catholics. The story they were told was that the chateau was to be used for super-secret Opus Dei meetings designed to revert France to its Catholic faith from communism and materialism. A significant and continuing burse was also provided to the local parish.

"Finally, an ENE employee named Simon was given significant funds to establish some sort of operation in Merced well after the ENE pullout last summer. In the envelope were extensive receipts, memos, and other supporting information. I have placed this envelope, carefully copied, into the 'dead drops,' sort of as Pierre's last will and testament.

"I have since learned from Interpol that Simon was killed in a house explosion near San Diego, California, with both his hands missing. Fortunately, he had some dental work done, which was tracked back to a Merced dentist and hence Simon's name while he was working for ENE in Merced.

"Shortly after Pierre's death, Victor was reportedly accidentally killed in a trek in Kenya after falling into a gorge. It was days before a rescue party could get there, and by then the animals had eaten almost all the evidence.

"I have made quiet inquiries, and have learned, and not to my great surprise, Victor is now living in the Montrichard chateau under the name Gerard Rousseau."

Jean paused for effect. "This offers us an enormous opportunity. We know now that Victor/Gerard was one of this secretive group that at the very least possesses the power to dominate minds and is willing to kill to maintain its secrecy. We also know that it was expending significant resources in Northern California for a project that clearly had him worried about something. Finally, we know that he continues to be active. He was seen two weeks ago trolling for young men in the gay bars in Amboise on the Loire River. I have notified the local police to be alert for missing young men or woman, based on the Paris pattern.

"Now I want to turn the meeting over to our German colleagues. After they have finished, I want to summarize what we know or suspect. Fritz?"

Fritz stood at the front of the room, clearly once an athlete but now, though still impressive, becoming pudgy.

"Thank you, Jean. We work for the Bayer Group, which has an electronics division that on occasion has worked with ENE. We really had no inkling of a problem until the strange case of Otto Willmes. Otto was originally a Rhinelander who joined the company about five years ago as a management trainee. He was a rising star, highly effective in all sorts of tasks, and was deliberately moved about the company to get wide exposure to our programs. We all thought he was being pushed by someone in the directorship, but no obvious connection was made to any one director. His powers of persuasion were formidable, and he generally got whatever he really wanted from his colleagues. I can't say he was very popular. There was a hard and ambitious streak in him that didn't make for casual friendship.

"It was roughly a year ago when suddenly Otto was required to leave the company headquarters for a new confidential project at some unknown site. We were all told that his absence was to be for six months or more. Two weeks later, he turns up at the Frankfurt airport on a plane from San Francisco, a broken man, babbling in terror at the sight of strangers. The company immediately arranged for him to go into a psychiatric hospital near Munich, close enough so that he could have visitors once the doctors thought it was allowed in his treatment.

"However, one week later, before any of us had had a chance to visit, Otto was found dead in his room. The police were very interested in the Otto case, and checked to make sure that the hospital had used proper procedures. All the anti-psychotic medicines that Otto was receiving seemed suitable, although one was a rather old-fashioned drug not in current use, but still allowed under a doctor's care. However, in the inquiry, the night nurse who had administered that last dosage at 10:00 p.m. the night Otto died had retained a scrap of paper recording the required dose, because the medicine was not one she recognized. On the scrap of paper, the dosage was carefully written at exactly 10 times the dosage in the computer and in the doctor's prescription, and fully capable of causing a cardiac arrest. The inquiry found the nurse to be negligent, and she lost her license to practice. The company did not press charges, however, and she shortly was able to resume nursing in a small country clinic under close supervision since the error was found to be understandable.

"In the course of the investigation, the police found written records in the hospital guard's files that showed that three of the Bayer directors had been visiting Otto regularly, once each morning, another each evening, including the evening of the fatal dose. I am providing these names for the record.

"While this was worrisome, what followed was that there was a complete removal of all records of Otto's work from the Bayer computers. It was as though he had never existed. In particular, there was never any acknowledgement that he had ever been in San Francisco, and when I checked a week later, all that information was lacking in the Otto file, although we had heard for ourselves the original reports.

"Four of us, close friends for years, were discussing this during a hike in a local forest park. We soon found that each of us had seen some strange doings on the part of our directors, with the same three names that visited Otto appearing repeatedly. In some cases, one of us had been barred from deserved promotion by a requirement to promote Otto, and when the record was checked against original files, the original file was found to be sealed and confidential. In other cases, we had been asked to do tasks, at the personal request by one of these directors, that were against company policy, yet without a murmur, we had done it. It was always at a face-to-face meeting, never by a written order, and we all had this feeling that we had done something good and important that would eventually further our careers. Yet when we tried to explain it rationally to others, despite the strict requirement of confidentiality, we could not justify what we had done.

"Last month, Jean, with whom we had worked earlier on ENE business, came for an unofficial visit and told me of his efforts to track surreptitiously some strange ENE equipment that had gone to Bayer. I found that just after it arrived at Bayer, there was a shipment of drugs to San Francisco, and an ill-described electronics unit that might have been the instrument was on it. When we realized that date was just one week before Otto disappeared, on the way to San Francisco, all these amorphous worries started to jell into a serious conspiracy theory. We were clearly being manipulated against our wills by at least three senior Bayer executives into non-authorized tasks with no clear company goal. Otto had been sent for some task, predicted to be lengthy, but had been mentally destroyed immediately in a way hard to explain for a man as mentally tough as Otto."

"I have provided Jean with all sorts of additional documentation, much of which I have no idea what it means, but all of it suspicious."

A long pause followed. A fire had been kindled, and the only sound was its cheery crackling. Gradually, people returned to the lattes and pastries, but still with no conversation. Each was deeply absorbed in the profound implications of these doings, and a sense of fear and foreboding permeated the room.

Finally, Jean broke the silence. "The implication of all this is that we have in our midst a small group of powerful men capable of enforcing their will on others, masters of hypnosis or psychics of some unknown source that lies outside of science as we know it.

"These psychics, for whom we have not yet found a better term, are engaged in many activities, and are totally unafraid of committing murder when it suits their purposes. What bothers me is that the circumstances of the two known murders, Pierre and the gay man in Montparnasse, are so different. The Monparnasse murder, with the terror etched on the dead face, seems to be attributable to some group activity in torture and murder. The Pierre murder eliminated one of Victor's trusted associates, followed by Victor's faked death. Something seems to have gone terribly wrong with Victor's ENE operations. Perhaps this is tied to activities involving what appears to be a secret war with others in Northern California. On the base of the Otto experience, it appears they may be losing this war.

"We have several options:
1. Do nothing. Destroy these records, and go on our way avoiding these dangerous individuals.
2. Go to the police. Take all the records, and give them to the proper authorities. Certainly, there are individuals in these services who have

been marginally aware of these activities, and we could doubtless help them deepen their investigation. But based on prior experiences, such as Victor's faked death, they would flee, only to arise again with vengeance in their hearts for all of us.

3. Get allies. Find credible experts who are willing to help us uncover these monsters who kill so casually. Initiate research to better understand what they can and can't do, including, if necessary, kidnapping one of them. One variation of this is to try to find out what is happening in Northern California that has them so worried. At the very least, a search of California newspaper articles and the like would be useful, focusing on two areas:

a) the circumstances surrounding the deaths of Professor O'Neal and of Simon, and

b) the period between Otto's departure and return. Since this would involve no danger to any of us, I would recommend at least this action.

4. Go public. Take all these records to the press, and start major inquiries in all of the press. We could in principle do this without exposing ourselves, but the nature of the information would be such that many of us would immediately come under suspicion. However, confidentially sending Pierre's packet to the press might have the proper impact without involving any of us.

"The latter option has a certain attractiveness. I think that these individuals need secrecy for their own survival. If it became widely known that there were murderous psychics prowling Europe with powers unknown to science, there would be an avalanche of publicity that would sharply restrict their activities now and in the indefinite future. The value would be greatly enhanced if we find strange doings in Northern California about the same time, as this would energize the international press."

In the discussion that followed, the key point was how dangerous it was to have people with these special powers running around undetected and unchecked. A generic name was chosen for these creatures, Warlocks, and the group decided to call itself the most mind-numbing and boring name conceivable, and settled on "The Assembly of Organizational Auditors," with code names: supplies auditor (SA), travel auditor (TA), equipment auditor (EA), through to benefits auditor (BA), with numbers as needed.

The need for total secrecy was affirmed, to the death if necessary, as well as an effort to never, never be one-on-one with any of these Warlocks. It was decided that most of the group members lie low at any time, and that only small two-person teams were to make inquiries or do other actions at any time. TA and EA, Jean, and an ENE colleague were to check the web for news clippings in Northern California. They were also to start laying the groundwork for the Montrichard chateau surveillance.

A new meeting place and time was decided upon, January 15 in Metz, Germany, where there was a trade show to act as cover.

CHAPTER TWO

Metz was bitterly cold, and the rural inn chosen for the second meeting of
the Auditors was not up to the task of keeping the meeting room warm.
Still, it hardly mattered, as nervous energy was sky high. As promised,
there had been no contact between any of the Auditors for a month, except
for Jean's colleague, so anticipation was rife. They almost hoped that
somehow all these events would turn out to have an innocuous explanation.
It was not to be.

Jean began, "Big news. Almost immediately after the departure of Otto,
four businessmen with faked credentials were expertly kidnapped from
a house in Tiburon, California, on San Francisco Bay. When the police
began inquiries, it turned out that all aspects of their documentation were
completely fake, including letters of credit from a German bank. Rough
descriptions of the four men were provided, and one closely matches Otto.
Two weeks later, Otto is placed on a plane to Frankfurt, one-way ticket,
paid in cash. The flight attendants remember that he was accompanied
to the airport by three people, one man and two women, who mentioned
that Otto had been working on a big project and needed sleep. In fact, he
appeared very sleepy, and slept all the way across the Atlantic.

"The police report goes into great detail on how the kidnapping took
place, remarking that it was an exceedingly professional job. There was
a brief scuffle and some blood was found on a table edge. Pistols with
silencers were used to kill two Rottweilers, there was careful blockage of
electricity and phone lines, and other signs of foul play were evident, all
just one day after the men had moved into the rented house. All this was
covered in the press. There was one note that a strange electronic unit was
found in hall closet, and appeared to be some sort of radio of a unique
design. When tested, all it generated was noise. The police have it still in
the evidence room. It appears to be one of the three missing ENE units
Pierre was working on.

"As far as the police know, no trace of any of the men has been found.
They know nothing of Otto's return. Something else I had not seen
before. Pierre's packet mentions that the mysterious 16th Arrondissement

apartment in Paris was sold the very day after Otto's return.

"What can we make of this? Clearly, there was some sort of joint ENE-Bayer project of the Warlocks in Northern California that went horribly wrong. The competence of the unknown people, let's call them Ghosts, was extreme. They clearly could have killed them all, but we find instead Otto returned to Frankfurt a mentally broken man. Was he sent back as a warning of the power of these Ghosts? A warning not to try any incursions into their territory? And then why did the Warlocks kill Otto? Were they afraid he would talk, alerting the hospital staff of his Warlock status?

"So now our problem is compounded. We have these local Warlocks in some sort of conflict involving Northern California, using and developing ENE technology, which clearly did not help them when push came to shove. We have an even more powerful presence of Ghosts in Northern California. Strange instrumentation is being developed for purposes we do not know. Sacré bleu! What have we gotten ourselves into?

"I for one offer any of you release from our promises for your own safety. All records of your meetings with us will be destroyed. You can go home and try to ignore what has happened. I, for one, am frightened but extremely curious. We appear to have stumbled on an entire world running in parallel to ours but in complete secrecy."

There were no defections.

The German teams also had a report. They had made discreet inquiries into the three suspicious directors who had visited Otto. They indeed had a long history together, with a sudden improvement in the status of performance when the first two found themselves in the same division of Bayer. Progress had been rapid, aided by the untimely deaths of two people who would have blocked rapid advancement. They had several projects that were completely confidential. They occasionally took trips almost simultaneously, and their vacations often seemed to overlap. Looking more closely, it appears that the official record in the Bayer archives is somewhat at variance with open official record, including what looked like a murder indictment, later squashed, on one of the directors years ago. But there was nothing more that could be found in the open files.

A general discussion then ensued as to how the new findings complemented the earlier programs in Merced. It was agreed that Professor

O'Neal was a key player, but that his death (murder) was tied to the present conflict. If Professor O'Neal had been key, his purported loss had not obliterated his organization.

Alexis, coded as travel auditor #1, or TA1, was in the publicity department of ENE. It was his job to generate press releases on new products, real or imaginary, but in all cases exaggerated. He had come to ENE from the *Figaro* newspaper, a conservative but prestigious daily with strong ties to business and the government.

Alexis volunteered to travel to Merced with the cover of writing a freelance article on how the death of Professor O'Neal had destroyed a potential France-United States collaboration. Since they were uncertain whether or not there were any more Warlocks in ENE, one of the Auditors proposed that he use as cover a vacation in Majorca in March, with secret tickets to San Francisco, the largest city near Merced. The group decided that while in Merced, he should operate openly as a reporter.

There was a lot of negative comment on this scheme, since the Ghosts would probably recognize his presence and could respond like they did with Otto. However, Otto was clearly in the enemy camp, while Alexis was simply curious. In the end, it was decided to let him go on with the plan, but with backup cover by Jean in the nearby city of Modesto, which was also the home of the largest newspaper that covered the Merced area as well. His defense would be that, if he disappeared, a full record of everything learned about the Ghosts would automatically be made public.

238

CHAPTER THREE

By mid-March, all was ready. Jean left for a meeting in London, Alexis for a vacation in Majorca, then both flew to San Francisco for a meeting with tickets paid in cash. At the airport, a car was rented, and with abundant maps from MapQuest and Google Earth, they had no trouble getting to Modesto. Jean and Alexis found two motels, well apart. On the next day, Alexis went to the headquarters of the *Modesto Bee* to begin the research. Each day, they met well away from the city, and prepared a short report to be phoned back to Paris by Jean from a Modesto pay phone.

Day No. 1

The *Modesto Bee* was full of articles on Professor O'Neal, who was clearly a local celebrity of sorts. His work was pioneering, and a string of international visitors came to his lab in the physics department. In the past two years, rumors of breakthroughs in thin-film superconductivity were reported, with hints that this was the type of research that made Nobel Prizes. His students were in high demand, and went on to the most prestigious universities. There was some comment as to why O'Neal himself didn't leave, as he could easily have gone elsewhere. However, he seemed content, his lab was large and beautifully equipped, he was soon above salary scale at the full professor rank, he had a large circle of friends, he was involved with students at the local Catholic Newman Center, and his wife was just finishing her Ph.D., so it appeared that UC Merced was pulling out all the stops to keep O'Neal.

Day No. 2

For a backwater, Merced started to have a series of strange events about four years ago, with fatal car accidents, a murder, fires, exploding houses (four), student disappearances, and other unexplained activities swirling around the town and university. The *Bee* was full of these stories. A story about the murder of a young student called Bonny had a note that no cause of death was found on her, but her face was frozen into a mask of horror that one could never totally forget. That very day, five unknown men had been killed in a flaming car crash close to the scene of Bonny's murder. The parallels with the murder of the young gay male in Paris were obvious. If these five men had caused the death of Bonny, which the papers assumed, then their death was consistent with a secret war between Warlocks and Ghosts. There was nothing, however, that tied these events in any way to Professor O'Neal.

Day No. 3

By now, Jean and Alexis knew they had hit the jackpot. They realized that this was the focus of the Warlocks' attention. For example, there was an attempt on O'Neal's life in San Diego by an unknown bunch of Europeans, supposedly in search of his technology. Alexis pulled down the full record in the *Modesto Bee* of the ENE's move into Merced and the abrupt departure after the death of O'Neal. In the beginning, it was played up as a big move, raising the level of technology in Merced and promising a close university-ENE association with mutual benefits. Jean and Alexis knew how false these claims were, but the locals seemed delighted.

The untimely death of Professor O'Neal only a few weeks later was awfully suspicious. However, it had been fully investigated, and corroboration was gathered from a number of independent sources. The ENE departure followed shortly thereafter. Memorial services for O'Neal were extensive, first at the university, then a funeral at the Newman Center. The eulogies were reported in some detail, including many comments from students about what an inspiration O'Neal was to them in their spiritual growth.

The legitimate cover of the inquiry would naturally require Alexis to meet and discuss events with the Physics Department chair. After discussion with Jean, Alexis decided that she would attempt that the next day.

Day No. 4

A meeting was finally arranged, late in the day, with Professor Buchanan, who was a female faculty member. She was only too happy to mention that even after Ken's death, work was progressing very well with a new group of assistant professors recently hired, two of whom were Ken's students. Further, there was an excellent collaboration with a similar group in the UC Davis Physics Department, under yet another of Ken's students. The point is that she would welcome the return of ENE to Merced, and could assure them of a close and fruitful collaboration that was still doing world-class work in thin-film superconductors. She then toured Alexis through labs that included a high-power room-temperature superconducting cable, the best (she claimed) in the world and the key to remote siting of nuclear power plants, thus addressing greenhouse global heating problems.

Back in Modesto, Jean was intrigued by the reception Alexis had received. Perhaps an ENE front could be re-established in Merced to help investigations of the Ghosts.

Day No. 5

Alexis and Jean spent this day in Modesto, looking over the press reports on the strange doings for the past four years. The name of Sergeant Morales came up in some of the reports, and while Alexis proposed to check with him, Jean opposed doing so due to lack of a rationalization for his interest because he had no obvious ENE connection. However, a better timeline was established on the strange doings in Merced, which had all the aspects of a major Coven-Ghost war, with serious casualties. On the face of it, it looked like the Ghosts were losing.

Jean and Alexis gained more information on the dual house explosion last summer in Merced, one day before Simon was killed in a similar explosion in San Diego. Exploding houses seemed to be a consistent pattern in this inquiry. The most obvious reason would be to either kill the homes' occupants or to hide evidence such as fingerprints. Interestingly, there were conflicting reports in the newspapers and the police reports on the bodies eventually recovered from the wreckage. Originally no bodies were reported, then four, including two women, but they were all so shredded that identification was impossible. It was found that the first house belonged to a commercial psychic named Rosa, a Spaniard probably of Gypsy extraction, who had moved into the community a few months before and had a thriving practice with many satisfied clients who swore by her powers. It had been blasted by Claymore mines in the wall of a neighboring garage, and then obliterated by bombs under the floorboards that detonated as the house burned. But in the wreckage, fire and law enforcement investigators discovered that the house had redundant destruct mechanisms in place, with secure wiring to the second house about a block away. The electronics were sophisticated, doubtless ENE, but all code numbers had been erased.

"I would have never stayed knowingly in a house that was a bomb," mused Jean. "I wonder if Rosa knew about the explosives? Was she bait? And note the psychic connection."

Day No. 6

This day was dedicated to trying to obtain additional information on the kidnapping of Otto and his team. They found little of interest that had not already been put into the press. There were some loose ends, and it was notable that expected records seemed always to be missing. For example, the mileage on the rental car used by Otto's team indicated a serious trip just before they were kidnapped, but the location of this trip was never identified. There were no records of rentals of any boat large enough to hold the required people. This was pretty much a dead end.

They returned to Jean's motel about 7:30 p.m. after a frustrating day driving around the Bay Area. It was a Friday night, and traffic was atrocious. Jean was learning how to drive in California with a little less Gallic verve, as they had to talk themselves out of two potential tickets for rapid lane changing, which is a birthright among the French.

At their motel room, they kicked on the light, and two men, one a uniformed police officer, the other sort of professorial-looking, were ever so casually lounging in the only two comfortable chairs.

The policeman got up, flashed his badge, and said, "Please come in and make yourselves comfortable. I will order in a pizza if you don't mind. We need to have a little talk." Jean and Alexis had no choice but to accede, but an awful fear spread through their bodies at the thought of how quickly they had been uncovered. The mere thought of pizza was nauseating under the circumstances. On the other hand, there were four glasses on the table and a bottle of Napa Valley Pinot Noir, so it didn't look like their days were over yet.

"Please call me Juan," said the policeman, and the professorial type chimed in, "And call me Sam." It was clear the way the names had been spoken that they were fake. But there was not much they could do about it. They sat down on the bed while Juan dialed up a Round Table (the last honest) pizza, Italian sausage and onion.

Juan started, "We are a little sensitive to inquiring strangers around here right now, and we have real doubts about anyone French after the ENE program at the Merced physics department. There are still those who think ENE was somehow behind the tragic death of Professor O'Neal, and it became clear that ENE's main effort was to strip data from every UC Merced source, open and confidential, doubtless for its own reasons.

"The strange double house explosion was tied to an ex-ENE employee, Simon, who then perished in a similar explosion in San Diego. One would think that there was something inherently unstable about California housing construction, until one makes an estimate of the total tons of explosives smuggled into the United States for these pyrotechnics. Lots of high-level Gallic electronic equipment was strewn around the wreckage of all three houses, most likely of ENE origin. You aren't by chance ENE employees, are you?"

Silence. Minutes passed. Somehow neither Jean nor Alexis wanted to lie to these people who already knew so much.

Finally, Juan spoke, "Well, now that that has been established, why are you here? And while you are at it, why did you travel such separate routes, Madrid and London, if you both came from Paris, only to be reunited in San Francisco? There are lots of Paris-to-San Francisco flights, I'm sure you know. You were clearly trying to hide your trail on both ends of this jaunt. I have a feeling you are very worried people, perhaps even frightened."

Sam leaned forward in his chair, and seemed to be thinking or listening to something no one else could hear. "You should be frightened," Sam said quietly. "Perhaps it is time you should know what we all are up against in the Covens, which you call Warlocks."

CHAPTER FOUR

It was five days earlier when Roberto called Ken in Winters and said, "We may have company." Jean and Alexis had hit not one but several automatic triggers at the *Modesto Bee* archives, triggers carefully emplaced in the back issue search engine. A small team was sent down to Merced using a new safe house in the oak savannas, east of the city near Catheys Valley, and soon had the flight plans, motel rooms, and good surveillance photos. After the Day 1 report, bugs had been placed in both the motel rooms and the pay phone that Jean always used (patterns, the sign of amateurs). By Day 3, Omega had a pretty good rundown on Jean and Alexis, although they hesitated to initiate inquiries in Paris for fear of Coven surveillance. The invaluable Gypsy contacts were actually rather weak in Paris, but they remained a major asset for the future.

By Day 4, Omega was being overwhelmed with details, as the Frenchmen talked incessantly and freely in their Modesto motel room each evening. It became clear that they were researching strange doings in France and Germany, including Otto's return. New details were learned by Omega on the German Coven, and the neat dispatch of Otto. This nicely confirmed what the Gypsies had been told.

Jean and Alexis were reporting to a 10-person group of mixed French and German mid-level scientists and administrators who call themselves "Auditors," while they had coined the name "Ghosts" for the mysterious Northern California enemies of the Warlocks, as they called the Covens.

"Well, this event poses certain problems for us," said Ken. "The Auditors suspect that Coven powers are psychic and dangerous, but they don't know if the Ghosts are psychic. If we leave them alone, they would go back to their colleagues possessing knowledge that there is something mysterious around here that the Covens hated and tried to eradicate. There would be further investigations, and other facts might pile up to bring them to the conclusion that a different psychic group, the Ghosts, is also in existence. They have reasoned out that full public disclosure is the last thing Warlocks – and probably Ghosts – want, and have prepared 'dead drops' to make everything public should Jean and Alexis, for example, disappear from the face of the Earth.

"So what is the best we can hope? I think we should try to recruit them. We can be reticent about the nature of our powers, and emphasize instead that we are developing technology that threatened the Warlocks. My appearance to them would be a shock, and hopefully bind them to us more closely. I think, however, that they would not simply drop everything at this point, as they have learned enough to be scared and perhaps angry at these secret and ruthless power brokers, pulling strings and casually killing. I think we should tell them about Coven 'feeding' practices.

"I propose that Roberto and Jonathan should make the first approach in Modesto before Jean and Alexis leave to go back to France, and after their next telephone report, as long as they are still in the dark about our powers. I propose that Jill, Michelle, and I be in the next room of the motel, in wireless contact with Jonathan via an in-ear radio.

"Let's see how honest they are, while reinforcing the danger they are in playing with the Covens. We in turn could offer some level of information and protection, while they could be useful to us in our European programs next year. But they have to realize that the information we are giving them endangers both them and us."

Thus, it was five days later when Jonathan said, "You should be frightened." He got up, walked to the door, and let in a tall man of an indeterminate age (35? 45?) and two nice-looking women – one was quite young and very attractive.

"I am Kenneth O'Neal, and we need to talk. For obvious reasons – I am supposed to be dead. I will make myself scarce when the pizza arrives. But you are into this thing so deeply that if we do not help you, and soon, you will all be dead. My colleagues are Sergeant Roberto Morales of the Modesto Police Department and Professor Jonathan Campbell of the Department of Physics, retired. You have probably seen these names in the stories you uncovered."

"Pizza and wine. Not too bad," Ken started. "You have guessed a lot. We have had your room and the pay phone bugged for five days, after you triggered several different warnings embedded in the *Modesto Bee* back issue search engine."

Alexis looked totally crestfallen. It was so obvious! And he had been a newspaper man, after all. He should have known.

"I am an expert in thin-film superconductors, and I am using them for a series of new very sensitive electromagnetic sensors, including from electronic emissions of the brain. My work came to the attention of a group of psychics in San Francisco – Warlocks you call them – a Coven is their name for this group, with typicallly 12 to 18 members. They live just below the radar with their psychically enhanced powers of persuasion; rich, powerful, but shadowy figures who use others to do their dirty work for them. Regretfully, they can enhance their powers by jointly 'feeding' on the brains of certain sympathetic or sensitive individuals, leaving a corpse with an awful mask of terror etched on their face. Pierre saw one in Paris. You never forget that look."

Jean was ashen. So Pierre had been given the job of covering up for a Coven "feeding" in Paris. No wonder he was becoming anxious.

"I also have been working with a group of altruistic young students at UC Merced, trying to enhance psychic communication with my technology. My attempts to enhance interpersonal mental contact or telepathy by technology have been a complete failure."

True as spoken, thought Jonathan. Revealing some, hiding much.

"A five-person Coven team was sent down from San Francisco about four years ago to evaluate whether I was making any progress, and while in Merced, had a 'feeding' on a young student named Bonny at a site up in the hills east of the city. On the way back, the driver lost control of the van, probably because, as we have since learned, that Coven minds are numbed and sated by the 'feeding,' and they went off the road into a canyon. All were killed, and the Coven blamed me. When Bonny's body was found by the police, with no mark on her but terror etched on her face, and the time tied the death to the mysterious five men and their forged identities, I became aware of the Coven and began to prepare defensive capabilities.

"This began a war, and we learned a lot as I used my technology to bug the Coven-associated non-psychic teams sent down to investigate the wreck. In the process, we have developed an obvious barrier to Coven psychic probes – any thin conducting sheet blocks the electromagnetic waves of the brain – since we knew all brain emanations had to be electromagnetic. But I also invented, by a complete fluke, a powerful noise generator that interacts with Coven brains and renders them almost incapable of rational thought, sort of like how a powerful high-pitched sound affects the ear.

"The Coven tried to kill me and my students, and eventually kidnapped Jonathan and took him to a safe house in Los Angeles, actually the old Jack Benny home that burned up three years ago. Yes, that was us, rescuing Jonathan while the Coven was writhing on the floor in psychic torment, then using liquid hydrogen released into the room to make an untraceable explosion. We killed 15 Coven members that night, emasculating the California Covens and buying us some peace.

"The attempt on my life by European Coven members in San Diego convinced me that my future prospects were dim indeed. One of these attempts would eventually succeed. Thus, we were very suspicious when ENE suddenly decided to set up shop in Merced. With the help of Jonathan and Roberto, we faked my death, again hoping to buy more time to develop my technology but at the same time happy to damage any of these Coven monsters we encountered.

"I moved to Winters, a town near UC Davis, incognito, but worked secretly but closely with one of my colleagues, a former student, who was following in my scientific footsteps. Several of my Merced student trainees came with me. So it was on one fall day that one of my students, working as a waitress, saw four obviously European men descend on a local but regionally well-regarded restaurant in Winters, the Staghorn. We immediately instituted electronic and even personal surveillance. They chattered away for two hours, talking mostly about trivialities, but without prior knowledge, we learned that they were clearly a Coven team about to re-constitute the destroyed San Francisco Coven with its rich 'feeding' grounds of psychics in the gay community."

Jean said, "That would explain the extra mileage on the rented cars."

"You have done your homework well," said Ken, ever the professor.

"We could not tolerate any more 'feedings,' so that very night, with the aid of the psychic noise generators, we kidnapped all four of them. Yes, that mysterious ENE electronic radio mentioned in the police reports was an ENE attempt to match my technology, since they didn't know whether we had any psychic powers, natural or electronically enhanced.

"We killed none of the men. The three are living under loose but effective surveillance in New Zealand, with the secure threat that we would use our technology to drive them insane, as we did with Otto when we pushed him too far in our efforts to learn about Coven activities in Europe. But we used enough persuasion so that as of now none of them has attempted to revive their Coven activities. They are strictly enjoined never to even meet each other, as it takes about three Coven members minimum for a 'feeding' attempt.

"Indeed we learned a lot, and put Otto on a plane back to Frankfurt. He died about one week later, but I don't think it was in response to our technology. We expected him to gradually recover."

"He was nicely murdered by three high-level directors of Bayer," said Alexis. Ken knew this fact, of course, from Karla, but wanted to see how open Jean and Alexis had become with what they knew.

All this time, Michelle and Jill had been sitting on the floor with their backs leaning on the bed, as chairs were scarce in the now-crowded room, eating pizza, drinking wine, and saying nothing.

Ken stopped, and paused. "I feared this wouldn't work," he said. "I am a lousy liar."

"You never had much practice," chimed in Jill, "for which I am grateful. Otherwise it would have been harder to accept your growing harem."

Their chat seemed to cause a lot of joking and laughing, but the implications were completely lost on Jean and Alexis.

"We have been reading your mental states. No, we cannot read your minds but we can sense current thoughts pretty well, and especially emotional responses. You are scared to death. You suspect we also are psychic, although you accept what I have told you, which is all true but by no means complete. Yes, my experiments with electronically enhanced telepathy have all been failures, but a group of telepathically connected individuals has arisen in Merced, mostly young, largely female, loving, and altruistic. Your suspicions are so profound that we have to trust you, for our sake and, I assure, yours."

Michelle and Jill got up, and stood side by side with Ken facing Jean and Alexis. Ken continued, but each word came sequentially out of the mouths of Jill, Ken, and Michelle.

"Michelle and I had the first breakthrough, and we found we could train and recruit a few others. Our powers were very different from those of the older, largely male Coven members, who needed periodic 'feedings' to maintain their powers."

Jean and Alexis were mesmerized. If this was a trick, it was a good one.

"No, Jean, it is not a trick. Members of Omega, which we call ourselves, are in total contact one with the other. Alexis, there are no hidden radio transmitters, and anyway, that could not explain how we can read your thoughts. Jean, think of a number, any number. Cute. The square root of minus 1. Truly an engineer at heart. Alexis, you just thought of your mother's maiden name, Polanski."

Slow acceptance started to penetrate Jean's thoughts, although Alexis was still fighting this new reality with every argument he could muster.

"This is all we have," continued all three. "No telekinesis, no past thoughts, no future predictions, just telepathy, but that is more than enough for us. We can put thoughts and pictures into people's heads, and that is how the first Coven members died in the car wreck. The driver thought the road was straight and flat. But they were racing back toward Merced, away from the crime scene so they could use their cell phones. They had learned from Bonny that some sort of spiritual group existed in Merced, and who some of the members were, including me. We would have been exposed and certainly killed if their information became known to the Coven in San Francisco.

"The European Covens attempted to trap us with Gypsy cooperation, but the Covens betrayed the Gypsies and tried to kill us in Rosa's cottage. We have since made peace with the Gypsy kingdoms of Europe. A very few Gypsies indeed have some telepathic capabilities, and we are now allies against the sworn-enemy Covens. These are still very powerful and well connected in Europe. You would have certainly, and already may have triggered their alert networks, personal and electronic. We are surprised you have managed to stay alive so long, which is probably a consequence of the Coven losses in Paris in general and ENE in particular.

"If it makes you feel any better, neither of you is what is called a 'sensitive,' and thus not a candidate for a 'feeding.' I assure you, almost any other form of death is preferable to that."

Jill and Michelle returned to their wine and pizza. Ken speaking alone, said, "What other questions do you have?"

"How many of you are in the Omega?" asked Jean. "That I will not tell you, but the numbers have been steadily growing for the past four years, and we have teams in many cities in California, especially around universities. Psychic contact requires a combination of great intelligence, high altruism, and deep yearning. Finally, there is a training and then a group 'awakening.' In complete contrast to a 'feeding.' which is bestial and awful, an 'awakening' is transcendentally beautiful. We will make sure you are present at one, although you will always be the best men, never the groom."

"What do we do now?" asked Jean.

"Pack your suitcases, grab your books, and we leave within 30 minutes. We will wait outside, allowing you a little time to discuss things between yourselves with us absent. But the sooner you disappear from the face of the Earth, the safer your lives will be.

"No, Alexis, if we had wanted to kill you, it would have happened three days ago, and neither you, nor the police, would ever know who or why. There would have been no pain involved, I assure you. But if you fire up that cell phone to call Auditor friends, probably Nicholas, you will be instantly tracked to this room. The question will then only be whether or not the non-psychic muscle hired by the European Covens and spread all over California will get you and us before the 30 minutes is up."

Alexis made his choice. "Good thinking," said Michelle.

CHAPTER FIVE

Jean and Alexis woke up to a splendid view of the mountains near Yosemite National Park. Neither had been to California before, and the view eastward from the Midpines safe house was awesome. The extensive lawn, trees, and playground made it resemble some pricey private school. There were about a half-dozen young children roughly 2 or 3 years old, playing in the sand box. A pair of really attractive women were in casual attendance to the children. Other than friendly greetings, no one approached or talked to Jean and Alexis.

A breakfast buffet was served, rich in California fruits and vegetables, yogurt, cereals, and if you wanted, various sorts of egg scrambles. The coffee was good, and if you added enough milk, it approximated a rather weak café au lait. Croissants would have been nice, but compared to the fast food they had been eating in Modesto, this was great.

Nothing more seemed to be happening, and no one appeared to be interested in Jean and Alexis. They, in turn, were full of unanswered questions, but no one seemed motivated to answer them. No one who had been at the motel was in evidence. Everything seemed so ordinary, but in their hearts they knew that everything would never be the same.

It was about 10:30 a.m. when Roberto showed up, in uniform. "Jean, you just got a money order in your name for 500 Euros delivered early this morning to the Modesto motel. What do you make of it?"

"Money orders? I have never gotten a money order in my life! I didn't know they still did such things," Jean said.

"Perhaps that is exactly why it was done," said Roberto.

There was a small explanatory text on the money order, stating that this was to allow Jean to move on to auditing ENE books in Vancouver, since they no longer needed purchasing supplies, travel, equipment, and benefits audits.

Jean blanched, "These were the code names for the four German Auditors. I think this means they missed our daily security call. They may be dead or missing, and that we should not return to France."

"My thoughts exactly," said Roberto. "I hope the rest of them can scatter in time. I expect they will find their way here, the last place that they know you were present. I expect they are in a state of panic about the dangers of being in Europe. Fortunately, the French Covens, at least in Paris, were badly hurt by the ENE debacle, and thus may be lying low, reducing their surveillance capabilities.

"We will set up surveillance around the Modesto motel, and elsewhere in the area. We will need names and descriptions to the best of your abilities. Jean, you, Jonathan, and Barbara will go to Vancouver, and set up surveillance there. I'll get you some help to hack the computer passenger lists. Alexis, you, Victor, and Gabriella, plus a second team with Diane and Michael, set up surveillance in San Francisco. It will be much tougher because there are so many international flights. Remember, they may land at some other city and take domestic flights to San Francisco. Your chances are small, but they will not know the area and will need help. Be sure to cover car rentals, because that is about the only way they can get to Modesto. Meanwhile, we will have a gathering of Omega, and you are the guests of honor."

The large dining room was by now filled with people, probably about 30 or 35 in all. It was notable that there were many more women than men, and most were young – late teens or early 20s. Jonathan and Ken were there, Jill and Michelle, and a number of young Hispanics. What was especially striking was that they all seemed so strong yet so happy, confident, at peace, and in a number of cases, clearly couples. "You would be hard-pressed to find such a joyous group anywhere in France," thought Jean.

Michelle laughed, "Perhaps we can change that someday."

Jean kept forgetting that these people read minds.

"And we can do more than that," said Michelle, finishing off Jean's unspoken sentence. "We can join or separate at will from the minds of other awakened Omega members, always only with current thoughts, and we are permanently and deeply in love with each other. When teamed up, our powers are pretty persuasive."

Alexis got up, walked to the middle of the room, and in unaccented American English, began singing an old UC Berkeley drinking song.

"Oh, they had to carry Harry to the ferry,
They had to carry Harry to the shore,
And the reason that they had to carry Harry to the ferry was that
Harry couldn't carry any more!
California, California"

Ken laughed, "Well done, Alexis! You may have potential as a sensitive. There are only about 30 percent of all people over whom we have little ability to control, and these are mostly middle-aged or old. Now how do you feel, Alexis?"

"I feel wonderful, proud that I have done something very good. But I have no recollection of what I have just done or why, and how I got to be standing in the middle of the room."

"Check with Jean on what you have just done, and on how you feel. You have had a tiny taste of what we feel in this semi-permanent group communion we call the Omega Project. The term is based on the book by a Jesuit, Theihard de Chardin, on the evolution of human consciousness and eventual growth into a single-thinking entity and eventually to be joined with God," said Ken.

Just then, one of the newer Omega members, Jeanette, got up suddenly and left the room. Tiffany stood up and went out the door with her.

"So, let's discuss your options. You now know essentially everything there is to know about the Omega Project. What you don't know is our recent pact with the Gypsies, who have always had some level of modest psychic sensitivity. They were recruited by the European Covens to spy and eventually help destroy us. They were appalled by the attempt on Rosa's life, and after a pivotal meeting, we now have a pact called the San Pedro Mártir accords for emasculation and eventually eradication of all Covens, largely as a way to stop their bestial 'feedings' on sensitives who might, in principle, eventually be able to be 'awakened' and join the Omega Project. We were just in the process of initiating this phase when you showed up. We assumed that you were Coven spies and operatives, but fortunately we were able to establish your true intentions.

"Because you have fallen into this predicament without any malice toward us, we can try to hide you somewhere in the world where the Covens can't find you. Out of France, and away from your friends and contacts, you are not much of a threat to them, yet. It is your choice, and you have 24 hours to make it. That is when we plan to set up the surveillance for your friends.

"We would of course be happier to have you join the Omega Project as non-psychic associates, like Roberto, Jonathan, and Frank, and four more, all of whom have done vital service for us, mostly because they believe in what we are trying to do. In addition, as non-sensitives, they are relatively immune to anything but the strongest Coven joint attacks. You have vital information on Coven activities in Europe, and we may be able to help your friends."

"Please feel free to walk around the grounds and talk to anyone." After he said it, it sort of echoed that famous song in the 1967 movie *The Graduate* about Mrs. Robinson. Hopefully, the French wouldn't know it.

Jean and Alexis wandered out by a large tree near a ring of chairs facing a fire pit. Michelle came out and joined them.

"Jean and Alexis, you may have noticed that one of our members, Jeanette by name, a stunning beauty even in a gathering this attractive, got up and left in some haste. Tiffany went out to help her. What had happened is that you, Alexis, had made a mental desire to meet with Jeanette and get to know her better, much better. You have to realize that with these women, you are seen as you are. Picture yourselves in that room filthy from head to toe, smelling of manure, with open scabs on your face and arms and drool dribbling down your chin. That is how you look to us psychically."

Jean and Alexis were stunned.

Michelle continued, "Your minds are a riot of deceit, greed, sexual hunger, pornographic images, causal brutality, profound selfishness, and self loathing. You people are a mess inside. You have no concept of mental hygiene. You are incapable of love, and everyone in that room knows it. We view you with pity, as we would an old, drunk, homeless man lying in a gutter. Your mental desire for Jeanette was like throwing a pan of dirty dishwater, or worse, in her face. Don't do it again."

Alexis was simply destroyed. All his Gallic swagger and self-confidence was eradicated. He looked back at his life with this new perspective and it wasn't a pretty sight. In the past, these were his secrets, sometimes dirty secrets, now hung out on the line like poorly washed laundry for all to see.

Jean was more philosophical. "What can we do? I personally want to be part of what is truly a unique evolution of human consciousness, even if I am associated at the lowest rung of a ladder I can never climb."

Michelle responded, "I really don't know. Most of our members came in as altruistic youth, most deeply religious. Recently, we have had some success with mothers and their babies, because it may trigger those who are marginally sensitive into full 'awakening.' The older associates, all religious, usually had had a lifetime of altruistic behavior. We don't know what to do with people like you, steeped in self-loathing and cynicism, traits common in France and probably elsewhere. Is it possible to totally reform, not just externally but internally? Is your redemption possible? I hope so. You are our first two tests. But we have had a few older associates who ended up marrying one of our members, and I can assure you their happiness transcends anything you ever thought of.

"If you come to love and believe in the Omega Project and our members, would you be willing to give up your life for the cause? Think about it," she said as she left.

"Well, maybe I laid it on a little thick," thought Michelle. None of us is perfect, but let's see how they respond to this slap in the face. Actually, a kick to the balls is probably a better analogy. She smiled ever so slightly as she went back in the house to help Jeanette.

CHAPTER SIX

The first impression was pain, pain in his arms that were being held back in an unnatural position. He tried to move, and realized he was bound tightly to a chair. His hands were numb from lack of circulation. He opened his eyes, and saw a very ordinary room in what looked like a modest country house. The furniture looked like someone had done a hasty run through some discount store, grabbing the cheapest stuff available. There was no sign of any care in placement, no sign in fact that the place had ever been lived in. The air was very cold. He could see a fireplace over to the left, but there was no fire in it. Heinrich was tied to a chair near his, head still slumped forward, unconscious. Still, he could feel no wounds on himself, or see any on Heinrich.

Fritz remembered what had happened, and the next emotion was profound regret for his stupidity. The entire German Auditor team had carefully and individually left Bayer, planning to use diverse routes to eventually join in a small town of Schwarzburg about 30 kilometers northeast. There was a small auto rental place in the town, and after a phone call from a booth on the street outside of the headquarters, they arranged for a car for the trip into France for the report on how the California team was doing. The coded message had indicated new and exciting findings.

In Schwarzburg, their car was indeed waiting for them. They all got in, and headed down the back roads for France. Just outside of the town, there was a steep hill that forced them to slow down. Suddenly Fritz had felt faint, steered over to the shoulder of the road, and ….

"Stupid! Stupid! Stupid! We were all together, and presented an opportunity to capture us all at one time. We had clearly been hit with an anesthetic gas timed to be released on the slow hill climb. Now the Warlocks had us all. I have failed us all!" Fritz was in despair. "Whatever happened next would not be pretty, and it's all my fault."

Heinrich sort of moaned, and stirred. Fritz called softly "Heinrich!" and was immediately rewarded by a hard blow to the back of his skull. His chair fell forward, and his head cracked on the wooden floor. The chair then fell to the side, and Fritz could see his attacker, a sneering young man holding a heavy walking stick, now somewhat bloody.

A scream came from the next room, and again, and again. It was Rudolf! "Shut up," the guard said to Heinrich. "Your turn will come soon enough."

Heinrich moaned again, and the guard turned and used the end of the stick to jab Heinrich, hard, again, and again, and then whipped the stick across Heinrich's face, probably breaking Heinrich's nose, as blood gushed forth. Heinrich cried out, and again the stick came down, this time on the back of his head.

Fritz twisted his body and suddenly realized that the back of the chair to which his hands had been tied had broken in the fall. He easily slipped his hands free, got to his feet, grabbed the heavy chair bottom, and brought it down as hard has he could on the back of the guard's head. The guard crumpled, and Fritz viciously brought the edge of the chair down on his head, probably with enough force to kill him. He reached down, slipped a pistol out of the guard's pocket, and began untying Henrich. Just as he finished, the door to the next room started to open. Fritz turned and fired twice at the gap in the door, and was rewarded by a cry and angry yelling. Pulling the still groggy Henrich to his feet, they staggered out the front door. Two cars were parked in front of the farmhouse, one of which was their rental. Fritz turned, and as the connecting door started to open, he again fired at the gap. The door was quickly closed.

Henrich by now was at the rental car, which was unlocked. Fritz sprinted to the driver's side door, and was rewarded by a set of keys still in the ignition. He turned, but the front door of the farmhouse remained closed. He then fired a single shot at the front tire of the other vehicle, a pricey Mercedes-Benz, he started the rental and raced down the dirt road. Soon they were past the bend, but Fritz careened down the road at a reckless speed, bouncing across ruts and though muddy places like a man possessed. At about 2 kilometers, they reached a paved road. Fritz turned right, headed down a hill and moderated his speed a bit. This was not the time to go into a ditch.

Five kilometers later, the view was becoming familiar. They were approaching Schwarzburg, and scattered houses were starting to appear. However, they were unable to get into the town square – the likely location for a police station – because of the Saturday farmer's market, by now in full swing. Wooden barriers blocked the road, and people crowded around.

He stopped the car, and with Heinrich holding a bloody rag across his broken nose, they pushed forward into the crowd. In about a block, the road opened into the square and opposite the church was a police station. They staggered in the door and to the front desk, where a police sergeant was sitting. Henrich sort of collapsed into a chair, and Fritz began to try to get action to rescue his colleagues still at the farmhouse.

Fritz placed the pistol on the sergeant's desk, stating, "I grabbed this gun from the guard when I struck him, and fired several shots at the other men to allow our escape. I think I hit one, and heard a lot of yelling in the next room. There are several men, and they are holding two of my colleagues, who they appeared to be torturing."

The desk sergeant asked for identification, and Fritz reached into his pocket to find, to his amazement, that his wallet was still there with abundant identification. Heinrich likewise provided his, and by now five officers had arrived and examined the pistol, which still smelled of burned powder. Orders were rapidly given. A nurse arrived and started to dress Heinrich's wounds. Fritz was put into a patrol car, and three cars left the village by a back route that avoided the square. With Fritz's directions, they reached the dirt road in about 10 minutes, and cautiously drove up to the farmhouse. The Mercedes-Benz, was as before, with the flat right front tire.

The police stopped, and spread out on both sides of the door. The sergeant led them into the front room, and noted the broken chair and ropes. The guard was lying on the floor exactly as Fritz had left him, dead. Moving cautiously, they pushed into the adjoining room. Two men were bound in chairs – Rudolf and George, both slumped forward, with Rudolf showing signs of a brutal beating. It was soon confirmed that they were dead. A fire was still burning in the grate, and a poker was lying next to Rudolf. There was a small amount of blood near the door. Unlike Fritz and Heinrich, no identification was found on either body. A radio call was made for ambulances and additional units. Roadblocks were to be established in all directions around the farmhouse.

A back door was open, and the police moved cautiously into the yard. A path led into the woods, running next to a small orchard and an open field. Two police officers stayed behind at the crime scene. Three police officers moved along the path and into the woods, which were damp and gloomy even near midday, with guns drawn. Twice, what looked like small traces of blood were found on flat areas of the path. In about a kilometer, they reached another farm road. Tracks were seen from a vehicle that had been parked at the end of the path, next to the road but hidden from view. Another radio call went out.

Back at the station, Fritz and Heinrich gave a detailed account of all that had happened, which was supported by abundant physical evidence. They could think of no reason for the kidnapping and torture, but hypothesized it might be associated with industrial espionage into new Bayer products and drugs. After about three hours, the police allowed them to leave, with the caution that they were to return to their homes and await further inquiries.

At the edge of the town, Fritz and Heinrich stopped the car.

"What can we do? We were obviously uncovered by the Warlocks. They were torturing Rudolf with that hot poker, doubtless trying to get details on the rest of the Auditors. I recognized the voice of one of them in the next room. It was one of our Warlock directors. I hoped I winged him," said Fritz.

Heinrich replied, his voice somewhat muffled by the bandages, "We can't go home. We can't go to the French Auditors, as we might somehow betray them or be swept up if Rudolf had told them too much. The French will miss the security call, and expect the worst. They will hopefully take the necessary precautions to protect themselves. As for us, we have to disappear from Europe, and immediately, before we can be stopped."

A quick check showed that their overnight bags, and those of Rudolf and George, were still in the car with credit cards and some money.

Fritz said, "I propose we go to Modesto in California, and join up with Jean and Alexis. We can travel overland to Amsterdam, buy tickets to San Francisco, and rent a car. There can't be that many motels in Modesto, a small city, as I understand. We will keep looking until we find them. However, by doing this, we will leave a credit card trail to San Francisco, but that is exactly the place where Otto and the previous team were destroyed. Perhaps the Warlocks will be hesitant to track us there. We can only hope that the good news Jean and Alexis have discovered can help protect us."

They crossed the border into Luxembourg, and then across small roads to Amsterdam. Tickets were bought on the next flights, which regretfully would require an overnight stay in Amsterdam. The city, once so familiar and friendly to the Germans in the old, innocent days, now was full of mystery and dark corners. They barely slept.

The next morning they were at the airport far earlier than was necessary. Their flight required a plane change in New York to get to San Francisco. Still, soon they were safely on the flight climbing out of Amsterdam and into a totally unknown future.

But every kilometer away from Europe relieved their fears.

CHAPTER SEVEN

Ken was just getting a report for the surveillance teams in Vancouver and San Francisco when the ever-efficient Roberto breezed in, plopped down into a comfortable chair, and instantly gathered everyone's full attention (as he had planned). "Company's here," he said, "and they are not French."

In the silence that followed everybody's minds were off in a dozen different directions. What next? Why can't people just leave us alone!

Roberto continued, "Two youngish (35 or so) Germans checked into a Modesto motel about an hour ago. I have had one of my Modesto colleagues check with the desk clerk, who noted that they appeared to be banged up, one with a bandage across his nose. They inquired about how many European tourists came to Modesto – in the winter? You must be kidding! – they were told 'precious few.' They then asked about two Frenchmen who were here last week. The desk clerk played dumb. As soon as they registered and left for their rooms, he called me. Their first names were Heinrich (with the bandage) and Fritz, which is so German as to sound like a made up name. But we know otherwise, don't we?" he continued for dramatic impact.

"So two of the German Auditors have arrived, searching for Jean and Alexis. Jonathan, let's pull Alexis back from the San Francisco stakeout and meet with the Germans this evening, before our boys do anything rash."

So it was at nine that evening that Alexis knocked on the door of Room 2005 of the Central Modesto Best Western Motel, saying in German, "Open up Fritz. It's me, Alexis. Please let me in."

Fritz opened up the door to see Alexis, Ken, Roberto in uniform, Michelle, and Jill.

Alexis continued, "These are my friends, and they can protect us from the Warlocks. But you have to leave this motel, now, this minute, because by using your credit cards to rent this room, your whereabouts have now been revealed to Warlock Associates known to lurk in this region. Come right now. Leave your car in the parking lot and leave the car keys on the desk."

Fritz and Heinrich, with scarcely a word, did exactly as told, and walked down a back stairway to two waiting SUVs with tinted windows. Two hours later, they were brought into the Midpines safe house and jammed into one room, as the place was by now pretty crowded. On the way, Alexis had briefed them on what was going on, and in turn got the story of the deaths of Rudolf and George, and their narrow escape. Their concern was now for their families, and that of Rudolf.

"We will intercede immediately," said Ken.

With hardly more than a few words of thanks, and exhausted by the trials they had endured, they went promptly to bed and to sleep.

Ken, Michelle, and Jill, and a few other members, sat around in the living room, cradling hot chocolates or tea. "What do you make of them?" asked Ken. "Their lives are less of a mess than Alexis'. The two German Auditors are pretty straight-arrow scientists, with wives and children, too, to which they appear to be faithful and for which they fear for their lives. That has to be our first effort, to protect the families. We are going to need Gypsy help, and fast. Luckily, the recently departed George was a bachelor with no close family ties, but Rudolf has a family."

A call was placed to Karla on the secure line they had developed. Karla was on the line immediately from Slovakia, where it already was morning. With the help of the information given by Fritz and Heinrich, Karla immediately deployed the hyper-efficient Gypsy hacker experts on the case.

"Give me about 10 minutes," said Karla.

The line went dead. Not a word was spoken, but all Omega members were working through the options open to them in a close communion.

In only eight minutes, the phone rang.

"There is no indication of anything amiss with Fritz's and Heinrich's families from our electronic sources. However, this morning, about 2:00 a.m., there was a mammoth arson-caused fire in a village near the Bayer headquarters, and an entire family was burned to death," Karla announced. "The arsonists used accelerants simultaneously in the front and back halls. There could be no escape. Mercifully, the fire was so intense, death was quick and probably by smoke inhalation. It was Rudolf's family. Is it possible that in their haste, the Coven directors didn't bother to get all the Auditor's names, and didn't know who the other Auditors were? After all, Fritz and Heinrich still had their wallets on them.

"Anyway, we have personnel moving to the other two families. However, when we get there, we will want Fritz and Heinrich to talk to their wives and alert them to the threat. They will never believe us. What do you propose as a plan?"

"Extraction from Europe," Ken said, "as their presence would be a serious threat via blackmail on Fritz and Heinrich. During the phone call, they can use the murder of their colleague's entire family as an example of what would happen when the other German Auditors become known to the Coven directors, as they certainly will when their absence is missed at work Monday. I would propose immediate transfer to a van, transport to an international airport, and a flight to San Francisco."

"So shall it be done," Karla said. "We will be in place in about 30 minutes at Fritz's house, 45 minutes at Heinrich's. Have them briefed and ready. I think we should try Paris, as our indications are that the French Covens are lying low, mostly in the countryside. Further, there are direct flights, Paris to San Francisco. We will arrange for enough 'cancellations' if the flights are full, which I doubt at this time of year."

"You never cease to amaze me," said Ken.

"The feeling is mutual," said Karla."

It was not easy to wake up Fritz, who had just hit the bed. But with some cold water and strong coffee, he was ready when in 35 minutes the phone rang, and it was his wife, Hilda. The call was surprisingly easy, as Hilda was in terror after what was clearly a murder of a close friend with all their children, and the total absence of contact with Fritz. In 20 minutes, Hilda and the three children were in the Gypsy van dressed for travel, aided by the fact that the kids hadn't left for school yet. Ten minutes later, the same pattern was repeated for Heinrich's family, and they were all in time to make an early evening flight from Paris.

Twenty minutes later, Karla called, "Could you please tell me what is happening?"

"Basically," said Ken, "a group of 10 curious amateurs, French (six ENE) and German (four Bayer) got wind of Coven activities, and started to make inquiries on their own, including an effort to identify just who it was in California that was causing the Paris Coven such heartburn. The German Coven reacted quickly and brutally, killing two of them. We have the other Germans and two of the Frenchmen here, and we expect to get all the remainder any day now. However, they developed some interesting data, and we now have the identities of four Coven members, including your old buddy Gerard, who is holed up in a chateau near Montrichard on the Loire, pretending to be an Opus Dei operative. The ENE group actually put some bugs in place. We can give you details once they show up."

"I always thought Gerard's death was awfully convenient, but we lost his trail," said Karla.

"The European Covens are not going to be happy about the escape of the auditors, and if they make inquiries and Gypsy assistance is suspected, the war may break out sooner than we had planned, or are really ready for. I fear for your people, my friend," said Ken. "I propose we get you some high-level Omega personnel and defensive capabilities immediately."

"Much appreciated. I'll get you details in a few hours, Sleep well. We will be ready when you awake. I will alert the kingdoms of the potential Coven threats. We already have pretty sophisticated anti-Coven defensive measures in place, and I'll make sure these will be activated."

CHAPTER EIGHT

The winter ski season was in full swing in Lauterbrunnen in the Swiss Alps, and the valley was filled with tourists from all over Europe. No one would notice, or care, that the valley was also the chosen site for a series of "business retreats," with lots of free time for skiing. There were also important tax breaks for the participants. Many old farmhouses had been modified to encourage this activity.

The Coven chateau had been an old farmhouse, well down the valley, away from the main road, and just beyond the tram to the ski town of Mürren, up on top of the cliffs. It had long been upgraded to a well-appointed second home for wealthy European businessmen who used the buildings for periodic business gatherings. They were generous with their neighbors, who ran the farm for them. The farm could sleep up to 35 people in a pinch. An old storage shed attached to the house, and originally used for winter hay for the cattle, had been quietly converted into an electronic communication center with significant capabilities, largely by secure satellite downlinks to a Coven-controlled Zurich company.

The room was set up in the typical Coven pattern with the Primes and A's sitting together on both sides of the fire facing a circle of chairs. One of the participants, German by appearance, had his left arm in a sling. In all, 32 members were present.

The clock struck 3:00 p.m., and a very old man, French by appearance, whose code name was Emil, initiated the meeting. "I would like to start by getting a report from our German members."

The German Coven member with the wounded arm, Johann, began, "We recently became aware of electronic attempts to access data from secure Bayer company records on our employment. These efforts were traced to a mid-level technical employee at the headquarters, named Rudolf. We instituted surveillance on Rudolf, and for six weeks could identify no unusual activities. It was possible that he was still resentful at being passed over for a well-deserved promotion by one of our newer Coven members. However last week, we became aware of contacts between Rudolf and members of ENE, with whom we had had some prior activities for the Coven, including shipping a noise generator to San Francisco on an otherwise legitimate Bayer shipment. The calls were intercepted, and seemed strange and unspontaneous, not tied to any legitimate – in the broad sense – Bayer activities with ENE, and possibly indicating some sort of coded information.

"When a good friend of Rudolf's named George made reservations on a Bayer account for a car rental in a backwater town about 30 kilometers from headquarters, we became suspicious. We went to the site in two cars, and installed an anesthetic gas canister in the reserved car, timed to incapacitate the driver in about 10 minutes outside the town. We were present Saturday when the vehicle was picked up, and tracked it until the car swerved to the side of the road on a hill outside of town and the motor stalled. When we arrived at the vehicle, we found Rudolf, George, and two more Germans. We quickly aired out the car, and drove all three vehicles to one of our safe houses conveniently near the town. One of our vans was pre-positioned on the escape route, as is our practice.

"When we arrived, we tied them up in adjacent rooms and revived Rudolf and George. Neither were in the least sensitive, so we resorted to more direct methods, torture with a hot metal poker, to gain information. Rudolf was being surprisingly reticent, despite serous pain, when suddenly we heard a noise from the next room. When we opened the door, we could see our guard flat on the floor, and two bullets were fired from the outside door, one hitting my arm. It turns out that one of the Germans had somehow gotten free of his bonds, flattened the guard with a broken chair, and had taken his gun. In the mêlée that followed, they escaped in their rental car, and flattened a tire on our Mercedes.

"At this point, we killed Rudolf and George, and escaped from the house to the retreat vehicle previously parked at the end of a 1-kilometer path through the forest, and left the area before any police activity was detected. We had already removed the gas canister set from the rental car. The guard had secure untraceable background from Czech sources. There was nothing in the house that could trace us to Bayer. Regretfully, the Mercedes was potentially traceable to Bayer and eventually to us. However, as soon as we got back, we immediately erased the assignment of the car from all Bayer records, and placed it in the care of a motor pool of a satellite rental car company whose records are deliberately messy."

After a brief delay, Emil responded, "You were wounded. There is blood, I presume, in the farmhouse that could be tracked back to you, should you come under suspicion for any reason." His humorless cold smile just hinted at the punishment he could deliver at will. Johann blanched, and a cold sweat beaded on his forehead. Emil sensed the fear, and found it adequate for his purposes. He needed information right now. Punishment could come later.

Emil continued, "What is your analysis?"

"I believe that based on the phone calls, four mid-level Bayer scientists were going to meet some ENE compatriots, probably somewhere in or beyond Luxembourg. I believe that these people had become aware of some of our activities, perhaps triggered by the Otto affair and the recent disasters in Paris, Johann said. "However, their level of spycraft was crude, and I don't see any sign of a guiding intelligence behind their activities. I think these people were amateurs, operating independently."

Emil paused before declaring, "There is something else."

Johann was by now verging on panic, but he continued, "We killed all of Rudolf's family three days ago in an arson fire, partially as a warning to any other amateurs, partially to destroy any notes he might have hidden in his house. George's apartment was also searched, with no information found.

"On Monday, we instituted checks on all Bayer employees, and detected the absence of two additional employees, both German, from the same division in which Rudolf and George worked. By noon, we had determined that they had no legitimate reason to be missing, and from their personnel and security badges, we had their photographs. They were the two other Germans we had captured.

"Both had families in the vicinity, but by 3:00 p.m. Monday, we found that both families had vanished from their houses that very morning, taking only bare essentials. We have found no trace of them since that time, despite checking all records of travel in the neighboring four countries. Further, no trace of the other Germans, Fritz and Heinrich by name, has been picked up yet, but we are combing credit card records for their names."

Johann paused. He really did not want to go on, but Emil's cold smile demanded total obedience and honesty. "Our inquiries of a neighbor established that they were spirited away in vans Monday morning early. One neighbor thought that the driver looked like a Gypsy."

Profound silence descended on the room like the pall of a dense fog. No one spoke or moved, as each pursued the implications of that statement. Minutes passed. Finally, one of the Swiss Coven members who had been at the Trieste meeting with the Gypsies felt compelled to speak up.

"We had recruited Gypsy assistance to infiltrate the Merced area and to try to find what had really happened to O'Neal and his student followers. All was going well when suddenly the house of one of the Gypsy psychics, Rosa by name, was destroyed in a massive bomb blast. Records in the Merced police department files show that several badly burned bodies, one most likely Rosa's, were found in the wreckage. One ex-ENE employee named Simon was traced to the blast, and was found dead the next day with four others in another house explosion in San Diego. Three Germans seemed to be involved in the San Diego explosion.

"The Gypsies were furious at us for killing Rosa. We explained at a meeting we called near Trieste that the Covens had nothing to do with it, but we suspected that it might be an independent German effort to avenge the mental emasculation of Otto. We are not sure they believed us.

"In the meeting, it also came out that Gerard had a homosexual lover at ENE, who had been used for a number of Coven tasks, including cleaning up after a botched Coven 'feeding.' That person, Pierre, was immediately killed by the Gypsies, but Gerard was allowed to live. Gerard promptly arranged his own demise, which is surely faked, and subsequently disappeared from our records. His location and activities are unknown, but there now is a gaping void at ENE. This may have triggered the inquiries at ENE, and perhaps the Gypsies are somehow involved in the recent German affair."

Another pause ensued.

Finally, Emil spoke, "This is serious. The Gypsies have never liked our 'feedings' but have tolerated our activities as long as their own people were not harmed and funds were regularly transferred into Gypsy-controlled front companies. Later you must tell me more about this Rosa affair, including why I was not briefed on it. I want a full and honest report when we return at 9:00 p.m."

He continued, "Let me work through the timeline. All four are captured Saturday morning. Two escaped around 11:00 a.m., and are not seen again. By late afternoon, they could be in Paris, Amsterdam, Zurich, or elsewhere in the region, by Sunday, anywhere in northern Europe, and by Monday morning, anywhere in Europe or North America.

"But the most likely explanation is that they continued on to their secret rendezvous with their ENE colleagues, and arrived in the afternoon of Saturday somewhere in France. Less than 36 hours later, carefully planned extractions occur for both families, with no trace left. This level of organization would not be easy, and especially not from the amateurs we know about. Clearly they had help, and it would be easy for the Gypsy kingdoms to perform the extractions and the later hiding. I am going to accept Gypsy assistance as the likely explanation, and the neighbors' observations as confirmation. We have to assume that our long-standing truce with the Gypsies has now been violated. How seriously, we do not yet know. But perhaps a salutary lesson is in order.

"I am assigning to the German team the selection of a viable 'feeding' candidate for the evening from among the population of Interlaken. I would suggest that the famous Flea Market be a suitable trolling area, and Gypsies suitable candidates. This will be a warning to the Gypsies that interference in our operations will not be tolerated."

Later that evening, as the Coven slumped in the post-prandial stupor after a satisfactory but minor level "feeding" on a gay Austrian tourist from Interlaken, Emil inquired, "I thought you were looking specifically for a Gypsy?"

Johann responded, "We sensed two suitable sensitives in the Gypsies at the Flea Market, but they were always surrounded by three to five people and there was no chance to go one-on-one with either of them. We even tried a diversion by dropping my wallet while walking away, but no one took the bait."

"Interesting," mused Emil. "Gypsy greed is legendary. Perhaps, just perhaps, they were told to take extra precautions against our activities. If so, this indicates that things have gone even further than I feared. We will institute discreet but thorough inquiries in the Gypsy matter from trusted non-Coven resources immediately. I think that perhaps we should reinforce the salutary lesson for the Gypsies with something more dramatic, something that could reignite their fear of us. That is all for now."

The Coven members started to get up and move to their rooms, bunks, or wherever a place to sleep had been provided. Emil sat by the fireplace in deep thought. But he was not thinking of Gypsies. Instead he was contemplating how his powers were starting to fail, although he was very careful to hide this from other Coven members. Further, the duration of the revival following each "feeding" became steadily shorter before the hunger returned. He had been glad that the "feeding" tonight was low level, because this time, just as he experienced at the previous mid-level "feeding," his thoughts and emotions had raced almost beyond his control. The madness of Friedman, a truly powerful A Prime in San Francisco, still bothered him.

It was more than an hour before Emil got up and went to his room in a house that was now as still as death.

CHAPTER NINE

Jean, Jonathan, and Barbara had barely reached the Vancouver airport when the first suitable flight arrived, an Air Canada flight from Toronto, the usual connecting city to northern Europe. They went to the central area beyond security where all passengers had to pass, and were promptly rewarded with all four ENE Auditors, looking distinctly nervous.

Jean walked up behind them ever so casually, and said "Looking for a ride to Merced?" All four whirled around in panic, primed for escape. This turned into delight and relief at seeing Jean. Many hugs and kissing of cheeks followed. Other passengers turned and smiled at such Gallic camaraderie. They were drawing a little too much public attention for Jonathan's liking.

"Jean! We are so glad to see you, and that you are all right. There has been some sort of disaster in Germany, with our teams not responding. We just learned that there was a terrible arson-caused house fire and Rudolf's entire family has been killed."

Jonathan cautioned, "This is not the time or place for this discussion. Our vans are outside. Get your luggage and meet me at the curb."

"What luggage?" Philippe exclaimed. "All we have is hand luggage and our passports. We left in maximum of haste. Where are we going?"

Jean said, "Let's start walking to the vans. You will learn in good time. I will introduce you to my companions when we are on our way. Your coded message may have tipped off the Warlocks as to the Vancouver rendezvous point. We will brief you on what is happening. Two of the Germans escaped, and they are here, and their families are on their way. Meanwhile, follow me."

Henri said, "I have a fiancée in Paris, named Jacqueline. We were very close and planning to get married. Is she in any danger?"

Jonathan responded, "Probably not, but we will extract her if she will come. You will call her when we get to our destination."

Fifteen hours afterward, late at night, a very weary group rolled into Mariposa, near Midpines, and was instantly and quietly shuttled into motel rooms pre-rented under false names. The clerk seemed totally satisfied with the arrangements, and never even caught sight of the ENE teams. Guards were posted around the motel, and the four ENE Auditors were told to expect a 10:00 a.m. wake-up call.

The next morning saw yet more joyous reunions as the German families arrived in San Francisco. They were driven to Mariposa, and put up in the safe house of the small Mariposa Omega cell. It was not really up to the task, especially when the ENE colleagues were brought over, but relief at being far from a suddenly threatening and mysterious Europe was universal.

In addition to Ken, Jill, Michelle, and Jonathan, Diane and Michael came down with their two children. It had been decided that honesty was the only policy. Introductions were made all around. Cups of coffee and small pastries were spread on a table. The German children were taken to the next room by Nancy, who was up from Merced helping the Mariposa Omega cell.

Ken addressed the four ENE newcomers and the Germans' husbands and wives, with Fritz helping translate when concepts were hazy.

"What I am about to tell you will destroy many of your ideas of reality. Telepathy exists – the ability to read the current thoughts of another. Further, we can put compelling thoughts in the head of another, controlling their actions. Trust me, it is all exactly as I will say it. We will provide further proof after the talk. But as a test, I want each of you, wives, Germans, and French, to write a single number on a slip of paper. Any number. Show it to no one, but fold the paper and put it in this bowl."

This was done. At which point, in quick succession, Diane, Jill, Michelle, and Ken read off the numbers, and the person who wrote it. The bowl was emptied, and the results confirmed.

"Alexis, are you ready to do another chorus of "They had to carry Harry to the Ferry?" Alexis actually blushed, and said to all, "They have other capabilities, too, but from all Jean and I have learned, this is about the most loving and altruistic bunch of people I could ever imagine. We are with them, to death if necessary."

Michelle smiled to herself. Better, much better. Maybe there is hope for him after all.

Ken continued, "Your husbands became aware of strange and disturbing activities at Bayer and ENE, a collaborating French company. Some of these activities involved efforts to kill me and my colleagues at the University of California, Merced, as they feared that our advances in telepathic communication and my new technology would threaten their activities. The activities included routine killings and psychic torture called by them 'feedings' that have been going on for centuries. They are psychics and need the 'feedings' to maintain their powers. For obvious reasons, they need secrecy. Your husbands threatened that secrecy, and some paid a heavy price. We too have paid a heavy price, and many of us have been killed by Coven attacks. However, we have had recent successes, and the Covens – that's their name for themselves, although your husbands used the term Warlocks, either of which is appropriate – can no longer operate freely in California. You are safe here, especially as long as your presence is unknown. But you cannot go back to Europe, at least right now, where the Covens are still strong. I can assure you, if any of us, especially our 'awakened' telepaths, are ever captured by the Coven, our fate will truly be worse than death.

"What we propose is to form an international and ecumenical Christian private kindergarten and primary school here in Mariposa, which is a nice area with good weather close to Yosemite National Park. We too have young children, like the children of Diane and Michael you saw this morning, and we need to have a school where these children are brought up in a safe environment. We can limit the initial enrollment to our children and yours. We will use you as teachers, including languages, and administrators. The local Catholic priest of the St. Joseph's parish is already an associate of the Mariposa Omega cell, and there are a couple of other ministers, including a young Lutheran minister, who are candidates for our school oversight board.

"We will buy each family houses back toward the small town of Midpines, close to our central location, which has a cover as a retreat for substance abusers. I propose to buy an old farm near the road that is large enough to house a small school, just big enough for our enrollment. The entire complex will be surrounded by sophisticated but inconspicuous electronic security, mostly against non-psychic 'muscle' that has been used against us in the past, as we are totally secure against any telepathic threats from the Coven, a fact that is well known to them by now.

"As a temporary measure, we will purchase two trailers for additional sleeping quarters at this safe house until we can complete arrangements.

This has all happened in a big rush."

Two days later, Jacqueline was reunited with Henri. To the delight of the Omega members, she had real potential as a sensitive, and Henri was not your usual French cynic. He was a professed but not very observant Catholic, while Jacqueline was definitely the more spiritual of the two. They were soon to introduce themselves to Father Murphy at St. Joseph's, and a wedding seemed imminent. They had actually decided to be celibate until that time, and the longing in both of them was noted and appreciated by the Omega members. This would make Jacqueline's "awakening" more probable, and it was scheduled for the day before their wedding. Jacqueline was given a room in the main Midpines safe house.

By the weekend, things had started to settle down. All six of the French ENE members were settled into rooms in houses adjacent to the Midpines safe house. One house was already available to Fritz's family, with their three children, while Heinrich had to do with a large apartment for the moment. To the delight of their children, snow had fallen on Friday night, and in the pines, it didn't really seem that different from suburban Germany.

Friday night, Karla called Ken, "How are things in California?"

"Better than I had expected," replied Ken, "including a new French sensitive."

Karla continued, "Thank you for Tiffany and Meagan, and the static devices. We are having them copied under the most secure possible circumstances, using only Gypsy technicians who are well aware that these devices may be crucial to our survival. They well realize that if their technology fell into Coven hands, they might find a defense for it before we are ready to use them. How was the prototype we sent you?"

"Not quite ready for prime time, Karla," interjected Ken. "The prototype you sent us had been subtly 'improved' by your people and it was much weaker than the ones we make. He doubtless didn't realize the importance of that feedback spark gap, because these are never used in modern electronics. Please get them back to the original design without, if possible, alerting them to the importance of the modification, as it is our most closely kept secret."

"Understood," said Karla.

He continued, "Tiffany has detected a 'feeding' at long distance in Paris, and is still shaken by the experience. The Coven is still there, and active. Meagan has been in Vienna for only three weeks, but so far has sensed nothing. She definitely has picked up a Gypsy admirer, named Alexander, who had been at the San Pedro Mártir meeting, and we may be seeing the first Gypsy-Omega marriage this spring."

Karla continued, "Things are deteriorating here vis-á-vis the Covens. We have instituted standard Coven defensive postures without trying to look obvious about it. However, there was a strange affair in Interlaken when the old dropped-wallet trick was attempted near one of our psychics in the Flea Market. We had plenty of support, and they went away, but the area seems to have a Coven presence that needs investigation. With your permission, I would like to run Meagan up to Interlaken."

"As you wish," said Ken, "but purely in a defensive mode until our resources are better. As support, I will send over Betsy to help Meagan. Expect her in about three days. You have a secure place to stay, I assume. But please alert your people never to turn on the psychic noise devices, because they would alert them to your presence miles away. They are only for emergency defense or planned attack."

Karla continued, "If the Covens think that we were involved in the German extractions, they may be sending us a message by resuming 'feeding' on Gypsies, with their higher fraction of sensitives. This would be a major mistake on their part, because with your assistance, we believe we are now able to defend ourselves better and perhaps eradicate the plague. A 'feeding' would turn the Gypsy nations red hot with anger, and we know enough about Coven members and activities to do them serious harm in Europe."

"We must remember," said Ken, "that when all this comes out, as it surely will, I want the Gypsy nations to get the credit for eradicating the Covens."

"Appreciated," said Karla. "Be careful my friend. And Marta wants to visit California soon. She is still in a hazy world of delight after what you showed her at San Pedro Mártir, and that requires a lot of Omega members working in concert."

"Can do. You set the date. But in two months, we will have a critical mass in Europe, too. In the meantime, we will be careful. Hector and Vlady will be keeping their eyes open here for non-psychic Coven actions, but Roberto will head to Europe soon."

The next morning, there was a general meeting of Omega at the Midpines house. Almost 45 people were present, many having come in from other cells, especially Davis. Ken went over all the recent events, and most cells had at least one representative.

With the situation stabilized, the effort to translate a good portion of Omega to Europe could be addressed. The original plan was for Ken, Jill, Betsy (because of her knowledge of Coven practices) and Michelle to go to Austria, meeting there with Meagan, Karla, and Marta. But the new information might make Interlaken a better choice.

The plan was still to send seven additional high-level Omega members and attempt their first passive scans for detection of "feeding" activity, first in Vienna, then Paris. However, Ken thought signs of a Gypsy-Coven war may hasten the need to increase the number of Omega operatives.

Ken said, "We have a new concern, however, not unexpected, but worthy of note. What we had originally expected is now beginning to occur. The married couples are starting to lose some of their performance on our annual psychic capability tests. We saw a little last year, but waited to this year to confirm. Diane and Michael, one of our premier pairs, are clearly so deeply in love with each other and their two children. Oh, sorry, Diane, I didn't know — two-and-a-half children. As a result, their range at mind reading and control are reduced to about 30 percent of what it was three years ago. Others are starting to show the same pattern, while some couples still show increases, such as Gabriella and Victor. In any case, we were not planning to send families to Europe, but this reinforces that decision.

"Our children, on the other hand, are almost all sensitives, and some even psychic after about the age of 3 years. We will watch this trend very closely. However, since they will have to live in the world, our new mixed school will provide a protected transition."

A general discussion followed, orally as was the tradition, although of course psychic contact was always there. As was usual, consensus was reached quickly, and the plans were modified. It was too risky to have just Meagan and Betsy at Interlaken, so it was decided that Ken, Jill, Jonathan, and Barbara would likewise go, and immediately. Something was stirring in Switzerland. There must be a major high-level Coven nearby, for this was the only location that had dared to attempt to capture a Gypsy psychic, in violation of decades of toleration and occasionally cooperation. Such a decision must have come from the highest levels of the European Coven. In addition, Interlaken was rather central in Europe, and one could reach pretty much all of Europe from there in one day.

The group decided to make the transition in March, toward the end of the ski season, when rooms became more widely available.

In the summer edition of the *Mariposa Tribune*, the headline read:

Mariposa Christian Academy planned for Fall

The board of the Mariposa Christian Academy of the Beatitudes (MCAB) held a press conference yesterday to announce the establishment of a new private school for kindergarten through sixth grade. One grade will be started each year, beginning with first grade, so enrollment is being taken for kindergarten through first grade. The board consists of several of the pastors of Mariposa churches, including Catholic, Lutheran, Episcopalian, and Presbyterian congregations, under the chairmanship of Father Murphy of St. Joseph's Catholic Church. The principal is Michael Callahan, with degrees in education from UC Merced, and the chief administrative assistant is his wife, Diane Tagliaferri. The board emphasized that the MCAB will stress the Gospel of the Beatitudes, full accord with modern science teachings like evolution, care for God's gift of the environment, and membership in the world community. Teachers from France, Germany, and Mexico are presently scheduled to teach, with a Spanish Immersion first grade planned. The size of the initial school quarters near Midpines are, however, so small that the initial classes are already filled up. As the expansion occurs, MCA looks to open its doors more widely to residents of Mariposa. There will be some tuition, but because of a generous initial endowment, the fee will be set low to allow all levels of society to participate.

CHAPTER TEN

Later in March, the Omega team members were united in Interlaken. They chose a hotel near the lake, just north of the town. During the summer, it would be prime vacation property, but in the mushy spring, it was deserted. The owners were delighted and surprised at the appearance of guests, mostly Americans, but with French and Austrians, too. They had all taken a European climbing vacation together five years ago, and this was to be a reunion, timed to overlap the spring vacation break at the University of California. There was some thought by the owners that the Americans had badly misread the weather conditions, but that didn't seem to dampen anyone's spirits.

In fact, a summer vacation house was being rented for the entire group, but it was not yet ready for occupancy. Even so, it provided a secure meeting place in the evening when the clean-up crew and repairman had left their tasks for the day.

The first meeting in the not-quite-ready house welcomed Karla, who had come over personally to oversee the Gypsy component of the project. As usual, he came prepared.

"We checked the records of missing persons in Interlaken, and came across the name of an Austrian tourist who was reported missing the day of the attempt on the Gypsy. He was a well-known gay from Vienna. He has not been seen since. We suspect he was the victim of the 'feeding'.

"We have surveyed all long-term gatherings of middle-aged men in the surrounding region, a task that was not as difficult as it seems due to the excellent Swiss records on occupancy and vacancy in this high tourist season. We have found nothing in this record that looks like a Coven gathering.

"We then looked at long-term second homes within about three hours of Interlaken, with the time chosen to match transport of the scheduled Gypsy victim to the 'feeding' site. This is ongoing, as records seem in many cases to be deliberately obscured. However, we have a number of candidates, relatively large properties, isolated, owned by non-Swiss entities, access to transport with multiple escape routes. The list grows shorter, and there now are areas that have a number of candidates.

"Then we surveyed the best caterers, looking for long-term (greater than one week) catering contracts for all meals, minimum of 15 persons.

"This list, which was now less than 150 candidates, was overlapped with the long-term housing list, and 24 candidates are now isolated. Eleven of them occur in the areas south and west of Interlaken, in the ski areas. The rest are spread around in every direction, but the ski areas seem to have the most promise. It is relatively easy to hide in a crowd, and that area is crowded this time of year.

"I propose a passive scan in this area tomorrow, basing the search at Lauterbrunnen and Grindelwald, with the latter the first focus because there are seven candidates up there. In the future, Lauterbrunnen looks good because it is the central rail hub for the area."

"Nice work, Karla," said Ken. "Let's give it a try. Have there been any more missing persons in Interlaken?"

"Not that we could find," replied Karla, "but it wasn't that long since the last one."

"I was just wondering whether they had left the area by now. After all, the Coven meeting in England was only supposed to be for five days. They may not stay in any area too long on general principles."

Meagan shuddered, as the memories flooded back. She now understood how close she had come to a terrible death, while instead she has now become a major asset in the destruction of these monsters. Meagan was not above saying a little prayer of thanks for the possible Divine Intervention. Or perhaps it was karma.

The next morning dawned gray and foggy, typical of the ugly transition between winter and spring in this area. It was a little difficult to perform an optimum search. They couldn't use convertibles in this weather, and trains would shield signals even worse than cars. They took the train to Grindelwald, a relatively new and wealthy area. There they met a Gypsy in a rental car to check potential sites, at which they were dropped off about one block away from each other. They sauntered past the sites in two pairs, Ken and Jill, then Tiffany and Meagan, with Jonathan, Karla, and a Gypsy guard staying in the car but within view. The Omega teams were in a total dark mind mode, but felt nothing at any of the sites. By 5:00 p.m., they were through with Grindelwald, and the light was rapidly failing in the deep mountain valleys, so they returned to Interlaken. Before returning to their hotel, which really was not yet set up to make a serious effort at dinner, they stopped in an old and famous restaurant along the river, by the old bridge (or a replica) that was the reason for Interlaken's location in history. The restaurant was not crowded, and they all could fit at two tables by the window. Two Gypsy guards inconspicuously stood at each end of the block, with radios.

Karla was exclaiming about the value of a Hungarian wine, when suddenly he saw all four Omega psychics simultaneously freeze. Their eyes had a blank and unseeing look, as it was not what their eyes saw that held their attention. A minute passed. He and Jonathan made small talk just to cover for their suddenly immobile tablemates.

Finally Ken spoke, "Two, standard probe-respond search, about two blocks west, moving away. One is wearing a maroon ski cap. Alert your guards."

Karla did so, and while on the radio, Ken said, "Entering a gay bar called Nepenthe. They have a candidate in mind." Karla quickly relayed the message.

Ken said, "Two more, in a car, three blocks south, but not in communication with the hunting pair. They are probably the getaway vehicle."

"They have struck. The candidate is following them out of the bar for what he assumes is a short trip to the Turkish baths off Geneva Avenue. The guy in the maroon cap is using a cell phone. The car is coming to meet them."

"What can we do?" asked Jonathan. "We have no vehicles!"

Ken ignored him.

"Get the car's license. We will track them as far as we can, since they are using a lot of unshielded psychic energy controlling their victim," Karla again spoke in the radio.

Ken, Jill, Meagan, and Betsy got up and left the restaurant. Karla watched them carefully separate themselves, so very casually, until they were all about 100 meters apart from each other. Then they simply waited, checking out the river, lounging by a light pole. Ten minutes passed, and then they came back, gathering outside the restaurant, talking among themselves.

Jonathan heard Karla's radio beep again, he listened, and then Karla spoke a few words in some eastern European language unknown to Jonathan. Karla then turned, "I have a car coming, an American Jeep Cherokee, but it will not hold us all. Jonathan, could you close the accounts at the restaurant, then get back to our hotel and alert the others? We are going to try to track the Warlocks." Jonathan noted that Karla had adopted the Auditor's name for the Coven members. Seemed reasonable.

"Got it," said Jonathan, and Karla left the table.

He joined the group outside. "Meagan and I both picked up a sense that they were going to take the Lauterbrunnen turn, but where they are going is beyond Lauterbrunnen."

"They can't go too far," Karla said. "That road dead-ends in the valley maybe 15 kilometers east of Lauterbrunnen, at the foot of the Jungfrau massif. I have a car coming that will just about take us all if we cram in. Jonathan is cleaning up here and then getting back to the hotel to alert the others."

After about the longest 10 minutes Ken had ever spent, a green Jeep Cherokee drove up with a single Gypsy driver. He got out, and went around and jumped into the cargo space. Karla got in to drive, with Ken on the passenger's seat. All three women got into the second seat. Jill turned to find the seat belts, but they were trapped behind the seat and clearly were not being regularly used. "Well, we have worse threats ahead of us tonight," she thought.

The Jeep wound out of the city and up the Lauterbrunnen road. Karla was driving fast but legally, as the Swiss police were hard on reckless drivers on snowy roads (the Spaniards in particular are a menace) and strictly enforce speed limits in tourist areas.

They were still just north of the town when suddenly all Omega psychics froze. Jill gave a little cry of anguish. Karla instinctively slowed down. For perhaps 40 seconds, no one moved. Then Meagan said, "Stop the car!" She opened the door, stumbled to the curb, and threw up.

Ken said, "A failed attempt at a 'feeding,' that suddenly ended. I sensed consternation among the Coven members during the 'feeding,' when their thoughts can broadcast for miles. They are all low-level, C-level and one D-level, and they were surprised when the victim went into anger, not fear. Fear is the 'mind destroyer,' the killer in 'feedings.' Then it stopped. I think the victim is alive but unconscious. It was up the valley well beyond Lauterbrunnen in a room in what looked like a spruced-up farmhouse. Where are your candidate houses? We must get closer."

"There are two up the valley beyond Lauterbrunnen," Karla said, "I'll get you there." Meagan climbed into the car, apologizing for her actions, but all around there was nothing but comfort. All knew how close she had come to the same fate. Betsy said nothing. The horror of her prior life flooded back. She was drenched in shame for what she had done. But she had fought out of it and survived.

About 10 minutes later, the victim awoke, only to find all four Coven members close and ready to attack the weakened and confused mind. The victim's screams rose as panic set in, then fear, then an awful death in total terror.

Jill could not restrain herself, "Unbelievably awful! So that is what a 'feeding' is. I will never get the hopeless fear of the victim out of my mind. How can we sense it so far away?"

"For these few moments, Coven members act as one, and a 'feeding' can be sensed miles away. Bonny was a full 10 miles into the hills and we sensed her, but those were high-level Warlocks. These people were barely capable, clearly a small group holding down the site after the big guns have left. But I strongly believe that this house is in steady use for high-level Coven meetings. This could be the break we have been hoping for," said Ken. "The Jeep was pushing up the valley, and yet still Omega could sense the sated psyches of the Coven as they gradually lost their mutual contact and relaxed, satisfied for the time being.

"The first one is just beyond the end station of the Mürren gondola. It is a couple of kilometers ahead, on the right," said Karla.

"That is it," said Meagan. "I can somehow sense the gondola in their minds."

"Same here," said Ken. "I got that, too. You are really good. I wonder if they are going up to Mürren for dinner or something. That would be awfully convenient."

Karla's radio beeped. He stopped the Jeep close to a road that led to the farmhouse.

"Get beyond the driveway, so if they do go to the gondola station, they don't have to pass us, Ken instructed. "I don't want to be too close to them. They might pick us up. It is hard to do 'dark mind' when we are all furious inside."

Karla did as requested, but all the while soaking up these insights into Omega capabilities and limitations like a sponge.

The Coven emanations were rapidly fading, and they were doing something to destroy the body of their victim. About 15 minutes later, a car was seen coming down the driveway.

"Company coming, kiddies," said Ken. "Be strong and be ready." Each dropped into their "dark mind" targets and held it until the car was well passed.

"Now what? Any ideas?"

Karla spoke up, "A second car is coming up with backup, but we have no electronic surveillance equipment available on such short notice."

"I agree," said Ken. "I want this house penetrated, but done very carefully. There will doubtless be all sorts of surveillance operational, probably including video cameras focused on the driveway entrance. I propose that we drive way up this road, and then come back perhaps two hours later, as though we had had dinner at someone's house. We have accomplished what we could, although we could not save the victim. Let's make his sacrifice not be in vain. Karla, call the other car, tell them our plan, and have them go back to the hotel.

"The bugging of this site will have to be done very carefully," Ken proclaimed. "If they detect our attempt to penetrate their security, they will abandon this site and we will lose them again."

CHAPTER ELEVEN

The meeting took place in a villa outside of Trieste. There were beautiful gardens wrapped around and through an extensive grove of old olive trees. In the distance a swath of the Adriatic Sea was visible. No other houses were visible in any direction, and in fact none existed within more than a kilometer. The room had a dramatic view of the gardens and the sea in one direction, but in all other directions, windows were covered and doors barred. A long and very narrow table was in the middle of the room, so placed that people on each side could reach out across the table and shake hands if they wished.

Rather incongruously, three long, low centerpieces of flowers were spaced evenly along the middle of the table, lending a cheery effect somehow out of place with the gravity of the reason for the meeting.

Around the table sat nine Gypsies – six men and three women, with the latter deliberately seated along the length of the table. These were representative of the dominant Gypsy kingdoms of Europe, the Spanish Calé, the French Manouches, the German Sinte, and the Eastern European Roma – by far the largest Kingdom.

Karla, clearly in a cold fury, announced, "I have called this meeting because of the events of last Wednesday. Gypsy traders in the caravan were going down to a rural fair near Turin when they were attacked and all captured. On the next day, a package was delivered to a bank in Milan that we often work with, with the eyeballs of all the Gypsies and a videotape. The videotape shows a Coven 'feeding' on a mid-level Gypsy psychic traveling in the caravan. It is appalling. You should all look at it.

"Yet I partly blame myself for these events, since it was I who recommended the cooperation with the Merced psychics of the Omega Project. Several of you were there; you know what we all experienced. So when they asked me in urgency to rescue two German families from incineration by Coven members, I took that risk. Since it was short notice, I was forced to use a Gypsy driver in one of the vans, and this was seen. I suspect it got back to the Covens. Yet there was no overt connection with saving these families and the Omega Project. It involved a bunch of non-psychic amateurs who got suspicious on their own.

284

"That our modest effort to save the lives of two German families triggered this massive Coven over-response is, I think, a measure of how worried they are about recent developments. It may also be a reaction to our termination of cooperative efforts against the Merced psychics after the Rosa affair. They needed our help, and we are no longer giving it, except for periodic and inconsequential reports from our Merced Gypsies. I don't know of any efforts at present to attack the Merced psychics, but I expect there are non-psychic actions happening. The risk of this course, however, is that non-Coven personnel become suspicious, as happened in the German case.

"There was also an earlier attempt on Gypsies. Shortly after this extraction, there was an attempt in Interlaken to lure a Gypsy psychic into a place where she could be captured. It failed, partially because we had instituted standard Coven defensive practices, and another young Austrian tourist was used for the 'feeding' of a high-level Coven meeting in Lauterbrunnen.

"We recruited members of the Omega Project to Interlaken. In the course of another Coven 'feeding,' and aided by extensive Gypsy computer-based research on the area, our Omega members were able to locate their secure meeting place, guarded by four low-level Coven members. We are working on a plan to carefully bug the site in anticipation of future meetings.

"My analysis is that the Italian outrage against our people was an attempt to pull us back into passivity and tolerance of their activities. I suspect that it was a once-only operation, and that they will now wait to see what we do. They know how to contact me at any time.

"The question is what should be our response? In this, I will open the meeting to all the kingdoms and await your analysis."

Victor of the Sinte spoke up, "I want to make sure our welfare is paramount in this affair. It is all well and good to help the Merced psychics, and they do offer us new avenues to increasing our capabilities. But is this worth an all-out war with the Covens? There are still a lot of cells in Europe, with massive non-psychic resources. We are given some of these resources to keep us passive. Loss of them alone would hurt our people, since we rarely are covered by European social benefits and health-care programs.

"I believe that in Germany, the Covens are strong enough to essentially

285

destroy the Sinte kingdom in the space of a week, with potential loss of one-quarter to one-third of our total membership, dead or imprisoned. I think the situation is similar for the Manouches."

Karla responded, "If the Sintes' and Manouches' kingdoms are so vulnerable to the Covens, perhaps Germany and France should be the first focus of our efforts with the Merced psychics. Perhaps we should focus on defensive efforts in Germany, and offensive efforts in France, where the Covens have been damaged and we have French non-psychic assistance. Further, one of their leaders, an A-level Coven member, is under our surveillance at present in the Loire Valley. I assure you, with the technology under construction in secure Gypsy laboratories right now, the Covens are extremely vulnerable, too. It is their non-psychic muscle we fear, but they might hesitate to use it for fear of our psychic capabilities.

"Remember also, the Merced psychics, even though few in number, essentially eradicated all the U.S. West Coast Covens and badly damaged those in the rest of the country, which are now scattered and hiding. The Omega Project is larger, now, and with our assistance, I believe we are far more powerful than the Covens. We are in the process of establishing Omega cells in Europe, with recruitment and training, and these will have a high Gypsy content."

For the next hour, a full discussion ensued, and the decision was made to wait a week for any Coven contact, while preparing defensive postures, especially in Germany. The Sinte would quietly move personnel out of threatened areas in Germany and into the Rom regions of the Czech republic, where they were much stronger and the Covens proportionately weaker. The Manouches would have a major meeting with Karla and the Omega Project in the south of France, in the hills east of Avignon, within the next three weeks.

Major efforts would be made to succor the relatives of the destroyed Gypsy caravan, with opportunities to join in any future offensive efforts. There was a blood score to settle. There would be an acceleration in the transfer of Omega personnel and resources into Europe, especially France, with the exception of Switzerland, because the Gypsies wanted the Covens to think that the Lauterbrunnen site was secure. No offensive operations would be undertaken, just reconnaissance. There was some discussion on methods to kill all Coven members in the Lauterbrunnen house, should that become necessary. Karla assured them that Professor O'Neal and his students had the capabilities to accomplish that in ways too oblique to readily conceive.

The meeting broke up on a somber note. It was realized by all that the status quo, Gypsy and Covens, was forever shattered by events, but it was not yet all-out war. The next few weeks would tell.

CHAPTER TWELVE

The five-man executive committee of the European Covens had chosen an upscale farmhouse that had been converted into a second home in the edge of wheat fields about 12 kilometers west of Chartres as their new base of operations. Two weeks had passed with no contact from Karla, or in fact any activity that they could detect. They had decided never to have "feedings" at the Chartres Centre because it was not well set up for disposal of bodies and there were few suitable sensitive candidates. Thus, they would periodically transport to a small chateau near Versailles to raid Paris, then retreat to the countryside. Emil, the senior A Prime in France and one of the most powerful Coven members in all of Europe, had decided he liked the location, and while he was not part of the day-to-day operations, they welcomed his presence even as they feared his powers.

William, the English Covens representative, had taken Gerard's place on the Executive Committee, and it was he who had the lead in the daily 3:00 p.m. briefing. Emil often sat in, but rarely said anything.

"The silence is deafening," said William. "Consider the response of the Gypsies when they thought we had killed one person, Rosa, which we hadn't. Now we kill seven Gypsies, 'feed' on another, and then send the eyeballs and the videotape to a Gypsy bank. The response? Silence. I don't like it.

"There are several options open to them:

1. Submit, come back to our prior agreements, collaborate against the Merced telepaths, and be safe (and rich) from our largesse.

2. Pull away from us, go their own way, cease to collaborate, and try to avoid crossing paths (at some serious loss of income).

3. Expose us to the world, which would seriously hinder our operations.

4. Attack our Covens at a time and place of their choosing to make us pay for the killings, which is a very Gypsy-vengeance response.

5. Join with the Merced telepaths and attack our European operations.

We can assume from the lack of contact that they have not chosen option #1.

"The other options are all distasteful at some level. Option #2 is the most likely. Option #3 could be a disaster for us, but proof would be hard to find and the Gypsies are known to be consummate liars. Option #4 would result in extinction of whole Gypsy kingdoms, especially in France and Germany, but also England and Ireland. The eastern Rom would probably survive, but damaged and poor. Option #5 would require a level of sophistication and collaboration that I believe is beyond Gypsy capabilities. Further, it is easy to see what they would lose and hard to see what they could gain in the struggle. However, that videotape, played throughout the Gypsy world, would generate both strong fear and strong hate. It is difficult to see which would win.

"I propose we make contact, and try to push the Gypsies into Option #2, perhaps even with financial subsidies. I would propose to say that we just learned of the actions in Italy, caused by a rogue German Coven smarting over their loss of personnel and blaming the Gypsies for helping the Merced telepaths and probably mentally emasculating Otto. I would offer an olive branch of continued collaboration and financial subsidies."

A discussion ensued, but the idea was supported. It was also important that the call be made, soon, and some details of the rogue Germans might be required. The rest of the meeting was focused on repairing the damage done to the French Covens by the ENE debacle. The German delegate surmised that the sudden absence of six ENE technicians was assumed to be tied to the German amateur effort, as they were heading into France for some sort of meeting. Inquires were made, and it became clear that one of them, Jean, had been a friend of Pierre, Gerard's now-deceased lover, while two others had been peripherally involved in the noise-generator research. They would have potentially known about the shipment of the noise generator to Bayer prior to its transfer to San Francisco. He noted that the press reports on the San Francisco abductions mentioned the generator and that it only made electromagnetic noise. They could have started to string together these events, along with the ever-so-convenient demise of the damaged Otto, into a causal string. In summary, this highlights the problem of using non-Coven personnel on anything remotely connected to Coven psychic activities.

The next morning Karla called Ken, still near Interlaken, and said, "I received last night a fascinating phone call from the Covens. We tracked the source back to France, but then there was some sort of isolation system so that we could never get a better location than that. In summary, it meets what you Americans call in the movies – good cop, bad cop."

"I can scarcely wait for the yarn they will spin," said Ken.

"Rogue Germans, mad at Otto's emasculation, guessing at Gypsy collaboration with the Merced psychics, decided to take things into their own hands. They have been ordered deep into Eastern Europe, and the Coven leadership sincerely regrets these unauthorized actions. The families of the killed will be compensated," said Karla.

Ken mused, "Not a bad effort. This allows the Gypsies some time to decide their own actions since the olive branch has been extended."

"We could ask for vengeance against the perpetrators. It is very Gypsy, and the Coven will never allow it, but it would keep a conversation going," Karla responded, "and then we could reduce our demands for the head of only the leader. At the very least, the Covens would probably up the compensation to the relatives.

"This is your show, and I will simply sit back and admire your touch," said Ken. "We have other work to do."

CHAPTER THIRTEEN

April in Paris is usually wet and dreary, despite what the song says, but early May is wonderful. It was with considerable enthusiasm, then, that a total of 27 Omega members and 12 associates arrived in the city and were placed strategically roughly every 2 kilometers in a grid. Omega personnel were always paired with Omega associates, such as Frank with Kelley, Meagan with Alexander (her Viennese Gypsy admirer), Jonathan with Betsy, and Tim and Jennifer up from Los Angeles. The six ENE members, provided by the Gypsies with impeccable forged documents, were spread around to cover the gaps in those areas in which they would not be recognized. All were in cell phone contact with Ken and Jill, on the west bank, Jonathan and Michelle in the 16th Arrondissement, and Barbara and Tiffany near Place de la Bastille. Gypsy muscle was spread throughout the city. Vehicles with Gypsy drivers were also spread through the city, equipped with anesthetic gas, and tranquilizing darts. A few were provided with the uniforms of the Gendarmerie. A safe house was found and bought through a series of transactions. It was located west of Paris, near Mantes-la-Jolie, on the River Seine.

The plan was to blanket the entire city with a network dense enough to pick up and locate any Coven trolling activity prior to an eventual "feeding," followed by capture, or if necessary killing, of the typically four to five Coven members. Of course, an actual "feeding" would be picked up even kilometers into the suburbs, and this eventuality also was anticipated.

Gabriella, Victor, Rosa, and two other Omega members simply could not stand being so far from the action. They drove up from Spain and decided to stay well south of Paris but close enough to help if needed. They chose the town of Chartres because of its beautiful cathedral. Michael suddenly showed up, sheepishly saying that Diana had given him permission since he was dying to be in on the action. Ken and Michelle noted that Michael, away from Diana and clearly missing her presence, had gained back much of his psychic potency.

Gypsy hackers had penetrated the police computers, and had marked the locations of all missing persons in the past decade. The sites were not exact, but two areas stood out – one near Montparnasse, and other at the West

Bank, Place Saint-Michel, near the Sorbonne. Pairs of Omega members were assigned to wander these areas in the evening, when the sidewalks were crowded.

After about a week, things had settled into a routine. Bugs in the communication net had been ironed out, some sites were changed to better ones, and everybody was eating awfully well. On the other hand, they were usually short on sleep since the net was very thin of personnel to maintain 24-hour coverage. Dr. Lucille Edwards found a way to join the team, and in fact they might need a doctor if things got nasty. She was paired with Michael.

It was Phyllis and Nancy who got the first contact. They were walking west from the Place Saint-Michel, just south of the Île de la Cité, in the early evening, when they both felt the dreaded cold, abusive inquiry of a Coven-trained mind, about two blocks away. "Into dark mind," said a quick-coded text message on the phone, and then very carefully they went in the direction of the signal. About a block away, they saw a somewhat older person dressed to look inconspicuous in this heavily student crowd, loitering outside of a chapel used for Catholic student services. There was clearly some sort of meeting inside, as the door was open and light was streaming out.

While they were watching, a second older man came up and had a few words with the first. Then a car drove up, turned around, and parked on the road along the bank of the Seine so that it could go back the way it came, away from the mob at Place Saint-Michel.

With scarcely a sound, suddenly Ken and Jill were there, standing behind Phyllis and Nancy. "We have cover to the west, too, since that is the way the car intends to leave. I may feel a Coven-trained mind in the car, but the signal is weak. We had better plan on three, with a likely fourth person nearby as a lookout."

Two young male students rollicked by, making vaguely suggestive comments to the girls, and quietly letting them know that a guard was behind them about 100 yards. "He is ours," they said. Then they left.

About 20 minutes later, a crowd of students started to stream out of the chapel. One young woman stopped, and laughingly entered into a conversation with the two Warlocks, as everybody was beginning to call them. A blast of Coven compulsion swept over all Omega members as the Warlocks were deluding the girl into thinking they were convivial companions with a special treat waiting for her in the car. Ken snapped on his radio, "They hooked one, a young girl. Wait until they pass that tree and move out of the light, then strike. We are right behind you. A local guard is being put to sleep."

Ken, Jill, Phyllis and Nancy started to walk toward the Coven members and towards the car. The Warlocks were so intent on their prize that they were oblivious to the people slowly converging on them, with interception just before the car. Ken was walking much faster, crossed the street, and was going to get opposite the car first. Omega members actually walked right up to the Warlocks, and suddenly the Warlocks were down. Ken hit the driver with a blast of compulsion, freezing him in place, while running up to the car. Luckily, the window was down, and an anesthetic injection did the rest. The three Warlocks were hooded with shiny material, just as a van drove up. All three bodies were put into the car.

"What about the guard?" asked Phyllis. "I don't see any way we can get him in the crowd and…." Just then, three tipsy students staggered up, with the middle one looking pretty limp. It was the guard, sedated by injection by the Gypsy backup.

"Nice work," said Ken. "Into the van." The Gypsies jumped into the Coven car. The girl was in hysterics, and Ken was afraid people would soon notice, so he jumped into the car with her. In less than 40 seconds, before anyone was close to the scene, they were on their way.

Jill held the student in her arms, saying again and again, "It is all right now. You are safe. What is your name?"

"Marie Celeste," the student sobbed, then in French, "They were in my mind. I had to obey them." Jill knew some French, and replied, "Marie, those terrible men are out cold. We will take care of them." Actually what Jill had said in her poor French was much funnier than that, but it had the proper impact on Marie Celeste, who was indeed a sensitive.

It was 45 minutes later when the car and the van approached the new suburban Omega safe house, on a bluff overlooking the Seine near the town of Mantes-la-Jolie (and incidentally with excellent sight lines in almost all directions). Four large cargo containers had been purchased and placed in a hollow behind the house, out of sight from all directions but the river, where there were trees to block the view. The containers had been painted in camouflage colors, so they were essentially invisible. The back half of each had been made into a featureless and well sound-proofed cell, with video and audio surveillance. There was a sink and a small toilet. A TV was behind a heavy Plexiglas partition. It was off. A bright light set into the ceiling was on. There were futon cushions on the floor, and one blanket. The entire cell had metal shielding to block telepathic thought. The sliding box that would provide the only routine contact for food and the like was doubly shielded, so the same mistake that happened at Planada would not occur again. However, each unit was provided with a hidden inlet for an anesthetic or poison gas cylinder that could be activated manually or remotely.

The Warlocks were stripped of all identification and dumped, one to each cell, on the futons. Each was provided with one pair of pajamas, a bar of soap, and a toothbrush.

The emotion in the Omega house was relief, not euphoria. They would now wait for the Coven response. Marie Celeste was actually curled up in Jill's arms, like a kitten. Jill was going major maternal.

CHAPTER FOURTEEN

The response was fury! Three Coven members and a guard had disappeared without a trace in the middle of Paris. The word went out all over Europe, and within two days, almost 30 Coven members were gathered in the safe house near Chartres. The background and plans of the missing members were reviewed, the place for the capture examined on foot, and yet nothing seemed out of place. The car had also vanished. Even more interestingly, no one was missing, according to the police.

Reluctantly, a call was placed to Karla. For once he was away, however, in India on some confidential Gypsy mission, and could not be reached. They expected him back next week.

For once, a feeling of helplessness oozed into Coven minds, like an acid eating away at their strength. Doubt, even a tiny bit of fear, began to intrude in private moments.

By the next day, the Coven was desperate for action, any action. It was decided to move in the Place Saint-Michel in overwhelming strength, psychic, and non-psychic. Among some of the younger Coven members, this was thought to be exactly what their unseen adversaries wanted.

Emil was quite aware of these doubts, and realized their corrosive impact on the Coven will and, indirectly, his leadership. At the 9:00 p.m. meeting, he encouraged a full discussion of options. One young Englishman, Peter, gradually took the position of the loyal opposition. Emil encouraged his comments, and Peter pushed on into dangerous waters.

"I believe that this capture was a trap, designed to move us into an area in which our adversaries, who are almost certainly the Merced psychics now in Europe, want us to go. I think that this is a mistake, and that we would do far better to lie low until their resources and patience wear thin, while assiduously trying to identify who and where they are."

Emil said smoothly, "You are thus implying that even in Paris, one of our charter cities, that this ragtag band of amateurs and do-gooders is more powerful than the combined European Covens, under my direction?"

Peter immediately saw where this thought was going, and desperately tried to backtrack. "No, of course, I will be 100 percent at your command once the decision is made. We need to be strong, united, and resolute."

Emil said smoothly, "Yes, you are so right. Strong. United. Resolute. And we get that way by 'feeding.'"

Peter screamed "No!" and then he froze under the iron will of Emil. "Place him in the chair!" A strong chair was brought up, with shackles, and Peter was installed and secured. Only then did Emil release his compulsion.

"No, I beg you! I will be your faithful servant for life. Don't do this to me!" Peter sobbed.

Emil said smoothly, "But you are my servant. Even now, I feel the power of the united Covens growing in anticipation of what is to come. You are strengthening us all, and in some way, you will be a key to the final victory."

"No, noooo!" Then the screaming began, piercing, soprano screams, and the Coven minds burrowed into Peter, and fed, fed well, on a torrent, a flood of fear. Fed, and fed, until nothing was left.

Members of the Coven looked around at each other, and their eyes glowed. They were strong. They would win. And then the "feedings" would be transcendental. There were no doubts now. And then the slow slump into the post-prandial daze.

Fourteen kilometers away, Gabriella and Victor were stunned. Such bestial horror, such abject terror. A high-level "feeding," and close, so close to Chartres. They quickly agreed on the direction, and Victor hauled out his cell phone.

Ken was about to go to bed when the phone rang. He listened intently, then hung up. "Gabriella and Victor have located their lair. There was just a high-level 'feeding' close to Chartres, with at least two dozen people involved, and we have the direction. Let me call our teams."

CHAPTER FIFTEEN

The fields around Chartres were green with young wheat. The sky was the robin's-egg blue so appreciated by the Impressionists. Puffy white clouds drifted in lazily from the west. The sound of roosters could be heard as they roused the flock for their morning debauch. The most cursory of investigations had established that the house on the hill was protected with an extraordinary level of redundant security, which had as a benefit establishing without a doubt that this was the Coven headquarters. However, there were only a few roads to and from the house. At the end of the long dirt road and driveway, any vehicle had only two choices, north toward the city and the freeway, or south deeper into the countryside.

Karla, Ken, Roberto, and Jonathan discussed their options. Because the house was unassailable, short of weeks of preparation, they decided to make the roads lethal. The road to Chartres was lined for almost a kilometer with a wooden fence protecting the wheat fields. The other side had a row of poplars. A quick call was made, and about 45 minutes later, a van drove up with Gypsy drivers. Small packages, each looking like a loaf of bread, were carefully attached to the top of each post, with the flat side toward the road. Eventually, the entire kilometer was lined every 10 meters with the packages. At the last moment, spray paint was used to disguise the objects.

Personnel were sent by a circuitous route with all the vehicles to block the south road where it was forced down into a gully, across a narrow bridge and up the other side. A few packages were dedicated to this stretch, but the main armaments were AK-47s and rocket-propelled grenades. About two dozen Gypsies and three Omega members manned this route. All the rest were placed beyond the mined kilometer, areas in which survivors might flee. In all cases, Omega members were supported by Omega associates and Gypsy muscle. Wildly diverse weapons were passed out, and concealed positions chosen.

About 10:30 a.m., a single van rolled down the road, and turned towards Chartres.

"Let it go," said Ken.

It was close to noon and getting hot. The buzzing of the insects was sort of soothing, and no one had had any sleep the previous night. Many a head

297

drooped, only to be jerked up, often by the other watcher at the site. By 1:00 p.m., Ken was wondering whether he ought to pull them back and get them at least water. Then there was motion at the house. Three vehicles, looking like Range Rovers, drove partway down the driveway and then turned west on a grassy road across the fields. There was no road in that direction for 5 kilometers, but on they went. Ken was in despair. "I should have known," he thought.

Then, several more vehicles came down the driveway, and continued onto the paved road. Two went south, but the other five turned north. Roberto was sitting at a laptop, gauging their progress. He wanted the south cars to start the fight since the north convoy was easier to hit. The cars heading north were making no attempt to look random, but were following each other perhaps 60 feet apart. Roberto squinted his eyes and did a quick calculation – 20 meters apiece, plus the cars. Perhaps 150 meters long for the convoy. The Claymore mines were set up in five independent groups – 200 meters long – each having its own frequency for ignition. The cars passed Claymore groups #1 and #2, and were just leaving group #3 and into group #4 when there were explosions and the rattle of gunfire from the south. Incredibly, the northern convoy continued north. Roberto could hardly believe that they would ignore an obvious attack. Still the convoy came, leaving group #4 and entering group #5. Then they started to slow, and the last car swung around in the narrow road, crosswise right at the transition between group #4 and group #5. This will have to do. Roberto glanced over to Ken, who nodded, and the laptop keys F4 and F5 were depressed.

Two sets of mines, 20 mines apiece, sprayed the entire highway with shrapnel, and the cars shuddered to a halt, riddled from end to end. Parts of one car was totally blown away. Even before the echoes had faded, Ken said, "Let's boogie. Remember, I want the two least wounded to survive. All others, dead or alive, get a single bullet in the brain."

Roberto started running down the road, shouting, "I need help with the unexploded mines. Everybody grab two or three mines. They are secured now. Then run south, covering your faces as you pass the driveway. They probably have active surveillance cameras."

Ken and Michelle ran out into the field, southeast of the road, and dropped into a small, dry stream bed that sloped down to the larger creek to the south.

Already sirens were screaming, coming from the direction of Chartres. Police and ambulances streamed down the road to what was obviously a major accident or crime scene. However, by the time the first one had arrived at the northern-most wrecked car (for some reason, none of them had actually caught fire), the rest of the Omega and Gypsy teams were long gone to the south, where the cars and vans were located south of the bridge. There, the scene was carnage. One of the two cars was in the creek, the other blown to shreds at the bridge edge, blocking the road. As they scrambled across the bridge and up the bank, Tiffany said, "We have one alive, British by looks."

In less than 12 minutes, the scene was deserted as every vehicle headed down the highway in prearranged escape routes. Omega members leaned out windows and made sure that anyone near the road was looking elsewhere when the cars passed. Soon they had fanned out, two north to Paris and the Mantes-la-Jolie safe house, two south into Spain, and the rest off to Vienna via Switzerland.

Ken and Michelle waited in the field, close but invisible. "Here he comes," said Ken. "Looks good," said Michelle.

A senior inspector of the Gendarmerie had arrived on the chaotic scene, Chief Inspector Reynaud. He was quickly briefed. Two men had been found alive, and they were being put into an ambulance for transport to Chartres. While the body count was not complete, it appeared that there were 16 dead bodies, all middle-aged men, dressed in deliberately casual and cheap clothes but most wearing Rolex watches. Their underwear was silk, one policeman noted.

Inspector Reynaud knew he was about to be part of the crime event of his life – one that could make (or possible break) his career. Five cars, destroyed by what must have been explosives, 16 dead men, each with a single bullet hole in the head even when it appeared that the subject was already dead, and two men carefully left alive.

This has a major right-wing conspiracy written all over it! President Royale, a good and effective Socialist, was uncovering vast amounts of income and wealth carefully hidden from tax collectors in her ever-more penetrating descent into the French way of fraud. Already heads had rolled at major French corporations, and the right-wing legislators were in orbit, thirsting for her scalp. Had he uncovered such a group of plotters?

A policeman came up, and said, "All the license plates are faked, as is all the identification we have found on them. Many are carrying cash to the level of thousands of Euros apiece. Carefully save all the evidence. Get me two additional police photographers here immediately. Cordon off the crime scene from at least 2 kilometers east. We have something really important here."

The gendarme saluted, and left. Inspector Reynaud was gradually gathering a serious number of police at his disposal, when a sudden thought occurred to him, "Where did those cars come from? Check that house over there to see if the residents know anything."

Because the road was blocked with wrecked cars, 12 police headed down the road on foot. Six went up to the house, while six continued down the road to the south.

Ten minutes later, the police radio crackled, "Another massive massacre site here at the bridge, about 500 meters south of the driveway. Two cars, six more bodies. Signs of bombs."

Inspector Reynaud picked up his radio, and said, "Get me helicopter air coverage. The situation down here is critical. Bar all roads around the area to a distance of 10 kilometers."

He was just turning to his subordinate, who was coming up with additional information, when a massive explosion blew the entire residence, and presumably six of his staff members, into a million shards. Fire immediately started in the wreckage. All were stunned, and were frozen for seconds as in some strange static tableau.

"Get ambulances to the house. Use the wheat fields." In his heart, Reynaud knew there was no hope for his men.

Who could have caused all this? The Communists could have had such capabilities in the past, but they were weak and fragmented. There were a number of vigorous young socialist youth groups, breathing smoke and fire at meetings, but the explosives and the organization are far too good for that. And the single bullet hole in the head of dead people! That sounded like vengeance. The fact that two were left alive for the usual thorough French interrogations is most interesting. It's as though whoever did this wanted the word to get out that the cabal existed.

A thought drifted into his head. The same right-wing groups were not only anti-socialist, they were also anti-immigrant, which in reality meant anti-Islamic immigrants. The Islamic fundamentalists have the explosive and have the capabilities; the young socialists have the knowledge to penetrate this cabal. It all started to make sense.

Ken looked at Michelle, and she nodded. They had given Inspector Reynaud plenty to sink his teeth into now, and he would be a bulldog in tracking down every (false) lead. It would be extremely interesting to see how the Covens would handle these events, especially when two or more of their members were in French custody, a custody sure to persist since they killed six policemen in their booby-trapped house.

Very carefully, Ken and Micelle slipped down to the creek bed, crossed at a shallow spot, and then up the bank and onto an old farm road. A Citroën "deux Chevaux" was waiting, with a Gypsy driver. Ken and Michelle got in, and left to the south. No one saw them pass, of course, because at key moments they were all looking elsewhere. Then in a roundabout route, they headed west, then north via Le Mans to Paris.

Two hours later – the traffic was awful – all the teams but Ken and Michelle were back at the Mantes-la-Jolie safe house, the Omega and Gypsy teams sprawled in exhaustion. Most of them had not slept for 24 hours, but there was still work to do. The English captive was put into the fourth secure cell, and the Coven associate guard for Saint-Michel was simply shackled to a chair in the outside room of the cargo container. Minutes passed, and all waited nervously. Finally, Ken and Michelle arrived, and relaxation and satisfaction could set in.

Ken gave a short summary of how they had planted ideas in the head of an Inspector Reynaud, who was both sharp mentally and in charge of the local Gendarmerie investigation. And then they set up the night guard schedule and everybody else gratefully hit the sack.

Well to the north of Chartres, close to the turn-off to Dreux, the three Range Rovers of the Coven Near Support Team, always required by Coven protocols in large operations, suddenly picked up intensive police activity on their scanners. It soon became clear that there had been a massive ambush, and most of the entire northeast group had been killed. Then came a short message for two ambulances, as two Coven members had clearly survived.

Emil frowned, looked into an old-fashioned day planner notebook, and told the driver, "Call Brussels on frequency 332.75.01. When you have contact, say Execute EXPCA. Head to Lauterbrunnen."

At the outer Autoroute belt in Paris, the lead Range Rover headed east, deviating from the original plan. The other two Range Rovers followed it unquestioningly. One did not challenge Emil's choices, as if any further proof were needed.

CHAPTER SIXTEEN

The Security Wing of the Chartres hospital was rarely used by the police, so the hospital had been in the habit of using it for private patients with optional surgery, such as the increasingly popular breast implants, mimicking an American staple. The funds from these activities were a significant fraction of the hospital's total income.

Thus, there was a flurry of activity when the police gave notice of two patients headed for the Emergency Room, and then to the Security Wing. When the patients arrived, physicians determined that although their wounds were serious, they were by no means life-threatening. After some minor surgery, they were moved into the Security Wing, which still had a faint odor of perfume. Inspector Reynaud initiated the questioning of the patients as soon as they were conscious.

The answers from the two victims, in separate bedrooms, were roughly similar, but differed in some important details. Both said they were on a top-secret government-sponsored program through ENE, and had just come for a meeting on the progress. They were required to travel with false papers and vehicles to maintain the high-security level, and they were prohibited from revealing their true names to police officers. All further inquiries must be directed to the Bureau de Sécurité in the Palais Royale in Paris. The responses were transcribed and entered into computers for analysis.

Upon analysis, it appeared that there were important differences. Each gave a different answer about where the cars were going, one to ENE Headquarters in Paris, and the other to ENE Research Labs near Versailles. There was likewise confusion as to where they had come from, the number of people at the meeting, and other points. The police knew they were being fed a story.

The Chartres District of the Gendarmerie requested support from the local police for increased security at the hospital. Two men were stationed in the lobby, and two in an unmarked car parked outside the hospital's sole entrance. They were to be relieved every four hours. Inspector Reynaud had two of his own men at the Security Wing's sole entrance.

It was about three o'clock the next morning when three men left a parked car in the hospital parking lot, and approached the hospital entrance. Both of the plain-clothed policemen in the car stepped out, walked over to them, and asked some questions. The police seemed satisfied by the answers, and the three men left toward the main hospital entrance. The police got back in their car.

The three men were soon joined by a fourth, who had come up unnoticed from somewhere behind the police car. The four men now avoided the main entrance and went toward the service entrance of the hospital. A soft "pop" was all that was heard as the back security camera was destroyed by a silenced pistol.

Ten minutes later, the four men were seen leaving in great haste. They passed the police car with the two unmoving policemen, got into their car, and left. Inspector Reynaud watched them leave, then quickly checked his GPS locator he had put on their car to make sure it was working. He watched the car leave the hospital grounds, then head north toward Paris. A quick tersely coded message into the police radio, and the Paris Gendarmerie would soon be in position to continue tracking the car.

Inspector Reynaud had not been aware of the Chartres police undercover stakeout, but was disgusted by lack of police support. They seemed to have fallen asleep on the job, and so he went over to their car. He opened the door, and caught a faint whiff of almond. Stepping back quickly, he realized that the policemen were both dead.

He went into the hospital, and inquired about the four who had just come in. The night nurse claimed that she had been on duty the entire time and had seen no one. Reynaud raced up to the Security Wing, where his two gendarmes were guarding the corridor to the rooms, awake and alert. They too had seen no one, and Reynaud believed them.

Curious and confused, Reynaud went down the corridor, and as expected found the rooms labeled but empty. He had secretly had the two suspects moved to a maternity wing, shackled to beds, and guarded by two other gendarmes. He went down to them, and all was well.

Returning to the entrance, he asked for and was brought into the room holding the security cameras. One had failed at almost exactly the time the men headed past him to go into the hospital – the one that surveyed the delivery entrance. So the night nurse was telling the truth. Checking on the camera on the Security Wing, Reynaud was pleased to find his two officers alert, but then suddenly they turned and faced the wall as four men came into view. Two men stayed directly behind the immobile officers, and two went down the corridor. About two minutes later, they came back up the hall in some haste, and all four left. As soon as they had left the view of the camera, the officers turned to their posts, chatting amiably as though nothing had happened.

Reynaud called the gendarmes down to the camera room and showed them the recoding. Both officers swore that they had no recollection whatsoever of these actions, with a vehemence that forced Reynaud to believe them. How had these men forced the officers not to see them? Some sort of compulsion? Instant hypnosis? Reynaud was clueless but deeply disturbed. What had they stumbled onto? It turned out that he was correct to understand that these two captured men, so carefully spared from the massacre, would be targeted by the cabal before they could be forced to speak. But the unusual actions of the two police on stakeout, and his own totally trustworthy officers, showed something else was at work here, something he did not even want to have to consider, but something he deeply feared.

It was by now abundantly clear that powerful forces would try again to kill these men. He would remain until morning, and then have the men taken to separate heavily guarded locations where the general public has no access. One could be the Centre d'Etudes Nucléaires de Saclay, just south of Paris, with its double barbed wire fence and guard dogs protecting national nuclear technology. He thought that the Special Forces Operations Center at Nancy might be another. These men must not die. He called his superior in Paris, Jacques Goudergues, the deputy director of the Gendarmerie.

The next morning, Inspector Reynaud was relieved to see three gendarme transport vans arrive, each with motorcycle escort. The deputy director himself had come down and congratulated Inspector Reynaud on an excellent effort, and assigned additional personnel and equipment to the task. He was pleased to report that he already had approval from Saclay for the transfer of one prisoner to the Saclay Infirmary, and he expected at any moment to get approval from Nancy.

The vans, prisoners, the two guards, and Inspector Reynaud were scheduled to leave the hospital grounds at roughly 9:15 a.m. While the prisoners were being collected and brought down, Inspector Reynaud became uneasy about how well things seemed to be going, he sat down beside the nurse at the front entry admittance station, plugged in his laptop, and e-mailed a highly confidential summary to a trusted colleague in the Paris division.

Twelve kilometers north of the hospital, Autoroute E50 swings down an incline into a valley and then curves rather sharply across a set of bridges before climbing out again. The gendarme convoy was spread out, with the motorcycle escort in front, then the three police vans. Suddenly, a tandem gasoline tanker drifted out of its lane during the turn and its trailing tanker forced the middle police van into the bridge railing at high speed. The last trailer flipped, spraying the entire area with gasoline. An enormous fireball erupted, incinerating all in the middle van.

Of course, it hardly mattered. Inspector Reynaud, the two Coven prisoners, and the two Reynaud gendarmes were already dead, and only the unsuspecting and betrayed driver died in the fire.

Almost miraculously, the driver of the gasoline tanker was able to leap from his truck onto the road and then into the edge of the creek, unseen by anyone because of the fire between him and the rest of the convoy. He gathered his feet, and ran as if possessed up the valley and into heavy brush, egged on by screaming sirens. E50 was closed for hours to clear the wreckage.

That morning, Victor and Gabriella, and two of the newer and more powerful Omega members from their San Joaquin Valley cells, Felicity and Jorge, showed up unexpectedly at the Paris safe house. Gabriella, always the most vocal of the pair, started in as soon as everyone was together. "We were monitoring the hospital from a fair distance away last night and this morning, when at about 3:00 a.m., we got evidence of psychic assault. The first was somewhere in the parking lot next to the hospital, and the goal seemed to be deception. Then about 10 minutes later, another and more sustained effort was detected, this one forcing both a physical action, and memory blanking. We were wondering if we should intervene when we saw four men leave the hospital in a car and drive north. We could sense no trauma in the hospital, no deaths, and we could sense the anger and frustration of the Coven members as they left. Whatever had been their plan, it hadn't worked.

"It seems your plan to leave two Coven members alive is bearing fruit already. The Covens are clearly worried. About two hours ago, there was a major police presence at the hospital, which ended with a convoy headed north, so we thought it safe to come here and report."

Roberto interjected, "Bad news! The police radio reported not an hour ago a massive accident on E50, just north of Chartres, with a gasoline tanker and police vehicles involved and a number of fatalities. No further details as of now, but E50 northbound is closed and expected to stay that way for hours."

Ken said, "Our boys clearly play for keeps. I would bet big money that two of those fatalities were the Coven prisoners, and I fear for Inspector Reynaud, who may have learned too much from the failed hospital kidnapping this morning. This shows a disturbing level of Coven non-psychic muscle. I wonder how they do it, maintaining loyalty in such conditions? Perhaps our guard may be useful after all. And Karla, could your fantastic Gypsy hackers tell us more about how the police response was staged?"

"Immediately. This response is pretty brutal and well executed. We want to know more about how they gathered and directed their resources for this coup at such short notice. Things done in haste often leave ragged footprints," Karla responded, and left the room.

In order to keep the tension minimal, it was a largely female team – Jill, Gabriella, Betsy, and Michelle, plus Ken and Victor – that brought the guard out of his cell and into a well-lit room. He was seated in a comfortable chair, unshackled, and offered some breakfast. He was not hungry, but took some café au lait in a bowl. He was simply drowned in abject terror inside.

Gabriella started, "We have no desire or need to hurt you. We know you work for the Covens, powerful and evil psychics who have awful ways to insure loyalty among their non-psychic associates. We oppose them, and are determined to rid the world of them. We just killed 22 of them near Chartres. We can protect you from them, forever. But you can help us to protect you by telling us all you know. As you realize, if the Covens ever found you, they would kill you instantly by the most brutal way possible. So let's start by telling us your name."

The Omega members instantly knew that his name was Claude, but they made no sign of this. Claude was silent, trying to think, and while doing so went back to his capture and initiation into the Coven network. Instinctively he thought of the left side of his left hand, burned and shriveled at Coven impulsion.

So that's how they did it, thought Gabriella. He was forced to fry his own hand under their compulsion. But there was something else.

But, thought Claude, the alternative was a "feeding," using the Coven term, and his forehead beaded with sweat and panic at what he had seen.

Ken started, "We suspect that the Covens have shown you their capacity to force people to do things they otherwise wouldn't consider. They doubtless also told you they have other powers, which they don't. Finally, they probably lied to you about the death by 'feeding.' They can only do that to other psychics, and you are not psychic. That was an empty threat designed to scare you into unquestioning and total obedience."

Claude was stunned by the level of knowledge these people had of the Covens. They knew the Covens had psychic powers, what they could do, and, it appears, what they can't do. Yet they claimed they just killed what had to be a significant fraction of the French Covens. How did they do it? Could they protect him? Claude had still not said a word. Finally his curiosity could not be restrained. Twenty-two Coven members? Those omniscient and powerful quasi-diabolical creatures. Twenty-two killed at once! Somehow he wanted to believe these people. He had to know.

Claude murmured, "How did you kill them?"

Ken said, "Your name, first, and information on your recruitment or, as we like to describe it, your enslavement."

"My name is Claude. They made me do this to myself," and held up his left hand. The side of the hand from the base of the little finger to the wrist was a mass of scar tissue. "They made me watch a 'feeding,' and they said they had the power to know what I was doing and thinking even when I was not near them. If I violated their least instruction, or mentioned a single word about them, they would immediately know and my fate would be a 'feeding.'"

Michelle said, "They lied to you. Their range of compulsion is no more than about 10 meters, and their ability to read minds is very poor. They sense emotions, fear, and use that. If you join with us, voluntarily, you will see how we have captured four Coven members and are holding them here. By this means, we are drawing the Coven into a trap."

She continued, "As to our recent success, we knew about their Chartres safe house, and we simply mined the public road leading away from it with more than 100 camouflaged Claymore mines. When a convoy of five vehicles used the road, we triggered the mines remotely. We operate on the basis of high technology."

Claude asked, "Which Coven members are you holding?"

Michelle answered, since Claude seemed to be opening up to her, a very attractive woman, "The three that were trolling for the girl at Saint-Michel, and a high-level British Coven member captured at the Chartres attack."

Claude replied, now more animated as he gained confidence, "The Saint-Michel team consisted of low-level members on a standard 'feeding' capture. I felt so sorry for the victims, but I was convinced that if I faltered in any way, I would be next. Could I see the British Coven member?" Claude inquired.

Gabriella and Michelle's eyes met above Claude's head. A small smile, a nod. He was theirs.

"By all means," said Ken. "By the way, the room and window are psy-shielded. He cannot detect you or us. In any case, we will be using a video camera."

They went to the next room, and checked cell #4. William was pacing the cell, unable to get any psychic readings of people nearby. He could be on a desert island, for all he could learn. But there was food, apples and bread, plus bottled water. They were clearly keeping him alive for some purpose. He had no doubt, however, that his future prospects were dim indeed.

Claude looked, and said, "I know him. I drove him in from the airport. He was the head of the British delegation, the top Coven leader in England."

Gabriella mused, "Well, well, well, now he is ours."

Roberto appeared at the door, and gestured to Ken, leaving Gabriella, Victor, and Jill with Claude, Ken, Michelle and Betsy, and returned to the main room. Karla and two of his men were already there. "Bad news. Inspector Reynaud and two of his gendarmes died in the crash with the prisoners. By the way, the truck driver appears to have fled the scene on foot, unharmed."

Ken turned, and asked, "Karla, is this something you could look into?"

Karla answered, "Will do! Incidentally, we have checked all the hospital e-mails and electronic transfers, and just before Reynaud left in the convoy, he e-mailed to a gendarme in Paris. We have his name, Tomas LaFitte. He is a mid-level inspector of the gendarmes like Reynaud. They were in a training class together last year. I think we'd better have a visit, and soon. Incidentally, our hackers erased the trace of the file from the hospital computers. We couldn't do the same in Paris because of a firewall."

"Great work!" said Ken. "Maybe Reynaud's death was not in vain."

It was only four hours later at the entrance to the Palais Royal metro stop near the headquarters of the Gendarmerie that Inspector Tomas LaFitte was sadly leaving work to go home to tell his young wife, Maude, that their mutual friend Reynaud had died in that terrible accident. Alexis came alongside him and said, "Reynaud was murdered because of what he and now you know. We should talk, now, at an inconspicuous site. You might be next. They trace e-mail, you know."

Tomas was stunned, "Who are you?" he asked. Alexis answered, "A friend of Reynaud's, and an enemy of the cabal he uncovered at Chartres. Let's walk toward Le Carousel. There are some benches there and this time of night, it is dim. You need have no fear of me, I am unarmed, and the place is still reasonably public. I fear for you, and I fear for your wife. We must get her out of the house, now, and into someplace secure. These people are powerful and desperate. Would she come down here if you asked her?"

"Of course!" was the answer. We are very close, and she loves to get out."

They walked past the edge of the Louvre and into Place du Carrousel. The glass pyramid of the Louvre glowed with lights, but the park to the west was dim. On the benches were two young women, Michelle and Gabriella. Alexis introduced them, by name.

They sat down, and Alexis explained, "Reynaud sent that e-mail to you because he was worried. The deputy inspector came down himself to pick up the prisoners, a most unusual event in itself. He had seen how an attempt had been made on the lives of the two injured businessmen, and by mysterious means. He was over his head, and worried. Thus, at the last minute, literally, he sat down and sent you his partially completed report. Then they got into the convoy, only to have his car obliterated by a gas tanker. Both prisoners died, too, as well as the gendarmes who were guarding the Security Wing.

"We have erased the record of your e-mail from the hospital records, but we could not do the same in your account here because of a firewall. They will search for any message from Chartres to Paris in the past day, and yours will surface – and maybe it already has. That will verify that you are the last person to know what Reynaud found, and you will have to be killed immediately. Please get your wife down here immediately. We can protect you at a secure house.

"I know we are asking a lot of you, but by now you see how these people play for keeps. You are the last threat to them."

Tomas nodded. Then he turned to the woman, "Are you part of this, too?"

Gabriella answered, "Yes. I was barely saved from a bestial enslavement, torture, and death by my friends. What Alexis has said is entirely fact. You and your wife are just a hair away from death."

Tomas nodded and picked up his cell phone. "Not the Palais Royal metro stop. Have her pick one near here, but not that one," said Ken. Tomas nodded. The call went out to Maude, very innocent sounding, mentioning a mutual friend in town and an early evening at a favorite brasserie. She agreed to come immediately.

Twenty minutes later, they were all together outside the Metro stop. Tomas started by saying, "Reynaud was murdered, but before he died, he sent me an e-mail this morning telling of this powerful secret cabal. Now I know, too, and they will certainly kill me and, if possible, use you to get me. We are in trouble."

Maude said, "I had just left the apartment and was down at the corner, when two cars drove up to our apartment block and about six men in suits jumped out and ran into the apartment. I heard glass break. I almost went back to look, but somehow I was scared of them, so I hurried to the Metro, and a train came in just as I hit the platform."

"Let's move, folks. Ken picked up his cell phone, and in 30 seconds, two cars drove up. All got in, and they were soon heading across the Seine, away from Palais Royal, and eventually west. In about 40 minutes, they drove up to the Mantes-la-Jolie safe house, and all breathed sighs of relief.

The arrival of Tomas and Maude in the room prompted rejoicing and hugs for all. What a nice-looking bunch of people, thought Maude. Who are they? Why are they so happy for us?

"Tomas, could you download that e-mail so we could see it?" asked Alexis.

"Actually, I printed a copy and then deleted it from my computer," said Tomas.

Jill was busy getting everybody something to eat. Rooms and beds were assigned – even couches, anything, because the house was so full.

Just then Karla burst in, "We have the driver of the gasoline tanker! My Gypsy teams flooded the region, looking exactly where the police wouldn't look, in the hedgerows, among the homeless, and we found him, scared and trying to get as far away from Paris as possible. He was a Coven Associate who was threatened with a 'feeding' if he didn't cause the accident. He will be here within the hour."

Tomas spread flat the e-mail text on the table. Ken and Michelle recognized pretty much of everything they had put into Reynaud's mind. But then there were the events at the hospital, Reynaud had become even more convinced of the power and ruthlessness of these men of the "cabal" as he named it, but with the additional very important point that they were able to convince his own men, fully alert, to face the wall and forget ever having seen them This was some sort of instant hypnosis, and it profoundly scared him. What was the use of even having guards if at any moment they could be blinded?

All this was in the e-mail, along with his plans to separate the prisoners on really secure military sites. The last recorded entry at was at 6:00 a.m., when he heard relief was coming.

Ken said, "Reynaud had done well, protected his men, and was betrayed by the deputy director himself."

Ken thought that it was highly likely that the deputy director was in fact a Warlock, and doubtless so were others on his staff, so that they working together could control people. He also realized that the prisoners Omega held were potentially invaluable. The next morning, it was time to have a conversation with the British Warlock.

Ken smiled and said, "I think that Meagan should be present and very active in the discussion." Now they were getting somewhere.

Jill had taken Maude under her wing, with Tomas sort of trailing behind. Soon they were set up in relatively private quarters (some of the Gypsy men were exiled to tents behind the house to make space, but that didn't bother them a bit. They had lived most of their lives under canvas).

Silence fell over the safe house, as the exhausted teams slept.

Roberto was wandering the rounds and checking electronic security, as the 10:00 p.m. to 2:00 a.m. security. He somehow felt that all these sleeping people were his children, in his care. A new creature was being born, born in love and altruism, and if protected in its infancy, it could grow and change the entire direction of a troubled world.

The next morning, they awoke to find additional Gypsy teams camped on the lawn, and with them the truck driver.

He was almost limp with exhaustion, as the hours of dread panic had sapped his strength. He no longer cared what was going to happen to him any more. He knew he had killed important people, and that he had no friends in the world. Everybody would kill him on sight, Covens and outsiders. He sat hunched over his café au lait, trying to enjoy these last few moments of his existence. Just please not a 'feeding!'

Then they brought in the guard from Place Saint-Michel, who sat down and also had café au lait. They didn't know each other, because it was Coven practice to have each Associate tied to a specific Coven member to discourage them from building lateral ties with other Associates.

"There will be no Coven 'feedings' on Associates, and there never were," said Claude. "They can't feed on non-sensitives, and you and I are non-sensitives. Also, their powers don't extend much more than 10 meters on the average. They can't read thoughts well. And these people are willing to protect us, even after all we've done for the Coven."

"Pretty good summary," thought Ken.

Karla came by, and said, "I have to get back to Slovakia. I am supposed to take a Coven call over the Italy massacre today, in the evening.

"For communications, use land lines, not cell phones or satellite phones. Our new ENE helpers are proving to be ever so useful, as they set up Coven wire intercept systems. However, there were so few Coven members, they could review only a tiny fraction of the intercepts, and the filters were extremely tight. Here is a printed list of the words they search for, in each language. These were chosen, by the way, by Gerard personally. Avoid these at all costs. I have written next to them our alternatives.

"I have also called Hector and Vlady back from Merced. Nothing seems to be happening there, your own security seems more than adequate, and the action is here. They will be useful, including their excellent skill in languages, a skill sadly lacking in most American Omega members."

Ken laughed, "Well done. How are you going to handle the Covens in the phone call?"

"I will use your ever-useful American good cop, bad cop," Karla answered. "I will have the Spanish Calé red hot with Latin anger, and barely constrained by the rest of the kingdoms. I will totally deny involvement in the German extractions, after deep discussions with the Sinte, saying the driver might have been a Turk. Germany is rife with them. I'll brief you after the call. What are you going to do here?"

"First, Victor has set up a small passive intelligence operation at Chartres, in case we could learn something more. Second, our hardware for the Lauterbrunnen penetration is almost ready, and will be shipped from California next week. You will like it. Third, we will data mine our captives.

That alone will take weeks," said Ken. "I think a period of quiescence will cause the Coven anxiety beyond measure. The quick extraction of Tomas and his wife alone will indicate serious capabilities in Paris. I expect there will soon be a lot of discussion, and I hope it will take place in Lauterbrunnen."

Karla and a lieutenant left, and the high-level Omega members conferred. This included Meagan, who was now way up the capability chart, and Betsy, who continued to develop. In the wide-ranging discussion, it was decided to start by simply removing some of the psy-shielding from one area of the Coven cells. There, unseen, would be two Omega members, two support teams, a digital audio recorder, and a static protection system. The work would always be continually monitored by camera in the main house. An anesthetic cylinder was placed in the room with a triggering device in the room or back at the house in the surveillance room, should somehow the Coven member get control. All personnel were to be in "dark mind" mode as long as they could hold it, probably about 30 to 40 minutes at a time.

They started that afternoon with one of the Place Saint-Michel Warlocks. Relatively little was learned in his rambling mental excursions, dominated as they were by self-pity for his inevitable demise.

The next morning, they tried the British Coven member, whose name was William. He was another matter, entirely. He was scheming, examining all options, and running through potential ways his whereabouts could be learned and his rescue accomplished. There was a nagging thought that if they couldn't rescue him, they would have to kill him. He had no idea he was being read, and consequently he made no attempt to withhold names and places, which he revealed in elaborate detail. Fortunately, he did not dwell on his 'feedings.' He did run through an analysis of that Irish girl's escape, and started to think that somehow that was behind their present trauma. He still had no idea that the northern convoy had been eradicated, thinking that his small group of vehicles was targeted because of him specifically.

After 40 minutes, the teams left the room, maintaining dark mind, and then downloaded what they learned. It was in awesome detail – locations and names of British Covens were gathered with scrupulous precision, including even code words for a telephone contact if William ever got away.

They also learned that in the dark period each was allowed for eight hours a night, he was working around his cell, checking the very bottom of the container because he found serious rust in several joist welds. Perhaps he could force enough apart to escape.

The Omega team was exhausted, but their penetration of the British Island Covens was essentially complete. A surprisingly high number of the Warlocks were in and close to the government. This was going to be tricky.

The next day, the process was essentially repeated, but little more was learned. On the other hand, the detail was confirmed, extended, refined, and a possible weakness was identified – "feeding" was not easy in London because of a tight police presence, so they quietly moved to a safe house near Liverpool where gay sailors were common.

The following day, the loudspeaker in William's cell, until now silent, came to life.

"Please name the A-level Coven members in the combined European Covens. The degree of your honesty and completeness will determine the degree of punishment or reward. We must tell you that you are only one of many Coven prisoners, and the Covens, under the deputy director of the Gendarmerie, just incinerated two high-level Coven members that the police had captured in the recent raid at Chartres. You too will be dead if they ever find you, and your death may well be worse, much worse, than incineration."

Just outside the room, Omega members strained to catch William's racing thoughts. They are trying to identify Emil, William thought, so they still don't know the organization. Maybe I can string them along, get some reward, and learn more about them. He decided to see what they would accept.

"His name is Gerard," William said.

Instantly, they turned off the lights in the room, and the gentle flow of cool air from the vent ceased. He soon learned that the water was also shut off.

William, completely unaware that he was being read like a book, then ran through the entire European Coven to see who he could name that would satisfy these unseen people and still cover for Emil. To even mention Emil's name and position was punishable by death, and William still thought that

316

there might be a chance to get away.

On the other side of the wall, Omega members were at their memory limits, and in about 15 minutes, they had to break off and compare notes. It took almost two hours, but at the end of the time they had a pretty good depiction of the European Coven, or at least the western component. There was another whole component in Eastern Europe and especially now Russia, powerful and rapidly expanding in the chaos of the post-Soviet Union era.

In the cell, William by now noticed that neither the water nor toilet was operational, and the room was getting stuffy. He began to think he may have made a mistake. These people clearly knew a lot.

By the next day, William was starting to really suffer from thirst. No food or drink had come. He simply could not get his mouth wet any more, and he was starting to fear for the oxygen content of the increasing stuffy air.

At the same time of day, the lights came on and the speaker came to life, "Please name the A-level Coven members in the combined European Covens."

He could feel the air start to flow, and he raced over to the faucet to find water was flowing again. He drank and drank, washed his face, and decided that he had to cooperate. Next time it might be longer, and he was totally in their power.

With a sigh, and a sense that he was about to pass a barrier that would mean he could never go back to his prior life, he began, "The A Prime Coven member is called Emil. Neither I nor anyone else knows his real name, his age, or where he was from. All who once knew are now dead. He looks very old, is about 185 centimeters high, thin, but I am told he is really not much over 60 years. His powers are awesome, and he can kill by thought alone. I saw a person strangled to death by Emil by thought alone. Whatever he says is law, as he seems to have the power to read minds. No one dares oppose him. The other A-level members are way below him in power. There are two Germans, one of whom has recently had some physical ailments and we don't see him much any more. Neither the Italian nor the Spanish or Austrian Covens have an A-level member. I am B-level and would not dare to aspire to A-level status. That might be a sure route to an awful death. Emil does not like competition."

317

Once he began, William continued at length, punctuated by inquiries as to what benefit this would get him, and what protection he would be provided. However, he did not know many details outside of the British Island Covens, and the feeling was this ignorance was a deliberate Coven effort for security.

Still, his food was immediately upgraded, and BBC was put on the TV under his control. One morning he woke up to find a cot in the cell with him. How it got there, he had no idea, but it made sleep better.

Two days later, Nicholas of the ENE, who was often on night surveillance duty, mentioned to Ken that even with the cot, William was not sleeping well. "While the lights are out, we of course maintain infrared scans, and he spends a lot of time tossing and turning. Occasionally he cries out or moans. I think he has nightmares. None of the others behave that way."

Ken replied, "Thank you. I'll check this one out myself. I am not sure I want anyone else to partake in the nightmares of a high-level Coven member. Wake me next time it happens."

It was about 2:30 a.m. when Ken got the call from Nicholas. He went out into the warm summer night, smelling flowers. There was a good slice of moon showing, and he could pick his way to William's prison without using his flashlight. He quietly opened the door to step into the anteroom. He stopped, backed up and shut the door. He went by Nicholas's post, and said, "You were right. He is having nightmares about his 'feeding' victims. This is important to us. Nice going." Nicholas beamed. Somehow praise from this group made you feel so good inside.

The next morning, over breakfast, Ken said, "William has pretty brutal nightmares about the suffering of his 'feeding' victims. Let's see what we can do with him."

It was about one week later, when Omega members had learned about everything William knew, that they decided to do one more test. The Lauterbrunnen surveillance equipment had arrived at Rouen, and Roberto, and two ENE scientists went down to pick it up. Thus, soon the operation would have to relocate to Switzerland. The Omega members decided to conduct a test to see how docile William had really become.

On the last day, at about the usual interrogation time, the door to his cell was opened, and William walked out. He could now see that his cell was about the last third of an oceanic cargo container. In front of him was a single chair facing a table. Five people sat across from him at the table – two men and three women. One woman looked somehow familiar.

"Sit down!" Meagan ordered. William sat. This group was not at all what he expected. And the woman.

Meagan continued, "Perhaps you remember me from the Sussex Coven meeting. I was to be dessert, if I recall."

Suddenly William remembered – the Irish serving girl, a sensitive, who was scheduled for the final "feeding" and had escaped. Here she seemed totally in charge and confident. A wild mix of emotions swept through his brain – anger, shame, wonder, curiosity.

"How did you escape us?" he asked.

She ignored him, and said, "What are we to do with you? The consensus seems to be to shoot you, as you are still Coven-trained, have participated in perhaps 60 ghastly 'feedings,' and if liberated, you could rapidly return to your old ways. We do not want to go to the effort to mentally emasculate you as we did to Otto. In the course of this, we were forced to experience his foulness up close. It is a price we do not wish to pay again. It is hard to find any reason whatsoever to keep you alive. Any suggestions?"

William's forehead beaded with sweat, even though the room was cool. He could think of only one reason – to stay alive helping this group eradicate his Coven companions. That he was not willing to do.

"You have made your decision. Goodbye, William. Roberto," she said, nodding subtly. Roberto raised his pistol, and prepared to fire.

William shouted, "You have not heard what I have to say!"

"But we have," said Meagan. "You decided that you would not help us eradicate your Coven companions."

"You don't know that," William cried.

"But we do," said Meagan, and she smiled.

"Are you telepathic?" William asked in wonder?

"You have no idea," Meagan replied. Suddenly William knew that these were the Merced psychics, and they could read minds. No wonder the Coven was losing. But they were mostly women? How could that be?

"We have felt the terror of your victims as you shredded their minds. You are a monster. While we dislike killing, we make an exception for

319

monsters," said Meagan.

"I'm sorry," sobbed William. "I didn't like the 'feedings' but it was necessary. It has always been that way, and most of the victims were doomed gay men with AIDS."

"But you made an exception in my case," commented Meagan dryly.

"We were required to find a 'feeding' candidate for a Congress of the European Covens. That is always the duty of the host country. We went to Galway because there are a lot of sensitives there, regretfully including a lot of young women."

"Regret, you say? Not regretful enough, I feel."

"I feel regret every night. The 'feedings' come back to me in nightmares. I was trapped into a system. I would have never grown from a D to a B without the 'feedings,' and I so wanted to be part of and joined with these powerful men. 'Feeding' was necessary, I was told. By the time I found out what a 'feeding' was, I was committed for life."

"And a shortened life it shall be," Meagan shot back. "Do you at least have the courage to make your last thoughts a plea for forgiveness from your victims?"

"I'm sorry, I'm so sorry," William sobbed.

Ken looked at Michelle, and nodded. At that very moment, William was hit with a psychic assault far more powerful than any he had ever experienced, even from Emil. His legs jerked to straight, and the chair went over backward. He was suddenly awash with pity for his victims, a floodgate was opened into the nightmares of his dreams, the suppressed memories of "feedings." He cried out loud and writhed on the floor as the pain of his many victims flooded into his conscious memory. Instinctively he curled up into an almost fetal position.

All Omega members quickly pulled silvery mesh caps down over their faces, and left. Roberto alone remained with the sobbing William, gun so casually cradled in his right hand.

It was probably 15 minutes before William could gather himself. "Get up, and pick up your chair!"

William did exactly as he was told.

"You will help us remove this scourge from Great Britain," said Roberto.

"Yes, yes, yes," sobbed William. "Even if it means personally killing all of your Coven colleagues?"

"Yes, yes, this 'feeding' must stop."

"Well, there is just a possibility that the 'feeding' can stop and the Coven members can remain alive, if you help us in your mind, your body, and what is left of your soul. Omega hates killing if there is any other way. You may provide that way."

Thirty minutes later, William was returned to his cell. He was drenched with sweat from head to toe, and stripped down to wash himself. Roberto left and went up to the house. "He is ours," said Roberto. Ken, Meagan, Michelle, and Gabriella were sitting sort of slumped into their chairs. They looked tired, and sad.

Ken said to the rest, "Thank you for what you just did. It was brutal to us all, forcing William to consciously relive these 'feedings,' but by doing so we may have avoided having to kill almost four dozen people, monsters though they be."

The other three Coven members were brought forward for trials, complete with defense attorneys and juries of ENE staffers and the two ex-Coven Associates. The defense tried to find extenuating circumstances. Betsy was especially good at this. Yet each had willingly joined the Covens, and had equally willingly done the most awful acts. None of them had the slightest trace of regret for the victims. All would have instantly returned to the Coven ways if released. Each was found guilty, and executed.

By the next morning, Omega was ready to leave for Lauterbrunnen, with three people left behind to guard the safe house and monitor electronic conversations in Paris, especially concerning the suspect Gendarmerie Coven.

William was let out of the cell, willingly accepting a radio anklet monitor. Omega was united in perceiving that there had been a profound conversion on his part.

He began drawing up plans to roll up the Great Britain Covens, following the very innovative Omega suggestions.

CHAPTER EIGHTEEN

Lauterbrunnen in August is a zoo. The valley itself is small, like Yosemite Valley with the floor in agriculture – almost all small dairy farms. Dusk comes quickly, even in high summer, as the cliffs put much of the valley into shade by 3:00 p.m. This is most welcome on hot summer days. The cows are in the high country for summer, but this place is taken by tens of thousands of lederhosen-clad Germans and mini-shorted Scandinavians hiking on every conceivable path, both up on the high country near Mürren on the south and Wengen on the north, and in the valley itself, with little respect paid to private property and "Mad Dog on Premise" signs. A few of the most naive were deterred by the "Take care – vipers" signs, and every winter the locals share their experiences over their beers on which signs work best.

The net effect of this chaos was to make Coven security well nigh impossible. There were scores of intrusion alarms every day, the surveillance cameras were in constant action, including on occasion sexual frolics behind the relatively discreet front hedge wall bordering the primary road up the valley. The only positive factor was that the valley was filled with students, some of whom were sensitives, and for these two months, and these months alone, the Coven was allowed to take one victim every 10 days. There were so many missing-person reports at the Lauterbrunnen police station during these months that they were simply put in a pile, awaiting fall. If someone contacted them in October, they would haul out the report and make a desultory effort, but the vast majority resolved themselves.

Seventeen Coven members had slipped into the Lauterbrunnen safe house, no more than two at a time. Word was spread among the valley's caterers that 20 meals per day, including box lunches and gourmet dinners, were needed for a sales force retreat, and that caterers delivering the best service would be rewarded with complimentary vacations.

Two weeks after the Chartres massacre, the Coven members received the first report from their investigations. The deputy director of the French Gendarmerie, Paris Division, gave the report in person.

"The attack on the Covens was brilliantly planned and executed, with only a single operational flaw. By means unknown at the time, the location of the Chartres safe house and the presence of a major Coven gathering became known to the assailants. They simply mined the roads from the safe house, both north and south, and out of range of the surveillance cameras at the driveway, with small Claymore mines that direct their shrapnel in a forward direction. When the convoys left for the Paris operation, the support team went west on farm roads and were not harmed. The rest left and when they hit the paved road, they split up, five to the north, and two to the south. The mines opposite the vehicles were fired two minutes later, when the cars were about 1 kilometers from the safe house. The mines were triggered, probably by radio, disabling all the vehicles and killing many of the Coven members.

"A team of our enemy then ran down the convoy, placing a single bullet in the head of every Coven member, dead or alive, except for the two least injured members, who were deliberately spared.

"We must come back to this point.

"They then picked up the unused – which numbered about 100, we estimate – from the fence posts, went to the south group, picked up a single but important captive, William, head of the Great Britain Covens despite being only a B-level psychic, and left on back roads. Rather amazingly, and disturbingly, they were never seen again, even though these small roads went by numerous farms with people in position to see any passing cars. They just vanished.

"This is a point we must also return to.

"Inspector Reynaud of the Chartres Division of the Gendarmerie took initial charge of the investigation. In the course of this, he sent six of his men to the safe house, visible on a nearby hill. We had left no one in the house, so when upon hearing no answer the gendarmes broke regulations and attempted to jimmy the front door, the automatic destruct sequence obliterated the house, and the six gendarmes. If our assailants had found a way to disable the autodestruct and enter the house, they would have found information potentially devastating to our European operations.

"Inspector Reynaud came up with a hypothesis, young Socialist firebrands attacking a pro-business opposition group supported by Islamic extremists furious at the opposition's anti-Islamic immigration policies.

"The support group, spared by use of the back roads, called for assassination by the Brussels Coven of the two surviving Coven members in the hospital, but Reynaud had moved them from the Security Wing. However, our immobilization of his guards was noted by Reynaud, who had personally staked out the hospital grounds.

"The next morning, I arrived to take charge, having delegated a fatal accident to my colleagues. However, unknown to me, Reynaud used about a 30-second gap to send his incomplete report, with many of his observations and his theories, to a colleague of his in Paris, Tomas LaFitte of my bureau. Once in the selected van, anesthetic gas followed by lethal injections killed them all, followed by the tanker crash, which regretfully also eradicated one of my unsuspecting Associates.

"There are two more points worth noting: One is that the truck driver, a Paris Coven Associate, survived and fled the scene on foot. In our attempts to track him down, we found that a few hours before the area seemed suspiciously rich in Gypsies. The other is that when I became aware of the Reynaud e-mail, it was about 5:00 p.m., closing time, and most of the staff had left. I immediately instituted a search for LaFitte, and never found him. Worse, his wife suddenly left their apartment – which we know because the soup she had been making in a pot was still hot – and she likewise disappeared.

"There are entirely too many mysterious disappearances to suit me, as our surveillance until now has been excellent in the region around Paris. Is it possible that the missing ENE "Auditors," as they called themselves, are at work?

"Since that day, there has been nothing of note. No attempts at wireless surveillance of our operations, no unusual phone calls – nothing.

"I await the judgment of this august group to direct me into my next duties."

The deputy director was always subservient to an extreme in the presence of Emil, for he was one of the few persons who knew something of Emil's background and thus was a potential "accident victim" if it was even hinted that he was becoming a threat. No one was entirely clear on the ability of Emil to read minds, but everybody suspected the worst and kept a high level of loyalty, and a major dollop of fear, in their thoughts when around

Emil. There followed about five minutes, when no one said anything. This was typical in Coven deliberations, and helped temper the subsequent discussion.

Emil spoke first, as was his right.

"I want this Gypsy business resolved, immediately. Where do we stand in the discussions?"

John, William's – preferably temporary – replacement for the Great Britain Covens, summarized. "We are in active discussions, but are not yet ready for the key meeting. They claim that the Spanish Calé are all for an open war, but the rest of the kingdoms have held them in check until all the facts are known. We are arguing for a rogue German connection, based on presumed Gypsy support of the Merced telepaths.

"Make it so," said Emil.

CHAPTER NINETEEN

The meeting took place in a villa outside of Trieste in early September. There were beautiful gardens wrapped around and through an extensive grove of old olive trees. In the distance, a swath of the Adriatic Sea was visible. No other houses were visible in any direction, and in fact none existed for more than a kilometer. The room had a dramatic view of the gardens and sea in one direction, but in all other directions windows were covered and doors barred. A long and very narrow table was in the middle of the room, so placed that people on each side could reach out across the table and shake hands if they wished.

Three long, low centerpieces of flowers were spaced evenly along the middle of the table, lending a cheery effect somehow out of place with the gravity of the reason for the meeting.

With their backs to the closed wall and a view of the sea sat nine Gypsies – six men and three women, with the latter carefully placed along the length of the table. The women were there to check on truthfulness, and it was because of them that the table had to be so narrow. On the wall behind the Gypsies and thus quite far from the table and well out of Coven compulsion range were three Gypsy men, each holding at the ready an AK-47 fully automatic rifle.

On the other side of the table were seven members of the European Covens, all looking distinctly nervous. John from Great Britain was to be the spokesperson, because the French cluster was in such disarray. They had been asked to remove their coats before entering the room, and were expertly frisked for hidden weapons. It was they who had called for this meeting at a time and place chosen by the dominant Gypsy kingdoms of Europe.

John began by bringing forward four boxes, each the size of a small suitcase, and placed them on the table in a neat row. "We are determined to clear up any and all issues between us. The most important is the Italian massacre. We have traced its source to a very high source, indeed, in the German effort."

He opened the first box, and there was the carefully preserved head of Herman, one of two German A-level telepaths. "Herman was the trainer and mentor of Otto. It was he who was behind the Italian massacre, aided and abetted."

He then opened the next two boxes, and two more heads appeared. "You see before you the entire Coven effort. These heads are yours."

"There were also four Coven Associates, all of whom have been executed with severe prejudice in order to discourage future independent operations. No one associated with the atrocity is alive."

Finally, he opened the last case, and revealed neatly stacked bills, dollars and Euros, in large denominations. "The total in there amounts to 7 million Euros in untraceable notes, in order to recompense the relatives of the victims."

The Gypsies were stunned. No one had ever dreamt of killing an A-level Coven member, and in fact it would be difficult to do so at close range because of their powers. The money was nice, but the evidence of the heads appealed to Gypsy sensitivities and need for a physical object for revenge.

Marta, sitting next to Karla, made a slight motion of her hand. Karla noted it, then said, "John, we will take this message to all Gypsy kingdoms, and promise to resume cooperation with Coven activities on the previous basis. However, I would recommend not operating in Spain and Portugal this year, as sensitivities are running very high. I will continue to act as spokesman for the combined Gypsy kingdoms for the next year, but then my turn is up."

John said, "Emil would like to offer you the hospitality of one of our safe houses where you can discuss with us activities that would benefit the kingdoms."

Karla would never agree to get close to Emil, for he feared his powers, but he lied and said, "I look forward to the opportunity, perhaps this fall," while counting on the fact that the relatively low-level Coven members present were not good at mind reading.

Then Karla spoke, "As an indication that our collaboration has been truly renewed, we have some information for you. Your supposedly deceased member, and number two man in the French Coven, Gerard, is presently living in fine style on purloined ENE funds in a small chateau, called Chateau Guillard by the locals, 14.5 kilometers southwest of the old church in the small Loire Valley town of Montrichard. He has started trolling for potential victims in Amboise, and even psychically scanned one of our Gypsy sensitives. He cannot have a 'feeding,' however, until he gets at least two other Coven members of level B or better. However, he is hungry, and has begun surreptitiously contacting selected old friends in some of the rural Covens near Paris, specifically Orsay. I trust that you will use this information to your benefit while avoiding another incident with a member of our kingdoms."

"We appreciate this information," said John, "and I will assure you personally that your people are safe."

The meeting broke up in a relatively positive tone, and the Coven members left in a block.

When the Coven members were gone, the chairs were rearranged in a more comfortable array.

Marta said, "Lying through their teeth. The massacre was in fact instigated by Emil to cow the Gypsies, who he believed had helped the Northern California mystics. This was also the first time I have ever felt dissent among the Coven members, just as there are differences of opinion among the Gypsies. They were truly surprised at the news of Gerard, and seemed appreciative."

A general discussion followed, but the group agreed to retain the existing Gypsy decision to try to keep on good terms with the Covens while weakening them in collaboration with the Merced psychics. The major success in the Chartres attack was proof of the vulnerability of the Covens. Marta was both vocal and powerful in this discussion, and her opinion was accepted as important by all members. They had always trusted her judgments in the past, and would do so in the present. But many feared a bloodbath for the Gypsies if things went wrong.

Back in Switzerland, summer was coming to an end. The last weekend of summer before the beginning of the fall terms at the universities brought a larger than usual crowd of students into the Lauterbrunnen Valley. The Lauterbrunnen house had fixed cameras on the driveway approaches and two roaming cameras, up and down the valley, to zero in on suspicious activity. These were monitored 24 hours a day, but usually only by one person. The up-valley camera saw much less activity than the down-valley camera, because it was from the town of Lauterbrunnen or from the Mürren gondola station 2 kilometers away that most hikers came.

Sometimes the activity was interesting, indeed. Dusk was falling on Saturday night, a dusk enhanced by the steep valley walls, when two comely young women slipped behind the hedge and began to disrobe. The camera operator increased the magnification and the light level until the screen was essentially filled with two glorious bodies enmeshed in a passionate lesbian encounter. For about 30 minutes, they arched and writhed in a slow-motion arabesque dance, until they both lay exhausted side by side on the grass, naked to the sky but unseen from the road just over the hedge.

However, it was getting quite dark, and the night down-valley cold wind from the Jungfrau ice fields was making the valley too cool for naked bodies. Mary and Nancy, now married for the past two years and becoming very powerful psychics, got up and helped each other dress, with continued signs of physical affection. They then strolled hand-in-hand through the gap in the hedge near the driveway, and back toward Lauterbrunnen.

"I certainly hope that no one made a tape of that and puts it on a web page," said Nancy. "We would be more famous than Loni Anderson."

Omega members gathered in the newly rented chateaus in Wengen, high in the cliffs on the opposite side of the valley from Mürren, much closer to Lauterbrunnen, and with an excellent view of the upper valley, including the Mürren gondola base and the Coven farmhouse. It was on the rail line to Jungfrau, and thus had regular daytime train service down to Lauterbrunnen. They dispersed themselves to every comfortable chair near enough to get warm from the fire. Ken and Jill had made raclette, a local dish of Swiss cheese, onions, potatoes, and pickles, and various ciders, beers, and wines were available.

Ken started, "Mary and Nancy, well done! You gave someone a real show. The down-valley camera was focused on you two the entire time, and the up-valley camera was directed straight up the valley, leaving the small grove of pines just up valley from the driveway uncovered. We were able to get our fake tree branches attached with a clear view of not just one, but two windows, one in an alcove near the phone. The infrared CO_2 lasers will read vibrations of the window panes and allow us to record every conversation in that room, even when the drapes are drawn, which is usually the case.

The data will be continuously or periodically downloaded to the second infrared laser beam that we can intercept using this mirror, now on our porch. We have a video camera with a monster lens upstairs in the loft window, recording all traffic on the road into their safe house.

"This is really timely, because we expect a report from the Trieste meeting with the Gypsies tomorrow or Monday."

It was in fact Monday when one of Karla's Viennese Gypsies, Alexander, who always seemed to be around when Betsy was around, came in with a report. "The caterer has been asked to up the meal to 50 per day for five days beginning on Wednesday. It looks like we are about to have serious Coven company."

Ken said, "Call in the troops. We are going to have to make an important decision. In words of one syllable – what's next?"

By Monday afternoon, the Gypsy and Omega members from all the posts were crammed into the Wengen chateau.

Ken started, "First, the intercepts. They were speaking in French most of the time, so perhaps Jean could do the report."

Jean began, "The system is working perfectly. We have weak coverage at the far edge of the room, near the wall, and we have had to filter out a low-level hum from the vibration of the window in wind, but by and large, we can read the room well. We have spectacular reception in the alcove near the phone, but most phone calls are very cryptic and in code, so we don't learn much. In addition, they often use their satellite cell phones from anywhere in the room. Nevertheless, we actually dug down one night and found the landline, only to see that it was in an armored conduit that we could not easily penetrate. Further, if the conduit were to be pressurized with an inert gas, any penetration would ring an alarm signal at the house. We closed up the dig, and camouflaged our efforts.

"The big news confirms Alexander's report – there is what appears to be a meeting of all Western European Covens, with observers from Eastern European Covens. We could not see into the room, but there was a rather characteristic French speaker who always led all discussions."

Betsy chimed in, "That would be the highest-ranking psychic, normally an A or, if they have one, an A Prime."

"Emil," murmured Ken. "We have the infamous Emil."

Jean continued, "Much of the talk has been about beefing up security, including having Coven Associate presence at all points of the valley, with heavy weapons, strengthened by Coven pairs on an active and passive psychic interrogation mode. Two ENE noise generators are being brought up Tuesday, although their ineffectiveness in San Francisco does not make them very confident in their capabilities. One crew will be posted at the base of the Mürren gondola. Finally, there is going to be a gas explosion under the main road in the valley Tuesday night, which will effectively close the main road past the house for six or seven days. All vehicles will have to use the alternate route on the other side of the valley. There was also some talk on at least identifying any Gypsy presence in the area.

"Ken, the first speaker – you called him Emil – seems very smart and in absolute control. He seems dangerous. Every suggestion he makes is followed to the last detail. If he is an A Prime psychic, what powers would he have?"

Ken replied, "All the usual ones, but enhanced, plus a better ability to read minds. He could sense our presence at perhaps 100 meters. He could disable a person at perhaps 15 to 25 meters and kill by thought alone. We have only encountered one in our experience, although another was close to A Prime level. I don't want to do it again, partially because their thoughts are both powerful and vile. You would have to see images from 1,000 'feedings,' and you would never really sleep soundly for months or longer. One we had to execute. However, the one case involving an A Prime under our joint attack tried maximum use of the powers, and his mind collapsed to an imbecilic state. There are also reports of A Primes going mad."

Ken continued, "What if we could kill them all while they are at this meeting? Your thoughts, Gypsies and Omegas?"

Karla spoke first for the Gypsies, "Let's assume that the meals are for the Coven members who must remain protected in the house and that the Associates would be free to eat anywhere in the valley, actually enhancing their effectiveness as spies. If we were able to kill Emil and 49 other Coven members, together with the eradication of the Great Britain and Irish Covens orchestrated by John, they would have lost so many members that it would be almost impossible to have 'feedings' and the remainder would have to migrate east or lose their abilities, in the gnawing hunger. Further,

331

if one could do that, we would have put such a fear into the Covens, especially after the disasters in the United States, that they would probably be scared to ever move back."

"I consider such an outcome an absolute triumph, if it could be done. You would save perhaps 1,000 people a year from 'feedings' in the western half of Europe."

Michelle commented, "This would also allow us to build up Gypsy and non-Gypsy Omega teams in Europe itself, so that should anyone try to have a 'feeding' in the future, they would be broadcasting their presence to waiting Gypsy and Omega teams."

"Other comments?" asked Ken.

"Is there any way we could do to them what we have planned in Great Britain and Ireland?" asked Meagan.

"Unlikely, but worth a shot," said Ken. "At the very least, it means we have done all we could. Let's hold the option open if we find anyone with the internal misgivings of William. I propose that we should set up teams, perhaps three independent teams in easy-to-defend sites near the one road into Lauterbrunnen from Interlaken. Perhaps three Omega teams, in dark mind mode, with two Gypsies and an ENE technical support member with computer and recording capabilities. The cars will attenuate the signal, and we will have trouble telling one from another, and finally some may be asleep. Still, with three such teams, we should get a picture of them.

"Meanwhile, I will move with Karla and colleagues on the eradication concept. I am not sure how we can do it, but we have two or three options to examine.

"Please self-select into the teams, but Michelle, Gabriella, and Meagan should not be on the same team. We need to spread them out. Also, each should have a male Omega member, too, since their capabilities are slightly different than the girls."

Jill affectionately bopped Ken's head at the deliberately casual reference to "the girls," because to her it made the whole operation look like a teenage slumber party.

"Karla, have your people find the sites, ideally within 15 meters of the road. Places on hills where the cars must go in single file and slow down are preferred if you can find them," Ken directed.

"Jonathan, Frank, Karla, Betsy, Kelly, and I, and some of Karla's best people, will examine the eradication options. All who can will make a report tomorrow at the same time. Be careful out there! This place is filling up with lethal muscle. Karla, we need your people more than ever.

"I will put Alexander in charge of protection. After all, there is no way he would want Meagan harmed, I can assure you," said Karla. With her fair skin, Meagan's blush was easy to see, while Alexander's was more discreet.

CHAPTER TWENTY

It was Wednesday in the second week of September. The crowds were gradually leaving Lauterbrunnen, the weather was cooling down, and this was the best time of the year (according to the locals) in the calm before the winter madness.

The room in the Coven safe house was set up in the typical Coven pattern with the A Primes and A's sitting together on both sides of the fireplace, facing a circle of chairs. In all, 47 members were present, exceeding the comfortable capabilities of the farmhouse and requiring cots, couches, and other furniture.

The clock struck 3:00 p.m., and Emil initiated the meeting. "I would like to start by getting a report from our German members."

German Coven member Johann, sitting on the other side of the fireplace as befitted the other A-level Coven member, spoke next.

"We have much to talk about in the next five days. I propose we start with the Gypsy situation, since that was Emil's most pressing concern." Even though Johann was powerful enough to fend off Emil if push came to shove, deference was always a wise policy.

"John was in charge of the Gypsy meeting. Your report?"

John started, "All indications are that we have patched up our differences with most of the Gypsies, although the Calé are still a problem. We should leave them alone for a while. The physical presence of the severed heads was very Gypsy, and they responded to them in a way that nothing else would have accomplished. The money was secondary."

"In return, Karla told us that Gerard was still alive, in some comfort, in an ENE-supported chateau in the Loire Valley. We have made some inquiries, and it appears that Gerard is trying to reconstitute his own rural Coven, with 'feeding' opportunities in Orleans, Tours, Amboise, Angers, and Le Mans."

"Let us invite Gerard to be here by tomorrow morning," purred Emil.

"He had also mentioned during the meeting the problems the Gypsies were having with Islamic extremists, who view Gypsies as thieves, prostitutes, and Devil-worshippers, worthy of obliteration in the name of Allah. As you all know, we have never found even a single Islamic sensitive."

Emil asked, "What have they learned about the Merced telepaths?"

John answered, "Not too much. As you know, the Gypsies maintain two Gypsies in Merced, at our request, who periodically report to us despite our differences. So far, there are no strange events to report. The Merced telepaths seem to be lying low in Merced. However, perhaps it is so quiet because they have moved operations into Europe.

"They appear to have instituted long-range investigations into ENE, based on the obvious ENE interest in O'Neal and on electronic intercepts, and they are worried that the Gypsies are helping the Covens as a result of the strange Rosa case. They also feel that there is Merced involvement in the disappearance of the ENE and German Auditors, as they called themselves. They too feel that the Chartres massacre was a Merced telepath attack, perhaps in retribution for the German killings. As you know, the technology of the attack was rather basic."

But, Emil interjected, "What about the missing Coven member, the two carefully spared Coven members, and the strange ritual pattern in the deaths in the convoy? Karla thinks that the Merced telepaths were trying to get Coven members into French hands for questioning, which could unravel Coven operations without any risk on their part. After all, they have been badly hurt by Coven attacks in the past, and may be wary."

Emil mused, "That has always been our 'Achilles heel.' We have to have secrecy to dominate in the shadows. They realized that, and did everything they could to make our operations public. Fortunately, our response was adequate."

"Thank you, John. You have done well," intoned Johann, and passed on some psychic reward. John, appreciative, smiled, bowed, and retook his chair.

Emil was not nearly as sure as John and Johann that things were going all that well with the Gypsies, but clearly they were trying to stay on good terms with the Covens. Perhaps, after events, that is the best they could achieve.

"Now let's discuss the captives. Do we have any word of William and the three Paris Coven captives? I also recall we lost an Associate, too.

"We have an ongoing investigation of the entire event, based on a missing-person report on a young female Sorbonne student, associated with a bunch of Catholic do-gooders and thus possibly a sensitive and probably the victim. Jacques and the last few members are due tonight, late, and we can have him report tomorrow morning."

Johann, who was in charge of physical arrangements for the meeting, said, "We will get the first large catered dinner tonight. Regretfully, I have had to expend funds for beer and wine, which we will not use but our Associates will appreciate. Otherwise people would wonder about us. I propose we re-convene with our full membership tomorrow at 10:00 a.m. I expect the remainder of the members to arrive late tonight or tomorrow very early. Jacques said he will be here around 8:00 p.m. As deputy director of the Gendarmerie, he has considerable resources, has been very active in the investigations, and seems to have news."

Back at Wengen, the results were analyzed. All three teams had been able to scan perhaps 25 new Coven members as they drove to the meeting. The search for a conflicted or wavering Coven member was universally negative.

"These people are uniformly slime," said Gabriella. "I can see hardly any redeeming values in the entire lot. They have felt all-powerful for so long that they feel that standard morality does not apply. They view the rest of the human race as sheep asking for slaughter. I'm sorry, Meagan, your concept was worthy. We will keep it up tomorrow, but this had better be a nicer bunch. My mind won't be clean for months."

That pretty much ended the discussion. There was no sign of, nor news from, Ken and Karla's team.

Late that evening, Jonathan got a call. "We are in southern Germany. We can do it. You have to give the OK, based on the Omega consensus there after Meagan's survey. Sort of reminds me of Lot's argument with God over Sodom and Gomorrah. What have you learned?"

Jonathan replied, "Big meeting tomorrow at 10:00 a.m., with the last few arriving this evening or early tomorrow. We still have one team on the highway for late arrivers. There will be a report from the French Gendarmerie on their investigation into the captive Coven members."

"Jonathan, here is my satellite number, which has never been used and is not traceable to us. Use this for the call," said Gabriella.

Not 10 minutes later, Michelle came in from the last stake out. "Problems, people, Michelle declared. "The deputy director is on to us. He was dying to give his report tomorrow. The Place Saint-Michel operation is gaining traction, and has started a survey of all possible places west of Paris that could possibly hold groups and captives. The French record-keeping is very complete, but often on paper and dispersed. Still, he has assigned almost 60 officers to the case, and they will probably identify the safe house in two or three days. We will have to alert William and the team to make the Great Britain move immediately, two weeks before we had planned."

Jonathan placed a call, checked a notebook, and a few words were spoken about a wine shipment. He hung up the phone. "Message received. They will be out in the morning," Janathan said. "William continues to be extremely cooperative, both superficially and deep in his mind. He is viewing the whole operation as his one chance at redemption. However, we can't move the containers that quickly, although we will do our best to have them out tomorrow. Wonders can be done in France if cash is involved in adequate quantities. I assured him we would pay any price for this rare wine. Other than that, the last attendees are even viler than the first. I would give Ken a 10:30 time for whatever he is planning. What will he want us to do?"

Jonathan keyed the code, listened, then hung up.

He announced, "Everybody but Jean is to be out of here by 7:30 a.m., beyond Interlaken by 9 a.m., and then by the pre-selected route to Vienna. By 10 a.m., switch your license plates and modify the vans as planned. Use the pre-selected crossing point Karla has given us.

"Jean, your job is to monitor the Coven meeting, then key the auto-destructs and pick up our last equipment here, and leave on your own. See you in Vienna.

"Alert the troops and start packing up. Another sleepless night, I fear," said Jonathan.

"I hope that whatever Ken and Karla have planned, it destroys any possible tapes of our X-rated show. I would hate to see it as evidence in some trial," said Nancy.

"Just think of the residuals," laughed Jill.

CHAPTER TWENTY-ONE

Sergeant Gilbert Johnson keyed his pass, took a retinal scan, and entered the control room as he had done so often in the past two and a half years. It was far, far nicer and much safer duty here in the Bavarian Alps on a NATO base than in the Middle East, still festering after the war in Iraq. Because of staffing problems, the control room was not even being staffed during nighttime hours, and the eight-hour day and eight-hour evening shifts were really just to check out and maintain the 24 long-range non-nuclear cruise missiles. The control room would be fully staffed, 24/7, and on one-hour alert, if the base went to DEFCON 3 or a higher alert. But right now, it was on DEFCON 2, and things were pretty relaxed.

He went to fire up the coffee pot, only to find that the evening shift, LeRoy, had neglected to refill the coffee. Gilbert had to rinse the grounds, fill the pot, and start the operation, grumbling about lack of consideration for fellow sergeants, who are, after all, the backbone of the army. Still, LeRoy had never screwed up before. Sergeant Johnson wondered if it was some replacement.

Finally, with coffee in hand, he started the missile-by-missile checks. By about 10:15 a.m., he had ensured that all was well with propulsion. The normal next step is a check on targeting. He switched consoles, and fired up the computers on missiles #1 and #2 – a dual launch pair designed for high-value targets.

The screen showed that the coordinates were loaded, the status was excellent, and they were ready to go on a moment's notice. Something nagged at the back of his mind, because the coordinates seemed strange. Had they been changed overnight? He would look at the operations log to make sure they had been done correctly. He keyed in the checklist on blast doors at the missile silo, and ... They were already open! What had LeRoy done? That was the worst sort of blunder, for then a single button could launch the missiles.

Sergeant Johnson quickly pushed the key to close the doors, immediately there followed the muted swoosh of a cruise missile launch 200 meters away. In 10 seconds, a second swoosh. Two missiles were off to destinations unknown. There was no way that the blast door closure should have launched the missile, unless there was some wiring screwup. Oh, shit. There will be hell to pay. Thank God the warheads had not been armed. That required actually going to the missiles and pulling the arming strap, which meant getting into a shielded bunker.

He called on the phone, and got the base duty officer, Edward. "Two unarmed cruise missiles launched by an electronic short – he was lying but he could not admit any more this side of a court martial – on the revised coordinates entered on the evening shift."

Minutes followed. Heaven knows where the commanding officer was on this small base high in the mountains. The desk sergeant replied, "Ill try to get some brass up here. Not much luck. Where do you think they are going?"

"They both are headed to 46° 33' 31" north, 7° 55' 50" east, with a very high terminal angle as if they were avoiding a mountain," said Johnson.

"My God," said Edward, "that's in Switzerland. Who the hell put in those coordinates? Hold it, we have brass in sight. There will be hell to pay for this. They aren't armed, are they?"

"No way," said Johnson. "I was just doing the normal maintenance checks when I noticed that the blast doors for #1 and #2 were open. When I tried to close them, they launched."

"Which means that anyone could have climbed in the open blast doors and pulled the arming straps," said Edward. "I think we have a carefully planned terror attack. We are now on DEFCON 5. I will ask the colonel to confirm and notify Switzerland, which is not, as we all know, a member of NATO."

Across the mountains and in Switzerland, Ken's team watched with pride and sadness as the missiles streaked across the valley toward Lauterbrunnen. "We left lots of clues that this was not LeRoy's fault, but that of a nighttime penetration of Islamic fundamentalists," said Ken. "LeRoy will have no memory whatsoever of our control of his actions. Karla, your assistance in getting this Islamic evidence on such short notice was much appreciated."

"Based on the problems they are causing my people all over Europe, it was a real pleasure," replied Karla.

"Anyway, I hope it's adequate so they don't fry LeRoy's ass. By the way,

Frank, you had those coordinates for the Coven house awfully quickly. How did you do it?"

"Google Earth, the professional version, not the free one, is preloaded in my laptop. I can even see the driveway in the picture. I had LeRoy program it so one would strike about 10 meters east of the other, to reduce the entire main room to an enormous crater. These were bigger than usual warheads, too."

CHAPTER TWENTY-TWO

The room in the Coven safe house was set up in the typical Coven pattern with the Primes sitting together on both sides of the fireplace facing a circle of chairs. In all, 52 members were now present, one of the largest Coven gatherings ever attempted.

The clock struck 10:00 a.m., and Emil initiated the meeting. "I welcome the return of our dear colleague Gerard, who can now take his rightful place next to Johann. But I must say, Gerard, you are not looking too well. Lack of 'feedings,' perhaps?"

Gerard, clearly nervous, said, "I feared for my life from the Gypsies, and always planned to return once that threat was resolved. When I heard about the Italian massacre, I hunkered down a little longer until it could blow over."

Emil responded, "Your dereliction of duties in Paris has caused repercussions with ENE, which your presence could have stopped. An amateur effort by some of your ENE staff seems to have brought in the Merced psychics. We will go into this later, and propose ways you can stanch the hemorrhaging, as we have lost 22 members killed and four captured."

Gerard blanched, "That many? That's a tragedy. I didn't know."

"Jacques has done a wonderful job keeping the details out of the press. And perhaps we should hear from you first, Jacques, since I understand you have news."

Jacques stood at attention, very much the deputy director of the Gendarmerie. He knew power when he was in its presence. "We have done a full analysis of the Place Saint-Michel capture of three Coven members, an Associate guard, and the woman victim. There were actually quite a few witnesses, and we have a full reconstruction of the events. If I may," Jacques said.

He pulled out his laptop, and plugged it into the projector. All curtains were drawn in any case. The first picture showed the Place Saint-Michel.

"We have identified two young women, not French, probably American, who had been seen walking around Place Saint-Michel for several nights. We have identified that they were walking west when they would have come into sight of two Coven members waiting outside of the Catholic chapel. They would have been about here, at that time. As you know, it is hard to have our people look like students, so they may well have recognized a Coven stakeout.

"According two protocols, we would have had a car, and indeed one was seen to drive up, make a U-turn and illegally park under a tree, in heavy shadows. At that point, an older couple arrived, young middle-aged looking, very American, and talked to the young women.

"About 20 minutes later, a crowd of students started to stream out of the chapel. Our members were seen talking to a girl, who was laughing, and then she walked off with the Coven members toward the car.

"The four Americans then started walking toward the Coven members and toward the car. The man walked faster, and was opposite the car, about here. The other three Americans walked right up to the Coven members and the girl, and then the Coven members went down. Someone appeared and lifted them to their feet just as a van pulled up.

"No one saw what happed to the driver of our car, but another young man was seen jumping into the car. Just then two other young men, looking like students, were seen weaving across the road with a third between them looking very drunk. That may, or may not, have been our Associate. The van and the two cars left heading west. The entire act took less than 30 seconds.

"There are several points to note. The Americans had been staking out the area for days, waiting for a Coven capture. They know that this was a prime hunting area. They were waiting for us, determined on capturing our members.

"Second, the Coven members simply collapsed, according to our one witness close enough to see. No blow was struck. Just collapsed. It looks like a psychic attack, especially because they were putting out maximum effort controlling the girl. As soon as they collapsed, the girl started screaming, which gathered some attention to the scene.

"Third, if we assume the drunken students were involved, we see seven people involved in this effort, a serious and well-planned kidnapping. I fear we are being hunted by large and capable teams, including the Merced psychics," Jacques concluded.

"Your analysis," said Emil dryly.

"The Merced telepaths have relocated to Europe, and are bent on our eradication," Jacques declared. "They certainly have allies in ENE and Germany, and I am not entirely sure that there isn't Gypsy involvement. There are an awful lot of slim, dark-looking people involved in these matters.

"I believe that we are threatened by an intelligent and powerful group that can overcome our defenses. Based on my analysis, their number is not large, but with the help of the ENE and German Auditors, and perhaps Gypsies, they can be devastatingly effective. I am trying to find where they are holding the captives.

"My analysis is that we should immediately terminate this meeting, disperse to safer areas farther east, and re-group. A gathering like this, even in a secure site as we have here, would be an irresistible target if we were to be discovered."

Emil, suddenly worried, said, "I appreciate your analysis, and I agree that we cannot linger here. Too many people are here, and some may have been traced via their cars. We must leave, immediately, before any actions can be taken against us.

"Make it so. You may even leave in a convoy, and then split at Interlaken."

There was a flurry of activity, and a scent of fear in the house. "Fear is the mind destroyer," mused Emil, "and now we fear."

A German tourist, a retired professor now free to travel any time he wished, and his comfortable-looking wife were having a late breakfast at a café in Mürren. The weather was ideal, the tourists largely gone, and the prices low. And the view from the patio was awesome – the long, beautiful valley with its neat farms now awaiting the return of the cows from the high pastures, and the looming white bulk of the Jungfrau with its snow fields. At the western end of the valley was Wengen, where waterfalls as high as 300 meters cascaded. Surely this is one of the most beautiful sights in the world.

A humming sound became louder, but the tourist and his wife couldn't see anything that would make it. Suddenly not 50 meters over their heads, a cruise missile was diving toward the valley below. Stunned, they could not move a muscle, until just seconds later, a deafening explosion rocked the valley.

Echoes bounced off the walls of the gorge, but before the echoes had died, a second missile, closely following the first, dived past them to the same unfortunate target below. The second exploded, like the first, but now there were also flames and smoke from the valley below. In seconds, they could hear the screaming sirens, but the obvious route to the bombed site was blocked because of major damage to the road from a gas explosion on Tuesday. As the fire and smoke rose ever higher, blowing up the valley, they didn't think the extra 10-minute delay would matter much. Nothing could have survived that explosion. Cruise missiles? In Switzerland? Gott in Himmel. What was this world coming to?

The limited resources of the Lauterbrunnen fire department could do nothing, especially because of ongoing explosions that occurred as the flaming wreckage in the Coven hideout detonated demolition charges one after the other. In all the smoke, flames, and falling debris extending more than 100 meters from the house, no one noticed the scattered debris, including what looked like electronic components strapped to a single shattered branch of a pine tree that would have had a good view of the house.

CHAPTER TWENTY-THREE

The island of Colonsay lies off the west coast of Scotland. South from the tiny main town of Scalasaig lies Cable Bay, where a high ridge protects the area from the strong Atlantic gales. An abandoned RAF site sits in the lea of the hills, facing east, with trees planted to provide protection from the wind. It had been an emergency base for seaplanes in the Battle of the Atlantic, and had recently been turned into a pricey private sanitarium for terminal AIDS patients. Because of this, the area was shunned by the few hundred residents of the island, aided by an effective fence designed to keep the patients from wandering away. The island residents, however, were always happy to sell to the sanitarium the limited produce of the island and the abundance from the surrounding seas.

William, complete with white coat as head administrator, sat at his desk in the Annex reviewing the records. Presently, there were 52 patients, all ex-Coven middle-aged men or older, in his care. They were not, however, doing very well, and many were suffering from various withdrawal symptoms from lack of 'feedings.' All were under various forms of sedation all the time, and their lives, though limited, were not unpleasant. William himself was doing better than most, aided by medication.

He felt he had done exactly as he had promised to Omega, with their help rolling up all Great Britain Covens without a single fatality, and placing them in physical and psychic isolation here on Colonsay. Now he was dedicated to their care. He had just finished installing a new outer belt of automatically triggered psychic noise generators from Merced, which now allowed the patients to stroll farther through the grove of trees, including rhododendrons of amazing size, and a number of other woodland species, protected by the wind-shaped eucalyptus.

His staff was exclusively composed of ex-Coven Associates, and they were allowed the freedom of trips to the mainland within the limited range of their thigh-embedded GPS locators.

Today was a special day for him, because Meagan was the Omega member on this week's rotation, and she was arriving today on the twice-a-week ferry. She would be accompanied by her newly awakened apprentice, Marie Celeste. They would have long talks about the growing Omega Project cells, mostly in Ireland, and the thin but effective screen of Omega cells in many major cities, but especially London. No evidence of "feeding" activities had been seen in years.

William would have for Meagan the latest details of the rate of loss of patients into dementia, a rate much higher than in the general population. It appeared that the "feeding" activities were indeed mind-damaging, a conclusion the Gypsies had surmised more than 500 years ago, when they stopped the practice.

Today William was going to recommend that one of his most effective Associates, Robert, from Edinburgh, be placed in formal charge of the facility. William was not doing as well recently, and now that things were on a stable footing, he was tired and wanted to drop into a supporting role, away from day-to-day operations. The problem would be to convince Meagan that the pent-up anger of the Associates against the Coven members, founded on their years of fear and subservience, would not result in degradation in patient care.

This might well be Meagan's last visit, because she was going to be a mother in only three months. Marie Celeste would take her rotation, but William would miss Meagan. He hoped that he might have the chance to see Meagan and Alexander's child. The children of Omega were so very special.

William was in a pensive mood. He had seen the Omega cells grow, and been present at an "awakening" near Galway. How different his life would have been if he had met these people first, rather that the sharks of the Coven. How he wished he had made the choice that Betsy had, before it was too late. She would be coming seven weeks from now for her week-long shift. They too had much to talk about. Betsy in particular was much more involved in present activities. With Omega's help, the Calé Gypsies had eradicated the Coven from Spain and Portugal, sometimes with "extreme prejudice." France was clear, and had numerous Omega cells, as did Bavaria and Austria. Italy, Croatia, Slovenia, Switzerland, the Netherlands, Denmark, the Czech Republic, and the western half of Germany were clear of Coven activities. At least, no "feedings" had been detected in the past year, although the Covens had learned to do "feedings" in metal-enclosed rooms that blocked most of the telepathically enhanced agony of their victims. The tense stand-off between Omega and the eastern European Covens continued, with no aggressive actions on either side. The prior Coven-Gypsy collaboration was now a thing of the past, even in Russia.

Well, whatever the future might bring, he was no longer part of it. He would do his duty, here, until he died, while finishing work on his book, **Revelation and the Dread Covenant**. This book will be published as total fiction with such a disclaimer in the preface, unlike *The Da Vinci Code*, which claimed that components of that book were based on fact. However, unlike *The Da Vinci Code*, this book would actually be a rather complete and fully accurate history of the European Covens, which because it would be interwoven with information about hundreds of prior unexplained disappearances, massacres, exploding houses, the recent cruise missile "accident," and the like, would be compelling. The book would emphasize the role of the European Gypsies in fending off the Covens and thus saving Europe, while downplaying the role of the Omega Project, which would now merely be the shadowy source of high technology, with no psychic powers. The book would, however, make future Coven activities in Europe far more difficult to hide, which was one of the reasons it was being written. William already had a publisher. Maybe there would even be a movie. He would love to have Leonardo Dicaprio play the role of Kenneth O'Neal, and he would want Scarlett Johansson as Michelle.

High on the hill, he thought he could hear the sound of the sanitarium's antique truck coming with the week's rations, newspapers, and hopefully Meagan and Marie Celeste. He got up, and walked out to the well-groomed lawns that cradled the driveway. A few more rhododendrons would be nice here, he thought, as the truck chugged into view.

CHAPTER TWENTY-FOUR

They were driving through a sepia world – gray skies, brown trees, dying grasses, in the early Russian fall. It had rained yesterday, but today it was just misty. It was the kind of cold, dreary day that made one long for snow. Three of the surviving Coven members that had somehow avoided the Lauterbrunnen massacre were carrying with them an offer from the Eastern European covens to powerful, shadowy forces in the new Russia who longed for the glories of the old Soviet Union. Such a meeting would never have been contemplated, except for the realization that the California psychics had technology that had made them powerful enough to decimate the western European covens. New allies were needed, and the age-old code of secrecy was about to be broken in these dire times.

They didn't know where they were going, but it appeared to be northwest of Moscow. The seemingly indestructible 2C2 from the San Francisco Coven, having recently escaped from his New Zealand exile, had seen a sign that he could translate as Kamenka about 10 minutes back, but the combination of the dreary day and the tinted windows of the official limousine made little else evident.

Soon the car slowed and turned left onto an inconspicuous but well-graded gravel road, similar to hundreds that led off the highway. But in a few hundred yards, the gravel gave way to paving in excellent condition, about the time inconspicuous guard towers became evident in the woods. Sweeping up to a sprawling dacha, they were greeted by what appeared to be about 100 soldiers, bivouacked in front of the mansion.

Sergei leaned over and said, "We will do a review of the troops, but stay next to me and point out two or three that you need for your demonstration." The last two words dripped with a sarcasm for what Sergei knew was going to be some sort of scam.

The soldiers snapped to attention, in a smart double line. Sergei saluted and started a quick review with 2C2 at his side. A gentle tap on Sergei's hip was the agreed-upon signal, and after the review was over, they went into the dacha with two of the soldiers in tow.

The main room was very large, and a fire burned in an enormous fireplace. A set of comfortable chairs and couches were evident to the left of the fireplace, but the people on them could barely be seen, because the lighting put them in deep shadows. The fully illuminated Coven members were left standing nervously in the middle of the room.

One of the figures spoke from the shadows. "Make your case."

Marcel, a surviving coven member from France spoke Russian, and started, "We are an ancient society that has over the centuries developed telepathic and control abilities that allow us to manipulate people. We always keep our existence hidden but are involved in all sorts of projects that make our members wealthy and powerful. Our lives are very pleasant, especially when one learns to use our powers to get the very most out of sexual encounters, but that is just a sidelight."

Very French, thought 2C2, although he knew it worked. It was also that behavior that first brought the California psychics down onto the Coven.

"Recently we came across a new group of telepaths from California that have developed some, but not all, of our techniques, and enhanced them by technical means. The result has been a disaster to us, with the North American and western European Covens decimated. We are still numerous [pushing the truth a bit] but need allies with technical capabilities who are willing to keep our secrets in turn for our assistance in your projects. Without secrecy we are lost, and would have to emerge from the shadows. We still have important secret resources to draw upon, including faithful servants in high places. We will show in a bit why they remain faithful to our way. The alternative for them could be ghastly. (So begins...) the BIG LIE – most people are not psychic enough to suffer a 'feeding'.

"To prove to you that we have such powers, your general has placed at our disposal two soldiers to enable us to demonstrate that we can compel almost anyone to do our will.

"Anyone?" mused Sergei. "Then why did they pick just two soldiers out of 100?"

Addressing one of the shadowy figures, Sergei said, "We actually have three candidates, Vladimir."

2C2 was stunned. Could they be in the very presence of Vladimir Putin, ex-KGB and president of Russia? We must really have gotten someone's interest if that were true, he thought. This dacha, however, has all the trappings of state power and Sergei, their contact, is a ranking KGB general.

Vladimir said nothing. Sergei realized he had made a mistake even using the name. Now nervous, he said "Bring in Alexander."

The soldier came into the room, and not really seeing who was in charge, sharply saluted Sergei. "Very good, Alexander," Sergei said.

Marcel asked, "Does he speak any language beyond Russian?" A quick conversation, and the expected answer came back. "No."

Marcel started, "Sergei, ask him if he is ready to execute your orders." Sergei did so, and Alexander responded in excellent Parisian French, "As you wish, my general." Then in American English, "What do I do next?" Then in Spanish, "At your command." A slight murmur came from the shadowy witnesses.

2C2 handed a large knife to Alexander. Marcel asked, "Step over off the carpet onto the wood floor, and slit your throat." Smiling, Alexander moved over to the wood and with one swift slash slit his throat from ear to ear, and then crumpled to the ground. A red stain oozed toward the edge of the carpet, and someone jumped up and threw a towel over it to stop the spread.

The tension in the room was now suddenly intense. No one spoke for over a minute.

Then Marcel said, "But this is not the worst we can do. Please bring in the next soldier. We will need him tied to a chair in the middle of the room. He must be fully conscious. Tell him that this is for his own protection."

The soldier came into the room, and sharply saluted Sergei. "Peter, so you won't hurt yourself, we need to have you restrained in this chair. It is for your own protection." Peter was not sure that this was true, but in the presence of such overwhelming authority, he had little choice but to submit.

The Coven members gathered around the chair, but left a gap so the shadowy figures near the fireplace could see clearly. 2C2, channeling all the rage he felt from the disasters of the last year, sneered at Peter, who responded with a growing fear. Sensing their opportunity, all three Coven members attacked, and Peter screamed and struggled, his face twisted into a mask of terror. On and on it went, perhaps 90 seconds or so, and the Coven members were tiring, but suddenly Peter slumped forward in his bindings, his face frozen in terror, and horribly dead.

The Coven members, with their powers restored and their telepathic abilities enhanced, turned as a unit and smiled at the audience. "We put these powers at your command, Mr. President, if you will but help us learn the technology to defeat the American psychics."

ABOUT THE AUTHOR

Thomas A. Cahill, Ph.D., is a professor of physics at the University of California, Davis. His early work at UCLA, in France, and in Davis, California, was in nuclear physics and astrophysics, but he soon began applying physical techniques to applied problems, especially air pollution. His data in 1973 on the impacts of airborne lead was instrumental in the final establishment of the catalytic converter in California in 1976. He proposed and supported the law to lower sulfur in gasoline in 1977. He was director of both the Institute of Ecology and the Crocker Nuclear Laboratory, which included work on analyzing ancient documents.

He spent the following 20 years designing, building, and running the aerosol network to protect visibility at U.S. national parks and monuments – now the national IMPROVE program. In 1994, he founded the UC Davis DELTA Group to work in two areas – aerosols and global climate change – for the National Science Foundation (NSF) and the National Oceanic and Atmospheric Association (NOAA). Additionally his group analyzed aerosols and human health impacts for the California Air Resources Board, American Lung Association, and the Health Effects Task Force for Breathe California of Sacramento Emigrant Trails. Because of this health-related work, a U.S. Department of Energy colleague asked Cahill and his team to evaluate air at the excavation project following the collapse of the World Trade Center towers in the autumn of 2001. Cahill was one of the first to warn that workers at the site were at risk of serious health threats from the toxic metals in the air they were breathing at the site. While he is the author or co-author of hundreds of academic articles and book chapters, this is his first work of science fiction.

Thomas Cahill at the World Trade Center site in 2002. Photo by Sylvia Wright.

CPSIA information can be obtained at www.ICGtesting.com
Printed in the USA
LVOW042112150712

290180LV00002B/3/P